CW01021898

# The Orphan With No Name

## BOOKS BY SHIRLEY DICKSON

*The Orphan Sisters*

*Our Last Goodbye*

*The Outcast Girls*

*The Lost Children*

*The Orphan's Secret*

SHIRLEY DICKSON

# The Orphan With No Name

bookouture

Published by Bookouture in 2024

An imprint of Storyfire Ltd.
Carmelite House
50 Victoria Embankment
London EC4Y 0DZ

Storyfire Ltd's authorised representative in the EEA is Hachette Ireland
8 Castlecourt Centre
Castleknock Road
Castleknock
Dublin 15 D15 YF6A
Ireland

www.bookouture.com

Copyright © Shirley Dickson, 2024

Shirley Dickson has asserted her right to be identified as the author of this work.

All rights reserved. No part of this publication may be reproduced, stored in any retrieval system, or transmitted, in any form or by any means, electronic, mechanical, photocopying, recording or otherwise, without the prior written permission of the publishers.

ISBN: 978-1-83525-998-6
eBook ISBN: 978-1-83525-997-9

This book is a work of fiction. Names, characters, businesses, organizations, places and events other than those clearly in the public domain, are either the product of the author's imagination or are used fictitiously. Any resemblance to actual persons, living or dead, events or locales is entirely coincidental.

*For my Wal.*

# PROLOGUE

## THE NORTH-EAST TOWN OF SOUTH SHIELDS, MAY 1943

As the siren ceased its warning, Polly heard them coming. The drone of enemy planes. Terrified, she scrunched up her face and squeezed her eyes shut. Hearing faraway thuds and guns blazing on the ground, she trembled. The roar of planes came nearer. Ear-splitting shrieks and explosions and, as the light from the lamp flickered and then went out, Polly heard someone screaming. It wasn't till she felt arms surrounding her and Daddy's soothing voice in her ear – though she couldn't make out a word he was saying – that Polly realised the screams came from her.

They sat on the bunk bed in the brick-built shelter at the bottom of the back yard, their neighbours, Mr and Mrs Thompson from the flat upstairs, sitting next to them on beach chairs. All the while, Polly pined for Mam, who was working an evening shift at the clothing factory.

The planes thundered overhead, wave after wave. Hearing the bombs whistling down and the thuds of nearby buildings tumbling to the ground, Polly could barely breathe. Dust, smoke and smells filled the shelter and Mrs Thompson could be heard 'coughing her guts out' as Mam would say. The thought of Mam, the comforting lavender smell of her, sent a rush of longing through Polly.

A bomb, directly overhead, came shrieking down and Polly, her body seeming to collapse inwards, didn't have the power to scream. There followed a long silence when she feared the shelter walls would fall in and, cradling her head in her hands, she cuddled into Daddy.

Minutes later, the raiders had gone, droned off into the distance. Only the sound of an ambulance bell and fire engines could be heard. Swallowing, noticing her dust-caked throat, Polly sat up. No one spoke, but rustling noises came from where the Thompsons sat. A match struck and soon the warm glow of the hurricane lamp cast shadowy shapes on the walls. Polly gazed around. Everyone was covered in dust – their faces, clothes, hair, and eyebrows. At any other time it would seem funny, but not now, not with their solemn clown-like white faces staring at her, looking as dazed as she felt.

Mrs Thompson shook her head as though trying to think properly. 'How about a cuppa?' Her voice came out in a whispery squeak. She brought out a flask from the black leather bag beneath her deckchair. 'There's not a lot to go around, but enough to wet dry throats.'

'That's the spirit, love.' Mr Thompson, his face stern, patted her shoulder. 'Don't let them bugge—' Mrs Thompson raised her eyebrows at him. '*Jerrys* get you down. We'll win through.'

Later, when the all-clear sounded, they emerged from the shelter into the early morning light to a ravaged world – Daddy's words. There were acrid smells from burning houses and all around the immediate area other buildings were blitzed beyond recognition.

As she stood in the street, taking in the scene, Polly felt stunned, as though nothing she saw was quite real. She was used to seeing bombed buildings but she never thought it would happen in her neighbourhood.

'Aye, this is what you get when you live in a town that's on the mouth of the River Tyne and littered with shipyards.' Mr Thompson's voice sounded quivery as he looked around.

Ambulance bells continued to pierce the air and the injured, lying in the back lane on yard doors taken off their hinges, waited to be ferried to hospital.

'Their war's over, God rest their souls,' Mrs Thompson said, nodding to where blankets covered a row of mounds on the ground.

*Dead people*, Polly realised with a shiver, wishing Mam was here to give her a hug.

Daddy ran his fingers through his hair, telling the neighbours, 'I'm off to find Jane.'

Mam worked in a clothes factory in John Clay Street where they made uniforms for soldiers. Daddy wasn't happy about her working, Polly knew, because she'd heard her parents' raised voices through the thin bedroom wall one night when she was unable to sleep.

She recalled the conversation, her mam's voice urgent. 'It's for the best, George. You've been told by the specialist you can't return to active service. Your pension only goes so far, so there's nothing else for it. I'm going out to work and that's that.'

Polly had been told that Daddy was classed as an invalid because he'd been injured during the war in Burma.

There had been a pause, then Daddy had mumbled something.

'George, there's no shame in it. Most women are out working these days.'

In the end Mam got her way, as usual, and it hadn't been so bad because at the start she only worked evenings when Polly was in bed.

'Will you manage, Mr Pearson?' Mrs Thompson's voice interrupted Polly's thoughts. Their neighbour eyed Daddy's crutches.

'I won't rest until I see Jane's all right.'

'Go on then, seek your wife.' Mrs Thompson's round face twisted in concern. She patted Daddy's arm. 'See that she's safe and sound. Don't worry about the bairn, we'll look after her.'

As though in a dream, Polly was led upstairs to their neighbours' flat, which always stank of fish, and through the scullery to the kitchen where she sank down on the sagging horsehair couch. It was only then she realised the windows were missing their panes of glass.

She must have fallen asleep because the next thing she knew, Daddy was kneeling by the couch staring at her, the whites of his eyes pink. Polly didn't know how much time had passed and, rubbing her eyes, she sat up and knew by the grave look on Daddy's face that something was wrong.

'Pet.'

Polly's fears grew: Daddy never called her pet. That was what he called Mam.

'Mam wasn't in...' His chin trembled. 'The building she was in took a hit.'

Polly struggled to sit up. 'By a bomb?'

*That was daft*, her mind mocked, *what else could it be?* But she didn't want to believe it.

He nodded.

*Mam's been injured and she'll get better*, her mind told her.

'Is she in hospital?'

Daddy shook his head. 'That's the thing, Polly. I've got some very sad news. Mammy didn't make it. She died.'

Died? Mam couldn't be dead.

It was as though Polly had turned into a puppet. She couldn't speak or move.

The misery she saw in Daddy's eyes told her what he said was true.

# 1

## SOUTH SHIELDS, OCTOBER 1943

The night started out like any other Monday, with Polly sitting at piano practice in Mr Cartwright's front room overlooking the street. The room was filled with heavy furniture, and he had the blackout curtains drawn, but the light from the solitary bulb hanging from the ceiling and the fire burning brightly in the hearth was adequate enough for her to see by.

'Bravo, Polly.' Mr Cartwright, towering over Polly as she sat on a mahogany piano stool, gave a rare smile.

She turned and grinned at Daddy sitting behind on the window seat, the strains of 'You Are My Sunshine' still lingering in the musty, tobacco-smelling room. She had been practising on the piano at home all week while Daddy went on his 'constitutional' walk after dinner.

Daddy struggled to a stand and, leaning on his crutches, he clapped his hands, telling her proudly, 'That's my girl.'

'I told Mr Cartwright the song was your favourite and I wanted to surprise you by playing it on your birthday.'

When Daddy was home on leave from the army, she

often heard him whistling the tune. After he was sent abroad, she was reminded of him whenever she heard the popular song.

'You have, thank you, pet.'

Though Daddy smiled, it didn't reach his eyes. Polly reflected that the Daddy of old was never like this; these days he sometimes just stared into space and he easily got irritated, though he always apologised afterwards. Even when he'd come home injured after last Christmas, when he easily got upset and his eyes swam with tears for no good reason, he had still been the same dependable Daddy, with Mam telling her at the time, 'We have to be patient. He's been through a lot and needs time to heal.'

But after the bombing, he'd changed. It seemed somehow as if he wasn't there, and he had a frowny face most of the time.

As she thought of that night when Mam was killed, a wave of sadness overcame Polly and, struggling to breathe, she tried to think about something else.

'Very wise, Mr Pearson...' Mr Cartwright's voice penetrated her thoughts. 'To take your family— erm... your *daughter*, to the safety of the countryside.'

'That's the plan,' Daddy told him.

*Move to the countryside?* Polly was confused and turned back towards Daddy. She looked at him for reassurance, but his eyes wouldn't meet hers.

Mr Cartwright, oblivious, went over and clapped Daddy on the shoulder. 'Many happy returns, Mr Pearson. And how are you celebrating your birthday?'

'I'm taking Polly to the pictures.'

'I'll be sorry to see you go.' Mr Cartwright sighed. 'You too, young lady.' He turned to Polly. His tone had lost its gruffness and was surprisingly kind and gentle. 'You've come a long way. But heed my word. You must only continue piano lessons if that's what *you* want to do.' He winked at her, then clamped his pipe between his teeth.

Standing in the inky blackness outside Mr Cartwright's front door, Polly heard a rustling noise. With no moon sailing in the heavens to lighten her surroundings, frightening thoughts – such as that someone, or a scary monster, might leap out of the claustrophobic darkness and grab her – ran through her mind.

'Here, Polly, take this torch.' Daddy's voice came from the blackness above.

The torch, whose beam was partially covered by layers of tissue paper in accordance with regulations, was handed to her. Light was forbidden at night outside so that enemy planes would be unaware they were flying over built-up areas.

'Remember to point it downwards.' Neither of them made to move and it was Daddy who broke the silence. 'I'm sorry that you found out that we might be moving like that, Polly. I did mean to tell you before, but it was never the right moment—'

'You told Mr Cartwright.' Polly heard the accusation in her voice and shrank because she didn't normally make a scene.

'Only because I thought it fair that he should know in advance what I'm planning.'

'Where are we moving to?'

'Your Aunty Jean's house in Leadburn for a start. You'll like it there. It's a big stone house in the middle of the village with a garden.' His voice sounded as though he was trying to convince her. 'Your Uncle Jim is in the navy and, with no family of her own, your aunt will be glad of the company.'

Aunty Jean was Daddy's only relative and though she sent Christmas and birthday cards, Polly had only met her once – though she'd been too little to remember her aunt and uncle's visit. Daddy had wanted Mam to take Polly and evacuate to Aunty Jean's when he went away to the war, but Mam was adamant she didn't want to live in the middle of nowhere with nothing to do all day. If only she had left then, things would have been diff—

Polly slammed her mind shut but still a painful heaviness tugged in her chest and tears threatened behind her eyes. Swallowing the lump in her throat, she willed her mind to switch to something else.

'Are we going to live with Aunty Jean forever?' she asked.

Daddy shifted to get more comfortable; his spine hurt if he stood too long.

'No, just until I find somewhere for us to live that's big enough for me to have my own business.' His crutches tapped on the pavement as he walked away, his torch guiding his path. 'Come along, Polly. We'll freeze if we stand here any longer. And you know how long it takes me to get anywhere. We don't want to miss the start of the feature film, do we?'

He sounded impatient and Polly suspected he didn't want to continue with the conversation. Normally Polly would be excited to be going to the pictures and badger Daddy to find out what they were going to see, but upset at the turn of events, she could think of nothing except that she didn't want to move away from Marjorie Binks, her best friend at school, or from the only home she'd ever known, which was filled with all her memories of Mam. Tears welled in her eyes and, sniffing hard, she stemmed the snot threatening to flow with the back of a hand. Argument out of the question, she obediently caught up with Daddy.

A thought struck her. 'What kind of business will you have?'

'The same as I do here. Cobbling shoes.'

Daddy worked in the washhouse out in the yard mending neighbours' shoes – heels that had dropped off, rips in the leather, but mostly he fixed holes in the sole. Shoes were on ration and because of a shortage of leather, they had to last.

'The thing is, Polly, we could make Leadburn our new home.' Hearing the finality in his voice, Polly's shoulders sagged. He went on. 'I want you to be safe in the countryside away from the bombs.' His voice cracked then, and Polly knew he too was thinking about Mam.

On they walked, until Daddy's concerned voice called out, 'Keep well away from the kerb, Polly.'

Although kerbstones were painted white, people had been known to trip over them and land in the main road in front of an approaching motor car. Polly's squeamish mind imagined the bloody scene and she recoiled. At least the glow-in-the-dark buttons Daddy had sewed on her coat, so she would be visible, gave her a small sense of security.

Keeping the hand that carried her gas mask in contact with the house walls, Polly experienced a tingle of anticipation. 'What's the picture called?'

'Wait and see.' Daddy's voice had a note of playfulness in it. It had been a long time since that had happened. 'It's a surprise. Afterwards, we're to have a fish-and-chip supper for a treat. I need fattening up,' he joked.

These days Daddy looked hunched, as if he didn't have enough strength to hold his tall figure upright. It saddened Polly as she thought of how he used to seem as big as a bear and how, with a belly laugh, he would throw her up in the air while she squealed with fright, even though she knew all along she was safe, and trusted that he would catch her. Tonight though, Daddy had brightened, and was more like the Daddy of old. She felt uplifted and wondered if it was the move and living with Aunty Jean that was making him happier. Or maybe it was the outing.

But surely he would miss home. Polly felt homesick already.

Following Daddy as he made his way up to Westoe Bridges, hearing the motors as they passed in the road, Polly scrunched up her nose at the sour smell from the nearby brewery. As they made their way along Chichester Road, Daddy didn't turn into Whale Street, where they lived, but continued along the street. It was then Polly understood which cinema they were making for and, realising what they were about to see, a flicker of excitement ignited within her. A few days ago, as Polly had returned home from school, she saw on the billboard outside the pictures the advertisement that *Dumbo* was showing. How she had wished she could see the film, but treats like going to the pictures were rare. Polly would rather Daddy used her piano lessons money for things like the cinema, but he considered the lessons a necessity for her creative development, whatever that meant. She found the lessons with the gruff Mr Cartwright dreary, but Polly never complained because it was the way of things that she'd always tried to please her parents.

Pushing open the cinema door, Daddy stood back, making way for Polly to enter. When they had their tickets, he led them into the darkened picture hall where the Pathé news played on the large screen. An usherette carrying a torch led the way up the short flight of stairs to a row that had two vacant seats.

'Put your gas mask and music case under your seat,' Daddy whispered.

Doing as she was told, Polly settled in her seat. When the news finished, the house lights went up. Daddy, rummaging in his jacket pocket, brought out a small paper bag. He offered the packet to Polly.

'Pear drops. I saved the coupons.'

Looking around the packed house, the sweety rattling on her teeth as she sucked, Polly searched the audience to see if there was anyone she knew. Then the house lights went out and, in the blackness, cigarette smoke billowing in the beam of light that shone from the whirring projector at the back of the hall, the feature film started. Over the next hour Polly sat engrossed watching the adorable baby elephant who, because of his enormous ears, was ridiculed by the circus troupe. As the story unfolded, she laughed and cried, but when Dumbo was forced into doing a dangerous stunt, unable to bear the elephant's plight, she peered through her fingertips.

When the film finished, she stood with everyone to sing the national anthem and then filed with the rest the of picturegoers as they made their way to the exit. Her vision blurred by tears for the little elephant who'd won through in the end, she accepted the handkerchief Daddy offered her.

'I hope you're not going to want a pet elephant for your birthday,' he kidded.

A warm glow of happiness that Daddy was enjoying himself, swept the happy sadness she felt for Dumbo away. But she didn't get the chance to answer, because at that moment a chilling noise came from outside.

The wail of the air-raid siren.

# 2

Inside the lobby, panicking picturegoers surged forward, pushing the doors open and swarming outside, and Polly, scared in their midst, was carried along. Surrounded by a wall of grownups, she felt suffocated and found it difficult to breathe.

Outside, the moon, now coming out from behind the clouds, was shining and Daddy's voice rang out somewhere in the din.

'Polly!'

'I'm here,' she cried, relief flooding through her.

Seconds later, a hand grabbed her shoulder, making her start. And there, by the light of the moon, she saw Daddy.

'Hold on to the back of my coat and don't let go,' Daddy's urgent voice commanded as people jostled past. 'We'll make for the public shelter in Dean Road.'

Grabbing the coarse material of his army greatcoat, Polly clung for dear life as he slowly moved along. The siren now stopped, and in the silence a new and terrifying noise could be heard: the far-off thunder-like rumble of planes. In the distance, guns fired incessantly from the ground.

'They're after the docks.' Daddy's voice was tense.

Faraway thuds could be heard and, as the roaring of planes came nearer, Polly felt frozen with fear. Then came an ear-splitting shriek as a stick of bombs came terrifyingly close, followed by a mighty explosion that shook the ground beneath her feet. Screaming with fright, she looked upwards to where the moon sailed high in the heavens and search lights criss-crossed in the sky as black blobs fell from enemy planes.

'The cinema's doors have blown in,' a lady shrieked as she flew past.

Screams followed as the crowd took fright and, running pell-mell along the pavement, bumped into Daddy as he made his labouring way along the street.

'Move on, mate,' a voice of authority called from behind them.

Polly saw an older man with a moustache standing there, with the distinctive white *W* on his helmet.

The air raid protection warden looked at Daddy. 'What have we here?'

'Daddy's going as fast as he can,' Polly blurted, then shrank behind her dad.

The planes thundering past growled into the distance, then an ominous silence followed.

'There'll be more,' the warden told them. 'Best you get to safety as quickly as you can.'

'It would help if you could take my daughter to the shelter,' Daddy told him. 'I'll feel better knowing she's safe. I'll follow behind.'

Polly, horrified, bit her lip.

Taking off his helmet, the warden, scratching his head,

observed Daddy's crutches. 'That I can do, but I'll have to be quick, cos I'm needed elsewhere.'

'No, Daddy, I'm staying with—'

'Polly. You'll do as you're told.' Dad's tone held a finality that told Polly it was useless protesting.

'Bonny lass, come with me.' The warden made off, ushering Polly in front of him.

'Keep me a seat in the shelter,' Daddy called after them.

Standing at the top of the concrete stairs, Polly looked down into the gloom.

'Away you go, bonny lass. Get yourself into the shelter. Your dad won't be far behind.'

'Aren't you coming?'

'Nah! There's work to be done, lass. Looking for incendiary bombs for one.' He nodded down the stairs. 'Mebbes you'll meet up with some folks you know.' Turning, he moved off, disappearing into the night.

Making her way down the dark stairwell, she hurried around the blast wall. As she entered the dimly lit passageway, she wrinkled her nose at the stinky smell that greeted her. It was cold and draughty in the shelter, but with her thick woollen knee stockings, hat and scarf Mam had knitted and her red winter coat, Polly was snug and warm. Her eyes landed on an old woman sitting by herself on the floor next to the passage entrance. She wore a skimpy black shawl around her thin shoulders, and she looked at Polly with an uncomprehending stare. Polly gave her a friendly smile then continued along the passageway where people were sitting on seats that folded down from walls or on blankets in groups on the ground. No one paid her any attention as she walked by into the next section, which she was loath to do as she worried Daddy wouldn't find her. But Daddy's instructions were to keep a seat for him and with no spots available here she was determined to carry on and do as she'd been bid.

She looked around, hoping for a place to sit. Crowds of people sprawled on the floor, families by the looks of things, surrounded by pillows, suitcases, flasks; men reading newspapers, babies crying. A man, wearing a worn and shabby jacket with patches at the elbows, and a cap that sat at a jaunty angle on his head, played a mouth organ.

She picked her way into the next adjoining passageway, where the same scene met her eyes. But then her heart lifted as she spied an empty seat at the end of a row. When Daddy showed up, she could sit on the floor. Making her way over, Polly sat next to a girl who looked a similar age. She was skinny and had blonde hair as well – longer than Polly's – and her cheeks were flushed and she kept shivering. Deciding the girl must be poorly, Polly felt sorry for her. She gave the girl a sideways glance, noting she wore wrinkled ankle socks, and a shabby and stained coat whose cuffs fell far short of her wrists. Looking up, she met the girl's accusing stare. Polly's gaze dropped then, and her cheeks reddened at having been caught staring.

Mindful of what she'd been told, to always make sure the gas mask she carried was safe, Polly placed it and her music case under her seat. Taking off her pixie hat, she placed it on her knees. As she unwound the colourful scarf from around her neck, the lady sitting the other side of the girl leant forward.

'By gum, that's a bobby dazzler of a scarf, isn't it, Jenny?'

The girl turned to look at Polly with dull disinterested eyes. 'Suppose so.'

'Will you look at all those colours. It must have taken the patience of Jove to knit. Did your mam make it, pet?'

At the mention of Mam, Polly tensed. 'Yes,' she managed to say. 'She unravelled all her old cardies and jumpers and even some of Daddy's wool socks.'

'Eee your mam's lucky. I wish I had the time, hinny.'

Still feeling guilty that she'd made the girl uncomfortable by staring at her, Polly had an idea. 'Here, you can wear this for now.' She held out the scarf.

'Are you sure?' the lady, who had a rather droopy sad face, exclaimed. 'It's cold enough to freeze the balls off...' Her hand clapped over her mouth. 'That is,' she said, her hand cradling her cheek now, 'it's very cold down here.'

'My coat's warm enough for now,' Polly told her.

The lady's face wrinkled into a smile. 'Eee! That's kind of you, love. We haven't been to the clothes depot for a while and Jenny lost hers. Go on take it, Jenny, you look frozen stiff. Straight to bed for you, my lass, as soon as we get you home.'

Polly had the urge to insist the scarf was only on loan, but decided that would be impolite as no way would this nice lady allow the girl to keep anything that wasn't hers. The lady, who called herself Sadie, seemed kindly, though Polly did wonder about the hairnet she wore covering the curlers in her hair. Mam would have been horrified. She thought wearing curlers in public common and only wore hers in bed at night.

Jenny didn't make a move and Sadie, shaking her head, took the scarf from Polly. 'Jenny's got a bit of a cold.' She wound the scarf around the girl's neck. 'And the last thing we needed was to be stuck down here in this draughty shelter. Anyways, pet.' She turned to Polly. 'How old are you? You're too young to be down here this time of night on your own.'

'I'm ten, but my birthday's next month.'

'Eee, the same age as my Jenny here.'

'My daddy's coming soon. He's slow cos he walks with crutches. I'm keeping him a seat.'

'That's all right, then, as long as you've got someone. What's your name?'

'Polly Pearson.'

'Stay with us, Polly, until your da shows up. Jenny here will keep you company, won't you, love?'

Jenny didn't look up, but gave a dutiful nod.

Sadie raised her eyes heavenward and, shaking her head, she turned to an ancient-looking woman with a very wrinkled white face who sat on the other side. 'See, what I mean, Mrs Turner? My lass has no interest in anything. She's been that way since we heard. I'm at me wits' end to know what to do. I suppose it's just a matter of time.' Her shoulders lifted as she heaved a heavy sigh and Sadie's thin face appeared to sag. 'That goes for me as well.'

'Yes, they say time heals.' Mrs Turner's beady eyes looked agog for gossip, as Polly's daddy would say. 'How did it happen with your old man?'

'His cargo ship was sunk by bloody U-boats off Hastings and my Jake was one of the unlucky ones.' Sadie's chin trembled.

'Oh, I'm sorry, lass.' Mrs Turner's face creased in concern as she patted Sadie's arm. 'How are yi' coping'? Have yi' got family around?'

'That's the thing. His family lives in Middlesborough and I've only got Mam and she lives here in Shields. Me and Jake uprooted and settled in Sunderland because of his work.' The lady rubbed her brow with her fingers. 'Trust me to visit Mam the same time Jerry decides to bomb Shields' yards.'

'At least you've got your mam, hinny.'

'If only. Poor thing's demented since me dad died some

years back. She's in hospital at the minute, that's why I'm here this time of night. See, I work during the day. I haven't told Mam about Jake.' She tutted. 'Not that she'd understand because she can't take anything in.'

The older woman's hands flew to her cheeks. 'Lass, what a time you're havin'.'

'Same as many a one these days. But I'm determined not to go like Mam and to stay sane for Jenny's sake.' She tucked in the scarf around the back of her daughter's neck.

'There's no chance of that, you're as—' Mrs Turner stopped and cocked an ear. The far-off drone of airplanes could be heard.

'The buggers are—' She looked at Polly and pulled a remorseful face. 'Are back.'

As distant crumps came from outside, far away at first then ever closer, Polly gasped. No! Daddy was still outside. In danger. Her thoughts turned to Mam, and how she died in a raid. Paralysed with fear, she sat frozen to the spot. She couldn't lose Daddy too. As planes shrieked overhead, it was Jenny's stomach-chilling scream that galvanised Polly. With only one thought on her mind – she must find Daddy and help him – she leapt from her seat and made for the passageway.

'What you doing, lass? Come back here,' Sadie yelled at her.

Polly, weaving her way through the people on the ground, disregarded the lady. On she ran through the remaining two sections until she reached the blast wall and an ear-splitting explosion from outside filled the passageway with dust and smoke. Polly covered her ears with her hands and sank to her knees. As bombs dropped and lights flickered, an almighty explosion shook the shelter walls. In that split second, Polly looked up and saw the old woman she'd seen when she entered the shelter. Her arms crossed over the shabby-looking shawl she wore, the woman gave the same vacant stare.

There followed an uncanny silence when Polly sensed something ominous was about to happen. As a creaking sound filled the air, her eyes travelled to the wall behind the old woman. Polly, transfixed with fear, realised the shelter wall was collapsing. She opened her mouth to scream but as the wall came tumbling down, dust in the air clogging her mouth, something heavy struck Polly's head and then... nothing.

# 3

When Polly awoke, she couldn't move. A weight held her down. She tried to shout for help but the dryness in her throat and something thick coating her mouth made speech impossible and she uttered only a croaky whisper. There was a crushing pain in her head, and for a while she succumbed to the merciful blackness again.

Sometime later, a light filtered behind her closed lids. Something cold and solid hemmed her in. A man's voice came, seemingly, through a long tunnel.

'There's another one here. She's alive, thank God.'

The weight was taken off her. Someone lifted her. It hurt but she was too weak to cry out. Then the darkness descended once more before the clamour of a bell woke her. But the excruciating pain in her head that made her feel sick had her craving the dark, and she welcomed it when it came.

The next time she awoke her body rested on softness, though her head still throbbed. There were noises all around. Talking. Wheels squeaking. The clatter of china. A man spoke but she couldn't catch what he said. She opened her eyes. The light hurt. She wanted to hide from the pain and sleep but some urgency prevented her from doing so.

'Hello there. You've been out for a while.'

*Out?*

'You've been injured,' said a soft voice. A woman's voice. 'Cuts and bruises, miraculously no bones broken, but you've had a nasty blow to the head.'

She felt disorientated, dazed. 'It hurts when I breathe.' Her voice came out in a whisper.

'That's because your ribs got bruised when debris fell on you. You need to rest.'

*Debris?*

'Can you tell me your name? I'm Nurse Todd.'

*Name?* She searched her mind but nothing came. Her eyelids heavy, they closed again.

'Losing your memory, Rosie, can happen when someone has suffered something we call concussion,' Nurse Todd, who had a smiley face and round spectacles and was dressed in a blue-and-white striped uniform, an apron and starched cap, told her. It was night and Rosie, used to the routine on the ward after a number of days, watched Nurse Todd as she did the rounds with the milky drinks trolley.

It was the ward maid who first thought of the name Rosie. The maid was mopping the ward's floor one morning when she looked up to where 'Rosie' watched on from the chair at her bedside. 'You might be poorly, hinny' – the maid leaned on the mop handle she was holding – 'but you've got lovely rosy cheeks.' A grin spread across her face. 'That's it. We've all been wondering what to call you, lass, since you can't remember, and Rosie fits the bill perfect.'

No one asked if she liked the name and calling her Rosie didn't feel right. Nothing did.

Though Rosie's head ached and she still had the curious ringing in her ears, she did feel better, especially when she'd stopped feeling sick. What upset her, though, was she was no nearer to remembering her real name, what had happened, or whom she belonged to. So she had decided that when it was her turn for a milky drink, to question Nurse Todd about memory.

'What's concuson?'

'Concussion,' Nurse Todd corrected, stirring a cup of Horlicks on the drinks trolley. 'In simple terms, means your brain was hurt when you got a nasty bump on the head.'

'When I was in the shelter?'

The lady they called Sister Purvis, who had a severe face and stood ramrod straight in her navy-blue uniform frock and who – Nurse Todd told Rosie – was in charge of the ward, had explained how there'd been a raid and she'd been found in the public shelter's entrance by the rescue squad.

'You're a lucky girl,' Sister Purvis had gone on. 'You escaped with only minor injuries and bruised ribs when the walls collapsed. We've been told you escaped the heavier masonry.' Looking decidedly guarded, Sister went on, 'There was an old lady close by who it's thought might have been with you. There was great confusion with causalities but no relative has come forward as yet to claim either of you. Meantime...' Sister gave that false smile grownups used to make you feel better, when they were at a loss what else to say. 'We mustn't worry about all that. For now, we must concentrate on you getting better.'

'What happened to the old lady?'

Sister Purvis's eyes clouded with regret. 'I'm afraid she died.'

'Did masonry fall on her?'

'No, she had a heart attack, probably from shock. She wouldn't have suffered, Rosie.'

The noise of her milky drink being placed on the locker top caught Rosie's attention. She told Nurse Todd, 'I can remember some things but not the things that really matter.' For instance, was that old lady who died a relative? Her grandma?

'It'll come,' Nurse Todd consoled, her hands on her hips.

'When?'

The nurse shook her head. 'I can't say. Sometimes it's a few days or weeks. Or it can take months. You just have to be patient and try not to get upset or it could hinder your recovery.' She smiled kindly. 'I suggest you drink your Horlicks and get some sleep. Things will seem better in the morning.'

As it turned out, things only got worse. Over the next few days, the pain from Rosie's poorly ribs when she breathed made her reluctant to move around much. But the nurses insisted a little exercise walking around the ward would do her good. Afterwards she was glad to sit in her chair by the bed and watch the goings on in the ward.

The cries from little children, as they looked through the bars of cots when their mammies left the ward, upset her. She felt better, and rather envious, by the thought that at least they did have a mam to visit them. There were toys and colourful pictures on the walls but most of the older children lay in cage-like beds looking sad and poorly.

That day, after dinner was served – sausages, lumpy mash and peas – the little boy with the blond curls in the next bed started to cry when Nurse Todd had told him that his mammy couldn't visit him this afternoon.

'You remember your mammy works in a factory?' The little boy nodded. 'Well, she couldn't take the time off today because they're very busy. And I bet she's just as sad as you.'

The little lad stopped crying but seeing his red-rimmed eyes and snotty nose, Rosie couldn't help but feel sorry for him.

Nurse Todd made for the ward kitchen, returning shortly afterwards with a cup in her hand. 'Drink this warm milk, it'll help you feel better.'

He drank greedily from the cup. Noticing the photograph of a lady on the lad's locker top, Rosie decided that she must be his mam because they looked similar. The lady held a baby in her arms and wore a big happy smile on her face.

Rosie started to wonder about her mam. *Why had no one come looking for me*, she thought. Surely someone would miss her. From what she'd overheard, people had been killed in the shelter and nearby houses including two ARP – Air Raid Precautions – wardens. What if, instead of being with the old woman, she'd been with her parents and they'd died in the raid? A mixture of loneliness and homesickness enveloped her, Rosie didn't know for who or what.

Looking down at the washed-out flannelette nightdress she wore, she remembered what Nurse Todd had told her. 'Your clothes weren't worth saving and were thrown away.' Did that mean she was dressed in rags when they found her? A chill went up her spine. What if she had been on her own in the shelter and no one cared about her? Why else would no one seek her out?

Closing her eyes, she stemmed the tears threatening to fall by pressing her fingertips on her eyelids. She didn't want to cry – she was tired of weeping.

'Has the little boy upset you, dear?' An older-looking lady, who had a posh voice and who was giving out second-hand toys and reading books, came across from the other side of the ward and stood by her bed. The lady had plump cheeks that bunched up when she smiled, and her eyes were green and sparkly. She wore a two-piece green suit with an embroidered badge above the cuff of one of the jacket sleeves.

Rosie knew the badge meant the lady was a member of the WVS – Women's Voluntary Services – but she couldn't fathom how she knew that and trying to gave her a headache. She shrank, finding it difficult to reply.

'He's called Malcolm,' the lady helped out. 'He's crying because it's his birthday and— oh, what's the matter? What have I said?'

It was the lady mentioning Malcolm's birthday that did it, made Rosie forget her resolve and cry. The sudden realisation she didn't know when her birthday was, or even how old she was, reduced her to great sobs that shook her shoulders. She cried because she had no idea who she was, or where she lived, or even if she had family.

The lady, placing the china-face doll she carried on the bed, enveloped Rosie in her arms. The sweet perfume she wore smelt familiar and made Rosie yearn for something in the recesses of her mind she couldn't recall.

'There, dear, you have a good cry. It'll do you good and make you feel better.'

Rosie forgot her shyness and, closing her eyes, sank her head against the lady's soft bosom and cried and cried until her stomach ached and she felt woozy with tiredness. Her sobs subsiding, she pulled back and, sniffing hugely, wiped her snotty nose against the sleeve of the cardigan she wore over her nightgown – another cast-off. The thought almost made her start crying again.

'I'm... I'm not usually a cry-baby, Mrs...'

'Wilkinson. Of course you're not, dear. Goodness, what you've been through would upset a saint. Besides, you're poorly and that makes us fragile.'

At that moment Nurse Todd, after having had a quiet word with Malcolm, moved towards Rosie. Taking hold of the floral screen, she pulled it, wheels squeaking, around the bed. 'Time for an afternoon nap, Rosie. You need some quiet time.'

Rosie was about to protest because she didn't want to be alone with thoughts that would torment her, but she did feel droopy and so succumbed to Nurse Todd's suggestion. Holding her side where it hurt, she crawled under the single sheet, which proved difficult as it was fitted tightly around the bed. Finally, she sank back into the plumped-up pillow behind her head.

At first, after waking with a start, Rosie didn't know where she was, but the flowered screen that wrapped around her bed and her sore ribs reminded her. She had woken in a dreamy, pleasant state but then remembered her predicament which came to cloud her mind and she was doused with despair, her thoughts going round and round like a spinning top, asking the same questions but never finding answers.

A lowered voice sounded from the other side of the screen.

'Mrs Wilkinson, you're still here.' Sister Purvis's voice. 'I see Malcolm's taking an afternoon nap.'

'He is. I finished my ward rounds distributing books, then came back to keep Malcolm company by reading him a story. He adores the *Peter and Wendy* book. The little fellow was asleep before I reached the end. Bless his cotton socks, he was fretting for his mammy and—'

'Hopefully, she'll be able to visit tomorrow. She works at

the munitions factory but sometimes she's allowed time off in the afternoon to visit.' A pause. 'Mrs Wilkinson, have you a minute to spare?'

'Yes, Sister. I'm due at the clothes depot but there's no rush.'

'It's about our earlier conversation. As I discussed before, it's time to discharge Rosie. We need the bed.'

Rosie swallowed hard. This was news to her.

'But she isn't fully better. Besides, there's nowhere for her to go.' Mrs Wilkinson sounded as concerned as Rosie felt.

'Bruised ribs heal themselves and usually take up to six weeks to get better. I'm afraid she can't stay here all that time. As I say we need—'

Rosie missed what was said next because there was a loud clatter from behind the screen.

'Good Lord, Malcolm must need his sleep, the sound of those books falling would be enough to wake up the dead,' Mrs Wilkinson's hushed voice said. A pause, then, 'I've passed the message on to the powers that be about Rosie. The trouble is everyone's working flat out after the last raid and temporary rest centres are now full. Emergency feeding centres are bulging at the seams, and clothes depots are struggling to keep up with demand.' A thoughtful silence followed. 'It is strange, how there's no relative come forward to say Rosie's missing.'

So, it wasn't just Rosie who thought it peculiar she didn't have family come looking for her.

'The constable who spoke to me,' Sister put in, 'assured me that the force hasn't given up trying to find out her identity and that of the old lady.'

Rosie squeezed her eyes shut, searching her memory to conjure a picture of a shelter and an old woman but her mind proved a blank.

'The constable said none of the survivors in that front section of the passageway knew who the woman was. Or noticed either Rosie or the woman arrive.' Sister Purvis sighed. 'As no one has turned up to claim the poor woman it can't be clarified if Rosie was related or not.'

'It's a mystery, that's for sure. But these days we have to think of the positives.' Mrs Wilkinson's voice didn't sound in the least bit positive. 'At least Rosie wasn't further behind, where the shelter was reduced to a pile of rubble and all those poor folks lost their lives. God rest their souls.'

Rosie tried to digest what was being said.

'It's happening all over these days.' Sister's tone was matter of fact. 'Unidentifiable persons for one reason or another after a raid.'

'What a to-do. Poor lamb, technically she's an orphan.' Mrs Wilkinson groaned as though she was heaving up from a sitting position. 'Is there a possibility you can keep Rosie here in hospital until we can arrange something?'

Sister Purvis said something Rosie didn't catch.

'It is a thought. I'll look into it,' said the WVS lady.

'That would be most helpful, please do.'

'It'll take time.' Mrs Wilkinson pondered. 'Can she stay here, meanwhile?'

'We do need the bed urgently. However, I'll ask if one of the women's wards have a bed to spare...'

As Rosie heard the wheels of the screen starting to move, she adjusted her sitting position, rested her head back on the pillow and closed her eyes, as she didn't want to be caught eavesdropping. The very idea of leaving the only place, the only people, she knew, especially Nurse Todd, filled Rosie with dread.

# 4

The very next day in the afternoon, Nurse Todd arrived at the side of Rosie's bed pushing a squeaky wheelchair.

'Hop in, you're on the move. You hold on to these.' She handed Rosie a brown folder of notes.

Rosie, feeling herself go weak, sagged. 'Where am I going?'

'Sister Purvis has arranged for you to go to the women's medical ward. Where, no doubt, you'll be spoiled rotten.'

With pitifully few possessions on her lap – *Heidi*, the book Mrs Wilkinson gave her to read and she was thoroughly enjoying, a change of nightdress, toothbrush, soap and hair-brush from the ward's store cupboard – Rosie was wheeled through the bustling, green-painted corridors that smelled of something familiar but what, she couldn't recall. Nurse Todd stopped at one of the wards and negotiated the wheelchair through double doors. Passing through a narrow passageway, the nurse stopped at another door and knocked.

'Enter,' a voice called.

Securing the brake on the wheelchair, Nurse Todd

entered the room, leaving the door slightly ajar behind her. 'Sister, I've brought the new patient,' Rosie heard her say.

'Er, yes,' came a voice that sounded as though the owner's mind was elsewhere. 'The bed on the left at the end is ready. I'll be down shortly.'

'Yes, Sister.'

Nurse Todd appeared in the doorway.

'Nurse,' Sister's voice shrilled, 'notes.'

Nurse Todd raised her eyes heavenward. 'Sorry, Sister, of course.' She took the notes from Rosie, then darted back into the room, only to return a few seconds later. Taking the brake off the wheelchair, she pushed Rosie onto a ward that had iron-railed beds either side where women, some reclining in dressing gowns on top of their bed, others sat knitting or reading at their bedside, looked up inquisitively at Rosie as she passed them by.

Pushing the wheelchair, her starched apron rustling as she moved, Nurse Todd headed to the farthest bed where, stopping alongside, she placed Rosie's belongings on top of the green counterpane. 'Out you get,' she said.

Holding her side, Rosie settled into the rather hard wooden chair by the side of the bed. Sister – Rosie knew who the lady was who bustled towards the bed because she wore a navy-blue frock with a white collar – came to stand at Rosie's side.

'Hello, Rosie.' Sister was tall with dark wavy hair under a frilly white cap. Seeming as though she looked down her nose at Rosie, she gave an attempt at a smile. 'I'm Sister Reed. Welcome to the ward.' She turned to Nurse Todd. 'That will be all, Nurse.' She dismissed her with a nod towards the door.

'Bye, Rosie. Take care, darling. I hope your memory

comes back soon.' Briskly pushing the wheelchair up the ward, Nurse Todd disappeared through the doors.

Rosie, watching her go, felt as if her heart took a dive downwards. Nurse Todd was a friend, the only friend she had in the whole world, and now she was gone.

Sister wrote something on the notes that hung on the bottom of Rosie's bed, then looked up. 'Nurse will be here shortly to settle you in, Rosie. But you must remember to be well- behaved at all times as there are sick patients on the ward.' As she strode to her office, Sister didn't acknowledge the women watching her go by.

'Take no notice of her, hinny,' a voice from under the covers in the next bed said. 'The woman might mean well but her bedside manner has a lot to be desired.'

Sitting up straight, gently rubbing her side as it hurt with all the activity, Rosie peered at the old lady who lay on her back, a starched white sheet pulled up to beneath her chin. The lady, who had grey straggly hair flowing over her pillow, had tired-looking eyes and a prominent black-and-blue bruise on the forehead, her bandaged hands resting on top of the counterpane.

She saw Rosie staring down at them. 'Silly old fool that I am, the chip pan caught fire and I thought I could put the damn thing out with a dishful of water. Next thing I knew I'm in here.' She cackled. 'It's the last time I make chips for me old man.' She cocked an eye at Rosie. 'What about you, pet? You're far too young to be in here with us old fogies.'

'I was in the shelter in the raid when it was hit and I got injured,' said Rosie, feeling a bit shy with the lady. 'And I've lost my memory since.'

The woman studied her as though deciding what to say. 'Then, I hope you keep on looking for it, pet.'

Rosie's brow creased as she tried to fathom out what the

woman meant. At the glint of fun in the lady's eyes, Rosie realised the woman was trying to make her feel better with a joke.

At that moment a nurse walked down the ward carrying a jug of water and a glass, then stopped at Rosie's bedside. She was quite young and pretty, and with a pretend expression of annoyance, she turned to the next bed.

'Mrs Spencer, are you causing havoc again?'

'Don't I always, Nurse Travers.'

The nurse gave a shake of the head. 'Hello, Rosie. Let's get you settled in. Take no notice of Mrs Spencer or she'll lead you astray.' The nurse proceeded to put the jug and glass on the locker top and put Rosie's belongings inside.

A little glow of happiness burst in Rosie. Being here on the women's ward wouldn't be so bad after all, not with the kindly nurse and Mrs Spencer.

Within a week Rosie had settled into the routine of the ward. Each day Matron did rounds, when there was a flurry of activity, bed linen straightened, pillows plumped, open ends facing away from the doors, locker tops tidied, flowers deadheaded and water topped up. Matron, a rather plump lady who walked with hands clasped in front, smiled and nodded as she passed each patient's bed. The ward was unnervingly quiet at this time; only the click of knitting needles from the ladies watching the goings on could be heard.

Today when Matron arrived, Sister Reed at her side, the nurses on duty standing behind them, Rosie, nervous, chewed the inside of her lower lip in agitation because she worried that Matron would stop and talk to her. As Matron approached Rosie's bed, she slowed.

'And how are you today—?' She glanced at Sister Reed.

'Rosie,' Sister prompted.

'Ahh! Yes. Rosie.' Again, she turned to Sister. 'Any recollections?'

'None that I'm aware of, Matron.'

'You'll be leaving soon, I hear.' Matron's grey eyes – eyes that missed nothing, according to Nurse Travers – met Rosie's.

Rosie shrivelled, forgetting to breathe. *Leaving?* This was the day she'd feared. The day she'd be told to leave the only security she knew.

Sister coughed. 'She hasn't been told yet, Matron.'

'Then, I insist she is.' Matron's brow knitted in a frown. 'It's in her own interest.'

Sister looked flustered. 'It's taking time to organise. Arrangements haven't been finalis—'

'At once, Sister.'

Sister Reed, lips pursed, cheeks pink, turned towards Rosie. 'Arrangements are being made for you to join the children from Blakely orphanage. You should be taken there next week.'

# 5

When Matron left the ward, Nurse Travers, her face concerned, hurried over to Rosie. 'It's probably only a temporary measure, Rosie.'

How Rosie wished the nurse had said, 'It's *definitely* only a temporary measure.'

Aware of the women in the ward giving her sympathetic stares, Rosie flushed with embarrassment because being the centre of attention was the last thing she wanted. She lowered her voice. 'Who are the children from Blakely orphanage?'

Rubbing her brow with her fingertips, Nurse Travers sighed as though considering how to go on. 'Blakely Hall was an orphanage here in the Westoe area. A place where children without parents live—'

'But I might have—'

'I know, Rosie, just hear me out.' The nurse knelt to Rosie's level and, with troubled eyes, she went on. 'You're getting better now and living in a hospital isn't right for you.'

'And you need the bed.'

'There is that but everyone only wants what's best for you.' She patted Rosie's hand. 'The first thought was that it might be nice... just until you get your memory back or it's found out who you are... for you to leave the town and all the bombing and be evacuated.'

A memory stirred in Rosie – she'd heard those words before but before she could explore her thoughts the nurse continued.

'It was Sister Purvis who thought it would be better sending you to an orphanage where there are children your age.'

Rosie saw the advantage. 'And this orphanage is in Westoe and so I'll be here when they find—'

'That's the thing...' A wary look crept into the nurse's eyes. 'When the war started the orphans at Blakely Hall were evacuated to the countryside in Scotland, to a place called Dunglen. The owner of the nearby estate agreed the children could live there.'

'Scotland!' That was miles and miles away. Rosie's chest constricted; it was difficult to breathe. 'I'm not going so far away. You can't make me,' she said in a rare display of stubbornness.

'Rosie, darling, there's nowhere else.' Nurse Travers stiffened, her eyes focusing to a spot over Rosie's shoulder. 'You'll have to go.'

Turning, Rosie saw Sister Reed's beady eyes upon them. Nurses weren't encouraged to chatter to patients.

'Trust me, Rosie.' The nurse stood up, smoothing her apron. 'It's for the best. Believe me, if your relatives are found, you'll be told wherever you are.'

Nurse Travers left to help another nurse haul a patient up to a sitting position in bed, whilst Rosie, troubled and distraught, made her way to the lav. She didn't need to go but felt the need to be alone in her misery. Viewing herself in the mirror above the sink, she tried with all her might to remember who she was. But the thin face with fine honey-blonde hair and blue eyes before her stayed a mystery.

It was dinnertime on the day of her departure when butterflies fluttered in her tummy and the greasy smell of lamb stew permeating the ward made Rosie feel sick.

One of the day nurses, collecting dishes, eyed her untouched pudding on the overbed table. 'You didn't eat your dinner either, Rosie. You must eat something.'

'I'm not hungry.' Sitting on top of the bedcovers, Rosie wore a grey pleated skirt with shoulder straps holding it up, a washed-out white blouse and knitted woollen knee socks.

The nurse's brow furrowed in concern. 'You've got a big day ahead. Try a little semolina pudding.'

The very sight of the milky pudding made Rosie's stomach heave. 'No thank you.'

The nurse shook her head. Removing the dish, she made to move, then hesitated. 'Mrs Wilkinson, the WVS lady, will be here shortly. Your suitcase is packed and ready to go.' She nodded to a small battered brown suitcase that stood at the bottom of the bed.

The ladies on the ward had been kind and given Rosie knitted garments they'd originally made for their children – gloves, hat, scarf, socks. Rosie didn't like to admit that the wool socks were the tickly kind that made her legs itch, as they had been such a thoughtful gift. Mrs Wilkinson had brought items from the clothes depot – liberty bodice, vests, knickers, two skirts and blouses, woolly cardigan, a tired-looking grey coat that swamped Rosie – and the toiletries she needed came from the ward stores.

The nurse must have sensed Rosie's dread of what lay ahead, as she gave a kind smile. 'Don't worry, you'll soon settle in where you're going, just wait and see.' She moved away and, stacking the dishes onto the dinner trolley that stood in the middle of the ward, she pushed it up the ward and through the open doorway, the crockery rattling all the way.

Sitting on the edge of the bed, dressed in unfamiliar clothes a size too big, the suitcase at her feet, Rosie's tummy felt hollow and she wondered if she should have tried eating something.

'Aye, it's all right for her to talk, isn't it?' Mrs Spencer, propped up in bed, called over. 'It's not her going to the back of beyond, is it?' She pulled a disgusted face. 'Take my advice, hinny, you only get out of things in this life what you put in. So, you make the most of wherever it is you're going. You're a canny lass and you'll be fine.'

Rosie didn't know how to answer and so just smiled and nodded.

Nurse Travers was on a late shift today and Rosie worried she mightn't get to say goodbye to her favourite nurse on the ward. So, when the ward doors opened and a beaming Nurse Travers made her way down to Rosie's bed, a burst of relief surged through her.

'I couldn't miss seeing you off, so I came in early.' She rifled in her uniform pocket and handed over a small parcel wrapped in tissue paper. 'This is for you. A little something to remember us by.'

Curious, Rosie opened the parcel that revealed a while handkerchief with a pretty lace edge.

'See what I've embroidered on it.' The nurse pointed to a red rose in one corner.

The kind gesture too much, a little sob wrenched from Rosie.

'Oh, I've upset you. Please don't cry.'

Sniffing hard, Rosie scrubbed away the tears with the back of a hand. 'I'm not upset. It's cos...' Her voice came out squeaky. 'You're kind. It's a lovely hanky, thank you. I'll keep it always.'

Nurse Travers looked shamefaced. 'It's not new, mind. It's a present I got off my nana last Christmas. It was too pretty to use and I wanted you to have it.'

Suddenly, all Rosie's fears came rushing to the surface like the big scary monsters she imagined at night that lived under the bed who would come out and grab her if she put so much as a foot out of the covers.

'What if the police forget about me and stop looking?' The squeaky voice was back. 'There'll be nothing in Scotland to remind me of who I am. What if people don't like me and I don't make frie—'

'Stop, Rosie.' Nurse Travers took her by the shoulders. 'Now you listen to me. Don't ever give up. You've got to trust you'll get your memory back.'

'Aye. Listen to the nurse, hinny,' Mrs Spencer called. 'She talks more sense than t'other one.'

'Promise me.' Nurse Travers's voice was firm.

Rosie, sniffing hard, wiped away the tears she hadn't noticed spilling from her eyes. 'I promise.'

'Cross your heart,' Mrs Spencer put in.

Rosie did as she was told.

At that moment the ward door opened and the WVS lady approached. Mrs Wilkinson wore a green overcoat with big lapels over her uniform and a matching felt hat. She was followed by Sister Reed.

'Are we all ready?' Sister Reed's voice was overly bright,

though her face drooped with regret. She didn't appear her bossy self.

It occurred to Rosie that Sister only made a show of being strict and it was like Mrs Spencer said: she meant well.

'Have you got everything?' Sister looked down at the suitcase. 'What about a gas mask.'

'All in hand.' Mrs Wilkinson held up a box. 'And her identification.' She pulled a piece of card out of her coat pocket. 'Oh dear, I've forgotten a safety pin.'

'Here.' Nurse Travers brought one from her uniform dress pocket. 'I keep one for emergencies.' Taking the card from Mrs Wilkinson she read out loud, 'Rosie Ward, care of Edgemoor General Hospital, South Shields. County Durham.' She smiled appreciatively at the WVS lady. 'Isn't that grand, Rosie. You've got a surname and an address for if you get lost.' She pinned the card to Rosie's coat that lay on the bed.

*What if I get lost?* Another fear came to torment Rosie.

'I hope you like the surname I've chosen.' Mrs Wilkinson looked at her uncertainly.

Rosie, mixed up as to how to answer, was relieved when Sister interrupted.

'Time's getting on and you don't want to miss your train.'

'Heaven help us if we do.' Mrs Wilkinson fussed, picking up Rosie's coat off the bed and handing it over to Rosie. 'Wrap up, dear, it's bitterly cold outside.'

Overwhelmed by events, a restless energy overpowered Rosie and she felt the need to be on the move.

'Goodbye, Rosie, good luck, take care of yourself,' ladies called out as she passed their beds.

As she walked along the corridor to the hospital exit, the impulse to run back to the ward and hide beneath the security of the bedclothes overcame her.

. . .

The day passed with Rosie moving in a world that didn't feel quite real. It didn't help that Mrs Wilkinson, between dozing and reading the *Gazette*, was no company. Rosie's memory was mostly of two wearisome train journeys that were no fun because as the afternoon progressed and it darkened outside, the blackout blinds shrouded the windows. There was nothing to look at except for an old man who sat opposite on the South Shields to Newcastle train who slept all the way with his mouth open, showing his yellow teeth.

Rosie's sore ribs hurt more as the day wore on, especially when she took deep breaths, but worse than anything was the fear that she would get left behind in one of the stations teeming with people, with no Mrs Wilkinson in sight, which proved more terrifying than even a monster living under her bed. However, the long journey on the Newcastle to Edinburgh train was highlighted by the plum jam sandwich wrapped in greaseproof paper and the lemonade bottle filled with water that Mrs Wilkinson produced, telling her, 'I came prepared. You never know when you might need a sandwich when you're travelling.'

After Rosie had eaten, her side still aching and also feeling tired all of a sudden, she settled back in her seat and in the cold blue light of the carriage, listening to the mesmerising chuff-chuff noise the train made, she fell asleep.

She awoke to Mrs Wilkinson prodding her.

'Rosie, we're approaching Edinburgh station, it's time to get off the train.'

So, here she was in Waverley station, and stepping from the train onto the platform, Rosie shivered as the cold air in the draughty station enveloped her.

'Stay close,' Mrs Wilkinson told her as she made off into

the throng. 'Visibility isn't the best but, would you believe, Waverley station has kept its glass roof, there's too much to remove apparently and it's mucky enough to block any light from below getting through.'

As the WVS lady prattled on, Rosie tried to keep up but still in a dozy state of sleep, she lagged behind. Weaving through the crowds, she heard a lady's voice come over the loudspeaker. Rosie strained to hear but the lady's speech was muffled, and she couldn't make out a word.

Suddenly, surrounded by hordes of people, families with squealing children, soldiers wearing army greatcoats and carrying kitbags slung over their shoulders, Rosie felt hemmed in by a wall of grownups and had a panicky sensation that she'd experienced this before. In her head she heard planes thundering above. But looking up all she saw was the glass roof Mrs Wilkinson had told her about.

Rosie's heart hammered in her chest, not from fear, but the certainty that what she had just experienced was a memory. A glimmer of hope lifted her spirit. Looking around to tell Mrs Wilkinson, she gasped in horror. The WVS lady was nowhere to be seen.

Her lightened mood changed as she realised that her biggest fear had become a reality. She was lost in the swarming crowds.

# 6

Forging her way through the throng, Rosie glimpsed a green hat not far ahead. Relief flooding through her, she could have cried. Wide awake now, she hurried as fast as her poorly ribs would allow, catching up with Mrs Wilkinson, who, it would seem, had been too busy looking for their platform to notice Rosie was missing. Holding on to the lady's coattail, Rosie felt safe as Mrs Wilkinson, threading through the crowds, led them to the entrance gates of a platform.

'We're just in time,' Mrs Wilkinson said as a train chugged into the station, coming to a screeching halt beneath a cloud of billowing steam.

Carriage doors opened and passengers spilled out onto the platform. A group of rowdy sailors wearing duffle coats moved forward to board the train but remembering their manners, they held back and insisted that Rosie and Mrs Wilkinson board first.

The carriage was packed with people standing or sitting on suitcases and the sailors started a game of cards as they sat on the floor in the corridor. Finding two empty seats, Mrs Wilkinson ushered Rosie into the window seat and then sat alongside her. Then a whistle blew and the train started moving slowly, before picking up speed and pulling out of the station.

'This is the last stage of our journey, Rosie, and won't take long,' Mrs Wilkinson reassured her. 'Then we'll be at St Boswell where we'll be met and taken to Teviot Hall estate, your new home for a while.'

In her mind Rosie argued she didn't want a new home, she needed to stay in her hometown and find out where she lived and who with. But the voice in her head that insisted she behave meant she could say none of these things.

As Mrs Wilkinson chattered on about Teviot Hall, Rosie tuned out her voice and considered that it would be late when they arrived at their destination. She wondered about Mrs Wilkinson's journey home as it was getting late and surely she... A thought flitted through her mind that made Rosie reel. As the reality that Mrs Wilkinson would be travelling home ALONE, without her hit her for the first time, she felt as though someone had punched her in the tummy.

'Are you all right, Rosie dear?' Mrs Wilkinson, studying her, gave a sympathetic nod as if she understood. 'Would you believe I get nervous at times? Especially when I go to a new place and I meet with strangers or I'm delivering a speech at one of the WVS meetings.'

Rosie was amazed. She could never imagine Mrs Wilkinson feeling jumpy and anxious like she was right now.

'What do you do?' she asked.

Mrs Wilkinson raised her eyebrows conspiratorially. 'I put on a brave face. Pretend I'm an actress playing a part. It's called *attitude*. Trust me, dear, it works. People believe what they see and treat you with respect.'

Rosie's brow creased; she kind of understood what Mrs Wilkinson told her. She liked the woman; she always spoke to Rosie as if she were a grownup. Rosie found herself wondering if the WVS lady had children of her own.

As the train hurtled through the darkened evening, the two of them fell silent, each deep in thought. Then a man in a uniform entered the carriage checking the blackout.

'Excuse me, sir,' Mrs Wilkinson called out, 'could you tell me please how many more stops it is to St Boswell's?'

'Aye, hen, that'll be the next stop.' Rosie recognised his accent as Scottish. 'I hope you've brought a torch, Mrs, it's a dreary night out there.'

'I've come prepared, thank you.'

The man nodded and moved off.

Mrs Wilkinson stood, heaving Rosie's suitcase from the luggage rack and placing it on the floor. She then searched in her shoulder bag and brought out a torch. As the train started slowing, Mrs Wilkinson picked up the suitcase.

'Come on, Rosie, best foot forward.' She started to make for the doorway.

Trudging behind, Rosie didn't want to put a foot forward, to step from the train into a scary world she had no knowledge of.

As the train shuddered to a halt, Mrs Wilkinson opened the carriage door to shadowy darkness and the moon shining high in the sky. Rosie, her fears rising to fever pitch, felt as though her legs would give way.

The icy air blasted through the open station freezing Rosie's face and found all the uncovered parts of her body. She shivered uncontrollably. No one else had got off the train and the only person she could make out standing on the platform in the semi-darkness was the figure of a man in uniform. He blew a whistle and, the noise piercing, Rosie covered her ears with her hands. As the train started up, slowly gathering speed, then huffing its way along the track, Mrs Wilkinson shone her dimmed torch on a building that loomed ahead on the platform.

'We're to be collected but as I don't see anybody, Rosie, I think it best we sit in the waiting room.'

In the cosy, deserted room lit by a hurricane lamp, Rosie noted a fire, burnt to red embers, glowing in the grate. There was a window with its blind down and a bench that ran around the walls.

'Thank goodness for small mercies.' Placing her shoulder bag and Rosie's suitcase on a section of bench, Mrs Wilkinson moved to the fireplace. Turning her backside towards the fire, she blew on her hands. 'At least we'll be warm while we wait.'

Legs still wobbly, Rosie came to stand by her. Realising this might be her last chance, she plucked up the courage to say, 'I don't want to be left here on my own. I don't know nobody.'

'Anyone,' Mrs Wilkinson corrected, then shifted uncomfortably. 'Rosie, it's not up to me, dear, it's been decided by the powers that be that this is what's best. It's safe here where there's no bombing. Remember how frightening that was?'

Rosie bit her lip. She didn't remember any bombing – she couldn't remember anything.

Tired and frantic, she forgot her reservations. 'It's not fair.'

'I agree, Rosie. This war isn't fair: making people homeless, killing innocent people.' Mrs Wilkinson's eyes glistened with tears. 'But we must all buck up and do our best and like those brave soldiers show our fighting spirit.' Mrs Wilkinson's voice had gone as trembly as Rosie's legs.

The room went quiet except for the little flames that swirled and crackled from the coals. After a while, the door swung open and a young lady appeared. She had a round jolly face and apple-red cheeks. Her clothes, a green jumper, sturdy-looking lace-up shoes, thick stockings that reached up to the knee of her brown trousers, made her look... *solid* was the only word Rosie could think of.

'Hello.' She came over to the fireplace and held her hands up to the flames. She told Mrs Wilkinson, 'I hope you haven't been waiting long. Miss Balfour was supposed to meet you, but Sir Henley's ancient Bentley is playing up and wouldn't start. Miss Balfour's a nervous driver and balked at the idea of driving the truck, so I was elected.'

Mrs Wilkinson looked taken aback at all the information she'd been given. 'Er, thank you. That's very kind—'

'Frances, Fran Patterson. Gang work forewoman of the WTC – the Women's Timber Corps – at Teviot Hall estate.' She stood erect and held out a hand that looked sore with cuts and blisters on it.

Mrs Wilkinson hesitated before shaking it. 'Mrs Wilkinson. And this is Rosie Ward.'

Fran nodded without looking at her. 'We'd better get going. Frosts are forecast.'

Rosie traipsed behind them feeling left out and unsettled. She didn't know what she'd expected, but not this lady who was a forewoman, whatever that was, and a Sir Henley. Her thoughts had only imagined children at the orphanage. It was all so new and very frightening. Rosie wished she could be like Mrs Wilkinson and pretend to be an actress and act brave.

Guided by the two ladies' torches pointing to the ground, Rosie was led out of the draughty station and down some steps to the roadway. By the light of a bluish full moon, she saw a truck standing at the roadside.

'Squeeze in,' Fran told them, opening the door. 'Give me the suitcase, I'll throw it in the back.'

She disappeared for a couple of seconds and when she came back, the truck tilted as she climbed aboard. Rosie, sitting in the middle, saw her start the engine. The truck revved to life.

No one spoke as they sped along in the semi-light of the shining moon. As the truck hurled around corners, Rosie heard Mrs Wilkinson give little gasps of fright.

'Don't worry,' Fran told them. 'I know these roads like the back of my hand.'

The speed of the truck did slow down after that, Rosie noticed. With nothing much to see outside apart from dark hedges and trees silhouetted against a silvery sky, the busy day caught up with her, and Rosie leant back and closed her eyes. Try as she might, she couldn't blot out the aching pain in her side which seemed worse in the cold.

'Nearly there,' Fran called out above the noisy truck's engine.

Instantly, fully alert, Rosie gazed out of the window to the scene outside the windscreen. The only things she could make out were the truck's two round beams of light focused on the ground and a row of trees, barely visible, loomed either side of the path. The truck slowed further as it drove along the bumpy road, and Rosie, jiggling in her seat, had nothing to hold on to.

'Potholes,' Fran declared. 'But Sir Henley has better things to worry about than fixing them.'

'Yes, I've heard, poor man. Dreadful.' Mrs Wilkinson

sounded sorrowful. 'I did rather hope to meet Sir Henley but under the circumstances, I suppose it's—'

'Out of the question, I'm afraid. He's staying with his sister, Lady Margaret.'

A silence followed and the only sound was the engine as it chugged along. After a couple more twists in the road, the truck stopped.

'It's been a long day for you.' As if she didn't expect a reply, Fran opened the door and climbed down from the truck.

Mrs Wilkinson had a struggle to open hers, then got out at her side. 'Hop down, Rosie. I'll get the suitcase.'

Rosie, shuffling along the seat, did as she was bid.

'Now, dear' – Mrs Wilkinson's voice was falsely bright – 'let's see your new home.'

Rosie walked behind Fran over the frosty sparkling cobblestones to a low-spreading brick building. Fran walked up a ramp and rapped on the wooden door. When it opened the three of them trooped into the dark inside. The door closed and a light switched on. A thin lady who didn't look at all welcoming stood before them. She wore a maroon dress buttoned up to her neck, black lace-up shoes, and her grey hair, scraped back into a bun, looked as severe as her expression. They stood in what appeared to be a large lobby. There were two doors either side, one marked *Office*, the other *Toilet*. There was also a closed door ahead of them, from where muffled noises could be heard within.

'This is Rosie, Miss Black,' Fran told her.

Ignoring Rosie, the lady addressed Mrs Wilkinson. 'It was good of you to escort the girl here. I expect you're hungry after your long journey.'

'We both are.' Mrs Wilkinson made a point of nodding at Rosie.

Miss Black's thin lips pursed. 'Has she been a good girl on the journey?'

'Er, yes.' Mrs Wilkinson's brow furrowed in consternation. 'Rosie's never any trouble.'

'Good.' The lady, lacing her fingers together, cupped her hands in front at her waist. 'Then she deserves supper.' She turned to Fran. 'Be good enough to escort our guest to the WTC canteen where you'll both find supper is being served. Meanwhile, the girl will eat here.'

'About accommodation,' Mrs Wilkinson cut in, 'I was informed I could spend the night here before returning tomorrow.' Two twin spots of pink showed on her cheeks and Rosie suspected she was as surprised and flustered at the reception they'd received as she was.

A friendly smile on her face, Fran addressed Mrs Wilkinson. 'Arrangements have been made for you to sleep at the big house tonight. I'll show you the way after supper.'

'Meanwhile you, child, will take a bath and have your scalp inspected.' Miss Black glared at Rosie, accusingly. 'I've heard that nits are rife in the town.'

'I can assure you,' Mrs Wilkinson, visibly annoyed, retorted, 'Rosie takes a regular bath and does not have nits.'

Miss Black bristled as though she was about to reply but then, apparently thinking better of it, responded, 'Miss Balfour will be here shortly. She'll see that you have a bath after supper.' Without another word, she moved to the door marked *Office* and disappeared.

'Goodness me,' said Mrs Wilkinson glancing at Fran, 'the woman doesn't mince words, does she?'

Fran shrugged, noncommittally. 'That's Miss Black's way. Her life is governed by the Old Testament. She doesn't shirk with punishment if she thinks it applies.' She regarded

Rosie. 'Don't let her scare you. Follow the rules and you'll be fine.'

The thing was, Rosie worried: she didn't know what the rules were.

Mrs Wilkinson gave a sad smile. 'It seems, Rosie, this is the parting of the ways for us. Never give up hope and be true to yourself.'

Rosie, looking at Mrs Wilkinson's tired and anxious face, did what she normally did on such occasions by formulating the words in her head to say the right thing, to keep the WVS lady happy.

'I'll be fine, honest.'

As Mrs Wilkinson smiled a relieved smile, Rosie couldn't help but feel the lady had let her down. That everyone had.

'There's a tap at the WTC huts,' Fran said, 'where you can freshen—'

At that moment the middle door in the lobby opened and a lady entered. Robust, with pink cheeks, brown shining hair framing her face, the lady gave Rosie a dimpled smile. She wore a similar frock to Miss Black's, only hers was navy blue.

'Miss Balfour,' she introduced herself to Rosie, then turned to Miss Wilkinson, her face apologetic. 'Sorry I'm late for your arrival but I've been organising supper.' She looked down at Rosie. 'Hello, dear, I expect you're tired and hungry. We'll get you something to eat then I'll take you over to the dormitory where you can settle for the night.'

'I'm supposed to have a bath.' Rosie worried she would be breaking some rule if she didn't and Miss Black would find out.

'I think we can leave that until tomorrow. You need your rest tonight.' Miss Balfour winked. 'I won't tell if you don't.'

Fran made for the door, addressing Mrs Wilkinson. 'We'd best get a move on.'

Mrs Wilkinson bent down to Rosie's height. 'I'll be off first thing tomorrow and mightn't see you.' She stroked Rosie's cheek with the back of her hand. 'Remember *attitude*, Rosie. Meanwhile, don't give up hope on your memory returning.' She nodded reassuringly. 'They say it's only a matter of time.'

Then the light switched off, the door opened and Mrs Wilkinson was gone.

'Come along, Rosie, I'll take you to meet the other children.' Miss Balfour opened the inner door she'd appeared from earlier.

Swallowing the sick feeling rising in her tummy, Rosie followed her into a chalk-smelling room. Observing the rows of desks and the blackboard, she was surprised to find she was in a schoolroom. Noises, sounding like cutlery clattering, came from behind a curtain partitioning off one end of the room.

'This building is Teviot Hall's Little Theatre,' Miss Balfour told her, making for the dividing curtain. 'Before the war, apparently, this hall was used by the local drama group to put on plays. It was also used for musical evenings and Burns Night suppers.' Her hand reaching out towards the curtain, she told Rosie over her shoulder, 'Sir Keith Henley, who owns Teviot Hall, had the stage pulled out and the hall divided into a classroom and dining area for when the children from the orphanage arrived.'

As the curtain was pulled aside, Rosie gasped in astonishment. The room, large and shivery cold, had green-painted walls, reminding Rosie with a pang of the hospital, and tall windows with the blackout curtains drawn. But it was the children – silent children of all ages – that caught her attention. They sat at long trestle tables, staring at her with dull, indifferent eyes.

All her fears confirmed, Rosie knew she didn't want to stay in this place and end up like these sad-looking children – but she also knew she had no other alternative. She could only pray that she would remember who she was as soon as possible.

# 7

Miss Balfour, giving Rosie a reassuring smile, addressed the children. 'Everyone, this is Rosie Ward, who I was telling you about.' She looked down upon Rosie. 'Go and find a seat, but first take off your coat and leave it here with your suitcase.'

Pleased Miss Balfour told her what to do, as Rosie felt agonisingly awkward standing there, she made her way over to a bench that had a space. Meanwhile, Miss Balfour walked to the side of the room where there was a food trolley outside a doorway, with three older-looking children forming a queue in front of it.

Feeling watched, Rosie was just about to raise her leg over the bench when a boy, with cropped hair and wearing a shirt beneath a knitted pullover, looking indignantly at her.

He whispered, 'You can't sit there. That's Bobby's place and he's busy being one of the food monitors. Besides, you have to sit with the girls.'

Mortified she'd done something wrong, Rosie saw that all the girls did indeed sit together, likewise the boys. She thought it safest to sit with the three little glum-faced girls at the end of the table nearest the curtain.

Miss Balfour glanced at her. 'Here, Alice,' she told the girl who was first in the food trolley queue. 'Take this bowl of broth over to Rosie.'

'Why me, miss?' She gave Rosie a black look. 'I'm looking after the little ones.'

There was a shocked gasp from the children.

'Because, Alice, you're nearest. Besides, Rosie is sitting next to the little ones. And please in future don't speak out of turn.' Her features softened. 'You know you'll only get into trouble.'

The girl, grudgingly taking the bowl offered to her, sauntered over to where Rosie sat, and with a pout of disdain handed her the dish of stew. The tense moment over, everyone got back to the business of eating and all that could be heard in the echoey hall were spoons clattering on china bowls.

'Thank you,' Rosie said.

With a jut to her chin, and without answering, the older girl walked away. She was stick thin with long legs and short curly red hair, but Rosie didn't like to stare for long because she was scared the girl with the hostile glare would turn on her.

At that moment the curtain opened and Rosie saw Miss Black walk in carrying what looked like a large black bible that had golden-edged pages. As the orphans shuffled to sit up straight, the atmosphere in the room became one of unease. Even the little kiddies on her table appeared as though they'd frozen. Miss Black headed for the top of the table where Rosie sat and she felt herself withdraw.

Her eyes surveying the room, the mistress spoke. 'Good evening, children.'

'Good evening, Miss Black,' they chanted in unison.

'Was grace said?' Her piercing eyes sought Miss Balfour's.

'It was, Miss Black. I thought it was wise to start as Cook had brought the trolley in and the food would get cold.'

A pause. 'We'll have the bible reading after the meal is finished.' She glanced down at Rosie. 'I take it you've introduced the new girl.'

'I have, Miss Black.'

The mistress sat down, beckoning to Miss Balfour with a hand to continue serving the food. In the unnerving quiet, save for spoons clattering, the only other sound that could be heard was the big clock ticking on the wall.

It was when the plates were cleared by two girl monitors, the pasty-faced little girl sitting next to Rosie, wearing a shabby washed-out frock with a white pinafore covering it, and navy woolly cardigan, raised wide, anxious eyes up at her.

Squirming in her seat, she whispered, 'Want a wee-wee.'

Rosie looked helplessly around. Seeing the little girl holding herself down below, Rosie put up her hand.

Miss Black peered at her. 'Yes.'

'Please, miss, the little girl wants to go to the lav.'

All eyes turned on her, Rosie felt her ears burning. She wished herself away from this horrible orphanage and the unpleasant people in it.

Miss Black's cold stare swept around the children, whereupon, eyes down, they continued eating their pudding.

'Miss Balfour, where is the help? This is her responsibility. The infants should have eaten before now.'

Miss Balfour, who had finished her duties at the food trolley, was now sitting at the opposite end of the table to Miss Black. 'Hazel's dad turned up in his van to take her home early as it's frosty outside and he didn't want her walking home in the dark and slipping on the pavement.'

Miss Black gave a displeased shake of the head, muttering the word 'mollycoddled'. Rosie wondered what it meant.

Miss Balfour nodded at an older girl with straight brown hair. 'Brenda, take Mary and the other two little ones over to the dormitory and help get them ready for bed. I'll be over shortly.'

Brenda nodded. Scraping back her chair, she made her way to the little ones, ushering them all out of the room.

The pudding finished – thick rice pudding that stuck to Rosie's spoon – she watched on as the food monitors cleared the tables before pushing the stacked trolley through the side doorway. Everyone then turned towards Miss Black, who stood, placed a pair of round metal-framed spectacles on her nose and picked up the bible that sat before her on the table.

Peering over the spectacles, she told them, 'The reading today is from the Book of Samuel.'

Rosie tried to stay interested but what with the mistress's dreary voice and words like 'thee', 'thy' and 'heareth', no matter how she tried, she couldn't concentrate. Looking around the fidgeting children, she realised neither could they. Eventually, Miss Black closed the bible and laid it back on the table. She paused for a moment, her stern eyes travelling across the children. Rosie felt herself shrink when the mistress's gaze stopped at her.

'Stand up, Rosie Ward.'

Rosie stood, feeling on show. She had a sensation that the hairs on her arms were standing up.

'Orphans, I want volunteers to tell Rosie what rules she must learn if she is to stay out of trouble.' Again, her eyes travelled the room. 'Very well.' She pointed to a young girl who had short black hair and a fringe. 'You can start, Pamela.'

Pamela, with a startled expression, looked helplessly around the room. 'To get out of bed at the first bell.'

Miss Black nodded, then her dark eyes travelled to Pamela's neighbour.

'The dormitories and washrooms are swept and cleaned each morning and inspected by monitors.'

So it went on and Rosie's mind felt swamped with all the rules. Then Miss Black nodded at the older girl with the red hair – Alice.

The girl smirked. 'To bite your tongue to stop you answering back.'

Miss Balfour gave a sharp intake of breath. Some of the older boys' lips sucked in to smother a laugh, but Miss Black's lips drew into a thin line of disapproval.

'You may think that's funny, girl, however, I do not.' She shook her head in regret. 'You have the devil on your shoulder, girl, and you must be taught a lesson.'

An uncanny hush descended on the room.

'Firstly, you will take on the responsibility of telling Rosie Ward all she needs to know about what is expected of her, and to show her around. Making sure she knows the rules and schedule here at Teviot Hall: homework time, mealtimes, the monitor system. If Rosie fails to know the rules, you will be held responsible.'

Rosie was upset she was being dragged into this but she was afraid of the consequence if she were to speak out. Alice, however, folded her arms and gave Miss Black a scornful look. Though her tummy trembled, Rosie couldn't help but admire the girl's nerve.

Alice tossed her head. 'And secondly?'

Miss Black picked up the bible. She told Alice, her thin

body bristling, 'Because you can't keep a civil tongue, your punishment will be to wash your mouth out with soap. Starting tonight when you'll come to my office after homework time.'

Alice muttered something under her breath. Rosie's heart sank and she stiffened as she saw Miss Black's eyes narrow.

'And if the new girl does make a mistake, your punishment will continue.'

It was unfair to burden Rosie like this, she wanted to argue, but she could tell that to do so would mean she'd be in deep trouble. The look of resentment she got from Alice made Rosie realise she was in bother with her too.

After Miss Black took prayers that took an age and everyone was dismissed, Alice approached Rosie.

'Come on, then,' she said with a scowl, making her way to the dividing curtain.

Rosie, collecting her belongings, hurried after her. Outside, she took a moment to look up at the sky where the moon, hanging in the darkened heavens, had a hazy halo surrounding it. Stepping carefully over the glittering frosty ground, she followed Alice, who was making for a building the other side of the courtyard.

'You'd better remember everything I tell you,' Alice said without turning as she too took care crossing the slippery cobbles, 'or else I'll be for it and it'll be all your fault.'

Rosie thought this unfair too, but decided it was best not to reply.

'Are you dumb?' Alice stopped at a building which had a brickwork arch with a door in the middle and peaked roof with sash windows beneath. At the far end of the building, stone steps with a handrail led to a door that Rosie gathered was the upstairs entrance.

Alice's face angry, Rosie knew she was intent on arguing.

'No. It's just I don't know what to say,' Rosie answered.

'For a start, that you'll do your very best to remember everything.'

'I promise I will. I don't want you to have to wash your mouth with soap because of me.'

'Good. You should have said so to Miss Black. I know I would if it had been me.'

The chilly air was biting Rosie's face and she wished they could go inside but she really wanted to know what Alice would have done. 'What would you have said?'

'I would have told the old hag she was being unjust bringing me into it.'

Rosie cringed at the thought that Alice might think she was a coward. It was clear Alice didn't care what she said or to who, and Rosie hoped she wouldn't call Miss Black a hag in front of the mistresses as she really would be in for it then. Though, if it was Miss Balfour, she didn't seem the kind of person who'd snitch on Alice.

'Where is everyone?' she asked, noticing the other children hadn't made an appearance.

'It's too early for bedtime. So we either do homework or read books in the classroom. Both are boring but the witch doesn't allow us to laze around or heaven help us, if we idly gossip when the devil would be at work.' Opening the door under the archway, Alice stepped inside.

Rosie, unsure what to expect, followed. As her eyes adjusted to the gloom she saw, by the flickering light of two lamps, a high-ceilinged dormitory with wooden cot beds either side, and more green walls. A warm glow came from a cast-iron stove at the bottom end of the dormitory.

'The washroom's through there.' Alice pointed to a door

at the other end of the room where noises came from within. 'The lavs are outside.'

'Who's in there?' Rosie gestured to the washroom.

'I would think Miss Balfour with the little ones. She left before prayers. Lucky her.' Alice made for the bed at the end of the row. 'You can have this one. Nobody's using it.'

Her side aching, weariness washed over Rosie, and after placing her suitcase on the end of the bed, she slumped down beside it.

'Actually, when I come to think about it,' – all signs of irritation gone, Alice sank down beside her – 'I'm rather enjoying this punishment. It's better than being stuck with the others doing homework.' Swinging her feet up, she lounged on the bed. 'They're so terrified of the witch they never have any fun.'

Rosie's sympathies were with the others, as she too was scared of the mistress. Changing the subject, she asked, 'Who's Hazel? The girl Miss Black was cross at.'

'Hazel Rutherford. Her dad, Ian, runs the newspaper shop in the village. Hazel serves in the shop of a morning, then in the afternoon she looks after the infants here that don't go to school. She's expected to stay and help them get ready for bed.'

They lapsed into silence for a while, Rosie digesting this new information.

Then looking around the high-ceilinged room, she wondered at the dormitory's size. 'What was this room before?'

'Miss Balfour says the building was once a coach house. The rooms upstairs used to be the groom's and coachman's quarters in the olden days. Miss Balfour lives up there now.' Alice sat up and put her hands behind her head. 'Sir Keith Henley, who owns this place, had it fixed up. See, the other side is the boys' dormitory.' She nodded to the end of the room.

On further inspection, Rosie noticed that it wasn't a wall but a wooden partition. Curious about Sir Henley, she probed, 'Mrs Wilkinson who brought me here was talking to Fran about Sir Henley. It sounded like something's happened to him?'

'Not him. His son, Fergus. Miss Black told us that the Halifax bomber Fergus was in ran out of fuel and crashed landed in a field not far from the RAF station. Fergus was one of the crew killed.' She gave a sad shake of the head. 'I like Sir Henley. He's posh but not stuck up.'

'Does he live on his own?'

Alice nodded. 'His wife died years ago before we came here. He always stops and talks when he sees us and seems interested in what we're doing.' She grimaced. 'You can imagine prayer time on the day Miss Black found out his son had died. They went on forever.' At the thought of the mistress, Alice's face clouded over. 'Sir Henley's gone to his sister's and no one knows when he'll be back. I bet if he's not here for Christmas the old cow won't let us have a tree this year.'

Rosie tried not to show her shock at Alice's name calling of Miss Black. 'Why won't she?'

'She thinks we'll all go to hell for forgetting what Christmas is really about and only thinking of our bellies and presents. Not that we'll get any of those now that Sir Henley isn't here.'

Rosie found her mind wondering about Christmases past. She tried to conjure up a memory of what they had been like for her but again it was useless. Rather than dwell on her woes as it would only upset her, she asked, 'Are all the children here from South Shields?'

'Nah! Not all. Some of them come from around here and have relatives or a mam in the area. But because they're poor, they put their kids away. And d'you know what?' She pulled a disgusted face. 'Those kids cry at night cos they want to go home. Stupid! Fancy crying over somebody that dumped you.'

It was too much for Rosie; she felt tears prickling behind her eyes. Maybe she had a mam who didn't want to find her. In her weakened state, it would have been easy to bawl but remembering her vow not to cry, she told herself: grow up. She couldn't imagine the girl lying idly next to her giving in.

'Have you got any relatives?' Rosie asked Alice.

Her good mood vanishing, Alice jumped from the bed as though a wasp had stung her. 'That's got nothing to do with you,' she hissed, and left Rosie dumbfounded as she stormed down the dormitory before slamming the door on her way out.

# 8

Miriam Balfour, hearing the dormitory door slam, opened the washroom door a crack and peered out. By the light of the lamp, she saw Rosie Ward sitting on the far-end bed but not a sign of Alice. Groaning, she wondered where the girl was, and if she'd kept her appointment with Miss Black to receive her punishment. Or was she being true to form and being her obstinate self?

Miriam worried over all her charges, but none so much as Alice. She never allowed herself to show any favouritism, treating each of the children as individuals, deserving of equal amounts of her time and energy – even though she did have a soft spot for little Mary as well.

Hauling her mind back to the job in hand, she concentrated on helping the three weary infants in her charge to get ready for bed. A short time later, closing *The Bounty Book for Tiny Tots*, Miriam eased herself as quietly as she could from Mary's bed and, checking that the other two little girls slept soundly, she tiptoed over to Rosie Ward's bedside.

'Are you awake, Rosie?' she whispered.

A head came from beneath the blanket. The girl looked upset, the white of her eyes pink.

'I know it's all strange, Rosie, but you'll soon settle in.'

'It's not that.'

'Then what is it?' The girl seemed reticent to say anything. 'Was it Alice with you before?'

Rosie nodded. 'I didn't mean to make her mad but—'

'What happened?'

Rosie struggled to sit up in the bed. 'I only asked if she had relatives.'

*Oh dear*, Miriam thought, *a touchy subject with Alice.*

'The thing is, Rosie, though Alice is quick to lose her temper she can just as easily get over why she lost it. I suspect that sometimes she regrets her outbursts.'

'But what if she has to have her mouth washed out with soap because of me?'

Seeing her anguished face, Miriam's heart went out to the child. But now was not the time to get into a discussion about such matters. 'Rosie, you must be exhausted. For now, all you can do is to try to put today's events out of your mind and get some rest. How are your injuries? Are you in pain?'

Rosie nodded. 'A bit.'

'Shall I get you a hot water bottle?'

'No thank you.' The child sank down in her bed.

Miriam had the suspicion she didn't want to be a bother, but respecting Rosie's answer, she pulled the blanket up to her chin. 'Night night, Rosie. Everything will look brighter tomorrow after a good night's sleep.'

Hark at her, Miriam thought as she moved from the bed. *If only I believed the things I trot out to make the children feel better.*

Making her way to the little ones' beds to check they were indeed asleep, Miriam despaired at the thought of what

Alice might be going through with Miss Black. But she couldn't intervene; her job would be at risk and what good would that do? Şhe wouldn't be here for the children then.

Alice was one of the oldest girls at Teviot Hall. Miriam had hoped she and the new girl would make friends as Alice's fiery behaviour frightened the other children. Rosie appeared such a ready-to-please young soul, and Miriam hoped the new girl would have a calming influence on Alice – even if their first meeting hadn't gone so well.

Miriam had learnt over the years that the orphans, because they had no permanency in their lives as staff and other children were never a constant, often didn't bond with anyone and came to depend on only themselves. In the case of Alice, her frustration at times getting the better of her, she would explode like a volcano in a rebellious tantrum.

She looked down at the little girls, angelic in sleep. Huddled beneath their coarse grey blankets, their little forms were far too thin. If only they were allowed a teddy to cuddle but such things were frowned upon by Mistress Black. Life at the orphanage was both strict and structured. No child was permitted to own anything and everything must be shared, toys put back in the cupboard at the end of the day.

Miss Balfour kissed her fingertips and placed them on each of the infants' foreheads. She hoped the picture story book she'd read to them earlier would leave them with sweet dreams.

'Night night, sleep tight.'

Closing the coach house door behind her, Miriam picked her way over the cobbles, the torch she carried guiding her way as the moon was veiled behind a cloud. Entering the darkened lobby of the Little Theatre, she noted the light shining from beneath the bottom of the office door. Entering the classroom, the chilly night air seeping into the room, her eyes skimmed the children at their desks, noting Alice wasn't amongst them.

'Bedtime, everyone. Put your homework away.' Her voice sounded as deflated as she felt.

'Yes, Miss Balfour,' the children chanted.

Desk lids were lifted and books put away, then multiple chairs scraped on the wooden floor.

'Be careful, it's slippy outside,' she told them as they filed from the room. It wasn't necessary to tell the children to keep quiet in the dormitory because the little ones were asleep, because silence at all times was drummed into them by Mistress Black. And to disobey carried the risk of punishment. 'It's your turn to lead the way with the torch, Agnes.'

Agnes, who wore a baggy polo neck jumper, kilt and knees socks that straggled down to her ankles, stood up, her young chest puffed out in pride at this privileged responsibility.

After the children left the room Miriam, rubbing off the writing from the blackboard, heard the classroom door open behind her. She turned to see Alice standing there, her freckles standing out in an ashen face. Clearly agitated, Alice struggled to keep her composure. Miriam found it difficult not to fuss – but knew Alice would detest such a happening, so she resisted going over to the girl.

'Stupid cow,' Alice blazed. 'Why Lifebuoy?' There were traces of red on her lips from the soap Miss Black had used and Alice wiped her mouth with the sleeve of the jumper.

Miriam balked at the idea of reprimanding Alice about her language, as she'd suffered enough for one day, but she couldn't resist saying, 'I know you're upset, Alice.' *And rightly so*, said a voice in her mind. 'But you must learn not to antagonise Miss Black. What if she hears you now?'

'I couldn't care less if she does.'

Miss Balfour inwardly groaned. How could she reach the child?

'Alice, Miss Black believes that—'

'You're taking her side.' Alice's expression hardened. 'She's an evil old cow who likes to terrify little kids and not you or anybody else can tell us otherwise.' Breathing heavily after the outburst, Alice's eyes widened, seemingly in shock at her loss of self-control. Turning, she fled from the room.

It was true, Miss Balfour accepted, but what could she do? The fear of losing her position and being homeless and, more importantly, not being there for the children, made her afraid to speak out.

Home to Miriam as a child was a sprawling vicarage surrounded by overgrown gardens, in the grounds of St Joseph's church in her hometown. Her mother died when Miriam was six from a heart problem and from an early age Father treated her more as his companion than his daughter. As she grew, her life became one of restraint. The picture house, according to Father, was a 'den of sin', dances 'dens of iniquity', and wearing make-up 'the road to damnation'. Though she had yearned to be like other girls, go courting, become engaged, get married, she had resigned her life to keeping house and helping Father serve in the parish.

It was when Miriam gave Mrs Rawling, a parishioner, a home visit after her fifth child was born that she first clapped eyes on Terry – Mrs Rawling's oldest son, who worked his apprenticeship at the shipyard. Two years her senior, Terry was a handsome, twinkly blue-eyed lad with a cocky manner and roguish grin that made the young Miriam's heart twist in rapture at the mere sight of him. To her mystification but increasing delight, Terry showed an interest in her and seemed as smitten as she was.

Father worried about his daughter visiting the Rawling household as he considered the area an unsavoury part of town. Miriam didn't agree; what she saw was a close-knit community where everyone looked out for one another. Plus, there was Terry.

Then came the day when Mrs Rawling insisted, 'You've been a godsend, miss, but it's time I managed on me own. I've got to see to the bairns meself sometimes, haven't I?'

But seeing Terry had become an addiction Miriam was helpless to do anything about. His insouciant ways had rubbed off on her and she felt liberated from the constraint of vicarage life. So much so that those clandestine meetings in the Rawlings' back lane when Father was out at parochial meetings continued, despite Mrs Rawling not needing her help, giving Miriam a devil-may-care attitude she'd never known before or since.

'We have to keep our love for each other a secret.' Terry's striking, boyish features were earnest and sincere as he spoke. 'Because if your da finds out there'll be hell to pay.'

Seeing those gorgeous blue eyes beseeching her, Miriam's heart melted and she would agree to anything once Terry had declared his love for her.

'You're driving me crazy,' Terry told her one October night as, pinning her against the lane wall in the darkness, he came up for air after one of those dreamy kisses where his tongue explored hers. He groaned, 'Seriously, I can't go on like this anymore. Here, feel this.' Taking her hand in his, he'd placed it over his groin.

Feeling something big and hard sent an exquisite tingle in her abdomen and instead of doing what Miriam knew to be right and proper, especially when she had a father who was a pillar of respectability in the community, she let her hand linger, enjoying the ecstasy of the moment. Then the knowledge she was acting indecently kicked in and Miriam resisted the longing to go any further.

Terry withdrew from her and in the darkness, she could feel the tension building. 'You can't love us as much as you say,' he accused; his words like a knife slashed her innards. 'Or else you wouldn't put us through this agony.'

God help her, Miriam, starved of love her whole life through, would do anything to keep him. So, one night when Father was out at a parish meeting, Terry came calling and she led him to her bedroom. Afterwards when she lay in his arms, instead of being sublimely happy, came the gnawing doubts and worries. She'd sinned and Miriam knew come the day, she'd have to pay.

As happens in close communities where tongues wag, Father eventually heard his daughter was 'seeing that young tearaway, Terry Rawling'. Outraged, he forbade his daughter from seeing Terry again. Such had been her submissiveness in the past he didn't question she wouldn't obey. But so strong was her love for Terry, the timid soul she was changed into one of rebellion.

'I love him,' she wailed.

'He's not the sort of boy I want my daughter associating with and that's the end of the matter,' Father barked.

Standing in the silent classroom, Miss Balfour closed her eyes. Transported back to that time when she had no control over her life, Miriam recalled the resultant behaviour to Father's unbending stance on the matter of Terry – her anger, resentment, the final shame. Father's fury at her behaviour knew no bounds, the aftermath being that Miriam was packed off to teacher training college at Alnwick Castle. He made it plain that from then on, she was expected to make her own way in life, which suited Miriam fine, especially when she heard he'd hired the trollop Mrs Teresa Hardy, a widow in the parish, to replace Miriam as housekeeper.

It was when her teacher training finished, the realisation she'd nowhere to live and no money to find a place dawning on her, Miriam, who by now had misgivings about her prior behaviour and the price she had to pay, lost her fighting spirit. So, when the position for a housemistress to be employed at Blakely orphanage was advertised in the *Gazette*, she duly applied and was thrilled to bits. Though she did find it difficult to work under the harsh regime which the mistress at the time imposed but with no alternative, she plodded on, and her religious convictions intact, Miriam pledged to devote her life to the orphans.

Shaken by the memories, like a book whose pages become too harrowing to read, Miriam slammed that compartment of her mind firmly shut.

But the ghost of Father, his bullying, still resided within her and it affected her in such a way that although she was loath to admit it, the previous mistress had intimidated her, and now so did Miss Black. At least Miriam had never lost her faith, but the difference between Father, Miss Black and herself was that she believed in a loving and forgiving God.

The first time Miriam ventured into the local Co-op after arriving at the estate, the villagers in the queue were agog with curiosity, wanting to know who she was and where the orphanage had come from. Miriam, answering their questions as best she could, was told by a middle-aged woman, 'I attended Dunglen school where Miss Black was headmistress. She was a nasty piece of work then. Aye and I feel sorry for those poor wee orphans under that woman's tyrannous rule.'

Miss Black, a spinster, had come out of retirement when there was a call in the local village for someone to run the orphanage.

'Her father was a local preacher,' Mrs Craddock, the shopkeeper, had told Miriam, her arms folded at her substantial bosom, a hardened expression on her knowing face. 'A bible-bashing man and his weans had no life. Though the youngest had a mind of her own and wouldn't be browbeaten.'

'She's still the same to this day,' the woman in the front of the queue said, laughing.

'Weans?' Miriam had asked, confused.

'His bairns.' The shopkeeper had shaken her head. 'You'll have to learn the language, hen, if you're to settle this side of the border.'

Crossing the courtyard in the frigid night air, Miriam now looked up at the darkened sky, the distant rumble of aircraft startling her. She tensed as the planes droned closer, then thundered overhead, but relaxed when she recognised them as heavy bombers, probably returning to the nearby airfield.

Her thoughts, as she opened the coach house door, were of Terry Rawling. His ambition had been to join the RAF. *Did he?* she wondered. Wherever he was, she prayed for him, as she'd forgiven Terry long ago.

# 9

Alice awoke next morning to the aftertaste of Lifebuoy soap. Lying in the darkened dormitory, she ran her tongue over the roof of her mouth and pulled a disgusted face. Images played back in her mind of the previous night when Miss Black handed her the tablet outside the toilet in the Little Theatre lobby.

'Wet the soap with cold water and wash your mouth out with it.'

Rage had coursed through Alice at the sheer indignity of what was expected of her, made worse by the fact the mistress watched on. A pounding came in her ears. She wouldn't do it. The cow couldn't make her. Then she'd seen the gleam of gratification in Miss Black's evil eyes: she'd expected trouble and possibly would resort to a far worse punishment for disobedience. Alice wouldn't give her the satisfaction. Wetting the soap at the little sink, she opened her mouth and put out her tongue, directing it at Miss Black. Then she licked the soap as though it was a lollipop.

The mistress's eyes had narrowed in her bony face.

'Mmm!' said Alice, desperately trying not to gag and inwardly feeling sick to the stomach. The smell of soap reminded her of the disinfectant that was put on wounds and she concentrated on the idea that it was doing her good.

*I won't be sick, I won't be sick,* she chanted in her mind.

'Enough.' The mistress was not amused.

Alice had got the upper hand but what could the cow do about it? Alice had done what she was told. *Ha!*

Her spine stiffening, the mistress made for the doorway. 'Let that teach you a lesson.'

Alice, giving the mistress time to go back in her office, lunged forward and, kneeling, put her head over the toilet bowl, and heaved from her toes. She hoped Miss Black hadn't heard.

Now, sitting up in the darkened dormitory, rubbing the sleep from her eyes, she wondered what the time was. The morning bell hadn't rung yet, so it must be before six. She shivered. The stove had gone out and the air in the dormitory was perishing.

A moment later the bell jangled outside, making Alice start. Then the dormitory door whined open and Miss Balfour's silhouette moved down the centre aisle. This time of year, the blackout wouldn't end until breakfast time, which was another two hours away. The lamps were lit and Miss Balfour carried a torch, her soft voice encouraging the infants to awaken.

A tinge of guilt poked Alice; she felt bad about accusing Miss Balfour of taking sides with Mistress Black. Like all the orphans, Alice was fond of Miss Balfour – though Alice was pained to admit to it. A committed Christian, Miss Balfour was the fairest person Alice knew. And though she appeared as afraid as everyone else of Miss Black, the teacher always put the children first – even if it meant crossing the evil witch at times.

Alice reached for her woollen socks and the garters to keep them up, and her thoughts strayed to Rosie Ward. She became indignant at the thought of the new girl being her shadow. Huh! If Miss Black thought Alice would kowtow to her wishes to show this Rosie the rules, then she could think again. The girl could read, couldn't she? The rules were everywhere. And they were recited by Miss Black at the beginning of every week. As far as showing this Rosie around, she had eyes, hadn't she? All she had to do was follow the rest.

Feeling better now that she'd found a way to outwit Miss Black, Alice smiled smugly and pulled up her socks.

---

A bell clanged, waking Rosie. She sat up, staring into the dark void. Though exhausted, she'd hardly slept a wink. Tossing and turning throughout the night, her mind wouldn't rest. She didn't like it here. She was afraid of Miss Black, Alice was mean and the others never played or looked happy, they just stared with big, frightened eyes – and Rosie didn't want to end up like them.

She wished she could remember something about her life. The scariest thing was not knowing who you were. But what if, her anxious mind asked, it's best you don't find out, because finding out would only make things worse?

A sudden noise distracted her. The lamps were lit and, by their glow, Rosie saw Miss Balfour walking down the middle aisle towards her.

'Good morning, Rosie. I hope you slept well. Time to get dressed.'

Though she couldn't make out the mistress's features, in the dim light Rosie heard the smile in her voice. Miss Balfour was nice.

Clinging to the thought as she braced herself to get dressed in freezing air, a natural curiosity for what the day would bring took over.

Teviot Hall orphanage had a tightly structured schedule, Rosie soon found out. The day started with Miss Balfour giving out duties in the dormitory.

When it came to Alice's turn, the housemistress said, 'Washroom and toilet duties, Alice. Take Rosie along with you. She's got poorly ribs, so perhaps you could give her the lighter jobs.'

'Aw, miss, it doesn't seem five minutes since I last did the toilets,' Alice complained.

Miss Balfour hesitated before answering, but then said, 'Everyone takes their turn equally, Alice. You should think yourselves lucky,' she addressed the children. 'The laird was kind enough to provide us with a decent place to wash, and outside toilets. Unlike the WTC women who have to make do with a tap outside and an earthen toilet. And remember' – she faced Alice – 'Miss Black makes spot checks.'

After giving out the rest of the duties – scrubbing floors, making beds, sweeping and tidying the classroom and dining hall, the older ones helping dress the little ones – Miss Balfour left.

Rosie, unsure, approached Alice. 'How can I help?' She heard the caution in her own voice.

Alice, busy fastening the laces of her scuffed boots, didn't look up. 'You're not deaf. You heard what we have to do.'

Agonised what to say, Rosie decided upon, 'If you tell me where to start—'

Alice stood and glared at her. 'You're not a baby. Just get started.'

Frustrated, Rosie had a mind to tell Alice what would happen if she didn't do as Miss Black said but felt that unwise because, intuitively, she knew that would only make matters worse.

She chewed her bottom lip; neither did she want to beg. 'I don't know what to do. Where things are.'

'That's not my problem.' Alice made for the washroom, collecting a lamp on the way.

Rosie, aware the orphans still in the dormitory were staring at her, felt uncertain what to do.

Alice's voice came from the depths of the washroom. 'You could make a start in the lav by cutting newspapers into squares. You'll find the newspapers and scissors in the basket on the floor. Then thread the squares on the string that's hanging from a nail in the wall. That shouldn't be too difficult for your poorly ribs.'

Alice poked her head around the door, and Rosie saw the smirk on her face by the light of the lamp.

'And while you're there, check the toilets. The infants can't reach the chain to flush.' She made to turn then, scowling, she added, 'But mind, I don't want you hanging around me all day. Is that clear? Just read the rules and follow the rest.'

A part of Rosie could easily hate the girl with the flaming red hair but looking deep into Alice's eyes, she knew the look that resided there. It was fear. Then Rosie's young heart understood. For all her bravery, Alice was the same as the rest. She wasn't helping Rosie by telling her what to do, but trying to avoid the anger of Miss Black.

A bell rang at eight o'clock, summoning the orphans to breakfast in the dining hall. Light now, they didn't need a leader carrying a torch to see by as they made their way over the cobbled yard.

'Eat everything up,' whispered the fair-haired girl who sat next to Rosie at the trestle table. Her eyes darting around the room, she continued, 'The mistress says it's a mortal sin if you don't and you get punished.'

Observing the lukewarm stodgy oatmeal gruel, with a blob of treacle in the middle, Rosie's appetite diminished. But fear drove her to pick up her spoon and she didn't stop, eating until her bowl was clean. After the unnervingly silent breakfast when only spoons clattered on dishes, prayers were said, and then Rosie trailed after the rest into the classroom.

Miss Balfour, standing at the front of the class, pointed to a desk. 'You can sit there, Rosie. I take morning class. In the afternoons the older children attend the village school where you'll meet the local children and other evacuees who are staying in the area.' She gave an encouraging smile. 'Don't worry, Mrs Murray takes you to school and Alice will be there to look after you.'

Alice, sitting the opposite side of the room, glowered at Rosie, whose heart sank.

'If you don't feel well enough let me know and you can stay here with Hazel and the little ones,' added Miss Balfour.

No matter how much her side hurt, Rosie was determined she wouldn't stay in the orphanage – not with Miss Black lurking around.

The morning passed quickly with Miss Balfour giving

them a history lesson but Rosie found she couldn't take much in because she couldn't concentrate in her new surroundings. Dinner was a rissole – a sort of sausage made out of what looked like oatmeal, dried egg powder and a scrap of minced meat, covered with breadcrumbs – served with a scoop of mash and peas. Pudding was again stodgy rice pudding that stuck to her spoon. After the meal was finished and Alice nowhere in sight, Rosie decided to do what the girl told her earlier and 'follow the rest'. So, trooping after the others, she found herself in the lobby where everyone was taking their coats from the hooks and bundling into them.

Finding her coat, Rosie turned to the fair-haired girl from breakfast, who was called Agnes. 'Is the village school far?' she whispered.

Agnes looked furtively around and, satisfied it was safe to speak, answered, 'Nah! It's not that far.'

'Who's Mrs Murray?' Rosie shouldered into her outdoor coat.

'She comes in every day, usually to help on a morning to look after the little ones. She's not so bad and allows us to talk on the way to school.'

As if on cue the lobby door opened and an older woman came in. She had a cheery, plump face and little lines fanned out from her eyes when she smiled. She wore a colourful turban-style headscarf, and little pearl drop earrings hung from her ears. Her coat, with its green and white stripes, looked as though it had been made from a hairy woollen blanket.

She ushered everyone outside, then seeing Rosie, she beamed. 'You must be Rosie. Come on, hen, catch up with the others outside and form a line. We don't want to be late for school, else we'll be for it.' She cackled as though she didn't have a care.

Rosie, warming to Mrs Murray, felt her chest slacken and even her sore side seemed to relax. The lady didn't seem the sort to be afraid of Miss Black.

Outside in the chilly afternoon, as the orphans walked along the path in crocodile style, the winter sun cast long shadows of their bodies on the ground. Rosie paired up at the end of the line with Agnes, who appeared about the same age as her. The others made off up the tree-lined road and when they snaked around a bend, Rosie saw Alice way ahead, walking on her own at the front. Rosie was glad she had Agnes as a partner to take her mind off things because the girl seemed willing to talk now that she was out of the orphanage, and it was as though the rules didn't count anymore.

'Did you live in the orphanage when it was in South Shields?' Rosie asked.

Agnes nodded. 'We came here at the beginning of the war when I was only five. Not everyone as there wasn't enough room. I don't know where the others were evacuated to.' She glanced at Rosie. 'I'm glad I was sent here though.'

'But why?' Rosie was confused why anyone would want to be here with Miss Black in charge.

Agnes gave her a look as though it was obvious. 'Because I wanted to stay with Miss Balfour.'

'Even with Miss Black in charge?'

'The mistress we had before was just as bad, if not worse.' She gave a little shudder at the memory. 'Anyway, it doesn't matter because I'm going to be adopted soon.' A faraway look came into her eyes.

'Really?' The thought of being adopted had never occurred to Rosie. What if that happened to her and the police stopped looking for her relatives. This new worry made her chest squeeze tight and she couldn't breathe properly.

Agnes, apparently, didn't notice her discomfort. 'Where are you from?' she asked.

'Same as you. South Shields.'

'In an orphanage?'

Rosie felt herself withdraw; she didn't want to talk anymore because her ribs started to hurt. She was saved from answering when Mrs Murray, at the front of the line, waved to them to catch up.

'Hurry up.' Agnes's expression grew uneasy. 'We're lagging behind. I don't know how but Miss Black always finds out if we do something wrong and I don't want to be in her bad books.'

Rosie held her side as they hurried to catch up with the others. Passing between two stone pillars whose gates were missing, Rosie found herself at a main road at the bottom of a hill with grim, stone-built houses either side. When she reached the top of the hill, the view opened out to reveal a lovely village with shops, houses, a post office with a red pillar box in front, all centred around an expanse of green.

'What's the tent for?' She nodded to the large tent erected under some trees in the middle of the village green.

Agnes shrugged. 'I heard Mrs Murray say billeted soldiers from the village got their tabs there. See that?' She pointed to a tall redbrick building that had a clock that had stopped at ten o'clock and was built into the walls above a high window. 'It's the old school. Mrs Murray says it's been requisitioned for the war.'

'What's requi— mean?'

Agnes shrugged. 'I don't know but we can't use the school anymore, we use the church hall instead.' She pointed to a building the other side of the green that had a tall steeple, a red arched front door and colourful windows. 'And that building' – she pointed to a shop that had a queue waiting outside – 'is the butcher's. See the black door next to it? That's the downstairs flat where Miss Black lives.'

Entering the hall by a side door, Rosie found herself in a corridor. She followed the line through a doorway at the end of it into a large musty-smelling hall with tall windows that let in lots of light. At the front of the hall, a blackboard stood below a raised stage that had forlorn-looking curtains either side. A grey-haired lady, wearing a grey suit and colourful scarf tied at the neck, stood in front of rows of wooden desks with cast iron legs.

Mrs Murray bustled up to the lady. As the two of them spoke, their eyes shifted to Rosie. Then with a satisfied nod, Mrs Murray turned and, making her way to the doorway, she smiled reassuringly as she passed Rosie. Meanwhile, everyone was taking off their coats, hanging them up on hooks on the walls, then sat down at their desk. Feeling conspicuous, Rosie looked helplessly around; she spied Alice, who sat in the back row. As their eyes met, Alice turned away.

'Rosie Ward.' The grey-haired lady sought her out with a caring look in her gleaming eyes.

'Yes, miss.'

'I'm Mrs Cameron, your teacher. Take a seat here at the front.'

Rosie did as she was told. The room had gone quiet and she could feel everyone's eyes upon her back.

'If you learn nothing else, Rosie, here at Dunglen school but the three Rs, then you'll do fine by me.' The teacher's eyes travelled the room. 'And what are the three Rs, children?'

'Reading, 'riting and 'rithmetic, Mrs Cameron,' the class chanted.

The afternoon went swiftly by. Mrs Cameron handed out slates and chalk to everyone and gave a spelling test. Afterwards they did sums where they had to add and subtract columns of pounds, shillings and pence. Then the slates were handed in and Mrs Cameron announced, 'Home time, everyone. Wrap up in your coats, the forecast on the wireless is for frost again later.'

Rosie, feeling a pressure down below, didn't want to stand out by asking where the lavatory was. She decided she could wait until she was back at Teviot Hall. Outside, the day darkening, the others formed a line and Mrs Murray appeared from the hall and started counting heads, beginning with Rosie. Agnes was in the middle of the line with a new partner, and Rosie, at the back on her own, crossed her legs because the sudden cold made her feel like she was dying to go.

It wouldn't take a minute, she decided – no one would miss her and she would be back before the line moved off because Mrs Murray was talking to one of the boys at the front. She knew she shouldn't but making a fuss and drawing attention to herself was something she couldn't cope with. Her mind made up, she stole back through the open church doorway and checked the doors in the corridor. Discovering only a kitchen, and a room stacked with chairs, she decided the toilet must be outside.

Back outside, Rosie was dismayed to find the orphans had already started to move. But the urge to wee was unbearable, and Rosie feared she might wet her knickers. Hurrying along the narrow earthen path to the back of the church, she put a hand between her legs, hoping to stem the wee threatening to flow. Looking around the small piece of overgrown land, there were two wooden buildings. Writhing in discomfort, she managed to open the door of the first one, to discover it was half full of coal. Sliding back the bolt on the next door, she opened it. The foul smell emanating from inside told Rosie this was the lav.

Wrinkling her nose, Rosie switched on the torch that was hanging from a nail on the inside and bolted the door. At the back of the hut was a wooden box-like structure with a hole in the top and a door beneath. She knew it was an earthen toilet. Wiggling around in desperation, Rosie worried she wouldn't get her knickers down in time. Holding herself below with one hand, she pulled her knickers down with the other. Sitting on the wooden seat, she closed her mind to the fact that other bums must have done the same thing. As she relaxed, having a wee never felt so good.

Finished, she wiped herself with the newspaper provided which made her think of the Teviot Hall toilets that morning. The reminder of the orphanage brought on the anxiety that Mrs Murray and the others had left, and that she had better be quick if she was to catch them up. As she pulled up her knickers, by the beam of the torch, she spied a big pot with a lid. Rosie knew she had to shovel the ashes inside it into the toilet as it was supposed to stop flies and the stinky smell, even if in Rosie's opinion it didn't work.

Struggling to unbolt the door, she was alarmed when it wouldn't budge. Panicking, the walls seemed to come in on her, and she sagged against the door. *Stay calm*, she told herself when all she wanted to do was burst into tears, *the bolt opened before.* She waited a few minutes, then, with a trembling hand she tried the bolt again and it slid back with ease. All she could think of as she hurried from the hut was that when she fell back against the door it must have slackened the bolt somehow.

Tired and shaky all of a sudden, she hurried as fast as she could along the path. It was while she closed the church gate that she realised she'd left the torch on the floor beside the lav, where no one could see it. Too much in a hurry to return, Rosie knew guilt about this would bother her for the rest of the night.

But that was to be the least of her worries.

# 10

As Rosie hurried down the hill, the late-afternoon gloomy sky was closing in. Breathing the frosty air, she coughed, which made a pain slice through her side. Seeing the stone pillars to the entrance of Teviot Hall ahead, she felt comforted knowing that soon she'd be toasty warm in front of the stove, and hurried along the path looking for the entrance to the Little Theatre.

But soon all she could see was the silhouette of trees that loomed way above her head. She stopped for a moment in the spooky silence before pressing on knowing the path that led to the courtyard must be somewhere ahead.

Looking to her left, she saw a building materialise in the darkened skyline. Teviot Hall. She had missed the path to the theatre. Retracing her steps, relief engulfed Rosie when she saw a path appear on her right. She hurried along it but became confused when it dived downwards and into the woods. Somehow, she'd gone wrong. She stood in the silent night trying to figure out her bearings but she couldn't remember now whether she needed to go left or right. Scared and anxious, Rosie knew she was lost. And her sore rib that she thought better was now beginning to ache.

'Help!' she called into the darkness. 'Somebody help!'

All she heard in reply was the wind blowing through the trees.

The darkness of the woods was intimidating and she feared something sinister might jump out of the dark depths and grab her. But then a memory flashed through her mind of a tall figure looming over her in the darkness, making her feel safe. Feeling bolder, common sense told her that she had to move as help was not far away. She plodded on, stumbling in her haste, prickly bushes on either side of the track scratching her bare skin.

'Hallooo, is anyone there?'

The voice startled Rosie but seeing the beam of a torch bobbing towards her, she made her way towards it.

'I'm here,' she called.

The torch's beam shone in her eyes, blinding Rosie.

'I thought I heard someone. Is that you, Rosie Ward?'

Rosie recognised the voice of Fran Patterson. She could have hugged the woman if she wasn't so reticent with strangers.

'What are you doing out here on your own?' Fran asked.

'I missed the others coming home from school and got lost in the woods.' Rosie, screening her eyes with a hand from the dazzling light, didn't feel the need to add she'd gone for a wee.

'I'm surprised no one missed you.' Fran thankfully left it at that. 'Good job I came back early as there's no one else around to hear you. Some of these tracks go on for miles and you could easily have found yourself deep in the wood and goodness knows when you'd have been found.'

At the thought of being lost in the woods at night, a cold shiver ran down Rosie's spine.

'Come on.' Fran started back, the beam of the torch lighting her way. 'They'll be worried about you.'

It felt good to be trotting alongside Fran, the torch pointing on the ground. Rosie asked because she thought it polite to say something, 'D'you live in Teviot Hall?'

Fran stopped and there was a rustling noise, then a match lit and a cigarette glowed in the darkness. 'Nothing so grand. I bunk up with the rest of the women in army huts.'

'You're in the army?' Rosie smelt the cigarette smoke.

Fran began walking again. 'Nope. The Women's Timber Corps.'

Rosie remembered Fran had mentioned the name when they first met. 'What's that?'

'It's an organisation that fells trees and runs forestry sites and it's managed by women. We're nicknamed Lumberjills. We provide timber for pit props, telegraph poles, coffins, all sorts of things.' There was a pause as Fran took another puff of the cigarette. 'It's important work but you wouldn't think so the way people treat us.'

Rosie didn't understand what Fran meant but decided not to be a nuisance and ask. They walked on in silence, Rosie nursing her aching side. She followed Fran as she crunched along the gravelled path in front of the big house. When they came to the entrance of the courtyard, Rosie reflected that though she didn't want to be in this place with the horrible Miss Black and so far from her hometown, it was a good feeling to be somewhere familiar.

As if Fran knew Rosie's thoughts, she threw her cigarette down on the cobbles and crushed it with a boot, putting a hand on Rosie's shoulder.

'Don't worry, they'll be relieved to see you. I'll stay until you're safely inside.' She knocked on the Little Theatre door.

For some reason Fran's kindness made Rosie quite teary.

The door opening, the pair of them stepped inside and when the light switched on, Mrs Murray appeared before them, her round face white as flour and her hands flying to her cheeks.

'Thank the Lord. Where've you been, hen? I've been worried sick. I trekked all the way back to the church hall with not a sign of you. Nobody knew where you'd—'

At that moment, the office door opened and Mistress Black stood there, her cold eyes sweeping over the three of them.

'Here she is safe and sound.' Mrs Murray's light tone of voice didn't match the concerned look on her face. 'I told you Rosie couldn't have gone far.'

Clasping her hands together, fingers intertwining, Miss Black's nostrils flared. 'She went missing in your care, Mrs Murray. Anything could have happened. See to it that it never happens again.'

'I can assure you it won't.' Mrs Murray, lips tightening, was obviously miffed.

The mistress nodded. 'That will be all, thank you, Mrs Murray, Miss Patterson. I'll take it from here.' She glared at Rosie, who felt herself quake. 'In my office, girl.'

'But surely I'm entitled to hear—' Mrs Murray began.

But the mistress, taking no notice, made her way into the office, leaving the door ajar.

'Of all the—' said Mrs Murray under her breath, her good-natured face fuming. Looking down at Rosie, her features softened. 'Off with you, hen, before you get into more trouble. I'll see what's what in the morning.' She looked at Fran. 'Are yi' coming?'

Fran, who looked dumbfounded at the goings on, nodded. Then the light went out and the front door creaked open. Feeling a blast of cold air, Rosie then heard the door slamming shut.

Standing in the dark, she made her way to the light streaming through the office doorway. The first thing she noticed when she entered the room was the fireplace on the far wall where a fire blazed in the grate. A large desk, with papers strewn over the top, dominated the room and a swivel chair with arms stood behind it. A bookcase stood on the back wall filled with ledgers and a hallstand was by the door with a pair of fur-lined bootee slippers beneath. Rosie could never imagine Miss Black wearing them.

'Girl.'

Rosie's head came up sharply.

'What have you to say for yourself?'

'I got lost, miss,' she mumbled.

'Mrs Murray assures me she counted heads.'

'She did,' Rosie confirmed. There was no way she would get the nice lady into trouble.

'What about Alice Blakely?' The mistress's eyes narrowed as she looked keenly at Rosie. 'She was supposed to be looking after you. She said you went off with someone else.'

Rosie felt a rush of heat flash through her. That was a fib but Rosie was stuck what to say. Because although Alice was mean and she didn't particularly like her, Rosie didn't want her punished on her account.

'I did, miss.'

The mistress bent down, and Rosie smelt mothballs on her clothes.

'Then how was it you got lost?'

Her heart beating wildly, she admitted, 'I went to the lavatory, miss.'

'So why' – the mistress's eyes probed hers – 'did Alice Blakely not notice when the line moved off that you were missing?'

'Because...' Rosie, suddenly weary, floundered. 'She didn't know I'd gone.'

'Why not?'

Rosie was afraid to go on in case she was caught out telling fibs. 'Alice... did look after me, but then I made friends with a girl... I can't remember her name,' she quickly put in. 'I wanted to walk back with her. Alice wasn't happy but when she saw I wasn't going to team up with her, she made off to the front of the line.'

The mistress glared at her and Rosie was convinced those stony eyes knew she was telling fibs.

'Then why did the—' the mistress began.

But Rosie interrupted. 'The other girl went off with someone else. I was at the back of the line by myself...' she improvised. 'I needed the lavatory by then and when I got back the line had gone.' Rosie, feeling uncomfortable telling all those fibs, felt her cheeks flushing but she was in too deep now to change matters. Besides, if the truth came out not only would Alice get into trouble, but she too would be punished for the deceit. Almost in tears because of the tangle she found herself in, Rosie squeaked, 'So, you see, miss, it wasn't Alice's fault.'

The mistress, while stroking the loose skin that drooped from her skinny neck, studied Rosie. 'Come with me,' she finally said, striding out of the room, her lace-up shoes clomping on the wooden floor, and opened the lav door on the far wall.

Rosie felt a cold shiver of fear in her buttocks.

'Here, girl, where I can see you.'

Alice emerged wearing a couldn't-care-less expression.

'Wipe that sullen expression off your face, girl,' Mistress Black barked, 'else I'll reconsider not having to punish you.'

A puzzled frown riddled Alice's brow as if she hadn't heard right.

'Surprisingly' – the mistress didn't look surprised but aggrieved – 'it would seem you were telling the truth. Rosie Ward did take matters into her own hands and walked with someone else and you couldn't have known she was missing.'

Alice glanced at Rosie with an astonished expression.

'I'll overlook your behaviour this time but mark my words, girl, you have a demon in you and nothing will convince me otherwise.' Miss Black nodded towards the lobby. 'Now go before I have time to reflect on your insolence.' She stepped aside to let Alice pass.

Alice's lips bunched as though it was a struggle not to retort then she darted a look at Rosie. 'What about he—'

'That has nothing to do with you. Go, before I change my mind.'

As she watched Alice make off, Rosie, shaken by the exchange, wondered what would happen to her.

'As for you ignoring my instructions.' The mistress's dark eyes surveyed Rosie.

'Miss, I didn't. I just never thought,' Rosie blabbed, fearing washing her mouth out with soap.

The mistress folded her arms. 'You caused an uproar with your irresponsible behaviour. I was at the point of informing the police.'

Rosie could taste the soap in her mouth. 'Honest, miss, I won't do anything bad again.'

The mistress took a long time to respond.

'In consideration of your injuries, I've decided to be lenient. You will go straight to bed without supper and reflect on how your actions affected others. Pray for forgiveness and that it will never happen again.'

'I will, miss, I promise.' Rosie nearly fainted with relief.

# 11

Later, Rosie, the only one lying in bed in the darkened dormitory, felt numb and disbelieving at the situation she found herself in. Maybe it was all a dream and she'd awaken with her memory intact knowing where she was and whose family she belonged to. She squeezed her eyes shut and then opened them again, finding to her distress she was still in the Teviot Hall dormitory.

She heard the door open, and by the lamplight she saw a figure loom out of the darkness. Alice.

Alice came to stand at her bed and then just stood there for a while, before she blurted, 'Nobody's ever done that for me before, 'part from Miss Balfour.' Her voice held a note of incredulity.

'Done what?'

'Stuck up for me.' Alice dived into the pocket of the worn cardigan she wore and held something out. 'It's not much, only cheese and a crust of bread.' She placed the food on the bedcover.

Rosie was still cross with Alice because this was all her

fault, but she knew she wouldn't argue as the timid side of her was a bit scared of her. Plus, there was a part of Rosie that admired Alice and wanted to get to know her better.

'I didn't want you to have to wash your mouth out with soap.' Rosie shuddered at the thought. 'You would have done the same.'

'I wouldn't,' Alice said with certainty. 'Neither would any of the others. In here, you learn to watch out for yourself.'

'Why?'

'Because no one else will.' Alice's face changed and reverted to that hardened look. 'Anyway, I didn't want you to go without anything to eat.' She made to go.

So, that was all she was going to say. No being sorry that Rosie was being punished because of her.

'But I told fibs for you,' Rosie protested.

'I didn't ask you to.'

Seeing Alice's couldn't-care-less expression annoyed Rosie.

'You could have helped me like you were supposed to, then I wouldn't have got into trouble.'

Alice shrugged. 'It's simple. Like I said. Just follow the rest and read the rules.'

Anger flared within Rosie and she felt the need to pick a fight. 'You don't care about anybody but yourself.'

'I told you that already.'

All of a sudden drained by the events of the day – getting lost, having to fib to Miss Black, now fighting with Alice – Rosie crumpled. Her vow not to cry forgotten, tears burnt the back of her eyes.

Hating that Alice watched on, she sniffed. 'Go away.'

Giving in to the unbidden tears, she pulled the thin blanket over her head. She cried, not just for herself but for all the orphans, who like her had no one to turn to, no one who cared. If only this was a story like in the book she'd read, *Heidi*; they'd all have a happy ending. But as much as she might wish it, this was not a story, it was really happening. The thought made her cry even more.

When her sobs subsided, Rosie cupped her face in her hands. She considered what Alice told her: that orphans had to watch out for themselves.

'It was mean of me to let you take the blame.'

Alice's voice startled Rosie.

'I didn't think about what would happen to you when I told the witch you were walking home with someone else.'

In the darkness of the blanket, Rosie's anger subsided; Alice hadn't exactly said she was sorry but she did agree she'd been mean. Rosie seemed to know this was a big thing for the girl to acknowledge. She came up from beneath the cover.

Alice shifted and looked at her feet. 'Why would you care if I got punished?' Her eyes looked uncertain, as if it was difficult asking such a question.

'I don't know. I don't like to see people unhappy,' Rosie answered honestly, because that was her way. 'I don't know if I've always been like this, but I think I probably have.'

'How d'you mean, you don't know?'

Too tired to worry about people finding out what had happened to her, Rosie admitted, 'Because I've lost my memory.'

'Really. Can't you remember anything?'

'Not before I was in hospital I can't. Except...' The little ray of hope returned within her. 'I've remembered some things but nothing to help me know who I am.' She blurted without thinking, 'And nobody cares enough to come looking for me.'

Alice, now sitting on the bed, wanted to know about Rosie's memory loss. After relating about the bombing and her stay in hospital, then being packed off to the orphanage, famished, Rosie began to munch on the hard and tasteless cheese.

'You can remember your name, though.' Alice spoke as though Rosie should be happy at that.

'It's not my real name. It's the name they chose for me on the ward I was in.'

'Ah! I see. Rosie Ward.' Sadness crossed Alice's face. 'Snap. Alice Blakely.'

Bewildered, Rosie asked, 'What d'you mean?'

'It isn't my real name either. Blakely Hall is the name of the orphanage I was in before.' Her jaw clenched as though it was difficult for her to admit and Rosie understood the feeling. 'I was found as a baby on the doorstep by a Nurse Bell. Her name was Alice.' She spoke as if every word was painful to say. 'I was dumped like a piece of rubbish. And I'll never forgive who did it.'

Rosie searched her mind but there was nothing she could think of to help Alice feel better. Besides, Alice's angry expression made her cautious to say anything.

'I've never told that to anyone, mind.' Alice's tone was sharp. 'So, I'll know it's you if anybody says anything.'

'I would never.' Rosie couldn't believe Alice had trusted her with such a big secret. But then, hadn't Rosie done the same thing? Somehow, she felt closer to Alice, as if their shared secret bonded them. She ventured, 'I don't want people to know about me either.'

'It's different with the others,' Alice said, as though Rosie's revelation was taken for granted. 'At least they know who their parents are, even if they were dumped here.'

'Their mam couldn't help it if she was poor,' Rosie defended.

'If I ever have a baby, I'd never give it up. I'd rather starve.'

Rosie thought it best to change the subject. 'What happened to the orphanage you were in before?'

'According to Miss Balfour, Blakely Hall took a hit during the bombings early on in the war. The old battle-axe who ran it and her husband didn't evacuate with us. He was killed and she survived I'm pleased to say but, apparently, she was in a bad way.'

*You see*, Rosie thought, *Alice does have a kind heart.*

'Did she get better?'

'I hope not. I was pleased she didn't die because it would have been too quick. I wanted her to suffer like she made us orphans do.' Alice grinned maliciously.

Horrified at the answer, Rosie was struck dumb. In the silence she noticed, by the glow of the lamplight, that deep in Alice's brown pupils there was no spite, only longing, the same as Rosie experienced when she felt sad and alone.

A sudden noise in the dormitory made them both look towards the door. Miss Balfour was making for Rosie's bed. When she saw Alice, she clutched her throat in surprise, shaking her head when she reached them.

'This really won't do, Alice.'

Alice rolled her eyes at Rosie and said, 'I took the trolley to the kitchen after supper and then skived off prayer time.'

Rosie gasped at her daring.

'What if Miss Black noticed?' the mistress tutted. 'You'd be in trouble again.'

'She didn't though, did she? She was too busy bible reading to notice. I couldn't abide listening to her voice spouting heareth and knowest another night.'

'Alice!' Miss Balfour shook her head once more, lost for words.

As the two girls stared at one another, a look of amusement passed between them and seeing the funny side of the ancient biblical words, Rosie's lips twitched. For no reason save that it was a relief to let loose some of the tension inside, she started to laugh. Alice, bringing her knees up to her chest, collapsed back on the bed and joined in.

'You do know that's blasphemy,' Miss Balfour was heard to say and though her voice was stern, her amused expression gave away how she truly felt.

Long after the stove had gone out and all Rosie could hear was the other children's soft breathing as they slept and the occasional snuffle as if someone was crying, she burrowed under the thin blanket trying to get warm. It had been good to have a laugh with Alice, even if she was worried about 'Blasfomy', that word the mistress used. In Rosie's mind it meant God would be angry with her. Fancy, though, her mind rattled on, Alice being left on the orphanage doorstep. What a horrible thing to live with.

*What about being left on your own at night in an air raid shelter?* a little voice in her mind said. *Kids aren't supposed to be out on their own at night, not if someone loved them and cared.*

Rosie froze at the realisation, and the thought that had been buried away came to gnaw at her brain.

*Maybe my family thought they were better off without me.*

# 12

## DECEMBER 1943

As the children stood and began singing a hymn of thanksgiving, Miriam looked around the tables that morning, and her gaze rested upon the two girls standing together. Though she cared deeply about all the children, and had committed her life to them, she was particularly pleased these two were becoming friends and dearly hoped their friendship would give them renewed strength to face the trials of life.

Rosie, the shorter of the two, had a reserved, shy look about her, but Miriam sensed a toughness in Rosie, which the child hadn't as yet discovered herself. Alice, taller, more robust, her freckled face pouting sullenly, kept her lips firmly closed in rebellion. But beneath her unruly exterior lay a hurt and troubled girl who Miriam prayed would find her rightful place in the world.

Hark at her, Miriam thought. She sounded like Father. But she comforted herself: unlike him, who never practised what he preached, her thoughts and actions were genuine.

The hymn finishing, the strains of childish voices filling the chilly air, Miss Black stood, bible in her hand, her bleak eyes surveying the children.

'The reading is taken from Deuteronomy, chapter twenty-seven,' she said in a reverent voice.

As if the orphans had the time, inclination or bible to check, Miriam found herself thinking before chastising herself for her cynicism.

Miss Black's voice droned on, and Miriam shook a cautionary head to little Mary, who'd started to fidget. When Miss Black read, '"Cursed be the man that maketh..."' and Alice looked at Rosie and grinned, Miriam made big warning eyes at her. Fortunately, Alice took the hint and was more composed by the time Miss Black looked around the innocent faces staring at her. There was hope for the girl yet, Miriam decided.

Then came endless prayers and a report informing on the state of the war. There followed more prayers – this time for the Greek island of Leros which was suffering airstrikes from the enemy causing great destruction. Miriam made a mental note to show the children on the world map where Leros was.

Later, while she was eating stodgy oatmeal (as there was insufficient milk and no treacle left, only a scraping of Cook's homemade jam which Miriam left for the children) she rehearsed in her mind what she would say today to Miss Black when Miriam went to the office and brought up the subject of the festive season. Christmas was by no means imminent, but the thought that the laird wouldn't be here to host the carol singing at Teviot Hall kept niggling at her. Pinching the skin on her neck in concentration, she acknowledged, for the orphans' sake, she must get this right.

. . .

'Away with you and see her ladyship,' Mrs Murray told Miriam in a delightful Scottish accent, her jovial face taking on a serious expression.

Miriam had shared her concerns about Christmas with Mrs Murray and revealed that she was going to raise the subject with Miss Black.

Mrs Murray had said at the time, 'Och, that's good to hear. Those bairns need something to look forward to.'

'I'll manage things here,' she told Miriam now, indicating to the class sitting upright at desks, hands clasped behind their backs.

She gave Miriam an accusing stare. 'By the way, why are the wee ones supposed to sit like that?'

'Miss Black insists that in the reading lesson each child takes a turn reading and it's against the rules for the others to turn a page before it's time.' Miriam shook her head in disgust. 'To avoid temptation, I've told them to sit with their hands behind their back.'

Mrs Murray's bushy eyebrows lowered and pinched together. 'I've never heard anything so rid—'

'I'll be as quick as I can,' Miriam interrupted, having seen the children's eyes go round with curiosity as they listened in.

'Take as long as you like, hen. As long as you jolly well tell her these wee bairns need—'

'I'll do my best,' Miriam said hastily.

Opening the door to the lobby, Miriam then rapped on the office door.

'Enter,' came the strident voice.

Smoothing her uniform frock, Miriam opened the door. 'Can I have a word, Miss Black?'

Sitting behind her desk on a captain's chair, a pen poised in her hand, the mistress frowned. 'This is most irregular, Miss Balfour, you should be in the classroom.'

'Mrs Murray is kindly covering for me.'

Miss Black placed the pen on the desk and sat back, forearms resting on the arms of the chair. 'This had better be important.'

Miriam took a deep breath. 'It is, rather. It concerns the children's Christmas. I thought perhaps we should prepare now.'

Miss Black visibly bristled, as Miriam suspected she would, but this was too important to back down. She crossed her fingers behind her back.

'Sir Henley usually has a tree erected at the hall so the orphans can sing carols around it on Christmas Day.'

The tradition started when the orphanage first came to Teviot Hall. A lavishly bedecked Christmas tree with a small gift for each child beneath it stood at the bottom of the grand and sweeping staircase in the entrance hall of the big house.

'I'm fully aware of the fact,' Miss Black remarked, a perceptive expression on her face as if she knew what to expect next.

'I know how you feel about being—'

'Christmas is a time of rejoicing the birth of Our Lord.' Miss Black pursed her lips disapprovingly. 'Allowing children to believe in Father Christmas is sinful and an offence to God.' With an annoying casualness she sat back in her chair. 'Whilst Sir Henley was here, and as he is gracious enough to allow the orphanage to reside on his estate, I had no choice but to abide by his wishes.' She interlocked her fingers. 'The laird is grieving this year and from what I hear he wants no part of this heathen ritual.'

'But they're only children and have no—'

'In answer to your unasked question: no, Miss Balfour, there will be no Christmas tree, wreaths, or presents, even if it was financially feasible.' Her steely eyes probed Miriam's. 'I will not be party to risking these children go to hell.'

'But that's only your op—'

As Miss Black stood, hand in the air silencing her, the words froze on Miriam's lips.

'I would tread carefully, Miss Balfour, as your employment here depends on your obedience to my wishes.'

Miriam, rattled, understood the uncontrollable rage that sometimes exploded within young Alice. But being subservient to her father over a lifetime had left its mark on Miriam and she kept silent. Besides, though she loathed her spinelessness, could she really risk being dismissed, leave Teviot Hall, the children? The thought was unbearable.

She swallowed her objections. 'I understand, Miss Black. I will of course abide by your wishes.' She left, avoiding Miss Black's gaze because the antipathy she felt for the woman would surely be plain to see.

As Miriam walked into the classroom, Albert, standing behind his iron-framed desk, a worn copy of *The Pilgrim's Progress* in his hand, was, as usual, stumbling over a passage he was reading out loud. Miriam forced herself to smile at the children, her heart twisting at their air of despondency, which should never be found in ones so young.

Mrs Murray, standing at the front of the class, book in her hand, raised her eyebrows questioningly. Miriam shook her head, and was thankful no one could make out the, undoubtedly, unrepeatable oaths Mrs Murray muttered under her breath.

As she observed those dejected little faces, a fire torched in Miriam's belly and she vowed that, somehow, she would make the festive season a happy experience for them all. But first, she decided, her conscience pricking, she must say a prayer for forgiveness for thoughts of animosity towards Miss Black. You never knew what drove someone to become the person they were – she of all people should know that.

# 13

Rosie awoke with a start and, staring into the pitch blackness, her befuddled mind reckoned it must have been the pouring rain that roused her. Rosie hated the creepy darkness, when her mind still imagined some evil that she couldn't see was ready to pounce from under the bed. The stove had long gone out and icy blasts found their way beneath the bottom of doors and around aged window frames. Shivering, she pulled the skimpy blanket up around her neck, but it did no good, and even though she wore her clothes in bed, she was still frozen. But the good thing was her ribs didn't pain her as much these days.

A beam of light further along the dormitory caught her attention. The only person she knew to own a torch was Alice and where she'd got it from was a mystery as she wasn't telling. But that was Alice. Miss Balfour said she was a law unto herself.

Since finding out they shared something in common – that neither of them knew where they came from or who their parents were – the pair had formed a friendship. Rosie was drawn to Alice and her daring nature, and though she knew she should stand up for herself, she felt protected by the older girl. But Rosie had no idea why Alice had befriended her.

She sat up and, squinting, she saw by the torch's beam that the clock showed it was two o'clock – four hours until the bell rang. She was now getting used to the strict routine at Teviot Hall, but the silence that was demanded throughout the day and the fear of punishment if you broke the rules was wearing. Worse still, Rosie still didn't believe she was an orphan, nor that she belonged here.

The torch's beam was getting closer.

'I saw you were awake,' Alice whispered as she stood by the bedside, her face looking ghostly in the eerie light. 'I can't get to sleep and being perished doesn't help.'

'We could keep each other warm.' Rosie knew bunking up together wasn't allowed. But spooked by the unnerving darkness, she wanted the comfort of company.

As a howling wind made the windows rattle and a gush of icy air blasted through the dormitory, Alice pulled back the blanket and climbed in the slim bed.

'Careful, there's not much room,' Rosie whispered, clinging to the other side of the bed.

Alice shivered. 'Oooh you're lovely and warm.' Her cold feet landed on Rosie's leg.

'Your feet are freezing,' Rosie complained. 'Where's your socks?'

'Me boots have got holes in them.' Rosie smelt toothpaste on Alice's breath. 'So I had to take me socks off cos they got soaked.'

Socks had to last the week and they took an age to dry on the stove. Boots got changed at the WVS clothes depot when they had the right size.

Rosie felt bad for Alice. 'Miss Balfour lit her coal fire this afternoon, you should have asked if she could dry them upstairs for you.'

Miss Balfour's room was one of two directly above the dormitories. But Rosie knew Alice could get huffy when they talked about Miss Balfour, and sure enough the next moment she felt Alice's body stiffen.

'How d'you know that?'

'When Agnes was poorly with a bad chest Miss Balfour lit her fire early and said she could keep warm by it until the stove got going down here.'

'And it was a good job Miss Black didn't find out, or there'd be ructions on,' said Alice.

'I don't see why. Miss Balfour was only being kind to Agnes.'

'She's like that with all the orphans.' Alice's voice was snappy. 'That's why they love her. But I've known her the longest.' Unlatching her arms, Alice lay stiffly on her side in sulky silence.

Rosie didn't know what to say to make things right and decided not to say anything. Alice sounded childish, Rosie thought, as if she was jealous.

After a time, Rosie thought Alice had fallen asleep, but she got a surprise when the older girl whispered in her ear, 'I'm warmer now, are you?'

Her voice sounded like she wanted to make up and Rosie knew this was Alice's way of saying she was sorry. She also knew Alice couldn't help being the way she was. It was the same for Rosie trying to be brave.

Before Rosie could answer, Alice yawned and said, 'But I still can't get back to sleep.'

They both went quiet for a while when all manner of things flitted through Rosie's head.

'What d'you want to be when you leave here?' Alice whispered, wrapping her arms around Rosie again.

'I won't be here that long. I'll have remembered who I am by then,' Rosie said.

'But what if you don't remember?'

Rosie was horrified at the thought. It had never occurred to her that her memory wouldn't return one day and that she would end up staying at the orphanage.

'Go on, there must be something you want to do,' Alice pushed.

There was only one thing Rosie wanted.

'I'd try and find out who I was and if I had a family.'

Again, Alice stiffened. 'Are you joking me?'

'Shh!' Rosie told her because Alice had raised her voice. 'Don't you want to know who your mam is?'

'Never.' Alice's voice was somehow a quiet shout. 'Selfish cow. Catch me wasting me time on somebody that dumped me like a bag o' rubbish on a doorstep for strangers to find. And not once returning to see if I survived.'

A new thought came to Rosie. 'When I was with Agnes once she said she was going to be adopted.'

Alice groaned. 'She's said that for years.'

'But could that happen to us?'

'It's wishful thinking. Agnes knows she'll never be adopted because she has a mam. Besides, people who adopt don't want older kids. They want babies or little ones.'

Rosie inwardly sighed with relief. She didn't want to be adopted when her family might come looking for her.

'What happened to Agnes's mam?'

She felt Alice shrug. 'Dunno. She's probably poor cos after Agnes's dad died, Agnes and Albert were dumped in here.'

Rosie felt sorry for Agnes and made the decision to be

extra nice to her from now on. She asked, 'Albert is Agnes's brother?'

'Yes.'

'I wish I had family here.'

'You can be mine.'

Rosie, stunned, didn't think she'd heard Alice correctly. But her friend continued.

'We could pretend you're my little sister...' A pause. 'If you want to, that is. And when we've both left here and I'm rich, cos that's what I want to happen after I leave, I'll buy a house and we can live together.'

Rosie didn't know what to say. If she did find her family, she would want to live with them. But she didn't want to upset Alice. And so she said nothing.

Rosie must have slept because when the bell rang, she started awake. Alice must have returned to her bed sometime in the night. Bleary-eyed and dishevelled in her clothes, she shivered in the frigid early morning air. Miss Black considered lighting the stove in the morning an extravagance as the orphans would be keeping warm by doing their jobs. The blackout curtains drawn, the lamps had been lit and as Rosie looked down the row of beds, she saw Alice making for the door, torch in her hand. Alice signalled to her and Rosie remembered it was their turn to be food monitors.

Stepping outside into the darkness, she saw Alice making her way over the cobbles.

'Blimey, Rosie, be careful. The rain's turned to sleet and made the ground slippy.'

Mrs Stewart, otherwise known as Cook, usually arrived earlier and unlocked the Little Theatre door. Taking off their coats and hanging them in the lobby, the pair of them made for the dining area where they headed for the door on the far wall that led to the big house. Walking along the dim passageway, Rosie noticed Alice's bare legs. She shuddered at the thought of wearing boots without socks, especially boots with holes in them, in this weather.

Entering the kitchen, with its chipped cream walls, dado rail, stone floor and gleaming copper pans that hung from the ceiling, Rosie relaxed as the warmth from the enormous black range cooker greeted her. Cook, a plump, harassed-looking lady wearing a white mob cap over frizzy grey hair, and a white pinafore with frills around the bib, stood at a wooden table in the centre of the room. Her face dour, she looked up from the loaf she was cutting.

'Morning. You can start by setting the trolley.'

'And good morning to you, Mrs Stewart.'

As Alice's face split in an exaggerated, overbright smile, Rosie inwardly groaned. *Please behave, Alice.*

Bread knife poised in the air, Cook went on, 'You'll both need to give me a hand this morning because Ellen's away registering for war work.' She clicked her tongue. 'Silly lassie. I don't know why, she's got months before she's eighteen.'

Cook couldn't manage on her own and Ellen, a girl from the village, was employed to do menial tasks, peeling mounds of vegetables, scrubbing floors, washing dishes.

'So why is she registering now?' Alice wanted to know.

'She says it's because lassies who enlist at seventeen can choose the service they want while at eighteen it's decided for them.'

'Did Ellen say which service she wants?' Rosie asked.

Her lips a thin line of disgust, Cook told them, 'Factory work apparently. Daft lass wants away from home. Fancy going off to God knows where at her age. *And* to leave me in the lurch.' She sliced another piece of bread.

Alice gave Rosie a warning look to keep quiet until Mrs Stewart was in a better fettle.

They worked in silence and when the oatmeal was simmering on the stove, the trolley set with white bowls, cups, bread, margarine and cutlery, Mrs Stewart declared, 'After you take the food trolley out, I'm away to put me feet up for a wee while. After breakfast, you two can make a start on washing the dishes. Tell Miss Balfour what's happened and that you'll be late for class.' Mrs Stewart shuffled off into the passageway leading to the big house where she shared a two-roomed flat with her caretaker husband at the far end of the building.

The girls trundled the trolley along the passageway and out through the doorway into the dining hall, where Miss Balfour and the silent orphans were waiting for them.

When Alice told the mistress the news she nodded. 'Doing the washing up will be such a big help to Mrs Stewart.' She took the lid off the pan of porridge. 'I'll expect you in class as soon as you've finished in the kitchen.'

'Yes, Miss Balfour,' Rosie replied.

'Did you notice I didn't answer?' Alice said to Rosie later in the kitchen as she placed dirty bowls into a half-full sink of water as that was another commodity to be saved.

'Answer what?'

'Miss Balfour when she said we have to join the class after we'd finished here.'

Taking a wet bowl off the wooden draining board and drying it with a tea towel, Rosie felt her throat constrict. She knew that audacious look on Alice's face meant she was plotting something.

The dishes washed and put away, the table scrubbed, tea

towels hanging on the brass rail above the range to dry, Alice's eyes sparkling with mischief, she told Rosie, 'How about we have a look around the big house?'

Rosie's eyes bulged. 'But—'

'No buts. We're not expected in class until we've finished the dishes and it took *such* a long time.'

Uncomfortable at the naughty grin on Alice's face, Rosie was unsure. She so wanted to see Teviot Hall but did she have the courage?

'Come on.' Alice made for the door to the passageway – where none of the children were supposed to enter. 'I dare you.'

Rosie knew Alice would never refuse a dare, but something inherent in Rosie, the need to please, prevented her from doing wrong. 'What if Miss Balfour comes to check on us?'

Alice rolled her eyes. 'We've finished the dishes early and it won't take long, honest.'

Rosie felt bad at the thought of ignoring Miss Balfour's trust. 'What if we get caught?'

'We'll get punished.' Alice grinned. 'But it'll be worth it to see inside the house.'

Rosie didn't want to lose face, but neither did she want to get punished. Agonising over what to do, Mrs Wilkinson's words played in her mind. *I put on a brave face. Pretend I'm an actress playing a part. It's called attitude. Trust me, people believe what they see and treat you with respect.*

She would pretend to be Alice.

She gulped. 'Go on then, you go first.'

Alice led the way along a carpeted passageway, the feeling of adventure driving on Rosie. The end of the passage opened to a vast entrance hall, whose floor was covered with a faded multicoloured carpet and which had two matching couches that stood against each wall. The stone archway that Rosie walked through led to a sweeping staircase that rose to another floor which had an overhanging balcony. She gave a sharp intake of breath.

'What's up?' Alice, at her side, sounded alarmed.

Rosie pointed to the side of the staircase where a grand piano stood, its lid propped up with a wooden stick. A tingle of excitement ran through her. 'I just know I can play the piano, Alice.'

'You can forget playing it for now.' Alice's tone was sharp. 'The Women's Timber Corps have offices here.'

'You didn't tell me that before.'

'I—' Alice froze as she looked up to the balcony.

'What are you two doing here?' a voice bellowed.

Looking up, Rosie saw a lady wearing a uniform, a bundle of papers in her hands, staring down at them from the balcony.

'It's Miss Fellows, the WTC officer in charge,' Alice muttered. 'Come on!' she called as she raced for the passageway.

'D'you think she'll report us?' Standing in the kitchen, Rosie agonised over the trouble they were in.

Alice shrugged. 'The best thing to do is turn up for class and deny we were ever in the big house.'

Another fib, then.

'But she saw us.'

Alice, by now, was heading for the doorway into the dining hall and with nothing else for it, Rosie followed. Entering the classroom, Rosie was surprised to see Mrs Murray up the front.

'Come on in, girls.' Mrs Murray's cheery face looked

glum. 'There's been an accident. Miss Black was summoned to a meeting in the big house with Miss Fellows' – for an awful moment Rosie thought this had something to do with them – 'and, unfortunately, the mistress slipped on the icy cobbles.'

Rosie breathed normally again as Mrs Murray continued.

'An ambulance was called and Miss Balfour has accompanied Miss Black to the hospital. We'll just have to wait and see what the damage is.' She nodded to the desks. 'Sit yourselves down. I was just telling the class that you have to put up with me until Miss Balfour returns.'

As they took their seats Alice grinned. 'We're in luck,' she whispered.

# 14

'Are you sure you don't want the fire on, Miss Black?' Miriam asked.

Miss Black, sitting in an aged, brown, leather wing-backed chair, her thin face ashen, shook her head. 'I do my bit by conserving coal; it's in short supply.'

Judging by the freezing temperature, Miriam wondered if the fire was ever lit. The room, with its dark and heavy furniture, marble fireplace, and religious pictures hanging on the walls, looked unlived in and had the distinct smell of mothballs.

A wave of sympathy washed over Miriam for Miss Black's plight. She'd had a nasty fall and after having X-rays, she was found to have broken her arm in two places and sprained her ankle. Her arm was now in plaster, and with her injured foot, she was finding it difficult to walk. Miriam had expected her to stay in hospital overnight but Miss Black, adamant, told the medical staff she intended to go home. It was only after she insisted that she had a sister living close by who could see to her needs that she was discharged.

An ambulance had brought them back to Miss Black's flat and Miriam, wondering what her next course of action should be, decided her first duty was to seek out the mistress's sister and tell her the news.

'Whereabouts does your sister live, Miss Black? Will she be at home this time of day?'

Miss Black thought for a moment, her brow creasing in perplexity as though worried her memory had been affected. 'Beatrice lives the other side of the green. Number twenty-six. The big white house next to the post office.' That look of puzzlement again. 'What day is it today?'

'Friday.'

'She should be in. Though it's Merchant Navy week, so she might be out collecting door-to-door for the WVS.' She pulled a face. 'I don't envy her as folk are sick and tired of flag days.'

Miriam was surprised the mistress knew the goings on in the village.

'Is there anything I can get you before I go?'

'Tea, if you'd be so kind.'

*Good gracious*, Miriam thought, *the mistress can be civil when she wants.*

Miriam was surprised at the woman who answered the door. She had blonde hair framing a homey face, laugh lines at her eyes and her gaze was one of friendly curiosity. If this was Beatrice, she wasn't a bit like her sister.

'Hello, I'm—'

'Miss Balfour from the orphanage at Teviot Hall.' At Miriam's questioning look, the woman said, 'The grape vine runneth over in the village.'

Reminded of Rosie and Alice's hilarity at ancient biblical

words, Miriam's lips twitched. It had been good to see them laugh even if it was at the bible's expense. Plus, the Almighty was forgiving.

The smile was wiped from Beatrice's face when she heard what had brought Miriam to her doorstep. 'Blimey, poor Gertrude. Of course, I'll come at once.' Disappearing inside the house, she returned wearing an enormous black coat that almost swept the ground and a large red scarf wound around her neck. 'I'm the youngest,' she prattled as they made their way around the village green, the air biting Miriam's cheeks, 'the mutinous one.'

Miriam wanted to know more but politeness prevented her from asking.

As they walked around the green, picking their way along the icy pavement, Beatrice told her, 'Ellen Rutledge, my neighbour's daughter, works in the kitchen at the big house. The reason I'm telling you this is because I know how ill thought of my sister is at Teviot Hall.' She gave Miriam a sidelong glance. 'I'm a plain-speaking woman, Miss Balfour, and though I don't agree with most of Gertrude's actions, I understand the reasons for her being the way she is. I know she's strict with the children but she is fair-minded and thinks it's her sole duty to save their souls. She was the same when she taught at school before retiring.'

Miriam felt pressed to say, 'You're very unlike each other... in attitudes I mean.'

'I'm the lucky one: being the youngest, I escaped Father's indoctrinating ways.' Her breath as she spoke escaped like steam in the chilly air. 'In my opinion, Miss Balfour, even though he was a man of the cloth, Father was an overbearing bully.' She gave a wicked chortle. 'As you no doubt can guess, we never got along and I left home at the first opportunity.

Poor Gertrude.' Her shoulders rose as she sighed. 'She didn't have a childhood – she was taught the bible before she started school.'

Stopping, she put a hand on Miriam's arm. 'There is another side to Gertrude, you know. She lives frugally and gives generously to the poor. I've known her buy and donate such necessities as food and clothing. She helps out at the local Red Cross where she tirelessly gives any spare time she has.' She shook her head. 'To some, like young Ellen, Gertrude is a tyrant and to others she's an angel of mercy. Personally, I abhor some of her ways but' – her transparent eyes met Miriam's – 'she is my sister.'

Making her way back to Teviot Hall, Miriam stopped to stare over the countryside, where, in the dusky light, she could just make out the snowy fields and stone walls that ran at the side of soaring snow-capped hills. In the invigorating, cold air, it felt good to be alive. Her thoughts turned to Miss Black, who knew no other way to live than her father's bidding, instilled in her all those years ago. It didn't escape Miriam that the pair of them had experienced the same kind of upbringing. But Miriam had escaped, though the memories ran deep, and she still bore the hurts and heartache from that time.

As her footsteps took her along the path, she heard a vehicle coming up from behind. Standing to one side, a truck with Fran Patterson at the wheel passed by. Two Lumberjills wearing overcoats and scarves around their head, sitting beside Fran, gave a little wave. Returning the wave, Miriam assumed they'd been to the railway station yard to deliver timber. Probably the last run of the day by the looks of their tired and dirty faces.

As she watched the truck trundle down the path, a sudden realisation hit her. Miss Black was told at the hospital her injury wouldn't be healed for weeks. A slow smile spread across her face. Seeing the Lumberjills had given her an idea.

The next morning, after informing Mrs Murray to supervise breakfast, Miriam left the courtyard and took the path that led to the wooded area. On she went and though she wore wellington boots and thick socks her feet soon got frozen in the snowy path. Following the track into dense woodland, she came to a clearing where several army huts, made out of metal and shaped into a half cylinder, served as dormitories for the Lumberjills. She made her way up the path to the hut that served as a canteen, opened the door and walked in.

The place, filled with high-pitched voices and music blaring, the Lumberjills sat at long trestle tables, was a hubbub of noise. Miriam spied Fran Patterson sitting nearest to the serving counter, and caught her eye, gesturing with a forefinger that she wished to see her.

Fran, nodding, rose from her seat and made towards Miriam. Opening the door, she led the way out to the contrasting cold air.

'Can't hear a word in there.' She inclined her head to the canteen. 'What brings you here, Miss Balfour?'

'Miriam,' she corrected as she always did the few times she'd spoken to Fran, someone of few words and who always got straight to the point of the matter – which suited Miriam fine. 'I want to ask a favour.'

Taking a packet of ten Woodbines from her trouser pocket, Fran lit one and drew on it. 'Go ahead.'

'Did you hear about Miss Black's fall yesterday?'

'Miss Fellows told me this morning.' Exhaling a billow of

smoke, a glint of something that could only be described as satisfaction gleamed in the forewoman's eyes. 'That'll be her out of action for a while.'

'That's why I'm here,' Miriam told her. 'The thing is, Christmas is fast approaching and the children are usually invited to Teviot Hall where Sir Keith provides a tree with little gifts beneath. But this year the laird won't be here – no doubt he doesn't want to celebrate Christmas when his only son's been killed.'

'So, how can I help?'

Miriam faltered. She knew it was an imposition to ask but the thought of the children not having a Christmas treat this year pulled at her heartstrings. Safe to say, Miriam thought, Miss Black wouldn't find out and if she did, it would be too late.

'I'm wondering if you could help by providing a tree that we could put up in the children's dining hall.'

Fran took another draw on her cigarette and, raising her head, blew out a perfect smoke ring. Looking at Miriam, she grinned. 'That I can do. I won't tell if you don't. Those kiddies deserve something to make them smile at Christmas.' Turning, she made for the canteen door, the sound of her whistling 'Jingle Bells' filling the air.

'Och! It's no use putting mincemeat on that list.' Mrs Murray folded her arms, a look of disgust on her good-natured face. 'I know we've got to put up with shortages and just making do but Christmas without mince pies is just not right in my book.'

Three days had passed since Miss Black's fall. Miriam, sat at the office desk doing a menu for the week, and making a list for the groceries needed, was only half listening. But Mrs Murray's staring at her prompted Miriam to ask, 'Why no mincemeat?'

The indignant-looking Mrs Murray, who hadn't yet explained her reason for calling in at the office, told her, 'I've stood in the longest queue in that downpour of snow to be told by Sheila Craddock at the village Co-op that there's none to be had in all three warehouses.' Mrs Murray gave a frustrated sigh. 'It's the same all over according to the wireless.'

Miriam sighed. She wished that was the only problem she had to worry about, but shortages were common for all food supplies. Miriam had wanted to change things for the better but with insufficient funds or resources, she didn't know where to start. With Christmas coming she'd had such grand plans which were now to be dashed when the realities were realised. It galled her to think she could do no better than Miss Black.

'I wonder how yon rich folk in London are coping.' Mrs Murray, as was her wont, came out with some irrelevancy that took her fancy. 'Did I tell you I once visited the capital?' A faraway look came into her eyes.

Miriam didn't interrupt because it was good for the soul to remember happier times.

'Me and Mammy stayed with an ancient aunt. Don't ask me when or why, or even who paid for such an extravagant trip. One day Mammy took me to see the sights and we ended up in Oxford Street, the height of busyness it was, with all its swanky shops and swankier folk.' She shook her head in regret. 'It grieves me to think of all those grand stores bombed by those Jerry blighters. I hear tell Selfridges and John Lewis caught fire and were reduced to a shell...' Her hand clasped over her chest. 'Aye, nothing's sacred in this war.'

Coming out of her reverie, she pushed a stray curl beneath her turban. 'I'll stop blethering and get on with the real reason I called in to see you.' As if the weight of her body was too much, she leant on the corner of the desk. 'I've had a word with Walter.' Walter being her husband, Miriam recollected. Too old to be called up, he had joined the Home Guard. 'I told him the situation here and that I'd like to lend a hand until her ladyship comes back. To be truthful I can't abide the woman.'

Miriam opted to ignore the statement. 'How d'you mean, lend a hand?'

'Running the orphanage and taking the class is too much for one person. I've worked out I can take class on a morning to leave you to get on with other things you need to do. I'm no teacher but I can read, write and do arithmetic. We could use the monitor system and the older girls could help. I'll have a word with Elsie, my sister, and ask if our Hazel – who by the way is fed up with Ian, her dad, monitoring every move she makes – can come in for a few more hours.'

Miriam frowned in puzzlement. 'D'you mean Hazel Rutherford, the help?'

'The very one.'

'She's your niece?'

'That she is.' Mrs Murray looked into the distance and smiled fondly. She then took a deep breath as if what she had to say next was of great importance. 'Furthermore, I've decided to move into the coach house. I could use the other flat above the dormitories to help keep an eye on things at night and be handy for the mornings.' She shook her head. 'Lassie, with the best will in the world, you can't do it yourself and it's not forever.'

Miriam was touched by Mrs Murray's deliberations but she had misgivings. 'Thank you, but you can't leave Walter to see to himself.'

'What's good for the goose is good for the gander,' she declared. 'Many's the night I sit on me own when he's out gallivanting at Home Guard meetings. There's me with nothing to do but worry myself sick about those two laddies of mine doing their bit for king and country in foreign parts I've never even heard of before.' She clasped her hands on her cheeks. 'Weekends are no better with the man out marching and training and, would you believe' – her expression was incredulous – 'my Walter is capable of unarmed combat and how to lay booby traps because the word is there's a spot by the reservoirs which they say is recognisable from planes and a place where Germans can parachute in men.'

Her ample bosom heaved as she laughed. 'Can you imagine if Jerry came sailing down from a plane, the villagers would run amok with hysteria. Don't get me wrong, my Walter is doing a grand job. And he's happy for me to lend a hand here because as he says, we all have to make sacrifices if we're to win this war.' Mrs Murry wiped her brow as if such a speech had taken it out of her.

Miriam was torn. She found Mrs Murray capable and it would solve such a problem.

'But what about his—'

'No buts, lassie. We've got it all worked out. Only thing is on Saturdays I'd like to be home at night.' She belly laughed. 'It's not what you're thinking; it's so we can go to church together on Sunday mornings.'

Miriam, unsure of the challenges she faced ahead, decided she couldn't refuse such an enticing offer. 'If you're sure, Mrs Murray. Having you here would be an enormous help, thank you.'

That was one of her prayers answered, Miriam thought. But the other would be harder. How to make Christmas special this year for the children without the means.

But Miriam hadn't reckoned on a letter arriving the next day that would change all manner of things.

# 15

Miriam was just about to open the morning's post when a knock came at the office door. 'Come in,' she called.

Rosie Ward entered, a look of tentativeness about her.

'Is anything the matter, Rosie?'

'Miss, I...' The child lost her nerve.

'Just tell me what it is, Rosie.'

'Have you heard anything about me from South Shields?' She chewed her bottom lip. 'Miss, d'you think they've stopped looking?'

Placing the post on the desk, Miriam moved to stand beside Rosie. She believed it best always to be truthful with the children, even though it hurt. 'I should think everyone has done their utmost to find your family, but as time passes and they're no further forward, I'm afraid there'll be no other alternative but for them to give up looking.'

Rosie choked back a sob.

'Listen to me, Rosie. You never know what's going to happen. Believe me, God does work in mysterious ways.'

Miriam herself held on to that hope. 'But it is strange why no one has come forward to report you missing. My hope is that one day when you least expect it, you'll regain your memory and the mystery will be solved.' She bent down to the girl's eye level. 'For now, you must be brave and do your best here at Teviot Hall.'

Miriam could tell Rosie was bitterly disappointed, but she bunched her lips trying to show courage.

'Off you go now, Rosie, and help to make the decorations.'

When Miriam had entered the classroom that morning and brought little pots of pasting glue, paint brushes and newspapers out of a message bag, the orphans' eyes widened in astonishment. But it was when she told them, 'This morning we're going to make paper chains to decorate the dining hall for Christmas,' excitement rippled in the air.

'And if I do hear anything,' she said as Rosie made to go, 'I promise I'll seek you out straight away.'

'Thank you, miss.'

Sat in the chair, elbow on the arm rest, chin in her hand, Miriam would have given anything to be wrong, but the chances that Rosie's parents survived the raid were minimal. Why else would they not have come forward to claim their child? She sighed. She wouldn't give up hope for Rosie Ward's sake.

Picking up the post from the desk once more, her eyebrows knitted together as she noted the topmost envelope was typed and official-looking. Slitting it open with a little paper knife, Miriam took out the page and read the letter-head: British Red Cross. Intrigued, she began to read.

*Dear Sir/Madam,*

*This letter is to inform you that the* Stars and Stripes *newspaper ran a campaign for American servicemen to sponsor British war orphans earlier in the war.*

*Donations to the War Orphan Fund enables US forces to 'adopt' orphans for the purpose of purchasing any extras that these children, because of tragic circumstance, are unable to enjoy. The goal, combined with the Red Cross, is to afford each orphan a certain amount of money a year. Money raised from the American airmen at your local airfield has been donated to the War Orphan Fund. It has been requested by the unit that the money raised is allocated to Teviot Hall orphans.*

*Part of the scheme is that those donating can specify the sex and age of the child they sponsor. That detail hasn't been given apart from the request that Mary Millard, who lost both parents during an air raid, is one of the orphans chosen.*

*When the campaign was launched the hope was to raise funds big enough to sponsor a certain number of orphans. Due to the hard work of the* Stars and Stripes *newspaper, funds raised were double the expectation and to date there are six places left. The selection is to be at your discretion and the children chosen for support should be full orphans i.e., those children who have lost both parents.*

*A representative will be in touch to discuss the sponsored orphans and to supervise how the funds raised will be used to meet the children's needs. The representative will require a photograph and history of each 'adopted' child to send to the sponsors who will undoubtedly be keen to hear of their progress.*

Finishing the letter, Miriam sank back in the chair. She'd

heard of *Stars and Stripes* and knew it to be a military newspaper read by the American forces in the UK. She marvelled at the goodness of the newspaper and the airmen, reflecting that in this time of war when folk struggled to prevail against hardship, death and despair, goodwill came to the fore. Then a thought struck her: how did the airmen know about the orphanage? Someone at the airfield must have told them, but who?

Reaching for a notepad and pen, she began the first of two letters. The first one was to the Red Cross, thanking them. She finished by saying:

> *I look forward to a visit from a representative from the Red Cross to discuss the money held in use for the sponsored orphans. I will indeed concur with the guidelines and my choice will be those orphans I consider will most benefit.*

And there lay the rub. Who to choose?

Miriam was at a loss how to begin the letter to the Dunglen airfield, then decided the best way was to say what she would if the person was sitting in her office. Envisaging an older, officious-looking man in uniform, she began:

> *Dear Sir,*
>
> *The Red Cross has been in touch to say American servicemen at Dunglen airfield have contributed to the* Stars and Stripes *War Orphan Fund and six orphans from Teviot Hall orphanage are to be beneficiaries. I am deeply touched and would like to thank the men on behalf of the children on this most generous gesture.*

She concluded that she would indeed keep the sponsors' units informed of each child's progress and if there was any further way she could assist, she hoped the airmen involved wouldn't hesitate to ask.

Fairly happy with the result, Miriam licked and sealed the envelope.

It was after dinner, when the orphans were having their daily dose of fresh air with Hazel supervising, that Miriam made her way over to the classroom where Mrs Murray was busily tidying up after morning class.

'I'd like a word if you have a minute, Mrs Murray.'

Stacking books on a shelf, Mrs Murray looked up, her expression one of uncertainty.

'There's nothing wrong,' Miriam was quick to assure, 'I'd like your advice on something.'

The older woman, looking relieved, gave a toothy smile. 'Fire away, hen. I'll help if I can.'

Miriam related what the letter from the Red Cross said.

'Och, that's some news.' Folding her arms, she gave an impatient shake of the head. 'Some folk in these parts have no time for the Yanks. They say they're too free and easy and disrespectful in their ways but that's what I like about them. They treat the ordinary man in the street the same as the gentry.' Her expression softened. 'It just goes to show those Yanks have hearts and that's all that counts in my book.'

'I must say I'm overwhelmed by the offer.'

'So, what have you decided?' Mrs Murray's arms relaxed by her sides. 'Have you given a thought about which children to choose?'

'That's what I want your advice about.' Miriam despaired. 'It's going to be difficult.'

Rubbing her chin, Mrs Murray thought, then said, 'How about a couple of the infants for starters?'

Miriam went on to say about the airmen wanting to sponsor Mary Millard and Mrs Murray agreed it was a mystery how they knew about her.

'How about Charlie too?' she went on. 'He qualifies. Poor wee soul, his daddy was killed at Dunkirk and tragically his mammy was killed in a road accident.'

'I agree. Then maybe a couple of older girls,' Miriam mused. 'How about Brenda Dawson? Her father's Halifax bomber went down in a raid and she didn't know her mam as she died when she was a baby.'

The corners of her lower lip drooping, Mrs Murray nodded. 'Aye. Poor wee lassie deserves a bit of good luck to come her way.' Quiet for a moment while she collected herself, Mrs Murray went on to say, 'Who else d'you think?'

'How about Alice?' Miriam was surprised at herself. She was careful to never show favouritism but here she was doing exactly that. But she truly believed that if Alice was shown people had faith in her, it could be the making of her.

Mrs Murray pulled a dubious face. 'Some would say she didn't deserve privileges the unruly way she behaves.'

'Alice can be difficult I know, but from an early age she's only known harsh treatment. Is it any wonder she reacts the way she does?'

'But she's due to be leaving soon, isn't she?'

'Yes, she's fourteen next June. Maybe we could afford her a little happiness before then.'

Mrs Murray shrugged as if she didn't agree but it wasn't her decision to make.

'How about two older boys as well?' Miriam suggested.

Mrs Murray nodded. 'I'm thinking Tommy and Alan. They're both bona fide orphans, poor lambs.'

Miriam nodded. Making her way back to the office, the high-pitched voices of the children outside tugged at her heartstrings. The responsibility of what had just been decided weighed heavily upon her. She prayed she'd done the right thing by choosing who she had.

# 16

The following Monday, a lady named Mrs Hunt, wearing the uniform of the Red Cross, sat opposite Miriam at her desk.

'In my opinion,' she told Miriam, her composed and business-like manner suggesting she could deal with any problem, 'servicemen who sponsor orphans like to meet up with the child as it gives the child a sense someone cares. Or, a unit might invite the orphans to their base, give them tea, show them around. Boys particularly enjoy this.'

She went on to explain how she would oversee the spending of money held in trust for 'adopted' orphans and that she would be in touch when necessary. When she left, Miriam was satisfied that Mrs Hunt had everything organised as far as the sponsorship was concerned.

The next day, a letter arrived later from Dunglen airfield. Sitting at her desk, a finger of sunshine shedding a beam of light through the window onto the wooden floor, Miriam began to read.

*Dear Miss Balfour,*

*I wish to express my thanks for your recent letter.*

*The men under my command take great pride in their efforts to raise funds for the* Stars and Stripes *War Orphan Fund and the opportunity of 'adopting' orphans who reside at Teviot Hall orphanage. Some of the men have families at home and find it an honour to help provide for those unfortunate children who have lost their parents in this time of conflict.*

The letter went on in the same vein and Miriam sensed a dignified yet disciplined man had composed the letter. It finished:

*I have recently written to Sir Keith Henley, who assures me that he is in agreement with the arrangement. Furthermore, it is the wish of the men to meet with the 'adopted' orphans and, if this meets with your approval, representatives from the unit will be in touch.*

*Sincerely,*

*Lt. Colonel Douglas, USAAF*

Miriam considered the least she could do for the servicemen was to arrange for them to meet with the orphans, after they'd been so generous. Placing the letter on the desk, she wrote back to the colonel to that effect.

The next Saturday morning, when Miriam was doing accounts, there was a rap at the office door.

'Come in,' she called and was startled to see two American servicemen in smart uniform enter the office. *Representatives from the airfield,* she thought.

Taking off his service cap, the airman with the sparkling green eyes spoke. 'I sure do hope we're not butting in on anything, ma'am. We're from—'

'Colonel Douglas has been in touch to say representatives might call.' She stood and gestured to the chair. 'Please, take a seat.'

The airman, whose eyes never left hers, sauntered over. Miriam's pulse quickened, which made her feel ridiculous.

Flustered, she said, 'It's good to see you,' then felt rather foolish at such a lame greeting. In her defence, Miriam often felt uncomfortable in male company, having had nothing much to do with them in her line of her work. Her mind dredged up Terry Rawling, and she quickly closed that particular door of the past.

The airman held out his hand. 'Clark Mitchell. Otherwise known as Mitch.'

'Miriam Balfour.'

His hand slid back, their fingertips touching as he let go slowly. Rattled, Miriam recalled what Mrs Craddock at the Co-op store had said about American servicemen. 'If them Yanks get any more laid back, they'll fall over,' Mrs Craddock had declared. 'You don't see our lads slouching or chewing gum.' She'd clicked her tongue in irritation. 'Charming all the lassies, they are. No wonder folks are saying they're overpaid, oversexed and over here.'

Despite what Mrs Craddock said, Miriam felt sorry for the Americans. After all, they had come to help them fight Hitler and here they were, far away from home in a foreign country with people who didn't understand their ways.

'This here is my buddy, Joe Marino,' Clark was saying,

nodding to the other man. 'Though he's not much fun these days as he has a wife and kids back home.' He raised his eyebrows. 'Would you believe he's trying to keep me on the straight and narrow.' To prove it wasn't working, the man gave an audacious wink.

Maybe, Miriam reconsidered, this airman fitted Mrs Craddock's description.

Embarrassed for Joe's sake, Miriam disregarded the other's impertinent behaviour and held out her hand. 'Pleased to meet you, Joe.'

'Pleasure's mine.' Shaking her hand, Joe gave her a pleasant smile. He was stockier than his colleague, and had olive skin and black hair. 'Take no notice of Mitch, nobody else does.' He gave the other man a friendly punch on the arm.

Clark – she couldn't think of him as Mitch as it was far too personal – told her, 'We're here representing our group who donated to the *Stars and Stripes* orphan fund. Me and Joe were the lucky ones in the lottery we drew out of a hat.' He had an attractive southern drawl.

There was no doubt Clark Mitchell was handsome, but, my, did he know it. Broad-shouldered with light-brown hair, he looked in his early thirties. He smiled and she glimpsed his gleaming white teeth.

Unsettled by the man, she tore her eyes away and addressed Joe. 'You had a lottery?'

'Yes, ma'am,' Joe said. 'The guys in the group all wanted to visit so we drew lots out of a hat to see who got to come.'

'And boy am I glad we won.' Clark's eyebrow arched in approval.

The man was an incorrigible flirt, Miriam decided. However, though her head said to ignore him, her quickening heart wasn't listening.

Joe's eyes narrowing, he gave Clark a 'cut it out' look.

'I'm afraid I've only the one chair,' Miriam blurted, trying to dispel the uneasiness that had crept into the atmosphere.

Joe sat on the visitor's chair, whilst Clark parked his behind on the corner edge of Miriam's desk, brazenly smirking at her.

When President Roosevelt declared war on Japan after the shocking news that the Japanese had attacked the US naval base at Pearl Harbor, Hawaii, Mrs Murray had decreed with a knowing nod, 'My Walter says Hitler's done himself no favours because that'll be the Yanks joining in and helping to win this war. Them bombers we see thundering in the skies are giving Jerry a hammering.'

Another time she had told Miriam, 'Our Hazel's been warned to keep clear of the Yanks but the young find a way. Especially when the biggest thrill these lassies have had in years is to dance with each other at the village hall because all the menfolk are away fighting.' She shook her head in despair. 'When they're off to the pictures all they see is the glamorous lifestyle some of the Americans have with them big cars and even bigger houses, and lassies' heads are turned.' She nodded with certainty. 'I've told Walter, it's trouble waiting to happen.'

*Nevertheless*, Miriam thought as she sat staring at the two men in front of her, *the American airmen do have hearts*; the proof being the money they'd contributed to the War Orphan Fund.

Focusing on Joe, she told him, 'I can't tell you how much of a difference this is going to make to these children.'

'I sure would like to think if my kids were orphaned, something like this would be available to them. All the extras I'd want them to have.' He reached into his pocket and pulled out a photograph which he handed to Miriam. It was of a young woman with long hair, holding a baby in her arms, a toddler wearing a frock at her side, head lowered, clinging on to her mother's skirt.

Miriam smiled. 'What a lovely family you have. You should be very proud.'

His face lit up. 'I sure am.'

'Where was this taken?'

'At the family farm in Alabama, ma'am. The folks are getting on in years and my wife and I decided to stay put and help out.'

Miriam experienced an ache of longing for what she didn't have. Handing back the photograph, she said, 'All the family in one place, how nice.'

'Yep. We get along just fine.' Joe, staring at the picture, gave a contented smile, then returned it to his uniform pocket.

Aware they were excluding Clark in this exchange, Miriam looked expectantly at him. 'What about you, have you got a family back home?'

If she thought any information about his background would be forthcoming, she was wrong. Miriam saw his jawline tense, his eyes harden. She'd touched a raw nerve, she realised.

'How about the orphans? Have they been told yet?' Joe delicately changed the subject.

'Not yet. I was waiting until I knew more about the sponsorship.'

'And to check us out.' Back on form, Clark had a devilish twinkle in his eye.

Joe gave Clark an exasperated shake of the head.

Ignoring his buddy, Clark told her, 'The Red Cross forwarded the orphans' photographs and their history that you sent them. Those kids all had a tough start in life. Little Mary, poor kid, and the others.'

Miriam was prompted to ask, 'How did you find out about Mary Millard?'

'Me and the boys met up with two swell dames at the village dance. Vivian and Fran. You might know them, they work here.'

'Yes. Fran's a forewoman and Vivian's a ganger on the estate here.'

Clark shrugged as if clueless as to what that meant. 'They got on talking about Teviot Hall and how the owner of the place had offered evacuee orphans a home. Fran explained what had happened to little Mary's folks. When we told the guys at the base, some who have family back home like Joe here' – he jerked a thumb at his buddy – 'they decided they wanted to help.'

'It was Ray, one of the crew,' Joe chipped in, 'who told us about the War Orphan Fund and that it had been going in the Great War also. Apparently, the paper relaunched the campaign in forty-two.'

'When they heard,' Clark took over, 'our group decided to adopt little Mary. Then the thing snowballed with other units chipping in and we had enough to sponsor another five orphans.'

'How exactly would you like to provide for the children?' Miriam asked.

'That is for you to decide. Whatever extras it takes to make the likes of little Mary happy,' said Clark.

'Tell her about Christmas.' Joe's lean face looked eager.

'I'm getting to that.' Clark took a packet of cigarettes out of his pocket and, shaking one out, offered it to Miriam, who shook her head. Taking one himself, he placed it behind an ear. 'Fran explained about the owner, the tough times he's going through and how he won't be around this year to give the kids the kind of Christmas they're used to. So, when we related this to the crew it was decided to hold a Christmas Day party at the base for all the children at the orphanage.'

Joe leaned forward in his chair. 'It would mean the boys would get to meet the orphans they've adopted.' He pulled a long face. 'We miss our children, especially this time of year.'

Miriam felt sad for him, far away from home at Christmas, and the fear he might never see his family again.

'Mrs Hunt, the Red Cross lady, said you'd want to meet the children you're supporting. And it'll do them so much good to know that someone cares.' Realising the orphans were to have a Christmas to look forward to after all, Miriam clasped her hands together and hugged them to her chest in delight. 'I don't know what to say to such generosity. Thank you seems inadequate.'

'Then don't say anything.' Clark stood and saluted. 'Pleased to be at your service, ma'am.' He took the cigarette from behind his ear, and lighting it as he inhaled, his green sultry eyes lingered on her.

The cheek of the man.

# 17

'There'll be no chores this afternoon because today we're going to decorate the dining hall with the decorations you've made,' Miriam announced to the children at dinner time, the following Saturday.

A collective gasp of wonderment sounded in the room. She noticed Alice and Rosie look at each other and grin. A wave of happiness surged through Miriam that Alice had made a friend at last.

Miriam kept the biggest surprise for later: that this year the children would have a tree to decorate as well. Fran Patterson had come to the office during the week to make arrangements.

'We met the airmen when we were at the pub,' she told Miriam. 'They told us about the Christmas party. When they heard about the tree that we're providing, they asked if they could help.' She raised her shoulders. 'I didn't see why not.'

'Which airmen were they?' Miriam couldn't help but ask.

Again, Fran shrugged. 'Don't ask me. I can never remember names. Does it matter?'

'Not at all,' Miriam fibbed.

Now, as she sought the decorations in the classroom cupboard, Miriam couldn't stand the suspense of waiting to see if Clark would appear – why, she couldn't fathom, seeing as she thought of him as a Casanova.

Early afternoon was taken up with finishing off the decorations, then the older orphans took turns climbing a ladder and pinning paper chains from the corner edges of the ceiling to the middle. While this was going on, Fran arrived. She moved over to where Miriam stood holding a ladder.

'They're here,' she whispered. 'Is it okay for them to bring the tree in now?'

The thought of seeing Clark again sent a tingle of anticipation through Miriam. 'Yes. But give me a minute to get the children ready.'

As Fran disappeared, Miriam clapped her hands. 'Listen, everyone' – the children, scattered around the dining room, stopped what they were doing and looked at her – 'take your place at the table because we need room. Quickly now. Tommy, come down from the ladder.'

The older boy did as he was told, wiping his nose on his sleeve – exasperatingly, he had a perpetual snotty nose. An air of expectation mounting in the room, the other children also did as they were bid. All eyes on the curtain as it was pulled aside, there was a collective gasp as Fran appeared followed by two uniformed Americans, who were carrying an enormous tree into the dining room.

As the sweet, refreshing scent of the pine tree infused the air, Miriam noted that it was Joe and the infuriating Clark and, maddeningly, the thrill of seeing him again overrode any other emotion she might have.

The American winked as he walked past. The gall of the man. He was nothing but an arrogant flirt, she reminded herself, and she was appalled at how she was behaving like an immature schoolgirl with a crush.

Yes, with his gorgeous green eyes and sinewy body, he was attractive… But he was also trouble – and Miriam had no time for him. No time at all.

Miriam was gratified to see the look of wonderment on the children's faces as they gazed in wonder at the Christmas tree that stood against the far wall.

'She's a beauty.' Joe's gaze swept the tree whose topmost branch bowed over at the ceiling.

'She sure is,' Clark drawled, gazing at Miriam.

The cheek of the man. And in front of the children.

Joe, looking their way, gave his friend an impatient shake of the head.

Fran had left by now and the three of them watched the orphans diligently but silently dressing the tree with cardboard stars they'd made earlier. The two men had provided glittering tinsel and little white candles to go in holders at the end of the tree's branches.

'Who will do the honours and put the star on the top?' Joe's gaze travelled the orphans, who stared wordlessly back at him. He gave Miriam a questioning look.

'They're not used to strangers.' Miriam didn't add the orphans had been taught by fear of punishment not to be forward and to only speak when spoken to.

'It's too high for them.' Clark made for the ladders. 'I'll do it.'

Picking up a large carboard star coloured with crayons from the table, Miriam handed it to him.

The children surrounded the tree and watched on as Clark climbed the steps. Miriam turned up her face and found herself staring at his taut buttocks straining against the material of his uniform trousers. She felt herself blush as she tried to ignore the sensuous thrill she felt from the sight. What was wrong with her? Every fibre in her being told her the man was a scoundrel and she should be wary, but still, like a magnet, she was drawn to him.

Clark, looking down at her, smirked, as though knowing her very thoughts. She blushed again.

The star in place, he descended the ladder and reaching the bottom, he observed the orphans who stared in silent rapture at the star far above. He and Joe exchanged a stare of disbelief. Miriam was uncomfortable as she knew this was not usual behaviour for excited children.

'Everyone, what do we say to these gentlemen?'

'Thank you,' they chanted in unison.

'Will there be presents underneath?' Alice looked directly at the airmen.

Rosie, flushing in embarrassment, nudged Alice in the ribs.

'I was only asking.' Alice's tone was indignant.

*Will she never learn*, Miriam agonised. Suffering a degree of disquiet herself, Miriam began to say, 'Alice, that's not—'

'Atta girl,' Clark pitched in. 'You won't get to know anything if you don't ask.'

Alice opened her mouth to speak but before she did, Miriam clapped her hands. 'Tidy up, everyone, then you can have time outside to let off steam after all the excitement.'

As they moved towards the table, Joe's eyes toured the orphans. 'Which one is little Mary?'

Miriam hesitated. 'She's over there, see.' She pointed to Mary, who followed the others as they made their way to the littered trestle tables. 'Please don't say anything about adopting her, as I haven't told them yet.'

'These kids sure act different.' Clark, at her side, was watching the orphans as, wordlessly, they put away the decorating paraphernalia. 'Don't they ever get excited and make a noisy nuisance of themselves like normal kids? I worry for them. They seemed cowed.'

Affronted by the word 'normal', Miriam stiffened. It certainly was true what the gossips said about the Yanks, that they were forthright with their opinions. Even so, the man's arrogance at meddling in matters he knew nothing about was nothing short of rude.

'I consider discussing the orphans off limits, Clark. But I can assure—'

'No need to get starchy, ma'am,' he drawled. 'And it's Mitch.'

'As I was saying,' Miriam said, her tone prim, 'the orphans have been taught to be well behaved and to have good manners.'

*But by what means were they taught?* her mind argued. Miss Black believed children should be seen and not heard and they were punished accordingly. Flustered that Clark had brought to the fore what deep down she knew to be right, she would never admit it. She was too ashamed she'd stood by and let it happen.

'I didn't mean to ruffle your feathers, ma'am, I just speak the way I see it. In my experience kids in trouble have no voice.'

Surprised at the vehemence of his tone, she wondered if the conversation had triggered a memory. She could have told him to mind his own business but instead Miriam decided to let the matter drop.

In a lighter tone, she told him, 'Let's hope they'll be as well behaved on Christmas Day, Clark, as they'll be so—'

'Mitch,' he corrected, his cocky self already returned. 'And you are?'

Flummoxed, she had no option but to answer, 'Miriam.'

That moment Joe strode over. 'Mary's a cute kid but shy with it. She reminds me of my Lara.' A wistful look came into his eyes.

Miriam told him, 'I intend to tell Mary and the other orphans about their adoption by your unit in the morning.' Seeing the children had finished their task, she made to move. 'It was good of you to give up your time and help with the tree.' She smiled appreciatively at the airmen. 'Many thanks.'

'Our pleasure, Miss Balfour.' Joe's voice was courteous.

'It's Miriam,' Mitch told him.

Joe, looking uneasy, rubbed the back of his neck. 'I'd prefer to stick with Miss Balfour.' He addressed Miriam, 'No offence meant, ma'am, but we've been told to mind our manners and not cause trouble while we're here.' He looked meaningfully at Mitch.

Miriam sincerely hoped Clark Mitchell would take the hint.

# 18

The next morning, Rosie, with the rest of the orphans, was making her way along the icy path towards Sunday school. Alice was pale and Rosie knew the truculent look on her face meant trouble. She didn't ask what was wrong because Alice, in this kind of mood, was better left alone.

In an attempt to cheer her up, Rosie said, 'I can't wait for Miss Balfour to light one of the candles on the Christmas tree today, can you?'

Miss Balfour had told them at breakfast that each night until Christmas Eve, she would light a candle on the tree.

Instead of answering, Alice stopped in her tracks. Good job they were at the end of the line.

'I'm going to be adopted.'

Shocked, Rosie stopped abruptly too. 'How d'you mean adopted? Who says?'

'Miss Balfour.'

Rosie watched as the line of orphans, walking two abreast in crocodile style, moved further away, Miss Balfour at the head. 'When did she say?'

'This morning in her office. She told four of us older ones those American airmen are going to adopt us as well as two of the infants.'

'Is it the Americans who brought us the tree yesterday?'

'Yes, and some others at the airfield.' Alice's troubled eyes met Rosie's. 'I got such a fright I can't remember what else she said.'

Rosie thought the Americans nice and friendly; they handed out chewing gum to share and the one called Joe was chatting to little Mary.

'I don't want to be adopted and nobody can make me. I'll run away.' Alice bunched her lips.

Worried she meant it, because Alice dared do anything once her mind was made up, Rosie couldn't think of anything to say to make things better.

The line of orphans had stopped now and Miss Balfour, walking up the line, called out, 'Hurry up, you two, or we'll be late for church.'

With nothing else for it, the two of them made for the line of waiting orphans. As the line moved forward, Rosie, upset, couldn't bear the thought of Alice being adopted and sent away. But her overriding thought was to make things right for Alice.

'Mrs Murray says Americans are rich.' She forced the words to sound light-hearted even though she felt miserable inside. 'So it would mean you'd be rich too like you've always wanted.'

'Stop trying to make things better.' Alice's face scrunched up in anger.

Seeing tears glistening in her friend's eyes, Rosie was shocked. Alice never cried.

'I don't want you to go either,' she blurted. 'You're my...'

Alice wasn't listening. Taking off, she headed back the way they came.

Looking down from the balcony at the back of the church where she sat, Rosie observed the congregation below all dressed in Sunday best, the women mostly wearing hats. Mrs Murray had once told them when she walked them to church, 'This here hat' – she pointed to the tattered straw hat she was wearing – 'might have seen better days but with this war on and this make do and mend malarky, this relic of a hat is the only one I've got.' She pulled a disgusted face. 'And no respectable woman would be seen at church without wearing a hat.'

Bending forward and looking along the pew, Rosie noted Miss Balfour wore a red beret. The mistress was smiling at something Mr Jackson, the organist, was saying. Biting her thumb nail, Rosie agonised whether she should tell her that Alice had run off. Worrying that if she did tell tales, Alice would never forgive her, Rosie decided not to say anything.

---

Playing truant from church was easy; Alice had done it before and caught up with the line outside the church when the service was over and before heads were counted. The thing was, she thought as she made her way over the village green's stiff grass, those occasions were planned and were in summer when the temperature wasn't freezing cold. This time was different because on the spur of the moment she'd decided to run away for good as she refused to let them send her away to America.

Disregarding the ache in her throat she'd had since early

morning, she wandered to the top of the hill, trying to plan how she could survive. Seeing the woods in the distance, an idea struck. Of course. She could go far away where no one knew her and pretend she was old enough to join the Lumberjills and work on an estate. That way she would be fed and have somewhere to sleep and she would be treated like a grownup with no mistress to boss her around. Guilt stabbed her when she thought of Miss Balfour's kindness and how she treated the orphans fairly; nevertheless, Alice was proud she'd worked things out so easily. But the awful thing was, she realised, it would mean leaving Rosie for good. Then she recalled going to America would be the same. A flash of anger coursed through her and Alice felt bitter that her life wasn't her own. Neither would it ever be because if she stayed here, she'd end up as someone's skivvy, and the same thing would happen if she found herself in America.

She paused to gaze in a shop window, something that was never allowed when the orphans were walking back from church. As she wandered down the hill, the deserted village had that boring Sunday morning feel. Passing the grim houses where smoke curled from tall chimney pots, Alice found herself wondering what it would be like to sit in your own home, toasting your toes in front of a roaring fire.

At that moment a girl, who looked a similar age to Alice and was bundled up in a green belted winter coat and brown lace-up boots, walked up the hill and, stopping outside a house, rapped on the front door knocker. An old lady with grey hair answered the door and, smiling with delight, ushered the girl in. A sense of longing overcame Alice, to be that girl to have someone pleased to see her with welcoming arms. That could never happen to her because she was trouble and nobody wanted her. If her own mam couldn't love her enough to keep her, how could Alice expect anyone else to. That's what the mistress of Blakely, her former orphanage, told her when she was younger.

Alice believed she was bad because of the rage that sometimes erupted inside, that made her do and say things she later regretted but had no control over. It happened when her and Rosie were talking about her being adopted, and the urge to flee had taken hold and without thinking she took off.

As the cold started to seep through her coat to her bones and shivering, a thought struck. She didn't have any money to go far away or any clothes to change into. Running was simple, she realised, but she'd never had to fend for herself and she felt helpless where to start. Unlike the girl in the green coat, she had no experience of the outside world.

Deep in thought, Alice hadn't noticed where she was going and was surprised to find her feet had led her through the entrance to Teviot Hall. Walking in the still air along the treelined path, passing the big house, she followed the track that led into the woods. The quiet, save for her breathing, was unnerving, then a sound in the distance made her stop. Singing. She stood for a while listening and when the singing finished, voices echoed from deep in the woods. The smell of woodsmoke filling her nostrils, Alice concluded that some of the Lumberjills must have skived church too and were having a bonfire.

Moving on, she passed the stables where one of the working horses poked its head out of the stable door.

'Hello, boy.' She stroked the horse's flat white nose down to its muzzle and the animal, whinnying, shook its head in objection.

Walking through the stable's entrance she wrinkled her nose at the smell of sweat, manure and hay that accosted her nostrils. Looking around the spacious building, she saw a ladder and climbed the wooden rungs to a loft filled with hay.

Tired and now a headache starting, she sat on the floor, her head resting back against a bale of hay. Even though it was cold, it was pleasant sitting here by herself with nowhere to go and no one telling her what to do. Alice had never experienced that before.

Sitting in the silence, drowsiness overcame her and chills went up and down her spine. As the realities of living outside the orphanage dawned on her fuzzy mind, Alice considered she would have to return to the orphanage and the only thing good about that was to have a warm bed and that she would get to see Rosie again.

But not yet, she decided. She wanted to experience freedom a little while longer, away from the rules and being amongst the orphans every minute of the day. Even if she did feel ill, she just wanted to be herself for a while and if she got punished then that was nothing new.

Her eyelids heavy, thoughts drifted through her mind – Miss Balfour lighting a candle, Miss Black's stern voice telling her the American family would dump her on the doorstep just as Alice deserved...

Her body jerked, giving her a shock, but then Alice's sleepy mind told her that she was falling asleep.

# 19

'She's here.'

At the shout, Alice jolted awake. She was in semi-darkness, a beam of light shining in her face. She held her hand up to shield her eyes. Her first thought was she was in the dormitory but smelling the sweet hay told her differently. Thoughts flooded her mind and she remembered where she was and why.

'A search party has been out looking for you,' a female voice said. A voice Alice recognised but couldn't place.

'Bring her down. I've sent Vivian to tell Miss Balfour you've found her,' someone else said from below.

'Are you okay to climb down the ladder?' the first voice asked.

Alice realised it belonged to Fran Patterson.

She couldn't believe she'd fallen asleep, then remembering her initial intention to run away, she snapped, 'Of course I can.'

'Hey! You'd better watch your tone if you want to avoid trouble. Everyone's been worried about you.'

With nothing else for it, groggy and disorientated, her legs wobbly, Alice followed the beam from the torch and when she descended the ladder and saw the light outside the stable door was fading, she wondered how she could possibly have slept so long.

'What d'you think you're playing at, girl?' a voice barked and Alice recognised the tall willowy figure of Miss Fellows, WTC office in charge. The officer continued, 'You should be ashamed. Miss Balfour's at her wits' end worrying about you. She was at the point of telephoning Constable McClew.' She turned to Fran. 'What was she doing up there?'

'Sleeping. If you ask me, I don't think she's very—'

'There's no excuse. She's flagrantly flouted the rules by taking off on her own after church. Miss Balfour realised when she counted heads. The girl's wasted everyone's time looking for her, including mine and some of the Lumberjills on their only afternoon off.' Miss Fellows came to peer down at Alice, whose head had now begun to throb. 'Oh! It's you. I knew when I saw you up at the house you were trouble.' The officer folded her arms.

'Hang on, Muriel,' Fran piped up. 'To be fair, we don't know the reason why she—'

Miss Fellows quivered with annoyance. 'That one doesn't need a reason. Look at her face, defiant as ever.'

Alice was mystified. Her anger deflated, her limbs as well as her head aching now, she wasn't aware of any kind of expression on her face.

Fran didn't reply but nudged Alice's arm. 'Come on, I'll take you back to the orphanage.'

'Make sure you keep an eye on her, Fran,' Miss Fellows called as the pair of them made their way along the overgrown pathway. 'I don't want her running off again.'

. . .

Standing in front of Miss Balfour's desk, all Alice could think was to get her punishment over and done with, as all she craved was to return to the dormitory and crawl into bed.

'Why did you run away, Alice?'

A tinge of remorse pricked her as she saw Miss Balfour's concerned face.

'I didn't run, I walked and I didn't get far.'

Miss Balfour gave that grownup look of disapproval that meant Alice had said the wrong thing.

'Please don't try to be clever, Alice. You've caused enough trouble. Why did you decide to miss church and return to the orphanage?'

Alice wasn't trying to be clever; she was telling the truth. Too drained, she couldn't be bothered to argue like she normally did; besides, it would only prolong things. Best to simply answer questions.

'I dunno, miss.'

Miss Balfour's brow corrugated into a troubled frown. 'How d'you feel, Alice? You're flushed and could be running a temperature.'

'I've got a headache and feel shivery,' she admitted.

'Sit down, Alice.' When she was seated, the mistress continued, 'Then why, when you're feeling poorly, did you miss church and roam around in the cold.'

Alice remembered the girl in the green coat she'd seen earlier, who had appeared to be without a care. *The girl was allowed out on her own,* Alice thought, *and probably no one would question her where she'd been.* The injustice of what life could be like if Alice wasn't an orphan caused the furnace of anger, burning just below the surface, to erupt.

Aches forgotten in the moment, Alice fumed, 'Because I was planning to run away.'

Miss Balfour, dumbfounded, simply gaped at her. 'Where did you plan to go?'

'Anywhere but here. I'll try again,' she threatened and meant it. 'I don't want no Americans adopting me and taking me back to live with them.'

Miss Balfour sank back in her swivel chair. Her face relaxed. 'Is that what this is all about, Alice? Dear girl, you've got the wrong end of the stick. The Americans aren't taking you anywhere. Adoption in this case only means a group of Americans are sponsoring you and will give generously of their time and money to make life a little better for you and the others during the war years.' A look of enlightenment on her face, she went on. 'Is it because you're hoping one day your mother will return and if you'd left—'

'Are you kidding me?' Alice gave a bitter laugh. 'Huh! That's the last thing I'm hoping for. She dumped me without a care.' Weak and wobbly, a lump swelled in Alice's throat. She swallowed hard, reminding herself that crying showed weakness.

A look of sorrow crossed Miss Balfour's face. 'You're only hurting yourself thinking like that. People have reasons for what—'

'I don't want to talk about her. I hate her.'

'Don't say that, Alice. Hate is a strong word.'

'Why can't I say that? I'll never forgive her.'

'Because—'

'No one can make me think differently.' Past caring about being punished, Alice placed her hands over her ears.

---

When all the orphans were in bed and Mrs Murray retired to her room, Miriam, sitting in front of an unlit fire, went over the events of her meeting with Alice. She was worried about her as, indeed, she did look ill. How Miriam had wanted to take her in her arms, stroke her fevered head, comfort her. Instead, she had given Alice a hot milky drink, then sent her to bed, her wrongdoing never mentioned, the reason being Alice had jumped to the wrong conclusion and had been distraught at the thought of being adopted. It seemed unfair to punish her for a mistake, even though she'd reacted by running away. An offense, no doubt, that would be punished if Miss Black was still in charge, but Miriam saw no good to come out of Alice being disciplined on this occasion. She sighed heavily at the encounter she was likely to have with Miss Fellows, another strict disciplinarian, who wouldn't agree with Miriam's lax – as the WTC officer would see it – handling of the situation.

Her mind returned yet again to the scene with Alice. The loathing on her face as she spoke of her mother. Alice's words rang in Miriam's ears. 'I hate her.' Overwrought, Miriam asked herself, *Should I have made her listen?*

If Alice hadn't interrupted when she spoke, Miriam was sure she would have divulged the secret she'd guarded over the years. That when Alice asked why she couldn't say she hated her mother, Miriam would have said, 'Because I'm your mother.'

# 20

Sitting in a daze of wretchedness, the scene Miriam had refused to visit for years unfolded in her memory. In the shadowy moonlight, she crept along the streets keeping to the obscurity of the walls; the baby in her arms swaddled in a shawl, its tiny pink eyelids shut, weighed hardly anything at all. She knew exactly where she was going as she'd planned this journey since the day Terry Rawling rejected that her baby was his.

Terrified Father would find out and ashamed of being an unwed mother, Miriam hid the evidence by wearing loose-fitting frocks and a bulky cardigan, and with only a small bump she got away with her disgrace not showing. Or so she hoped.

The night of the birth when water trickled down her legs, Miriam thought at first that she'd wet herself. The pain when it started was indescribable and, afraid and clueless, she stemmed her screams by stuffing a pillow over her mouth. She knew to cut the cord and wait for the afterbirth because when she called at Terry's house after his mam delivered her baby, Miriam overheard Mrs Rawling describing the home birth to a visiting neighbour.

Mercifully, the bloodied baby didn't cry for long and, taking the tiny infant from the bed, she wrapped it in a crocheted shawl. Leaving her attic bedroom, Miriam crept down the stairs, past Father's bedroom and, opening the front door, stepped into the warm night. Opening the front gate, some instinct made her look up at the vicarage windows but they were as dark as night.

Miriam, weak and wobbly, made her way to Westoe village. Passing through a gap in a wall she came to a road with fields either side. Through the trees, she followed a gravelled path and, opening a squeaking wrought-iron gate, Miriam stood in the grounds of Blakely Hall orphanage. Approaching the sweeping stone steps that led up to a substantial house, she noted the rows of sash windows were in darkness.

By the light of a malevolent-faced moon, Miriam opened the shawl and gazed down at the babe in her arms. That was the mistake she made. Staring down at her baby girl – the cute little nose, rosebud lips – who lay serenely in her arms, Miriam fell in love and the enormity of what she was about to do hit her. So busy had she been, hiding the evidence over the months, the clandestine birth, the frantic rush to have the baby safely out of the way, Miriam never stopped to think what it would be like to leave her baby behind.

But keeping her was out of the question. Father would never allow such a scandal as her keeping a bastard child.

*This is my baby, my flesh and blood that I can't keep.* The tears came then, falling down her cheeks, dripping from her chin and onto the baby's shawl. Resting her cheek against the baby's warm skin, Miriam whispered, 'I'm so very sorry,

Gabrielle, I have to give you away. I'll always love you and pray for you every day. Have the best life.'

Gabrielle. She'd always loved the name of God's messenger for the birth of Christ.

Dawn was breaking and, afraid someone would see her, Miriam kissed the baby goodbye, wishing she'd thought to bring something of hers for Gabrielle to have.

She made a promise. 'Somehow, some way, I will always be close to you.' Wrapping the shawl tightly around the little form, she placed the sleeping baby on the doorstep.

But Miriam couldn't leave, not until she knew her baby was safely in someone's arms. Traipsing down the stone steps, she walked along the path and out of the gate and hid behind the overgrown bushes and trees. After what seemed like an eternity, the house door opened. A young girl dressed in a navy frock and long white apron looked out. Hiding behind a chunky tree trunk, Miriam could hardly breathe. Peeping around the tree, she watched as the girl bent down and undoing the bundle on the doorstep she appeared to freeze.

Picking Gabrielle up, she ran inside calling, 'Mistress, Mistress, come and see.'

The door slammed shut.

Trailing home, emotionally and physically spent, Miriam was startled when she reached the vicarage to find Father opening the front door. He stood tall and erect, his face as white as his long-pointed beard.

'What have you done with it?' his rasping voice asked.

A shudder of dread reached down her spine. Father knew.

'I've left her at the orphanage.'

He nodded and went inside. From that day on, they

never spoke of the baby, and soon after the birth, Miriam left the vicarage.

Sitting at her desk remembering, Miriam knew it was wrong not to pardon someone's behaviour but from that day to this, she never forgave Father and when he told her never to darken his door again, that was fine by her because she'd already vowed that she would never speak to him again.

Leaving her baby at the orphanage was the hardest thing Miriam had ever done but she'd kept her promise and stayed close to her daughter.

*My daughter.* Miriam savoured those two words she could never use in public.

Soon there'd come the day when Alice would be leaving the orphanage and the knowledge she would no longer be involved in her daughter's life terrified Miriam. But she could never confess the truth to Alice, or else she would see the trust in her daughter's eyes die, to be replaced by pure hatred. *I'll never forgive her.*

Even if she did tell Alice the secret of her birth, and a miracle happened and her daughter forgave her, Miriam neither had the means nor wherewithal to support them both in the outside world. This, Miriam concluded, was the penance for her sin and she would suffer her sorrow with fortitude and pray, as always, that Alice had the best life.

# 21

Three nights later, after the supper dishes were cleared away and the trolley wheeled back to the kitchen, Miss Balfour moved towards the Christmas tree and, taking out a box of matches from her uniform dress pocket, she struck a match. As the mistress lit a candle at the end of one of the branches, Rosie gave out a sigh of satisfaction. This was the best part of her day.

The little yellow flame burning merrily at the end of each day uplifted Rosie – she was so looking forward to Christmas. It was a shame Alice missed the occasion, but she was poorly with a heavy cold and Miss Balfour insisted she stayed in bed until she was properly better.

With only ten days to go before the big day, Rosie didn't know what to expect as she couldn't remember past Christmases, and trying to search her blank mind frustrated her. Was anyone pining for her, she wondered, or was it a case of good riddance? That was the question that haunted Rosie.

'Christmas won't be as good as previous years, cos the

laird isn't here,' Agnes had told her dolefully one dinner time.

The orphans weren't afraid to speak now at mealtimes but the rule was only if your mouth wasn't full, which Miss Balfour said was good manners.

'Why? What happened when the laird was here?' Rosie asked.

'He played the piano and we all gathered around to sing carols and afterwards we were given a gift from under the tree.' Agnes's face sagged in disappointment. 'But because his son's been killed, the laird's sad and none of that will happen this year.'

Now, as she thought over what Agnes had said, Rosie wondered how, when she saw Sir Henley's piano that day in the big house, she just knew she could play it? Try as she might, she couldn't remember, though the answer seemed as though it hovered just out of reach.

Miss Balfour stood up and caught her attention.

'Everyone, I have an announcement to make.' She looked around the orphans with a twinkle in her eyes. 'As you all know Sir Henley has tragically lost his son and we must continue to pray for him. But he won't be with us this Christmas and so this year will be different.' Miss Balfour smiled and Rosie leaned in closer, hoping it was good news. 'This year we've been invited to Dunglen airfield on Christmas Day by the American airmen.'

Rosie, along with the rest of the orphans, gave an astonished intake of breath.

Harry Burton put up his hand.

'Yes, Harry?' Miss Balfour was always happy to answer questions unlike Miss Black, who would scowl her disapproval at being interrupted.

'Please, miss, will we be having Christmas dinner at the airbase?'

Trust Harry to be thinking about food.

'No, Harry, we're having dinner here, then we're going to the airbase afterwards to have a party in the canteen followed by tea.'

Rosie's mouth yawned open in surprise.

As she lay in bed that night, Rosie couldn't get to sleep as waves of excitement rippled through her. Yesterday, after school, the sponsored orphans were taken by an airman to the airbase. When Brenda Dawson returned, she told Rosie all about the visit and how friendly the American airmen were. The colonel, who had invited them and who was in charge of the airmen, had showed them around. The orphans were given cake and a fizzy drink called Coca-Cola in the canteen. Afterwards the boys had played with toy aeroplanes while the girls and some airmen played board games.

She must have dropped off to sleep sometime because the next thing Rosie knew, someone howling woke her up. She heard voices in the darkness and groggily realised she was in the dormitory but the howling didn't stop.

As a different noise started up, Rosie froze. Anti-aircraft guns were firing from the ground. While one part of her mind wondered how she knew that, another part registered that it wasn't someone howling at all – it was the air-raid siren alerting them.

Then a lamp switched on and Miss Balfour's voice was heard to say, 'Everyone stay calm. Remember the drill. Put your boots on and wrap up in a blanket and make for the shelter. I'll see to the infants. Everyone, hurry.'

Along with the rest, Rosie did as she was told, donning

boots without lacing them up and, hurrying to the door huddled in a thin blanket, she stepped into the moonlit night. Stopping on the cobbles, Rosie heard them coming, the enemy planes, a distant drone at first and then, as they came closer, the deadly roar of the engines. Heart pounding, she stood transfixed on the cobbled courtyard, her legs frozen. As the planes screamed overhead, she closed her eyes.

'Rosie, come on,' a voice yelled, 'don't just stand here, come with me.'

Rosie opened her eyes. Alice stood before her, wild eyes in an alarmed face.

'You're out of bed?' Rosie blurted. Then felt silly because of course Alice wouldn't want to be all alone in the dormitory with bombers screaming overhead. She allowed herself to be pulled over the cobbled courtyard, through the stone arch and along the path to grassy land where a shelter was built underground.

Rosie sat next to Alice on one of the long wooden benches against the wall and, smelling the stink of the dank underground shelter, she wrinkled her nose. Light came from the two lamps Miss Balfour had lit. The mistress fussed, making sure everyone was settled, then made her way to Alice with a blanket over her arm.

'Here, Alice, I've brought you this. We don't want you to get pneumonia now, do we?' She tucked the blanket around Alice and with a nod of satisfaction, the mistress went to sit on a bench beside the little ones. 'The raiders will be after the shipyards on the River Clyde,' she told them.

Before the words could sink in, Rosie heard distant gunfire from the ground. They came again, enemy planes, thundering terrifyingly close. Rosie crouched down, eyes squeezed shut, and put her hands over her ears. While the racket went on overhead, behind her eyelids her mind was transported to a dim passageway where she sensed she wasn't alone. The roaring noise outside stopped but the quiet was more frightening. In front of her was a wall, the top half beginning to move, as though it was about to collapse. Paralysed with fear, her legs were rooted to the spot. Seeing the wall begin to fall, terrified, she began to scream.

'Rosie, Rosie, stop screaming. It's all right. The raiders have gone.'

Her breath ragged, Rosie opened her eyes. Alice stood in front of her.

'You frightened me, yelling like that,' she accused.

As distant crumps could be heard, Rosie looked around the shelter in a daze, taking in the terrified looks of the orphans, the crying infants being comforted by Miss Balfour.

'Everyone, settle down,' the mistress called. 'Hopefully the raiders are just passing over.'

Rosie told Alice, 'I'm sorry if I scared you but I—'

'Not half as much as the raiders did.' Back to normal, Alice grinned.

Recalling the scene that played in her mind, Rosie said in awe, 'I was remembering when I was in the raid, when I got hurt.'

'Can you remember anything else?' Alice asked sharply.

'No. Only when I was in the shelter.' She went on to relate what she saw in her mind. 'Don't you see, it means my memory's coming back.'

Disappointingly, Alice didn't look as happy as Rosie thought she would.

'Was anyone with you?' Alice asked.

'I don't think so.' The thought she was on her own that time of the bombing, and nobody cared enough to come and seek her, upset Rosie. She watched Miss Balfour haul Mary onto her knee, the other infants gathering around as the mistress opened a story book. The realisation the little ones would grow up in the orphanage and never know what it was like to have a home of their own made her heart ache.

At that moment the siren gave a long continuous blast signalling the all-clear.

Miss Balfour, taking Mary off her knee, stood. 'Form a line, everyone, and we'll get you back to bed. Don't forget your blankets.'

Rosie looked up and asked Alice, 'Why did you run away when you thought the Americans wanted to adopt you? It would have meant you'd have a home.'

Alice chewed the inside of her cheek as though she felt awkward. 'Because if I lived in America, I wouldn't see you again. And you're me make-believe sister, remember.'

Rosie didn't know what to say to that but felt tears prickling behind her eyes. She nodded at her friend. But the part of her that begged to find out who she was and where she came from still nagged.

---

'I never thought it, but you were right.' Mrs Murray's eyebrows raised in amazement. 'We are seeing the better side of young Alice these past few days. I reckon it's Rosie Ward's good influence that's done it.' A small frown creased her brow. 'Though I wouldn't push our luck, she can be full of devilment when she wants.'

Miriam had also noticed Alice was changing and though she still carried a chip on her shoulder, the result of her resentment at being abandoned, there was evidence of change. Miriam was convinced too it was because of the friendship she'd formed with Rosie.

With only a few days to go before Christmas the two

women were in the office trying to figure out what to have for dinner on the big day. Both of them sat at the desk and a pad was placed before Miriam. Hazel was supervising the orphans in the classroom where they were knitting colourful squares that were to be sewn together to make scarves. Both the boys and girls had been shown how to knit, something Miriam had encouraged. The orphans were proud of their work, as it helped them feel they were doing their bit for the war effort.

'How about mashed turnip and carrot?' Miriam asked.

Mrs Murray, taking the pencil from behind her ear, nodded. 'And peas for a bit of green.' She grimaced. 'I've checked with Cook and she says there's only tinned Spam in the larder.'

Miriam sighed heavily. 'I see no point in standing forever in a long queue to see if the butcher's got anything on offer.'

'I agree. The last I heard, he was serving his regulars murkey. But not me.' She gave a knowing wink.

Miriam assumed Mrs Murray must be one of the butcher's favourite customers – those who got something special that he kept under the counter.

'What on earth is murkey?'

'Where've you been, lassie, to not know that?'

Mrs Murray's shake of the head made Miriam feel she was out of touch, which was true, she supposed, as she scarcely left the orphanage these days.

'Since there's no turkey to be had, stuffed rolled mutton is now its substitute,' the older lady explained.

'Oh, I see.'

'The good news according to Cook,' Mrs Murray went on airily, 'is we'll have Christmas pudding even though shortages are at an all-time high.' She pulled a disgusted face. 'The bad news is there's no eggs and everyone's forced to make the pudding with the dry stuff. And with no dried fruit to be had, Cook says she's using one of Marguerite Patten's recipes.'

Curious, Miriam asked, 'What so different about the recipe?'

'It includes grated carrots and potato, supposedly to moisten the pudding and make it have a taste of toffee.' Mrs Murray rolled her eyes in disgust. 'Blimey! If that's the case then Walter and me will make do with jam roly-poly this year.'

They were quiet for a while, Miriam thinking about the ramifications of Christmas dinner.

But Mrs Murray didn't like silences. 'By the by,' she said, 'have you heard the talk about the New Year's Eve dance at the airfield?'

Miriam hauled her thoughts from the topic of food to what had been said. 'A dance?'

'Aye, all the lassies in the village are on about it. Young Hazel told me. She says Ellen's going.'

Miriam frowned as she pondered. 'Whatever became of Ellen joining up?'

'She thought better of it, so she says.' Mrs Murray made a knowing face. 'If you ask me, it's her dad putting his foot down by telling her she's to wait until she's eighteen. He reckons her mam needs her at home. That man likes to throw his weight around and let them know who's boss in the house.' She tutted. 'Aye, he's just like Ian.'

'Ian?' Miriam, mystified, could never keep up with Mrs Murray in a conversation.

'Me brother-in-law, remember.' Her tone suggested Miriam should know exactly who she meant. 'The man's strict and I've told Elsie – that's me sister,' she reminded Miriam in case she'd forgotten her too, 'no good will come of his controlling ways. Especially not when it comes to me niece, Hazel. In my book it'll only make Hazel resort to deviousness to get her way. And that usually ends up in grief.'

Miriam was transported back to the past, to the lies, the deceit to Father to get her way so she could meet up with Terry. That ended up in heartache.

'Thing is...' Mrs Murray's voice brought her back to reality. 'Ellen has our Hazel fired up about this dance. But Ian's forbidden Hazel from going; says she too young and he doesn't trust them Yanks as far as he could throw them.' Her face turned plum coloured in indignation. 'I told him, he should be ashamed saying such things. We should be thankful to those lads coming over here to help fight Jerry and that they're willing to die in the effort.'

'So did you change his mind?'

'Huh! There's no telling that man. I even pointed out Hazel was a fifteen-year-old working lassie, for God's sake, and not the pushover he seems to think. But Ian still insists over his dead body will he allow her to go to a New Year's Eve dance on her own with all those airmen just out for a good time.'

'It is a pity she'll miss out on the fun. As you know, I've met some of the airmen and they're perfect gentlemen.' Miriam thought of Joe, a trustworthy family man, but skirted around the subject of Mitch. He might be a flirt and appeal to women who courted trouble but she knew by some primal instinct that Clark Mitchell was decent and would never take advantage of a fifteen-year-old girl.

Mrs Murray watched her keenly, a scheming look crossing her otherwise amiable face. 'So, our Elsie, Hazel and me got to thinking...'

When Miriam heard exactly what the others had cooked up, she was dismayed.

# 22

'I told them in the Co-op I didn't agree,' Mrs Murray said out of the blue, surprising Miriam.

It was Christmas Eve and the two of them were sitting companionably at a round wooden table in Miriam's sitting-cum-dining-room making Christmas crackers from recycled wrapping paper. Miriam only half listened as she was keeping an ear out for the orphans in the dormitories below.

'What didn't you agree with?' she asked, filling a cracker with scraps cut from old Christmas cards and a paper noisemaker.

'I was vexed at what people in the queue were saying about the bombings in Berlin last week.'

'What were they saying?' Miriam was starting to wish she hadn't entered this conversation.

'That after the ruthless attacks on London, and Coventry, it served the Germans right if Berlin was bombed to smithereens.' She shook her head in disgust. 'I told them straight, that it's not the rulers that start wars that suffer but the little people like us who have to endure the bombings. In the main they don't want this war any more than we do.' She wrapped a piece of thread around one end of a cracker then snapped it off with her teeth.

Miriam held back from replying as it was Christmas Eve and she wanted to forget about the war for once.

Mrs Murray had other ideas. 'It all started with Arthur Craddock mentioning the hundreds of bombers that were despatched to Berlin. He'd heard that when they returned it was a foggy night and the poor lads couldn't make out the airfields. Needless to say, some planes crashed and others simply ran out of fuel.' She shuddered. 'Just think how those boys must have suffered in their last moments. Poor souls, they'd made it back to Blighty and couldn't land.'

Miriam didn't want to think, it was too harrowing. A sudden thought popped in her mind and her stomach clenched. Joe, Mitch... were they involved?

'Which airfield did they operate from?'

Mrs Murray cocked her head as she thought. 'If my memory serves me right, Craddock said it was an airfield near York. Why?'

Miriam didn't realise she was holding her breath and, letting it out, she relaxed.

'No particular reason.'

She didn't want to encourage Mrs Murray because once she started on gossip, especially anything gruesome, there was no stopping her. Plus, Miriam particularly didn't want to mention the Yanks because it might remind Mrs Murray of the recent request that she'd made for the New Year's Eve dance.

But then the sight of Mrs Murray, with her stoic attitude, when she carried all the worry of her two sons – one in the army, the other in the navy – on her shoulders, made the compassionate side of Miriam want to help ease the woman's life.

'Are you sure Mr Murray is fine about you having Christmas dinner here? Cook and I can manage.'

'Och! Walter's meeting up with a fellow Home Guard who's a widower and they'll be chewing the fat over a beer.' Her cheeks bunching, she grinned. 'I've got a wee surprise for our tea later. While you, lassie, will be gallivanting off to the airfield, Walter and me will be gorging ourselves on a bit of duck. Don't ask where it came from.' Giving a telling wink, she gave a raucous laugh. 'Afterwards, we'll settle ourselves on the couch and listen to the nativity play that's on the wireless. It's called *He That Should Come*.'

It sounded so companiable and cosy Miriam felt quite envious.

With only a few more crackers to go, she was content to work in silence. But Mrs Murray, as usual, felt otherwise.

'Crackers are never the same without the bang, are they? But their little faces will still light up when they see them on the table.'

Miriam nodded, adding, 'And glueing the scraps they find inside into scrapbooks will hopefully fill the time till we go to the airfield.'

She inwardly groaned. Lordy, now she'd gone and done it, mentioning the Dunglen airfield.

'Have you given any thought, lassie, to my suggestion for the New Year's Eve dance?' Mrs Murray pierced her with an expectant stare. 'As I told you, even if Elsie and I wanted to take Hazel to the dance, which we don't might I add, the lass was adamant she didn't want a pair of old fogies like us chaperoning her. Which is why she suggested you.'

Miriam had procrastinated answering because she found it difficult to say no. It was out of the question her going as she would feel and look like a fish out of water. Besides, she admitted to herself, not for the first time, she'd feel awkward around Mitch, who surely would be there. The very thought made her pulse quicken. Blast the man.

'If Hazel had someone responsible with her – and who better person than her employer,' Mrs Murray was saying, 'Ian can't say no. I've told Elsie she should stand up to him but she never has and won't start now.' She gave a resigned sigh. 'To tell you the truth, there's no telling how Hazel will react because like young Alice the lass has spirit and won't take no for an answer. You'll be doing us a such big favour.'

'Mrs Murray, I'm terrib—'

'Elsie agrees with me,' Mrs Murray hurried on as if anticipating a refusal, 'young Hazel doesn't get much fun and this dance is too good an opportunity to miss. The lassie should be having a wee bit of jollity in her life. That applies to you too.' She shook a disapproving head. 'You never set foot away from this place and a few hours at a dance won't hurt you. You need to let your hair down for once.'

A peculiar saying, but maybe it was true.

'What about—' she started.

'Don't you worry about this place. Elsie and I can look after things here for a few hours.'

Hazel was young, Miriam told herself, there'd be other dances and in the scheme of things, missing out on this one wasn't a big thing. But as Mrs Murray waited for an answer, a look of eagerness on her face, Miriam lost her nerve.

'I'm sorry. With Christmas and all I haven't had a minute to think.'

Disappointment etching her face, Mrs Murray nodded. 'Mebbes after you've been to the airbase tomorrow, you'll be more enthused.'

Miriam felt bad at delaying to answer yet again but she

couldn't face a disagreement with Mrs Murray. Not at the moment; she had bigger things to think about. The letter she'd received from Miss Black in the morning's post loomed large in her thoughts.

*Dear Miss Balfour,*

*This is to inform you that I have received a letter from Miss Fellows informing me that Sir Henley has been in touch to say he would be returning to Teviot Hall after the New Year.*

*I feel it my duty to be there when he returns but in my present condition, regrettably that is an impossibility. Therefore, I intend to govern from afar. Each Friday I would like your presence here at the flat when I will go over the following week's programme – prayers, bible readings, menus, the general running of the orphanage – with you.*

*Rest assured I will be back at the helm at the earliest opportunity.*

*Sincerely Yours,*

*Gertrude Black*

Miriam had thought the orphans in for a decent respite from the harshness of Miss Black's rule. And she'd made plans which would allow the children more freedom – all now to be dashed.

Miriam inwardly railed at her immediate acceptance at the state of affairs. She was allowing herself to be browbeaten and was taking the easy way out. Why was she so pathetic where Miss Black was concerned? Was it really all about the worry of losing her job, or did her insecurities run deeper than that? While she loathed this inner weakness, she didn't know how to overcome it. Besides, she told herself, inwardly knowing she was making excuses, Miss Black was boss, her word was law.

---

Alice was woken by the sound of the bell ringing.

'Merry Christmas, everyone,' Miss Balfour called.

In the flickering lamplight Alice saw the housemistress, still in her long dressing gown. Shocked at the unusual sight, she sat bolt upright, oblivious of the cold.

The mistress told them, 'Today is a holiday with no work and so you can stay in bed until breakfast time.' There was a shared intake of breath. 'Afterwards, the older ones can collect holly outside to decorate the dining-hall tables. The younger ones will stay with me inside where they can play with the toys or do jigsaw puzzles until the bell rings for dinner.'

Groggily, the orphans sat up rubbing their eyes and, like Alice, it seemed they couldn't believe what they'd just heard.

Later, as Alice sat beside Rosie at the breakfast table and after prayers were said – thankfully not an agonisingly long-drawn-out affair but just a thank you to the Lord for all his blessings and for his son Jesus Christ, who was born today – Alice stared in wonder at the plate of food that was put before her. There was a real egg, sausage and bacon, bread, spread with proper butter.

'I can't believe it's real.' Rosie also stared at her plate in astonishment.

Alice didn't answer because, cheeks bulging, she had a mouthful.

Miss Balfour, who also looked surprised, raised her eyebrows at Cook, standing by the food trolley, her face flushed with pleasure.

'These are from yon airbase,' Cook said.

'But how? When?' Miss Balfour wanted to know.

'According to Miss Fellows, one of those open-topped Jeeps arrived yesterday and a Yank from the airbase hopped out and came looking for her. He said he'd been instructed to drop a special delivery to the orphanage.' She grinned. 'Wait till you see what else he brought. Something special for dinner.'

Alice could scarcely wait.

---

That afternoon found Miriam sitting in the cab of a truck, the wide-eyed orphans, supervised by Hazel (who couldn't contain her excitement at the prospect of visiting the American barracks), being jolted around in the back.

She asked the driver, who'd introduced himself as Taylor, 'Was it you who delivered the parcels of food to the orphanage yesterday?'

His eyes on the road as he manoeuvred round a sharp end on a country lane, Taylor told her, 'No, ma'am, I'm not in this crew so I've got no idea who organised sending the food. But what a swell idea.'

'Whoever it was, I'm grateful. The ham for Christmas dinner was a wonderful surprise, especially when we all expected tinned Spam.'

Taylor, a fresh-faced young man with long blond lashes and hair cut above his ears, frowned and gave a long whistle. His eyes never leaving the road, he told her, 'Boy, if that's the case, am I glad.'

As they drove, the view beyond obscured by a high hedge either side of the road, Miriam wondered if she would meet up with Mitch on their visit. And, of course, Joe, she reminded herself.

Approaching the airfield, nothing could be seen but a high metal fence and gateposts where two rigid-looking sentries in uniform stood guard, guns at their side. Taylor wound down the window and spoke to one of the sentries. The barrier lifted and Taylor drove the truck through the gap and along a narrow road, passing rows of corrugated Nissen huts, painted camouflage green. Looming way in the distance, Miriam could see the control tower.

The truck came to a halt in front of a low-spreading, concrete building with a peaked wooden roof.

'The mess hall.' Taylor opened the cab door, jumped down and disappeared around the back of the truck to help unload the orphans. A few of them held back as if they were shy. Rosie was one of them and Miriam saw Alice link arms with her and pull her along.

Miriam led the children into the mess hall which was cosy and warm from the stove that burnt brightly. Looking up at the soaring peaked roof, she saw American flags hanging from sturdy beams. Tables stretched across the length of the room, the nearest ones covered with white tablecloths and set with plates, cups and saucers. Through the hatch at the far side of the room, Miriam spied a kitchen where a man wearing a white apron and white chef's hat looked up from what he was doing. His good-natured face lit up at seeing the orphans and he gave a little wave.

A grey-haired man in uniform with an air of authority walked towards her.

'Miss Balfour.' He extended his hand. 'Colonel Douglas. Pleasure to meet you, ma'am.'

His handshake was firm and, smiling at him, Miriam reckoned her imaginings of a disciplined and dignified colonel had been correct.

'The boys will be here soon,' he told her. 'Meanwhile you and the kiddies make yourself at home.' He directed his gaze to the children then nodded towards the tree. 'Go take a look around.'

The colonel took a pipe from his pocket, a wistful expression on his face. 'My girls are older and I miss this stage.' He heaved a sigh. 'They'll be bringing boys home next.'

Miriam inwardly smiled at the thought of how he would scare the life out of any lad who came near his daughters. She could tell what a good father he was.

Sudden thoughts of her father, where he was, who he was with, played in her mind. Did he ever think of the granddaughter he'd never set eyes on? Switching her mind off any unpleasant thoughts, she concentrated on the children instead. Bundled in outdoor clothing, cheeks pink and glowing from the cold air outside, they gazed around in awe. Seeing the overladen, decorated Christmas tree with parcels beneath, their expressions changed to dumbstruck.

'Coats off first,' she told them.

At that moment the door opened and American airmen (Miriam counted nine including Joe) entered the hall, a babble of noisy males. Feeling a twinge of regret Mitch wasn't amongst the airmen, she scolded herself for caring. The man was a rogue, she reminded herself – followed by the unaccountable thought, *A lovable rogue.*

Colonel Douglas, drawing himself up, put his unlit pipe back into his pocket. 'Time I took my leave, ma'am. Duty calls. The men are a good bunch but if there's anything I can assist with, you know where I am.'

'Thank you, Colonel,' she said, knowing she would never bother him. 'That's very kind.'

The genial smile was back, then he nodded and, cap in hand, he made for the door.

The man who'd led the airmen in, and who sported a moustache, carried a wind-up gramophone player in his arms. Placing it on the table he looked around and, spotting Mary, moved over towards her.

'Hiya, honey, how are you doing?'

Mary's young face lit up in recognition and Miriam relaxed, realising these men were known to the sponsored orphans from when they visited the airfield. As the afternoon wore on the other children, helped by the caring and overly enthusiastic airmen, gradually thawed. An airman called Frank played popular songs on the harmonica; then the man with the moustache, Ray, played carols on the record player, including Bing Crosby's 'White Christmas', the men subdued and misty-eyed as they listened and, no doubt, thought of home.

Games came next, charades, consequences, then finally tea was served. Miriam couldn't believe her eyes at all the food: an assortment of sandwiches, the queerest sausages called hot dogs, which the orphans took some convincing by the airmen that they were made of beef and not actual dogs, Christmas cake and jelly.

Sitting at one of the tables beside Joe, she said, 'I can't thank you all enough. Christmas this year has been special for the children, and whoever thought to send those hams was so thought—'

'That would be Mitch,' Joe interrupted. 'He got the boys organised and got the hams from the base exchange store.'

Miriam was taken aback and felt sure it showed.

'He's a good guy where kids are concerned,' Joe assured her.

Was it Miriam's imagination that Joe stressed the word *kids*, with a 'take note' expression on his face?

He continued. 'In fact, ma'am, he's a regular nice guy when he drops the lover boy act.'

Just then the door opened and Miriam looked up. Her heart fluttered despite her common sense. Standing there was Mitch, the lovable rogue himself.

# 23

The wireless, switched on in readiness for the King's speech, was playing Vera Lynn's heart-wrenching rendition of 'The Little Boy that Santa Claus Forgot'. Listening to the words, the orphans' expressions changed from happy to sombre. And when the song came to its conclusion, and Vera Lynn sang, 'I'm so sorry for that laddie, he hasn't got a daddy,' Charlie sniffled then burst into tears.

'Switch the wireless off,' Mitch's voice commanded from the doorway.

Miriam rushed over to comfort Charlie and looking towards where Mitch stood, taking in his furrowed brow of concern.

As the wireless snapped off, Chuck, a friendly airman from Georgia that Joe had introduced her to, stood up and moved over in long strides to the food counter. 'It's Coca-Cola time,' he said in an overly eager voice.

Chuck and Ray began to distribute bottles of the drink to the orphans. Charlie was served first and, wiping his snotty nose on his sleeve, he received the bottle with big expressive eyes of delight.

Mitch's gaze travelled the room and rested on Miriam. Flustered, her cheeks turned pink. He made his way over and sat on the chair Chuck had vacated.

'What are you doing here?' Joe's dark bushy eyebrows knitted together. 'You're earlier than I expected. Aren't you supposed to be on maintenance with the flight engineer.'

With an assured expression, Mitch eased back in his chair, stretched his legs and drawled, 'We were practically done so I skived off saying I had a meeting with the colonel.'

Joe scowled.

'Hey, it's partly true.' As if expecting to see the man himself Mitch's eyes swept the room, then rested back on Joe. 'Besides, rules are made for breaking.'

Joe gave an exasperated shake of the head. 'Till you get caught, buddy.'

Miriam, sensing underlying tension, was relieved when Ray announced, 'Time to open presents. Come on, kiddies, gather around the tree.'

The children stared uncertainly at Miriam, who, nodding, gave a reassuring smile. The children all rose from their chairs and moved to stand by the tree. Chuck, one of the tallest men in the group, sank to his knees so he didn't tower above them, with the other men following suit. The mood in the room changed to one of heightened expectancy, and the children began sitting, one by one, cross-legged on the floor.

Ray did the honours by giving Charlie his present first and, to the delight of the men, the boy tore off the wrapping paper and gave a yelp of delight.

'Look what I've got!' He held the wooden aeroplane in the air.

Each of the orphans opened a present in turn, the older ones self-conscious, the younger ones shy. Miriam noted how eagerly Alice tore the wrapping paper from her present and the exclamation of delight when she saw the boxed, lace-edged handkerchiefs and green ribbon for her hair.

Mary was the last to open hers and when she saw the red frock with the Peter Pan collar and puffed sleeves, she looked unsure. 'Will it be too big?'

'If it is, you'll grow into it,' Ray assured her.

Her face crumpled. 'But I want it to fit now,' she wailed, nigh to tears.

Miriam, in a bid to save the situation, bent down beside the little girl. 'It's all right, Mary. We'll try the frock on after the party.'

'What if it doesn't fit?' Mary sobbed.

'Then one day it will.'

'But it won't be all mine till then.'

How Miriam wanted to kiss those chubby cheeks to make things better but after years of the strict regime of orphanage life where sentiment was frowned upon, she refrained. The kaleidoscope of unfamiliar emotions Mary was experiencing was all too much for the little girl.

The airmen looked at Mary with distressed expressions, and Miriam was at a loss to know how to comfort the little girl. Then she spied the ribbon inside the wrapping paper.

'Look, Mary. You've got another present.'

Her sobs subsiding into gulping little gasps, Mary rubbed her eyes with her fists and stared at the crumpled paper lying on the floor.

'Look. You've got a ribbon too. A pretty blue one to match the colour of your eyes,' Miriam told her. 'How about I make a bow and you can wear it now?'

Sniffing hugely and with a mollified little smile, Mary nodded.

The tense atmosphere in the room lifted and the relief of the men palpable, they attempted to reassure the unsettled orphans in cheerfully booming, American voices.

'How about a bar of candy, kids?' one of the men called out.

'First a photograph,' another said and, producing a box camera, organised everyone for a group picture.

Afterwards, Miriam, feeling thankful now the awkward moment was over, returned to her seat. It occurred to her that being brought up in an orphanage didn't prepare the children for the turmoil and spontaneity of the outside world. The thought of Alice leaving next year popped into her mind, but it was too much for her to contemplate. Erasing the preposterous thought, she decided to concentrate on the present, only to be flummoxed by Mitch's oval-shaped, green eyes, locked with hers in an accusatory glare.

'If you ask me, these kids have a problem.'

*Nobody asked you*, Miriam's mind declared as she watched Joe and the other Americans supervising a game of pass the parcel. The wireless was blaring, 'Don't Sit Under the Apple Tree'.

She decided to ignore Mitch's statement but Mitch continued anyway.

'What did Mary mean, the dress wouldn't be all hers?'

Lordy. Miriam squirmed. How could she explain without the facts sounding heartless? Which they were of course.

'The children often don't get the same clothes back after they've been laundered,' she improvised. Laundered sounded grand and not at all like the washed-out, limp clothing which returned from the wash house.

Mitch's eyebrows raised in bemusement. 'But the dress is hers to keep.'

There was nothing else for it than to be honest. Miriam took a deep breath. 'The rules are that no one in the orphanage is allowed to own anything. Toys and clothes are all shared on a first-come basis.'

Mitch thought for a moment, his features hardening. 'You mean little Charlie and the others aren't allowed to keep their presents?'

At his condemning stare, Miriam could only shake her head.

'That's outrageous. Who makes these rules?'

Miriam felt naming names was going too far. 'As I say, it's customary to sha—'

'You're in charge, you can change the rules.'

A dart of anger stabbed Miriam. Who did the man think he was, telling her what to do? Just because he broke the rules. Someone had to make the decisions and others had to abide by them.

'I don't think our orphanage policy has anything to do with you,' she said primly. 'Besides, I don't make the rules. I'm only temporarily in charge until my superior returns.' Her anger diffusing as quickly as it came, Miriam realised she'd shifted the blame to justify herself. What went on at the orphanage was wrong but she felt helpless to do anything. Miss Black made it plain Miriam would be dismissed if she didn't abide by her instructions. And it would be unfair to the orphans if Miriam relaxed the rules only for them to be restored when Miss Black returned.

*There you go again, making excuses to make things right*, a voice in her head rebuked.

Mitch didn't answer but, his chin working, he watched the children as the wireless was silenced and Tommy peeled off yet another layer of wrapping paper. When the music started up again, the orphans' faces were animated as never before as they handled the parcel, and Miriam saw how their lives could be in different circumstances. She realised Mitch wasn't only the ladies' man she had imagined; he had a serious side she should applaud. But did he really care or did he just like the sound of his own voice? Would he actually act upon his convictions?

Her gaze wandered to Alice, too old to join in the game. Leaning against the wall, hugging herself, she nodded along to the catchy tune that resounded in the room. She was soon to become a young woman and Miriam realised with suffocating dread that this would be their last Christmas together – and there was no one to blame but herself. Alice was right, Miriam was to be deplored for giving up her baby. If only she'd been stronger, stood up to Father, she could have manged somehow.

'If only I—'

'What!?'

She heard the spikiness in Mitch's tone. Surprised she'd spoken her thoughts out loud, Miriam, feeling awkward, shrugged.

'If it's about those kids' – he nodded at the orphans – 'they don't have a voice.' His green eyes, probing hers, had lost their earlier warmth. 'Someone needs to stand up to whoever is making the rules and speak up for them.' He glared at her, leaving unsaid, *That person should be you.*

A pang of guilt plagued Miriam because what he said was true, but how dare the man be presumptuous in thinking he knew what was right without knowing all the facts?

'I'll have you know, if I did speak out my employment would be terminated. And what use would that be to the children?' Her chin jutted, challenging him.

'What use are you now?' He raised an eyebrow. 'To say nothing is the coward's way out.'

The music stopped and Miriam, watching Alan unwrap the last layer of paper to discover a bar of candy, felt her temper rise.

'I'd appreciate you minding your own business.' She heard a catch in her voice and willed herself not to weaken. 'You're clueless as to what you're talking about and, as far as I'm concerned, this conversation or any other with you is ended.'

He opened his mouth to speak then, with a look of frustration, he stood, shook his head sorrowfully and strode away.

Coward indeed! Miriam seethed as she watched him go, even though deep down she knew what he'd said was true. She'd been too afraid to say anything before now for fear of the ramifications. Thinking of all the times she'd watched orphans being mistreated, first by the mistress at their former orphanage and now Miss Black, the guilt was unbearable. She'd kidded herself by thinking being there for them was enough. She had never done anything to better their lives.

But that was to change. Miriam knew what she had to do for the orphans' sake.

Chuck came over to give Miriam a bottle of Coca-Cola, but she held up a hand to refuse it.

'It's getting late and time to take the children back. You've all been most kind.'

'Gee, must you? The kids are having such a swell time. Just one more game. Ray has promised them to play pin the tail on the donkey.'

Miriam, who'd never had a party, let alone a party game

when she was a child, didn't have a clue what that was, but it did sound fun and she didn't want to deprive the children.

'Just the one,' she conceded. She took the bottle from Chuck's hand as it would be a great pity not to enjoy such a treat.

As they sat back in their chairs, watching Agnes being blindfolded with a scarf, Chuck asked, 'Are you coming to the dance New Year's Eve, ma'am? Us guys are looking forward to it and can't wait.'

Miriam rather liked the easy-going Chuck, who was plain talking. She replied, 'It's Miriam and no, I don't think so.'

'That's a pity. It looks to be fun, with a band arranged and everything. Won't you change your mind?'

'I can't,' she said, without thinking.

Chuck gave her a sidelong look. 'Hope you don't mind me saying but don't take Mitch too seriously, Miriam.'

She stiffened. 'I don't.'

'Don't get me wrong, he's one of the best.' Chuck stretched his long legs in front of him and carried on, oblivious. 'And no one can fault him on the job but' – he looked uncomfortable – 'he's a ladies' man.'

Miriam couldn't help herself. 'I'd figured that out.'

'I told Joe you were a smart lady.'

'Joe!'

'He worried you'd fall for Mitch's charms.' He did an eye roll.

Miriam was horrified at the suggestion. She'd fallen for the wrong person once and there was no way she would allow that to happen again. She wasn't in the least bit interested in the wretched man. Long ago she'd dedicated her life to the children and that's how it was and always would be.

'I can assure you, Chuck, that's the furthest thing from my mind.'

Chuck gave a goofy grin. 'I knew you had class the minute I clapped eyes on you.' He reached into his pocket and brought out a stick of gum which he proceeded to chew noisily.

She watched Rosie, who was blindfolded, inch forward, arms outstretched, until she touched the kitchen doorway where a picture of a donkey was pinned. *She's finally coming out of her shell,* Miriam thought with satisfaction.

Then, a thought nagging, she asked, 'Why is Joe so cross with Mitch?' She guessed Chuck would blurt the answer, being the insouciant type.

'Mitch got himself involved with a broad down south, the clingy type by all accounts.' Chuck scratched his hairline above his ear. 'Being sent up here was a godsend, according to Mitch. But she wouldn't let go and kept on writing, so he thought of a way of getting off the hook.'

'Why didn't he just write and explain his feelings had changed?'

'That's what Joe asked.' Chuck blew a bubble and when it burst, he shrugged. 'I dunno why. It's just Mitch's way.'

There was a burst of laughter as Rosie pinned the paper tail on the donkey's nose.

'So, what did Mitch do?' Miriam asked, intrigued.

Chuck grinned. 'He asked Joe to write a letter to her.'

'But I thought you said he didn't—'

'Joe was to write to say Mitch *couldn't* write as he'd been in a fire and burnt his hands and he was back home.' Chuck blew another bubble, then continued, 'The letter ended saying he wouldn't be able to write as recuperation would take a long time. And Mitch wished for her to get on with her life.'

Miriam sank back letting the words sink in.

'Of course, Joe being Joe,' Chuck said, oblivious of Miriam's shocked reaction, 'he refused, saying he didn't want any part of the deceit.'

'So the letter was never sent.'

'Yep, it was. Mitch talked young Taylor into writing it for him.'

Miriam's mind seethed. *Of all the despicable, underhand things to do, this takes...* To think the man had taken the moral high road about her decisions at the orphanage, making her feel bad, when he was guilty of something equally deplorable. She had a good mind to tell Clark Mitchell exactly what she thought of him, and she knew exactly when to do so. Plus, she would be doing Hazel a favour.

She turned to the gum-chewing Chuck and said, 'I've decided I will attend the New Year's Eve dance, after all.'

# 24

'Alice, you're not listening.'

Alice conceded she hadn't taken in anything Rosie had said. It was nearly lights-out time in the dormitory, and the two of them were sitting on Rosie's bed. Alice couldn't help the mournful little sigh that escaped her, and flopping back on the bed, she wished Rosie would let her be.

'Didn't you have a good time at the party?' In the lamp-light, Rosie's big, troubled eyes gazed down at her.

'Not really.'

'Oh, but why?'

'I just didn't, all right.'

'But I saw you laughing at—'

'I've told you before, stop trying to make things better.' Alice sat bolt upright. 'It's annoying and makes you look stupid.'

Alice hated herself for how she was behaving but she couldn't help this fury inside that made her react in such a way. Surprisingly, Rosie didn't respond like she normally did by going timid and apologetic; she simply stared at Alice with a hurt expression.

'That wasn't a nice thing to say. Do people really think that about me?'

Alice felt bad and struggled to find the right thing to say. 'Oh, I don't know. It's just me in a bad mood. But you do try to please people and it gets irritating.' She grimaced. 'I'm just as bad. I can't help getting mad and lash out and say whatever comes into my head and I get into trouble afterwards.'

'You should do what Mrs Wilkinson told me: be an actress and play a part. She told me it's called attitude.' She hung her head as if what she was about to say was awkward. 'Instead of choosing an actress, I chose you.'

'Me?'

'I envied you because you're not afraid of anything.' Rosie's blue brooding eyes brimmed with intensity. 'I wanted to be like you.'

Alice told her friend, 'You must be joking. I wish I was more like you.'

'Me!' Rosie exclaimed.

They both laughed.

'You're so thoughtful and care about people and I've never seen you lose your temper.' Alice appeared embarrassed at saying such things.

Rosie's face lit up. 'Maybe that's why we're such good friends. We're learning from each other.'

They lapsed into silence thinking about that.

Then Alice's conscience pricked her, and she lowered her gaze. 'You're wrong, though, I do get afraid.'

'Really. What about?'

'Lots of things. Punishments. Miss Black's nostrils when they flare. That I don't know anyone outside the orphanage.' That fear had started when she ran away from church and was still haunting her. That was why she couldn't enjoy the party. 'And the fact I'm fourteen next June and I'll have to leave to go to work. That's only six months away.' Her belly wobbled at the thought.

Rosie's brow crinkled in mystification. 'How did you know when your birthday is?'

'I didn't. The mistress at the orphanage where I was left as a baby decided June eighth as it was the day I was dumped on the doorstep.'

A look of horror flooded Rosie's face. 'Where will you go when you leave?'

At one time Alice had been blasé about leaving, imagining life with no rules and having a grand time doing as she pleased while she made her way in the world. But now, after the experience when she ran away and found she was helpless to do anything without money and no knowledge of how to earn any, gut-wrenching fear overwhelmed her.

'I'll probably be sent into domestic service,' she told Rosie. *Where there'll be more rules and punishments if I disobey the mistress of the house, or worse, I'll be thrown out on the streets.*

'Is that what happens to us?'

'Yes, if we don't have family.' In the shadowy light she saw the terror in Rosie's eyes.

'Oh, I wish I could make my memory return but when I try it's like searching down an empty tunnel,' Rosie wailed. Then a guilty look crossed her face. 'By then you'll be settled and wonder why you worried.'

Alice raised her eyebrows in a 'you're doing it again' fashion. 'Who knows where I'll be.'

Rosie looked near to tears. 'We'll write to each other and I'll know where you are.'

'The war will be finished by then and the orphanage

can't stay here forever.' Alice shrugged. 'Who knows where you'll be sent.'

'I might have found my family by then. And you might work close by.'

Alice wished she had Rosie's belief in life, but she could only see the black side and the future looked bleak. 'Or you might have left the orphanage by then and be in the drudgery of domestic service in a different part of the country than me,' she said.

Rosie stared in disbelief. 'But you never give up. There must be a way for us to make sure we can stay together.'

Alice knew solving the problem was impossible. Their fate had been sealed the day they'd entered the orphanage, but she felt bad for letting Rosie down when she had so much faith in her.

'There could be a way.' Rosie's eyes looked wary. 'You could try and find your mam and maybe you could live with her.'

'What!'

'You could ask the mistress at the orphanage where you were before, if she knows anything. Your mam might have left something and—'

'That cow wouldn't help,' Alice cut in. 'Even if there was something left, she's mean enough to keep it from me. Anyway, my mother is a selfish bitch, who washed her hands of me the day she dumped me.'

Seeing Rosie's appalled face, Alice regretted her outburst. Rosie only saw the good in people and believed the impossible could happen, while Alice knew differently. Besides, finding her mam would be impossible but there was no way she could shatter the hope she saw in her friend's eyes.

As if she knew Alice's defences were down, Rosie

pursued the matter. 'It's worth a try, Alice. Then there might be a way for us to stay together.'

'I'll try and think of something,' was all Alice could come up with.

Because, like a fish needs water to survive, Alice needed Rosie in her life, not only because there was no one else, but because the pair of them had bonded and become like the family she'd always yearned for.

---

'Try it on, you might be surprised.' Mrs Murray held out the frock draped over an arm.

Miriam had agonised over what she should wear for the New Year's Eve dance. She had nothing suitable and even if she could spare the time to go to the draper's shop in Hawick, she didn't have the necessary clothes coupons left out of the thirty-six she'd received for the year.

Mrs Murray, hearing of her plight, had solved the problem. Kind as she was, she'd had a word with one of her neighbours, a young woman called Ina. Mrs Murray said at the time, 'Ina's a canny lass and she's about your size with a fulsome figure like yours.' She nodded at Miriam's breasts whose ample size had always been an embarrassment. 'She's happy to lend you her frock and shoes to match as she doubts that they'll have another outing, the way she's popping out bairns.'

'That's so good of her. I'll write to thank her.'

'Lass, war brings out the best of some folk as we all have to pull together.'

Now they were in the office and for the umpteenth time, Miriam regretted telling Chuck she would attend the dance. As had happened before, her indecision was overshadowed by the anger brought on at the thought of Mitch's deceit. If she were honest, which was often Miriam's downfall, her wrath stemmed from disappointment in the man. Just when she was beginning to see his worthy side, his generous and caring side, especially in his dealings with the orphans, Miriam felt let down. Like Terry Rawling before him, Miriam had mistaken Mitch's true character. She was no more than a child when she fell for Terry but, Miriam scolded herself, this time around she should have known better.

All she knew was she couldn't get Clark Mitchell out of her thoughts. Why had she been smitten by him? she wondered in disgust. But after tonight, when she'd give him a piece of her mind, that was the finish of her foolish behaviour. Once bitten twice shy, she told herself.

Eyeing the frock held by Mrs Murray, she shook her head. 'I can't wear that. It's red.'

Mrs Murray's eyes danced with mischief. 'And so are the dance shoes.' Picking up her message bag, she produced a pair of red, high-heeled dance shoes with an ankle strap. 'And what's wrong with red?' Mrs Murray asked, looking at the frock as if there was something she was missing.

Miriam raised her eyebrows. 'Nothing. It's just I'll stick out like a sore thumb.'

'Take advice from an old woman.' Mrs Murray's voice held a sagacious note. 'When you're young, you're highly critical of the way you look, but at my age, when you see photographs of yourself, you're surprised at how attractive you were. So, Miriam' – she was surprised at Mrs Murray using her Christian name but Miriam found she didn't mind – 'why not be the Cinderella of the ball.'

Did she dare? Miriam's mind wondered. She had been lacking in confidence for as long as she could remember and just for once she longed to leave the critic within her behind and just to be, without censoring everything she said or did.

Mrs Murray's eyebrows drew together in concern. 'Lass, take my word for it, it's the things you don't do that you regret in your dotage. It's time you stepped out from the prison of duty you've built around yourself.' Her face brightened and she grinned. 'Go on, be a devil.'

Miriam was overwhelmed in a good way by the feeling of goodwill Mrs Murray exuded towards her. She was a friend indeed and Miriam wanted to show her how much she valued her friendship.

'You never told me your first name.'

'You never asked.'

'I'm asking now.'

Mrs Murray's face was a picture of pleasant surprise. 'It's Rita.'

Miriam held out her hands. 'Come on, Rita, hand over the dress and I'll try it on for size.'

The night of the New Year's Eve dance, as she gazed at herself in her full-length wardrobe mirror, Miriam drew a startled breath. The red taffeta wrap-around frock with shirt-waist top, capped sleeves and tiny box pleats around the waist fitted perfectly, showing off her figure. Miriam felt special as the frock was soft as silk. Her brown hair, swept back, boasted a victory roll hairstyle which accentuated her high cheek bones, and was created by Hazel, who insisted it was her way of thanking Miriam for taking her to the dance. Miriam felt bad considering she had an ulterior motive for going, but standing here, eying herself, a warm tingle of excitement radiated throughout her body.

A rap came at the door and, opening it, she found Rita

Murray standing there. (They were on first names now but only out of working hours.) Rita clapped her hands in pleasure.

'You'll be the belle of the ball and no mistake. But remember to hang on to those shoes and don't be coming back past midnight as we don't want that Jeep to be turning into a pumpkin.' Cackling, she added, 'Though we could do with a Prince Charming coming to sweep you off your feet.' Wiping her eyes on the coarse pinafore she wore, she sobered. 'Away with you now and have a good time. And don't you be worrying about those children. I've checked and apart from the older ones, they're all away to sleep for the night. Fingers crossed.'

'Are you sure your Walter doesn't mind you being here, it being New Year's Eve and all?'

Rita gave a hoot of laughter. 'Och no! Walter's first footing days are long gone. He'll have a tot of whisky early on and that'll see him sound asleep before the clock chimes twelve.' She pulled a knowing face. 'And that would be me sitting by meself staring at the walls.' She gave a firm nod of the head. 'You go out and have yourself a good time.'

Tripping down the steps, Miriam, wearing an ankle-length coat, black lace-up shoes and carrying the dance shoes in a bag, stepped out into the twinkling, star-studded night. She experienced a delightful feeling of expectancy and let out a satisfied sigh. Not only because she was attending her first dance since college days, but a new year was soon to begin. A year of promise and new beginnings, if the plan she hoped to achieve for the orphanage was put in place.

Waiting outside for the Jeep, she bent back her head to look up at the stars whose radiance was testimony to God's perfect design. As she stood staring at the starry sky, her spirits took a nosedive as she recollected that in the coming year Alice would be fourteen, when she would leave the orphanage and Miriam would say a final goodbye to her daughter.

The sound of an engine ticking and a dim set of lights drawing closer brought Miriam out of the doldrums. Aware of the dark shape of an open-topped Jeep, she made out figures sprawled on its hood. As it came to a halt outside the coach house door where she stood, Miriam had an impulse to return inside but then she remembered the reason for going to the dance and stood her ground. Tired of being submissive and fervently wanting to change, she recalled in her mind what Rita Murray had told her: *These days, lass, you mightn't have a tomorrow*. Miriam desperately wanted to change and be the confident, resolute woman she'd always admired, and tonight she vowed she'd start by standing up to the two-faced Clark Mitchell.

Climbing aboard the Jeep, she peered at the driver and was pleasantly surprised to see Chuck sitting behind the wheel.

'Hi, there,' Chuck greeted her, and Miriam heard the familiar pop of a chewing gum bubble. 'There's no room up top with the two Lumberjill gals but you can squeeze in the back with Vivian and Hilda.'

'Hazel,' a voice from the back corrected him.

'Hold on tight, gals,' Chuck ordered, then the Jeep took off. 'Are we all ready for a night of fun?' he called as another chewing gum bubble burst.

As the others cheered, a picture of Mitch's spectacular green eyes and angular chin played in Miriam's mind's eyes and she shivered.

Arriving at the airfield, the Jeep drove over what seemed like a field of grass, jiggling Miriam about, before stopping where a huge aircraft hangar loomed in the darkness.

Climbing in an unladylike fashion from the back of the Jeep, she followed two of the Lumberjills, while Vivian and Hazel, excitement emanating from them, tagged along behind.

'It's huge,' Vivian said as she passed through the main entrance.

'Wait till you see inside,' Chuck told them. 'The place has been done up for the occasion and the boys have been looking forward to this for some time.'

He led them into the large open unit that was clad with corrugated sheeting and had a concrete floor. The noise was incredible, and Miriam gasped when she saw how many people had attended. The place heaved with both servicemen and women and girls from surrounding villages, who wore colourful frocks with nipped in waists and padded shoulders. Miriam, feeling both self-conscious and positively spinsterish, had the urge to flee but remembering her vow to stay confident, she took a deep calming breath. After all, who would be taking any notice of her?

'Oh, Miss Balfour.' Hazel, coat over an arm and looking stunning in a bright-green dress that matched her aquamarine eyes, came to stand at her side. 'Isn't this wonderful.'

Miriam followed the young girl's gaze, taking in the colourful lights strung around the entrance and across the ceiling, the round tables circling a dance floor, while further down the hangar was a trestle table set up with bottles galore. Incongruously, at the far end of the hangar, the nose end of an aeroplane could be seen.

'Crikey! I feel like Aladdin entering the cave.' Hazel clasped her hands together. 'I can't thank you enough for bringing me. I would die if Dad had got his way and I'd missed all this.'

Seeing the youngster's enthusiasm made Miriam's thoughts drift to Alice. Would she get the opportunity to attend dances? Would Miriam be there to see her? With a heavy heart she conceded, probably not.

At that moment a band, positioned to one side of the dance floor, struck up and the melodic sound of saxophones filled the hangar.

'Oooh it's a foxtrot,' Edith, one of the Lumberjills, exclaimed as she made for the nearest empty table. 'Come on, lasses, put your dancing shoes on and let's get cracking.'

Miriam tagged along with the rest, her eyes searching the tables, but there was no sign of Mitch. Shrugging out of her coat and placing it on the back of the chair, she took the red dance shoes out of the bag. Feeling everyone's eyes upon her, she looked up.

'Miss Balfour, you look so diff— amazing. I've never seen you look so lovely.' Hazel, with an astonished expression, gaped at her. 'Doesn't she?' she addressed the others.

'Beats wearing your usual uniform frock.' Vivian, standing opposite, grinned.

Not knowing what to say and feeling on show, Miriam sat to put on her shoes.

The evening wore on and when popular tunes were played, Miriam and the rest of the girls were approached by servicemen who, after introducing themselves, whisked them off to the dance floor. It was hectic but fun and Miriam was surprised to find she was enjoying herself. Though her borrowed high heeled shoes, a tad too tight, made her feet ache.

The dance finished, she told her partner, a dark-haired British soldier with an intense gaze and southern accent who'd introduced himself as Brian, 'I'd like to sit the next one out, thanks. I'm whacked.'

Seeing Brian's disappointed expression Miriam felt bad but, she reminded herself, she wasn't there to dance. The sole reason she'd come was to challenge Mitch. But did she really want to spoil this lovely night by confronting that ignorant, insufferable bloke? Besides nothing she said would—

'How about I fetch you a drink, miss?'

Brian looked so keen, how could Miriam refuse.

'That would be lovely thank you.'

He made for the trestle table and returning carried a glass filled with caramel-coloured liquid. 'It's cola.' He placed the drink in front of her. 'I'll jazz it up a bit, shall I?' He brought out a hip flask.

'No thank you.'

Sipping the thirst-quenching drink, and listening to Brian's tales of life before the war in Eastbourne, Miriam's eyes strayed around the room. The band was playing 'Night and Day' and, spellbound, she was transported to another time when skies were filled with only clouds and not raiders intent on bombing and killing people.

It was at that moment she saw him. Mitch. And for no accountable reason, Miriam felt her heart rate increase.

# 25

Mitch, with a woman at his side, swaggered in and moved towards a table across the dance floor where a few of his crew were sitting. He pulled out a chair for the striking blonde who had a self-possessed air about her and, helping her out of her coat, Mitch slung it over a chair then made for the drinks table.

As the band ceased to play, Brian, leaning in close, continued to tell Miriam about his life, his family, his job as an accountant. Miriam tuned out and watched as Mitch carried two glasses back to his table. As he placed a drink in front of the blonde, she smiled up at him.

The room stilled as the band's pianist, joined by a saxophonist, started to play a mesmerising version of 'Bye Bye Blackbird'. Watching the dancers as they began swirling around the dance floor, holding each other tight, for some unaccountable reason rendered Miriam teary.

Brian at her side, oblivious, drained his glass. 'Can I get you another drink?' he asked, rising from his seat.

'No thank you.' As he made to move, she told him, 'And, Brian, please feel free to get someone else up to dance—'

'But I—'

'I'm not very good company and I don't want to spoil your night.'

It was true her enjoyment had been ruined by the appearance of Mitch, who, his eyes searching the room, now noticed her. He nodded and settled back in his chair, never taking his eyes off her.

*Typical,* she thought crankily, *thinking he is God's gift to women and I will swoon because he deigns to be interested in me.* Her face stony, Miriam purposely averted her eyes.

When the music stopped, the Lumberjills, hot and elated, left their partners on the dance floor and made their way over to the table.

'I'm pooped.' Vivian collapsed in a chair. 'But I'll be damned if I give in. I can't remember when I last enjoyed myself as much. Or danced till I dropped.' She looked around the room, suddenly doing a double take.

'You see that Yank over there? He's one of the airmen Fran and I met at the village dance.'

Hazel followed her gaze. 'Oooh, isn't he handsome.'

Edith raised her eyes in a *for goodness' sakes* fashion. 'Never mind him. I'm starved. When d'you think the food's going to be served up?'

Grinning good naturedly, Vivian told her, 'Now there's a surprise.'

'Look, the Yank's coming over here.' Hazel fluffed up her hair at the sides.

'Can I get you ladies a drink?'

The voice belonging to Mitch came from behind Miriam. She stiffened. The cheek of the man!

Hazel, doe-eyed, twirled hair around her finger as she gazed up at him. 'Ooh, yes please.'

The silly girl was flirting. And besides being far too old for her, Hazel didn't realise she was playing with fire.

'That would be smashing, thanks.' A playful smile touched Edith's lips.

Lordy, she was at it now. No wonder Mitch was swollen-headed if this was the reaction he got from women.

Mitch's face split into a wide grin. 'Your wish is my command. Four shandies it is then.'

'Not for me, thanks,' Miriam called as he made for the drinks table.

'Gosh, isn't he dishy?' Violet, a dark-haired Lumberjill, let out a desirous sigh. 'I've got first dibs dancing with him.'

'He has to ask you first,' Hazel remarked.

They watched him as he brought the drinks back to the table.

'Ta da,' he said, setting the drinks tray in front of them. 'Enjoy, ladies.' He flashed a smile, then made off back over the dance floor.

'He could have at least stayed and chatted.' Watching him approach the band, Violet's face mirrored her disappointment.

'I've decided he's a patter merchant.' Vivian scrutinised Mitch as he had a word with the band leader, who looked smart in a dark suit and a dicky bow tie. 'His type generally are.'

*She's got that right*, Miriam thought.

'Look out, he's coming back,' Hazel squeaked.

'Is he making for here?' Violet, with her back to the dance floor, wanted to know. Her posture stiff as if expecting a tap on her shoulder, she reached for a drink.

'I think so.' Hazel looked from beneath dark eyelashes. 'Yes, he is.'

The piano struck up and began to play the popular tune 'Can't We Be Friends?'. Convinced it was for her benefit, indignation rose within Miriam. Or was she being too self-centred?

But then he came and stood behind her.

'Can I have the pleasure of this dance?'

In the awkward silence, Miriam felt everyone's eyes on her as they waited for her to respond. But she didn't turn.

'No, thank you. I'd like to sit this one out.'

As the piano tinkled on, couples got up and, taking to the floor, started dancing together, their heads up close.

'I'd like to talk,' said Mitch.

Did she hear a pleading note in his voice?

'I've got nothing to say,' she said. And, suddenly, she hadn't. What had she been thinking? There was no way she could confront him at the dance and even if she did, the two-faced, egotistical moron that he was – Miriam was shocked at the vehemence of her vexation towards him – Clark Mitchell wouldn't care.

'I'd like to—'

'I'm finished dancing for the night.' She bent down and began unbuckling the straps on her shoes. She'd wanted to be confident, stand up for herself, but her insides had turned to jelly.

Vivian spoke up. 'It's fine, he's gone.'

Miriam looked around and saw Mitch walking back to his table, but the woman he'd arrived with had disappeared.

'You know him?' Violet accused.

'He's one of the orphans' sponsors,' Vivian put in.

'Ooh, kind and handsome,' Hazel said, a dreamy expression on her face. 'He's gone on you, Miss Balfour, I can tell.'

Fortunately, Miriam was saved answering by the band leader announcing, 'Ladies and gentlemen, can I have your attention.' Everyone turned to stare at him and a hush descended over the hangar. 'The food is ready.'

People stood up and started to make their way to the tables at the far end of the hangar.

Edith told them, 'The sausages are called hot dogs and the round things are hamburgers. And we're not depriving anyone, apparently, as the food's been shipped in from the US.'

'How d'you know all this?' Vivian asked, folding her arms and giving Edith a meaningful look. 'Don't tell me, you've been fraternising with certain airmen.'

'Is it my fault if they find me desirable? Besides, it keeps me in silk stockings.'

Vivian clicked her tongue. 'Honestly, you'll go with anything that wears trousers.'

'Are you suggesting I'm—'

'Look, there's a queue forming,' Miriam cut in, saving the pair arguing. 'You'd better get a move on as it's building up already.'

The Lumberjills, forever hungry, didn't need a second telling and made for the tables with Hazel, a look of disappointment written on her face because she wanted more salacious gossip, traipsing after them.

Miriam had lost her appetite and wished she had a form of transport to return to Teviot Hall. Tonight had started out promising but turned into a disaster. Not only had she failed in achieving what she'd intended but also, despite knowing what a cad Mitch was, shamefully, she couldn't deny there was an element of her attracted to him. It was as Father said when he found out Terry had deserted her all those years ago: 'You're the gullible type who falls for the wrong kind of man. It'll be your downfall because you'll never learn.'

In that moment clarity struck and she knew the truth of the matter – the reason why she reacted so vehemently toward Mitch, when she should simply ignore him. There was something about him, and it wasn't just his good looks. She sensed the man ran deeper than he portrayed and she was drawn to him. But she was also afraid she was making a mistake yet again.

Deep in thought, she didn't notice when someone came to sit next to her but when she looked up, Miriam saw it was the man himself once again. She didn't react but continued to sit glum faced. Setting his glass of Coca-Cola on the table, he made to speak, but before he could, Miriam gathered her wits.

'Go back to your girlfriend,' she said.

A puzzled look crossed his face, then a light dawned in his eyes. 'I didn't take you for the jealous type.'

She knew his teasing was part of his patter, and also that she was being childish letting his behaviour bother her, but she couldn't help reacting.

'Don't fool yourself. I wouldn't be interested in you if you were—'

'For your information,' he rudely interrupted, 'Chuck invited Bette. See? She's with him now.' True enough, the couple were sitting at a table together deep in conversation. 'I told him I'd collect Bette if he collected the Lumberjills as there wasn't room for everyone in the Jeep.'

Feeling foolish at her mistake, Miriam couldn't think of anything to say.

Observing her, his face crinkled into a smile. 'You look amazing by the way.'

Annoyed at his nerve, she told him, 'I told you I didn't want another conversation with you.'

He held up his hands in surrender. 'Why are you so spiky, woman? That was meant to be a compliment.' Gazing at her for a moment, as if trying to decide what to say next, he gave a heavy sigh and his shoulders lifted. 'Just hear me out and you need never see me again, if that's what you want.'

She saw the pleading deep in his gaze. Part of her wanted him to go, but a larger part couldn't help being intrigued at what he might say.

'You have until the Lumberjills come back.' Her voice, she was pleased to hear, held a no-nonsense tone.

Two little lines in his forehead above his nose creased. 'I can understand you being angry after what I said, it was wrong of me to call you a coward and I categorically apologise. I had no right.'

'You didn't. Especially after—'

'Listen to what I have to say.' Those intense hypnotic eyes locked with hers and, rendered speechless, she nodded her consent. 'I've decided the only way I can redeem myself is to tell you what drove me to say what I did.' His expression looked pained, as if indeed this was a difficult subject for him to talk about.

'Dad was a train driver. There were three of us kids and life was okay, or so I thought.' He shook his head. 'But what does a kid know. When it was found out that my old man was drinking too much, he got sacked.' Mitch ran a hand over his eyes as if trying to blot out the memory. 'Life changed. He changed. He was generous with his fists on us kids, or his belt. Mom found work wherever she could find it. Then one day she didn't come home and disappeared for good.' He trailed a hand down his face as if he still couldn't credit it.

'Life got worse. I was the youngest and I never saw either

my brother or sister after they came of age and left home.' He drew a deep breath and the furrows in his brow deepened. 'The thing is.' His face sobered and his eyes hardened. 'Someone must have known, must have seen the bruises. They could have said something. Teachers, neighbours... but nobody saw fit to get involved.'

As the words hung between them, Miriam noticed the Lumberjills were edging up to the food table in the queue.

'That's dreadful. I—'

'Believe me, I don't want sympathy. I don't tell anyone about my past but I wanted you to understand why I blew my top.'

Did she believe him? After all, he'd fibbed to that poor girl. Resentment returning, Miriam remembered the reason for coming to the dance.

She blurted, 'Chuck told me about the letter.'

His brow creased in a question. 'What letter?'

'The one you sent to that girl to say you'd burnt your hands.'

A light dawned in his eye. 'Ahh!'

'Is that all you have to say for yourself,' she railed. 'How dare you accuse me of—'

'I had no other option.' Infuriatingly, he gave a nonchalant shrug.

'What!'

'It was the only way I could think of letting Veronica down without her getting hurt.'

'You're joking? The poor girl would be distraught. You're a self-cent—'

'Enough!' His usual laidback demeanour vanished, and he sat forward, arms folded on the table, a vein pulsating at his temple. 'The truth is before the war I was engaged to my childhood sweetheart. I registered for the draft and we agreed the wedding could wait until I returned home. Then out of the blue came a Dear John letter.' Mitch seemed to stare into the distant past, remembering. 'She was sorry and didn't want to hurt me but she'd met someone else.' His eyes focusing again, he looked at Miriam. 'I went crazy for a while, dating women who were only out for a good time. Getting serious was not for me, I had decided.

'Then I met Veronica when I was stationed down south, an English rose as they say and not my usual type. She became clingy and was the controlling kind. When we were sent up here, I hoped that was the end of things between us. It wasn't. She wouldn't give up, bombarding me with letters and plans for our lives when the war was over.'

'So, you made up that preposterous story.' Miriam heard the recrimination in her voice.

Remorse in his eyes, he nodded. 'I blame myself. I should never have got involved but neither could I make promises I couldn't keep. But I didn't want Veronica to go through the hell of rejection I'd experienced.' He rubbed the back of his neck, sighing. 'Rightly or wrongly, writing that letter was the only way I could think to lessen her pain.' Regaining composure, he leant back in the chair and looked Miriam squarely in the eye. 'I'm ashamed of getting involved, but not about finishing things, or the way I did it.'

Miriam was dumbfounded on what to say. Yes, Mitch was a ladies' man and some would say a cad, but his reasoning for his behaviour, why he did things – even if he did go about them the wrong way – was sound. He'd wanted to spare this Veronica heartache. Something spineless Terry Rawling could never understand.

'Why are you telling me all this?' Miriam asked.

'Because I care about what you think. You're spirited and

I like that.' His expression mellowed. 'I'd really like to get to know you if only you'd give me the chance.'

Miriam didn't know how to respond. Was this just more patter? Did he see her as a challenge? Was she the gullible soul Father accused her of being, easily taken in by scoundrels?

Unflinching, she stared back, studying his face, deciding the level of sincerity she saw couldn't be faked. Besides, if he was heartless, why would he bother trying to redeem himself and make up such stories? And why would he care what she thought? There came a time when she could only trust her judgement and seeing the appeal in those mesmerising green eyes, Miriam decided the time was now.

As though understanding he'd overcome the impasse between them, Mitch's handsome face lit up with a disarming smile. Despite her resolution after Terry to not have anything to do with men, Miriam, charmed, was helpless to resist smiling back. She pondered on what Joe had told her, that Mitch's womanising was all an act. His honest expression as he looked at her instinctively told her this wasn't the case here. The man indeed had depth, Miriam realised with a start, and she found she wanted to get to know more about him too.

'I guess you understand now,' he was telling her, 'that when I heard the way the orphans were being treated and nothing was being done about it, I saw red. As I told you, I'm sorry for calling you a coward but I'm not apologising for saying someone should stand up for them.' He bit his lip, and it appeared he was apprehensive about what he was about to say. 'The truth is I worried that they were being mistreated physically.'

Miriam suspected her flush of guilt was enough to

answer his question, but she wanted to move the conversation on.

'I've decided I'm not going to be silent anymore,' she said. 'And when the laird returns after the New Year, I'm going to be honest with him and say how Miss Black runs the orphanage.' She gulped. 'How the orphans are punished, on occasion with the cane.'

He nodded his approval. 'What if you're shown the door?'

Miriam's insides clenched in alarm but hearing Mitch's story had affirmed her resolve to do what was right by the children. Someone had to speak out against Miss Black's harsh treatment of the orphans, and that person was her.

'Then so be it,' she told him. But the repercussions, she thought, didn't bear thinking about.

'What are you two cooking up?' Vivian approached the table, the others following with laden plates in their hands.

Mitch, leisurely stretching back, his hands behind his head, reverted to the tease he was. 'That's for us to know and you to guess at.'

# 26

## JANUARY 1944

As Miriam stood, with trembly legs, in the laird's book-filled study that smelled of pipe tobacco, she was so nervous that the carefully rehearsed speech she'd prepared flew out of her head like a migrating bird. But she was determined to speak out and inform Sir Henley about the abominable goings on at the orphanage under the rule of Miss Black.

The laird, formally a robust man with an imposing bolt upright stance, now looked gaunt and haggard. Though his bearing was still commanding, he appeared to have shrunk. His three-piece black suit looked to be cut for a bigger man, and his hair, once dark, was streaked with silver strands. His dull eyes, previously bright and lively with interest, showed the depth of the pain he suffered at losing his only son and Miriam found it unbearable to see. *That's what grief did to you*, she thought.

As if aware of Miriam's fear that her legs wouldn't support her, Sir Henley gestured to a high-backed chair in front of a meagre fire.

'Now, Miss Balfour, what brings you here?' he asked, sitting in a matching chair opposite.

Miriam took a deep steadying breath. 'I've come to discuss the running of the orphanage by the mistress, Sir Henley.'

He cocked an eyebrow. 'I presume you mean Miss Black.'

'Yes, sir.' Miriam gathered her thoughts and began by pointing out Miss Black's commendable attributes and her dedication to the orphans' Christian upbringing.

'Miss Balfour.' The laird's voice held a ring of impatience. 'I take it you didn't come here to point out Miss Black's admirable qualities, of which I am aware and are why she was employed.'

'No, sir.' Miriam felt herself go red.

'Then do get on with it.'

So, Miriam did. She told him how the orphans were unfairly treated, how their lives were governed by strict rules and severe punishments if they didn't comply.

The laird's brow puckered and his eyes darkened. 'What form do these punishments take?'

'Amongst other things the orphans have been known to have their mouths washed with soap and get the cane.'

The silence in the room that followed was an uneasy one. Sir Henley, trout-mouthed, stared intently at the space before him, deep in thought. Was it possible Miriam had misjudged the laird and he was one of the ilk that thought children should be subjected to a lashing to be taught a lesson?

'Miss Balfour.' His hardened eyes focused on hers. 'In my youth I attended boarding school and suffered the fate of many lashings. Some would say they didn't do me any harm but I would disagree. I still bear the painful memories of those days when no one stood up for me.' He stood and, shoulders back, he appeared to have grown an inch or two. 'I would suggest you return to your duties and leave the matter for me to think over. You'll be informed of the outcome.'

Miriam felt an icy finger slide down her spine. *What did he mean, informed of the outcome?* She would rather know now if her fate was to be dismissed.

'Sir Henley, if you disagree with what I've—'

'Later, Miss Balfour.'

With nothing else for it, she stood and made for the door.

'Miss Balfour.'

Miriam turned.

'On the orphans' behalf, I'd like to thank you.'

Surprised and amazed at this turn of events, all Miriam could think to say was, 'Thank you, Sir Henley, for your time.'

A few days later, a knock came at the office door and Cook's husband, Mr Stewart, stooped and looking put upon, stood there with a letter in his hand, which he handed to Miriam.

'It's from Sir Henley. I'm not waiting all day for a reply.' He shuffled off.

Back at her desk, Miriam tore open the envelope.

*Dear Miss Balfour,*

*Furter to our discussion the other day, I wish to advise you that Miss Black has handed in her resignation.*

*I would like to offer you the position of house mistress at Teviot Hall orphanage and if you wish to take up the offer, we will discuss the terms and salary at a future date.*

*Your early reply would be appreciated.*

*Yours sincerely,*

*Sir Keith Henley*

Barely believing her luck, and with a mixture of trepidation, Miriam wrote back to Sir Henley, notifying him that she was delighted to accept the post he had offered. Feeling proud, she told herself that having the courage to inform the laird how the orphans had suffered under Miss Black's harsh rule was one of the better things she'd done in life.

---

'Please, miss, what's the second front?' Tommy asked Mrs Murray, his hand in the air, as she was about to start morning reading class.

Weeks had passed and Alice couldn't believe how different things were at the orphanage now Miss Balfour was in charge. If Tommy had dared speak up to ask a question before, he'd have been punished for disrupting the class. But since Miss Balfour had announced over breakfast one day that, due to her injuries, Miss Black had decided to retire, things in the orphanage had changed dramatically for the better. The children were allowed to question things about the outside world and the older ones were able to read the local newspaper and go to bed later than the younger ones. The biggest change was having a wireless (given to them by their American sponsors) and listening to the BBC Home Service in the dining hall at mealtimes. While music played, the orphans were allowed to speak to one another – but not with their mouths full. Prayers were still part of the morning routine but they didn't go for so long that you thought you'd die from boredom.

It seemed too good to be true that Alice would never set eyes on Miss Black and for days she'd expected to see the witch enter the dining hall each morning, her face disapproving. But she hadn't. And the orphans, who once wore hunted expressions, as though at any moment they'd be in danger of Miss Black's wrath, now had lively looks on their faces and, like Tommy, they weren't afraid to ask questions.

Mrs Murray looked thoughtful as she told Tommy, 'Mr Murray would be better advised to answer your question but I'll have a go.' Forefinger pressing on her cheek, brow creased in consternation, she said, 'As I understand it, the allies, which as you know is our side, are going to invade Germany from the west, across the English Channel, through France.'

Tommy's hand shot up. 'When will we invade, miss?'

'Ahh, that's the burning question. Everyone's on tenterhooks wondering and waiting for it to begin.'

'How will we invade?' he persisted.

'I imagine by ships, aeroplanes and troops on the land.' Mrs Murray picked up a book from the table and, looking harassed, she told him, 'That's enough about the war. You can read first, Tommy.'

As Alice listened to him faltering over a section of *Little Women* (Jo in the book was her favourite sister; she wasn't afraid of anything and Alice's hope was to be like her) her thoughts turned, like they often did these days, to what would happen when it was time for her to leave Teviot Hall. Like most girls when they left the orphanage, she would likely end up a housemaid but, she reasoned, she didn't want to be a servant at the beck and call of the mistress of the house. Alice had higher ambitions. But with no training for anything and nowhere to live, it was hopeless.

The talk she'd had with Rosie about finding her mother came to mind and her chest tightened with resentment. She was appalled at the very idea. What was she thinking? What good would it do to find a mother who'd abandoned her baby on a doorstep to never return? She wasn't interested then, so why would she want to know Alice now? Besides, she might have other children and never have told them they had a sister. An ache of longing overcame Alice, taking her unaware, and she found herself despising the woman more than ever.

Alice didn't need a mother – she didn't need anyone. Except Rosie.

There had to be a way to stay together.

The next Sunday, after the orphans had been to church and were sitting at dinner eating mince (and voicing their disappointment because there weren't any dumplings), Miss Balfour stood up at her end of the table and, striding over to the wireless that was playing *Workers' Playtime*, she switched it off.

'Listen, everyone.' All eyes turned towards her. 'Firstly, there are no dumplings because Cook says the national flour doesn't last as long and it's gone maggoty.'

Groans and screwed up noses followed. The mistress looked around the tables, waiting for the noise to subside.

'The second notice is if you see a black cat, it's a stray and Mrs Stewart has taken it in.'

'Please, miss, what's a stray?' Harry wanted to know.

'A cat that's been abandoned and has no home. With rationing and food hard to come by people are finding they can't keep a kitty anymore.'

*So, they're dumped like me,* Alice thought.

'Lastly, the good news.' Miss Balfour's eyes twinkled.

'This afternoon, all of you are invited over to the airbase for tea.'

Alice, sitting next to Rosie, wasn't as thrilled as the others by the invitation. The airmen were kind by providing clothes and whatever the sponsored children needed. When little Charlie received an outdoor coat and cap and was told they were his to keep, he burst into tears at such luxury. And Alice was particularly delighted when she received a pair of black lace-up boots that fitted properly and didn't have a hole in them. The rest of the orphans weren't left out, and were given stamp albums, marbles for the boys, skipping ropes for the girls. But Alice couldn't get enthused at the outing because Miss Balfour would be taking them to the airbase, and these days she had been preoccupied, giving the children – giving Alice – less attention than usual.

Agnes had told her the reason why, and at the thought, the pang of jealousy within Alice intensified.

'Miss Balfour's gone on one of the Americans from the airfield,' Agnes had told Rosie and Alice in a conspirative whisper, as they all sat listening one night to the BBC Home Service before retiring to bed.

'Gone where?' Rosie appeared bemused.

Agnes rolled her eyes. 'Fallen for him. Hazel says that's what people do before they get married.'

Agnes had befriended Hazel, who knew about such things. But topics like this were taboo in the orphanage, and Rosie winced with embarrassment, while Alice was beyond words.

'It started at the New Year's dance,' Agnes informed them. 'Miss Balfour was sitting with him and Hazel says you could tell they fancied each other.'

'Fancied?' Rosie was open-mouthed.

'Hazel says it means attracted to someone. She's seen

*Casablanca*, a picture where two people fancied each other and then fell in love. Hazel said the picture has a sad ending that made her cry.'

'Did they kiss?' Alice had never been to the pictures and cringed at the thought of seeing grownups kiss.

'A long smoochy one, Hazel says.'

No wonder the housemistress was preoccupied if she was thinking about kissing this American. A feeling of being abandoned overcame Alice.

---

These days Miriam had so much to occupy her mind and the responsibility of running the orphanage weighing her down, she often found herself in a stupefied state, where she was unable to think let alone make a decision. But days like today when she saw the orphans' happy and eager faces as they anticipated the outing to the airbase made it all worthwhile.

One of the biggest challenges, she decided, reaching for her coat hanging behind the door on a wooden peg, was what to do about Rita. The poor woman couldn't be expected to continue sleeping overnight at the coach house indefinitely. And for sure Walter must be fed up with the present situation, though nothing had been said. But there was a need for someone else besides Miriam on duty, especially at night with the little ones. The only thing for it was to advertise in the local paper for a live-in help.

As Miriam buttoned up her coat, a rap came at the office door. Before she could open it, Rita barged in, plonking her weighty body in the wing-backed chair Miriam provided for visitors. Mrs Murray had come in after church to help the orphans get ready for their outing.

'I still can't get over how I can just charge in here without waiting for Miss Black's permission to enter.' She gave a broad smile. 'It does me heart good to see all the changes you're making, lassie; it's doing wonders for the orphans. Bless them, they needed a bit of good luck in their lives.'

Miriam smiled her appreciation.

'They're all ready and waiting for their jaunt this afternoon,' Rita informed her, 'but I wanted a word before you take them to the airbase.'

Miriam had a twinge of misgiving.

'By the by.' Mrs Murray tucked some hair under her turban as she spoke. 'You never did say what the colonel actually said in his letter, only that the kiddies were invited to the airbase this afternoon.'

'He just said they were all invited for tea and games. He didn't give a reason.' In the pause that followed, Miriam took the opportunity to speak to Rita about the future. 'We need to talk, Rita, about you continuing here. I really do appreciate that you've stayed on so long. The laird and I have discussed the matter and I'm consider—'

Rita held up her hand, a grin spreading on her face. 'Two minds think alike. That's why I'm here. Just hear me out.' She plucked at her heavy jowls. 'Me and Walter have been discussing the matter. With our two lads away in this war there's not much to keep us at home, where all the memories are a constant reminder of them.' Her jaw quivering, she took a moment to compose herself. 'Walter reckons it makes sense for me to continue working here where I'm needed and suggests instead that he comes to live here too. To be honest, I'm attached to those bairns and feel I'm doing my bit for the war effort in some small way and Walter appreciates that.'

Miriam, speechless, as she realised this would solve all her problems, started thinking of the logistics.

'Walter wouldn't be in the way,' Rita reassured, 'with all

his Home Guard duties and such like, he's hardly ever at home and he's a dab hand at odd jobs needing doing around the place.' She gave a brazen smile. 'This way I'd have my Walter keep me warm at nights.' At Miriam's obvious discomfort, she let out an uproarious guffaw. 'Aw, lass, just say yes and it'll solve all our problems.'

Miriam nodded. 'Rita, tell your Walter thank you, for being so willing to help.'

Rita let out a sigh of satisfaction. 'Life around here is certainly improving in all ways.'

Miriam mentally agreed. Now her mind could concentrate on this afternoon when she hoped to meet up with a certain airman.

# 27

Sitting at a table in the canteen, an unidentifiable smell of dinner lingering in the air, Miriam combed the faces in the packed and noisy room. A jab of disappointment poked her when she didn't see Mitch amongst them, but it did her heart good to see a group of younger children sitting cross-legged on the floor, looking entranced at an airman who was reading to them from a picture book. Further along, at one of the tables, there appeared to be a war enactment going on with some of the boys and the airmen, moving toy soldiers into strategic positions ready for battle. Part of her balked at the idea the children were taking part in war games but seeing how much fun they were having, Miriam resigned herself to the fact it was something the male species did.

'Ma'am, it's good to see you.'

A hand clapped on her shoulder, making her jump. She turned and, looking up, saw Joe standing there, his face etched with fatigue. Miriam had read newspaper reports about the raids by bombers on Berlin, with heavy losses by the allies. Every time she heard an aircraft thunder off overhead, she wondered if Mitch and his crew were amongst them. It made the bombing missions terrifyingly personal and reports of a crew being lost made her nervous that it might be them. She understood more now the torment that Mrs Murray and other families endured worrying over their loved ones. And her admiration grew for the likes of Joe, who were willing to give their lives for the better good.

He looked around the packed dining room. 'Boy, it's swell to see these kids coming out of their shells. The guys have remarked how much they've changed since that first visit.'

Miriam, refraining from explaining the recent ramifications that had changed their lives, smiled in agreement. 'You men have been wonderful and we're grateful for all you do. Especially for afternoons like this.'

He rubbed his cheek. 'It's a real pleasure, ma'am. It was Mitch's idea initially. He didn't want the orphans who weren't sponsored to feel left out. Chuck's suggestion was that we invite all the kids to the airbase every so often for tea and games. Everyone agreed.' He gave a broad grin. 'Those of us with kids enjoy playing Dad for a day.'

The afternoon wore on and Miriam watched as a cook wearing a toque and white apron began tidying away the clean tin trays from the serving counter. Then, surprisingly, one of the airmen appeared from the kitchen doorway dressed as a cowboy. He wore a wide-brimmed hat, checked shirt, a bandanna around his neck, and in his hand, he held a guitar.

'Howdy, there, folks. I'm J.D. and I'm from Texas. And as you can see from my guitar, we're gonna have a singsong.'

If he expected a cheer, the cowboy was disappointed. The orphans simply stared open-mouthed at him, though there was a ripple of raised expectancy in the atmosphere.

J.D. strummed his guitar and announced, 'This here is my favourite song that I sing when I'm riding my horse ol' Silver.' Some of the men raised their eyes heavenward in amused disbelief. 'It's called "Back in the Saddle Again".' He sat on a high stool and, strumming the guitar, started to sing.

Soon all the Yanks were joining in, their baritone voices singing the lilting melodious song, evoking sadness in Miriam. Her gaze swept the enthralled orphans, and settled on Alice, who would soon be leaving the orphanage. Alice would never know how much she was loved. Miriam made a vow that she would do all she could to help Alice as she entered the wider world, as she would for all the orphans. But especially Alice.

During the singing, Cook came from the kitchen bearing plates filled with various sandwiches, scones and pink blanc-manges, placing them on the countertop.

'That's it, folks.' J.D. stood up from the stool. 'Time for what us cowboys call chow.'

Groans came from the rest of the men.

It was while the children started to queue up at the counter, Miriam's attention was caught by the door opening and a figure wearing a leather flight jacket entering.

Mitch.

He looked around the room and made for where Miriam stood. He gave her that roguishly boyish grin that made her stomach curl but, like Joe, his face was etched with fatigue.

'Y'all having a good time?' He peeled off his jacket and placed it on the back of a chair. His hair mussed, she had the urge to reach up and smooth it into place. 'I hightailed it over because I wanted to catch you.'

'Me. Why?'

Raising his eyebrows, little lines riddled his brow. 'To ask you out tomorrow night. Say yes, I've got a forty-eight-hour pass. The alternative is to sleep the time away. Please, Miriam.'

'I couldn't possibly.'

'Why couldn't you possibly?' he teased.

How she was tempted to abandon her inhibitions and live a little for once.

'Come on,' he enticed. 'We'll have a swell time you and I.'

'I can't get away—'

'You could for the dance. Who looked after the kids then?'

She explained about Rita Murray.

'Leave it to me, I'll have a word with her.' A mischievous glint sparkled in his tired eyes. 'I've a way with older women.'

Inwardly, she groaned at his arrogance. But she couldn't deny there was something about him, a magnetism that drew her. Her resolve was slipping. Miriam knew she was falling for him.

The stern voice of her father played in her head. 'You're a fool and always will be, involving yourself with the wrong kind.'

A sudden abhorrence for Father, the way he undermined her confidence to this day, made Miriam listen to her inner voice of reason. The time had come to rid herself of his control. *Besides*, she thought in dismay, *how many tomorrows does Mitch have?*

'Where would we go?' she asked.

His weary face lit up. 'I'm partial to one of your cute village pubs with a cosy fire.'

'I mustn't be late back.'

. . .

The next evening, as the pair of them entered the low-ceilinged Black Horse pub, a hubbub of noise greeted them. Smelling the log fire before she saw it, Miriam felt Mitch's hand grasp hers. He threaded them through the crowded bar to the opposite side of the room where they found a vacant table in a darkened corner. Pulling out a chair covered with a threadbare tapestry material seat, Mitch helped her out of her overcoat before she sat down.

'Am I passing the test?' He grinned.

'What test?'

'Of being an English gentleman.'

She laughed. 'We'll see.'

He didn't seem his assured self, as if he worried that he wouldn't get things right, and she was touched he cared so much.

Aware he was staring at her, she looked at him with a questioning frown. 'What?'

'I'm admiring the view.' Realising that sounded like a corny chat-up line, he quickly added as though wanting to come clean, 'If I was going to give you a chat-up line, I'd do better than that.'

'Such as?'

He cocked his head and put on a mock acting face. 'Hi, it's me. I've met you only in my dreams so far.'

She groaned. 'And these women really do fall for it?'

He leant forward, telling her, 'They're not like you, Miriam. They haven't got class. And you look a million dollars.'

The air charged, as though he was surprised at what he'd said. He sat up and gave an embarrassed cough at getting sloppy.

'Anyway, these women,' he mimicked, 'are only looking for a good time too and that suited me fine back then.' He looked startled, knowing he was digging a deeper hole for himself.

She wanted to reassure him but she didn't approve of his manner towards *these women.* So instead, she said, 'You're incorrigible.'

'Oh, but you can reform me.' Realising the words could be misread, he rubbed the back of his neck. 'Holy moly, I'm not good at this, am I?'

This man was not used to sharing his inner feelings, Miriam could tell. She sensed that like her, he was afraid of getting hurt. They were two of a kind, she realised.

'No, but at least you're trying.' She gave him a cheeky grin.

'What would you like to drink?' He changed direction.

'Erm... cider.'

'You don't sound sure.'

'I'm not. The last time I came to a pub was years ago, in my college days.'

Mitch looked taken aback, as though such a thing was unheard of and he was right, she thought, even the Lumberjills, as tired as they were, took time off to walk to the pub and enjoy themselves.

As Mitch stood and made towards the bar, she thought about his background. Both the women in his life he'd loved had deserted him – no wonder his trust in women had gone. Especially his mother, who— Her mind snapped shut. She was getting dangerously close to her own predicament.

Besides, what had really stuck in her mind was when he'd said, 'That suited me fine back then,' as though it wasn't the case anymore.

. . .

The night was pleasant and relaxed, and Miriam found Mitch's company pleasurable. Gone was his brazen side to be replaced by his more attentive, steadfast self and she enjoyed getting to know him. It was later, when the men in the pub became mawkish and loud – some of the older men from the village got merry and gave tuneless renditions of 'Roll Out the Barrel' and 'I'll Be Seeing You' – Mitch abruptly stood and, taking her coat from the back of her chair, he held it out for her. About to retort she wasn't ready yet to go, seeing his look of disgust, Miriam realised what had upset him. He didn't see the scene simply as friends having a good time but a bunch of drunkards out of control – reminding him of his dad.

Following Mitch out into the cold night air, the thought occurred that he hadn't finished his half pint of beer. On reflection she realised he had only drunk Coca-Cola at the dance. Was his abstinence the result of his father's drunkenness? Indeed, she reflected, she was right. Mitch was more complex than she first thought.

They made their way to the waiting Jeep, parked on the road beside the village green. Earlier, Mitch had revealed he'd done a deal to clinch getting the Jeep for tonight but never disclosed what the agreement entailed.

In the moon's eerie light, she saw his lean frame make for the passenger side, whereupon he opened the door. Her heart melting, she acknowledged that despite the night having ended with an intrusion of sadness from the past, he was taking the trouble to ensure she was treated right and having a good time.

Driving back to Teviot Hall, they didn't speak. Glancing sideways at Mitch, Miriam saw by his clenched jaw that he was still struggling with his emotions.

Touching his arm, she found herself saying, 'I understand because my past has left an indelible mark on me too.'

As the moon slipped behind a cloud, the night became swathed in darkness, the only light from the Jeep's two beams, directed to the ground. Travelling beneath the tree-lined path, the Jeep slowed then came to a halt.

Mitch turned towards her and, as though a silent consent passed between them, he took her in his arms and, his warm lips meeting hers, Miriam surrendered to his lingering kiss.

# 28

'It's happened again,' Rosie told Alice as they wandered from the dining hall to the grounds at the front of the Hall, leaving footprints in the crunchy virgin snow.

Dinner over, the orphans were taking their 'daily dose of fresh air', as Miss Balfour described the half-hour break before attending school. Bundled in outdoor coats, woollen hats and mitts, the two girls made their way down the slippery terraces towards the frozen lake that could be glimpsed through trees whose branches were bowed low under the weight of snow. In the claustrophobic atmosphere, muffled shouts could be heard in the far-off distance as the older boys had a snowball fight.

'What's happened again?' Alice wanted to know. Her eyes watering in the arctic blasts, she pulled the scarf she wore further up her face to protect her cold lips.

Stopping in her tracks, Rosie faced Alice. 'I've remembered something.'

Alice didn't trust herself to speak.

'Remember the other day when the airman was reading to the little ones?'

Alice nodded.

'The picture on the cover of the story book was an elephant that had enormous ears and he was flying.'

'So, what did you remember?'

'I saw the elephant in my mind last night when I was lying in the dark. And I felt happy-sad for him. I just knew, Alice, that I've seen him before. And something else...'

'What?'

'Someone was with me. I thought hard but they stayed in the back of my mind.'

Seeing Rosie's distressed face, Alice felt bad for not wanting her friend to get her memory back. Deep down, Alice knew it wasn't fair to think like that; Rosie always tried to make things better for people.

She forced herself to say, 'Don't worry. One day you'll remember who you are and who you belong to.'

'D'you really think so? But what if they don't want me?'

'Of course they will.' Seeing the hope in Rosie's eyes made Alice feel good about herself. 'Come on let's go down to the lake and see how thick the ice is.'

The pair of them slithered down the extensive terraced slopes to the lower-level grassy terrace, coming to a halt as they approached the lakeside. Surveying the landscape, Alice saw in a clearing, standing between two tall, skinny trees, an older gentleman who wore a long, shapeless coat with turned-up fur collar, and a tartan scarf wound around his neck. Alice recognised him as the laird. She nudged Rosie, nodding to the man. Staring at him as he stood still as a statue gazing out at the lake, they were startled when, as though he felt their eyes on him, he turned to stare right back, hesitating, as if wondering whether to speak or not.

'Hello. It's cold for you to be out,' Rosie called.

Alice was amazed at her daring, then realised she didn't know the laird. Still, at one time Rosie wouldn't say boo to a goose. Alice stifled a giggle at the silly saying.

The laird's lined, sober face brightening, he smiled. Using a stick that had a bird's head with a long beak on the handle, he walked towards them. 'It is but I needed fresh air.'

Alice tried to catch Rosie's eye to warn her but she was intent on gazing at the laird.

'Miss Balfour, our mistress, sends us outside every day for some fresh air.' She tilted her head queryingly. 'I haven't seen you before.'

'I've been away.' His tone was abrupt.

'Do you live here?'

'I do. In the big house.'

'Oh, do you work there?'

Alice cringed. 'Rosie, it's time we—'

'Yes, sometimes,' Sir Henley interrupted.

'You'll know Mr and Mrs Stewart then, do you?'

'Splendid people.' He made to move, then thought better of it. 'D'you ice skate?'

Rosie screwed her face. 'I don't think so.'

'My son was an excellent skater.' A faraway look came into the laird's eye. After a moment he continued. 'You must try. I'll send the skates over to the Little Theatre.' He glanced over at Alice. 'You too. But keep to the lake's edges where you'll be safe.'

'Thank you' – Alice struggled to remember what to call him – 'sir.'

'Won't your son need them?' Rosie asked.

Looking down, Sir Henley paused, then taking a deep breath, he looked up at Rosie. 'Not anymore. He died, you see, in the war.'

'Oh, I'm so sorry.' Tears sparkled in Rosie's eyes. 'You'll miss him so much.'

He nodded.

In the silence that followed, as it dawned on Rosie who the gentleman was, she made big eyes at Alice.

The laird cleared his throat. 'Tell me, what's your name?'

'Rosie Ward.'

'And yours?' He turned to Alice.

'Alice Blakely. They're not our real names. We're orphans.' She felt daft stating the obvious to him.

'And how old are you?'

'Thirteen, sir, nearly fourteen.'

'Nearly time for you to be leaving the orphanage, eh?' His thick, bushy eyebrows met above his nose as he frowned. 'You've got family, grandparents, to go to?'

'I don't know, sir. I was left at the orphanage.'

'Ahh! A foundling.' Sir Henley, leaning on his stick, stood for a while, apparently lost in thought.

Alice, wondering if they'd been dismissed, was just about to move when, shoulders back, he straightened as though he'd made a decision.

'I'll say good day to you both.' Nodding again, and using his walking stick, gingerly, he made his way up the slopes towards the big house.

'That was the laird, wasn't it?' Rosie's crimson face showed dismay.

'Yes, Sir Henley.'

'Fancy asking if he works at the Hall.' Rosie gave a nervous titter.

'Especially when he owns it.'

Alice tried to suppress the giggle threatening but her eyes must have given her away because, Rosie, staring at her and seeing the funny side too, started to laugh. They laughed and laughed until Alice's cheeks hurt and belly ached.

'Stop!' she cried.

'I can't.' Rosie wiped her eyes. 'I keep thinking of me saying...' Her lips pressed together, she tried to smother another chortle. '"*I haven't seen you before*" – as though he shouldn't be here when he owns the place.'

They both dissolved into helpless laughter.

---

After breakfast the next day, Miss Balfour clapped her hands for silence and announced in the classroom, 'Listen, everyone. Mrs Stewart has just delivered these from Sir Henley.' She pointed to three sets of ice skates sitting on the table.

A collective gasp of surprise filled the room.

'Sir Henley wants us to make use of them but only the older children. Hands up those who would like to have a turn.'

Rosie was one of the first.

Later, after dinner, ice skates in her hands and remembering the laird's words to keep to the edges, Rosie looked out over the frozen lake, which shone like glass in the afternoon sunshine.

'Here.' She handed Alice the skates. 'I'm scared I'll fall and hurt my ribs when they're just getting better.' As Alice was taking off her boots, Rosie said, 'I feel sorry for him.'

'Sorry for who?'

'The laird.' Rosie sighed. 'He's got no one now he's lost his wife and son. He's ancient with nothing to look forward to.' She gave a sad smile. 'We're lucky, when we leave here things can only change for the better.'

'I wouldn't count on it,' Alice, ever the pessimist, said.

# 29

Alice was to remember her words a month later when Miss Balfour announced in the dining hall, 'Alice Blakely, report to my office after breakfast is over.'

When Alice rapped on the office door, she decided that even if she had done wrong – though she couldn't imagine what – Miss Balfour would treat the wrongdoing fairly.

'Come in, Alice,' called Miss Balfour's welcoming voice.

*Miss Black's gone*, Alice reminded herself. There'd never been a time before when she entered the office without the fear of harsh punishment, but at the sight of the mistress's smiling, though pensive, face, Alice felt relief flood through her.

'Come in, Alice, sit down.'

Sinking into the comfortable wing-backed chair, Alice was surprised as she'd never seen it before. It showed the pleasant changes Miss Balfour was making.

'I've called you in for us to discuss what will happen after your birthday in June. Arrangements will have to be made.'

Alice's heart felt like it had plummeted.

'I've decided what might be a good idea is to find employment for you in South Shields where you originally came from.'

Alice knew there would be no discussion really, so what was the use of giving an opinion.

'What d'you think?' Miss Balfour, picking up a pen from the desk and fiddling with it, appeared edgy.

Surprised at being considered, Alice shrugged. 'I suppose South Shields is as good as anywhere.' Then it occurred to her that if Rosie's memory did return and she was reunited with her family she would go back to South Shields. She gave a firm nod. 'I'd like to work in South Shields.'

'Good. I'll make arrangements.' Miss Balfour appeared to relax. 'I'll find a suitable family for you to work with, one with children that need looking after.'

All her biggest fears slowly dispelling, Alice realised leaving the orphanage mightn't be so bad after all.

---

Miriam sank back in the swivel chair. The meeting had gone better than she'd expected, as Alice could be difficult when she so desired with fixed ideas of what she wanted, even though she'd never had any control over her life. This plan could be the best solution for everyone involved, Miriam concluded, the anxiety in her chest releasing.

After the war ended and the orphanage re-established in South Shields, Miriam would get in touch with Alice on the pretext she intended to keep an eye on the orphans' welfare after they left the orphanage – which in all probability would be true, when she came to think on it. She closed her eyes, thinking of the future, when she would be like a favourite aunt to Alice, always remembering birthdays and

Christmases and more importantly being included in her life.

Gazing into a satisfying storybook future, Miriam's mind turned the page to one that included Mitch.

An exquisite thrill surging through her, Miriam revisited in her mind Mitch's occasional visits to her flat above the dormitories. The two-roomed flat was the first place she could ever call home, and a place where she had invited Mitch at night when the orphans were tucked up in bed and he had a rare pass from the base. If the Murrays in the adjoining flat knew about the clandestine meetings they didn't let on, though that was unusual for the outspoken Rita, who had now become a close friend.

At first, sitting on her two-settee couch sipping Ovaltine, they put the world to rights, then, before he left, they had dreamy ardent kisses, when Mitch's hands roved her body and, reluctantly, she flapped them off. When things got more serious and petting led to Mitch exploring her body, Father's disdainful face materialising in her mind, Miriam, tensing, pulled away.

She knew Mitch's interpretation was that she was naïve in such matters, but when he told her in a hoarse whisper, 'Honey, you're driving me crazy but I can wait until you're ready,' she loved him all the more.

# 30

## MARCH 1944

Planes screamed overhead, sounding as if they were skimming the rooftops and Miriam, cleaning the blackboard, automatically dipped her head and crouched down.

As the aircraft roared off into the distance, Rita, who had covered her ears with her hands, exclaimed, 'Them Yank planes frighten me to death, zooming over like that.' Removing her hands, she told Miriam, 'On Tuesday, when I was standing in the Co-op queue, them bombers went over – by the by, my Walter says they're known as a B-17 Flying Fortress. Anyway, young Renee Dent, who is eight months pregnant, said later when we could hear ourselves think, that she'd nearly dropped the bairn she was carrying on the spot. Silly lass.' Rita pulled a knowing face. 'If only having a bairn was that easy.'

Miriam didn't reply; she didn't want Rita to go off on a graphic tangent on how babies were born. Besides, she couldn't concentrate on anything other than what to do about Alice.

Miss Fellows had agreed that Miriam could use her office

telephone to speak to someone at South Shields' employment exchange about securing Alice a job as a nursemaid. But it had been more difficult than Miriam had imagined.

The woman on the other end of the line she'd spoken to had told her brusquely, 'Most young children have been evacuated, some mothers going with them. Those who haven't aren't in any position to employ a nursemaid.'

'How about a housemaid?' Miriam refrained to let her voice convey how disgruntled she was at the woman's hoity-toity attitude.

'It's a case of supply supersedes demand. I would suggest you consult the employment column in the local paper.'

The telephone receiver clicked, leaving Miriam dismayed.

'Sheila Craddock from the Co-op got above herself yesterday,' Rita was telling her. 'She told the queue, in that put-on refined voice of hers, that those planes at the airbase wouldn't be there for long.' Before Miriam could reply, she carried on. 'You should have seen the commotion it caused. Folk wanting to know where she got her information from and what more did she know.' Rita gave an exasperated click of the tongue. 'Silly woman said her lips were sealed and quoted the poster that said, *Loose Lips Sink Ships*.' Rita rolled her eyes in disbelief. 'As if there'd be any spies in the Co-op queue.'

Suppressing the smile threatening her lips, Miriam placed a rock on each desk for the children to compare and learn about in this morning's science lesson. After Miss Black's controlling rule over them, Miriam was keen to introduce a different approach. She explained to the older ones about the three kinds of rock, igneous, metamorphic and sedimentary, and how they were formed. She then encouraged the children to describe their rock to the class and say what it felt like and what it might be used for. Everyone was nervous to speak at first but as interest for the subject grew, so did their confidence. She told the younger children they could draw their rock on a slate and that all the drawings would be displayed on the table at the front at the end of the lesson.

Though she did consider the three Rs important, so too were the creative arts. And so she had introduced free expression, dancing to music from the wireless, mime, play acting and physical training as part of the morning curriculum. The result being the orphans were becoming inquisitive and imaginative and beginning to express themselves freely, which gladdened Miriam's heart.

Now, as the children attended to their morning jobs and the two women were setting up class, the smell of food drifted from the kitchen. Sausages, Miriam deduced as she sniffed the air, but unfortunately not for the orphans and more likely for Sir Henley's breakfast.

Rita continued, 'The consensus of opinion in the queue after Sheila wouldn't budge telling what she knew (which personally I don't believe was anything worth telling)' – Rita took a sustaining breath – 'is the general belief the invasion will happen any time now. Some even suggesting it might be the weekend as the moon and tides will be just right.'

That struck a chord with Miriam, who was now writing the nine times table on the blackboard. She turned towards Rita. 'Really, as soon as that?'

'Och aye. Walter reckons so. He's been talking to Fred James, who he plays darts with at the pub. Fred's in the National Fire Service and he says most of his company have been sent to Dover. And Sheila Craddock deigned to tell us that one of the travellers told her that with miles of convoys blocking the roads to the south, no goods whatsoever could be despatched.' Rita scratched behind her ear. 'Makes you think, doesn't it?'

A cold finger of fear traced down Miriam's spine. Mitch. Because of all the recent missions, she hadn't seen him recently and the fear that *Alabama Beauty* (the name the crew had chosen for the bomber's nose art) might never return kept Miriam awake nights. The times she had seen Mitch, she had begun to see past the roguish part of him and get acquainted with his sensitive side. She considered he was still a rascal, but he was her loveable rascal and Miriam wanted him safe and sound by her side.

She ruminated. Mitch had made it plain by the desire in his eyes that he wanted her to give in but Miriam had made that mistake once and never again. Terry Rawling had been after only one thing and young and foolish Miriam, in love with him, had yielded. But this time around, she needed to hear those three little words. Besides, Mitch's home was across an ocean while hers was here. What future did they have? She couldn't leave even if he asked her to, even if she wanted to, as there was always Alice to consider.

Breakfast over, and the food monitors busy clearing the tables, Miriam watched as Rita shepherded the orphans into the classroom. A tap on her shoulder made her turn. Mrs Stewart stood there wearing a prim, tight-lipped expression.

'Not only am I the cook but the laird has now delegated me to a messenger.'

Used to Cook's complaints, Miriam took no notice. Besides, Mrs Stewart was devoted to Sir Henley and though she could grumble, she would be quick to defend the laird if anyone dared to say a word against him.

'Sir Henley requests you and Alice Blakely to go to his study after breakfast.'

Dumbfounded, Miriam asked, 'Did he give you any idea why he wants to see us?'

'I haven't the foggiest. The laird isn't in the habit of discussing his affairs with me.'

*Lordy, Cook really did get out of the wrong side of bed this morning.*

Miriam pasted a smile on her face. 'Thank you, Mrs Stewart, for passing the message on.'

'I had no choice,' she grumbled, 'if that husband o' mine did his job properly and could be found this morning, it was his job to be messenger.' Turning on her heel, she left.

---

'I've no idea why Sir Henley wants to see us,' Miss Balfour told Alice as they walked along the narrow and musty smelling passageway. 'Have you?'

Alice wasn't unduly worried because she'd only met him that one time with Rosie by the lake and she hadn't done anything wrong. Besides, that was a couple of months ago. But then a sudden thought made her flinch. What if he heard the two of them laughing and thought it was at his expense? Why just her though, and after such a long time?

As Miss Balfour stopped at the second door along the passage and knocked, Alice took a deep breath in readiness to justify whatever she was accused of.

'Come in,' boomed a deep voice.

Miss Balfour led the way and Alice found herself in a room that had dark wood-panelled walls and floor-to-ceiling bookcases with a ladder that reached to the topmost shelf of books. In front of a marble fireplace was a round table with a model of a ship (that Alice knew was called a schooner) on top of it.

Sir Henley, pipe in his mouth and wearing brown corduroy trousers and tweed jacket, stood behind an enormous desk that had a red inlaid top, piled with papers. Removing his pipe and knocking the bowl on an ashtray, the laird looked up. 'Ahh! Good of you to come.'

As if they had any choice, Alice thought, but she was relieved to see Sir Henley had a benevolent smile on his face. Though she still couldn't relax. Miss Balfour appeared flustered too, as if she knew she should say something but was unsure as to what.

'It's good to see you too, Sir Henley,' she said lamely.

'Please, sit down.' He gestured to a faded leather couch, at one end of the fireplace. Placing his pipe in the ashtray, he came from behind the desk, slipped his hand in his tweed jacket pocket and began pacing the room.

Sitting perched and alert on the couch alongside the mistress, Alice deduced the leather seat was as rock hard as it looked.

'I have something to propose.' Sir Henley stopped pacing, pinning Miss Balfour with a stare. 'And I thought the girl... Alice, that is, should be present as it concerns her.'

Surprised he remembered her name, a burst of worried adrenalin rushed through Alice.

'Proposal?' Miss Balfour repeated, a concerned look crossing her face.

'Let me explain. I met Alice and her friend down at the lake.'

Alice stiffened. *Here it comes.*

'Alice, here, told me she was a foundling. It occurred to

me that since she has no surviving relatives, she will no doubt go into service that has the benefit of accommodation. Am I right?' He looked quizzically at Miss Balfour.

She nodded.

'I've been in touch with Lord Douglas Wetherington's secretary. He has a house in London and as providence would have it, his housekeeper is searching for a suitable girl for the position of housemaid—'

'But Sir Hen—'

'No buts, Miss Balfour.' The laird's voice held a sharp edge to it at being contradicted. Brushing the side of his mouth with a thumb and forefinger, he continued, 'My proposal is that Alice takes on the position. How's that for a plan, my girl?' Looking rather pleased with himself, the laird pierced Alice with a glare.

Her brain trying to understand what she'd just heard, Alice could only stare back.

'It's good of you, sir, but...' Miss Balfour appeared to flounder. 'I'm busy organising employment for Alice at this moment.'

Looking rather disgruntled at her lukewarm response, Sir Henley responded, 'Locally?'

'Er... no. In South Shields where she was left as a foundling.' Miss Balfour's cheeks turned tomato red.

'Miss Balfour, surely it's best for the girl to be in a household of such an esteemed person as Lord Wetherington, where we know she'll be treated properly.' His voice held a critical note, his expression that of one who must be obeyed.

A look of dismay crossed the mistress's face but she knew better than to contradict. 'Of course, sir. It's good of you to take an interest.'

'Excellent. Then it's settled. I'll correspond this instant

to Lord Douglas's secretary and inform her of the situation and that the housekeeper's search is over. As for you, young lady.' He smiled down at Alice. 'Work hard and you'll do well. The changes will take place after your birthday.'

Alice was outraged that they spoke about her as though she wasn't present and her say in the matter was of no consequence. Which, to be truthful, had always been the case living at the orphanage. The thing that frightened her – and had done so ever since that time she'd attempted to run away – was the thought of venturing into an unknown outside world where she knew no one. Feeling cowardly at admitting such a fact, she knew there was nothing she could do to alter the laird's plans. Being part of a household, she admitted, was the best way forward. But London...

Swallowing her earlier indignation, she mumbled the only appropriate answer the laird was waiting for. 'Thank you, Sir Henley.'

'London,' Rosie exclaimed. 'That's hundreds of miles away.'

They were sitting on Alice's bed waiting their turn for the washroom. Alice felt defeated. Her fighting spirit had deserted her. Nothing she did would change the fact she had no say in her life.

She told Rosie, dispiritedly, 'It doesn't make any difference how many miles away I am. I'll be in service and it'll be like here where I'm told what to do and where I can go.'

'But you always think of something.'

The hope she saw in Rosie's eyes annoyed Alice. 'Well, I can't now.'

'You could still find your mam.'

'Yes, Rosie. Somehow, I could make it all the way back

from London on my afternoon off and magically find the bitch who's never wanted to know me.'

Rosie recoiled at her reaction. 'Sorry. I never thought. It was a silly idea. But promise you'll—'

Alice knew when she was beaten. 'I'm not promising anything. And I don't want to talk about it anymore.'

# 31

## APRIL 1944

Morning sunshine streamed through the classroom window and Rosie, sitting at her desk in the sun's warm rays, her belly full of bread and dripping, found it difficult to stop her eyelids from drooping. For in the middle of the night, the siren had blared and the orphans, still half asleep, had collected gas masks and blankets and made for the outdoor shelter, only to hear the all-clear sounding half an hour later.

'The general consensus of opinion,' Mrs Murray told the drowsy class, 'is that the siren going off must have been an accident as there was no sign of enemy aircraft in the vicinity.'

The damage was done though as, like the other orphans, Rosie had trouble getting back to sleep. She'd lain instead with upsetting thoughts swirling in her head. Mainly she thought of Alice leaving in two months' time but she never dared broach the subject because Alice was a crosspatch whenever the topic came up – and who could blame her. Besides, Rosie was at a loss to know how to help.

'Jerry's been out in force in the Hull area, so I've heard,'

Mrs Murray was telling the class, keeping them up to date with war news.

Rosie wished she didn't as it made everyone jittery and jumpy to hear about bombings.

'Mr Murray says the attacks are part reprisal for the devastation of German cities by the allies.'

'Please, miss, what's reprisals mean?' Tommy wanted to know.

Mrs Murray's brow furrowed. 'I suppose repaying us back for bombing their cities. But don't worry, Mr Murray reckons because of the windy weather and inaccurate target markings, that's probably why none of them Jerry bombs landed on Hull and—'

At that moment Miss Balfour entered the classroom.

'Good morning, everyone.'

The mistress had missed breakfast, leaving Mrs Murray to take morning prayers which usually meant only saying the Lord's Prayer and praying for the safety of our boys away at war.

'Morning, Miss Balfour,' they chorused.

'I have some news.' The mistress's gaze swept the classroom. 'Sir Henley wanted to see me and what he had to say concerns you all.'

Seeing Miss Balfour's eager look, Rosie relaxed as it had to be good news.

'The laird enquired about our Christmas last year and was pleased that in his absence you were all invited to Dunglen airbase. Sir Henley wants to thank the airmen by inviting them to Teviot Hall.' The mistress smiled broadly. 'It's this Sunday and he wants you all to attend. We're invited to tea and there's to be a singsong to replace the carol service he missed last year.'

The room buzzed with excited chatter.

'Now, everyone,' Miss Balfour called, silencing them all, 'we can't expect Mrs Stewart to do all that needs doing and so I'd like volunteers from the older ones to assist with preparation and serving.'

Hands shot up and shouts of 'Me, miss,' resounded around the classroom.

'Please, miss.'

Everyone stared at Albert, who had spoken up.

'Have we enuff food for the men to eat? We always get loads off them.'

Miss Balfour nodded. 'Mrs Stewart claims she has some flour that needs to be used and she reckons there's enough' – she looked at Albert and smiled – 'and remember to spell the word when writing it with a with a "gh" not "f" ending – to make cheese sandwiches and ginger biscuits. We have plenty of tea but sugar is short.' Her brown eyes twinkled with fun. 'So let's hope, shall we, the men don't take lots in their tea.'

Everyone laughed and the atmosphere lifted.

'Please, miss.'

Rosie was surprised when Charlie put his hand up in the air as he was usually loath to bring attention to himself and she knew the feeling.

'I only take one spoonful but the men can have mine.'

As Miss Balfour's face sobered, Charlie looked at her in surprise as if wondering what he'd said to make her look dewy-eyed.

'Thank you, Charlie,' she told the little lad. 'That would be most kind.'

---

As she sat at her desk, Miriam reflected on the unfairness of life that Charlie had evoked within her. She thought of all the little Charlies who, because of this 'bloody, bloody war' – she blasted at the far wall – were left orphans to find their own way in the world. And parents like Sir Henley, who'd lost his son… It was unimaginable what heartache they must suffer. Unnerved at the strength of her feelings to cause such a verbal outburst, Miriam reflected, shamelessly, she felt better for it.

She considered, it was as though recently Sir Henley decided to be able to live with the pain of loss and Miriam believed meeting the two girls at the lake that day had something to do with it. It was as if he'd found purpose in life: that of being responsible for the wellbeing of the orphans at his home.

The change in Sir Henley had untold ramifications for Miriam because his concern for the orphans affected Alice. Miriam had to admit that Alice could do a lot worse than finding herself employed at Lord Wetherington's residence. But *London*? How could Miriam possibly keep in touch apart from the occasional card? Alice would become absorbed in her new life in the big city and Miriam would be only an occasional afterthought.

The words sprang into her mind that she had consoled many an orphan with in the past: *Believe in God's plan for your life*. How trite that sounded now – and if it was true how could denying a mother her daughter be the act of a loving God?

This was blasphemous talk, she rebuked herself, but Miriam had worked herself up to such a frenzy, she didn't care anymore. She sank back in the chair, recognising she was being as rebellious as she had been in the old days with Father. Despite her torment, the thought that Alice was a chip off the old block made Miriam smile.

But in truth, she couldn't deny Sir Henley's worry for the

orphans' welfare was having a positive effect on their lives. When he found out Brenda was having piano lessons provided for by the sponsors, Sir Henley had the piano in the Great Hall tuned so that she could practise after tea. At great sacrifice to himself, Miriam knew, as he'd bought the grand piano for Fergus, who, according to Mrs Stewart, had become an outstanding pianist. After his beloved son's death, the laird had forbidden the piano lid to be opened.

In other ways too Sir Henley had been generous, arranging croquet on the lawns and fishing in rowing boats on the lake to name but a few. And though Miriam saw wistfulness in his eyes at times, the laird gradually was returning to the imposing stature of the man he once was.

Sitting erect, she planted her hands on the desk. If Sir Henley could get up every morning and face the day, when the son he adored had died at such a young age and would never have a family or grow old, she could put up with watching Alice from afar becoming the woman she was intended to be.

Couldn't she?

Miriam shook off her doubts. It was time she got on with her life and even though she could never desert the children, she would no longer hide away in the orphanage. Life was for living. A picture of Mitch, the handsome, unpredictable rascal of a man she'd fallen in love with, came to mind, making her smile. A tingling pleasure flooded her body at the thought she might see him on Sunday.

---

Sunday couldn't come quick enough and when Rosie, with the others, filed into the great entrance hall, she felt giddy with anticipation. The American airmen, striking in their uniforms, congregated around the piano set aside at the bottom of the sweeping staircase. Some were familiar but she didn't know their names except the two men who had brought the Christmas tree, who were called Mitch and Joe.

'Children' – Miss Balfour's voice, raised above the din of excited orphans and deep booming male voices, held a commanding tone – 'be seated on the floor.'

'When do we eat, miss?' Harry wanted to know. He eyed the trestle table, stacked with cups, saucers and plates at the far end of the hall, beneath the balcony.

Miriam told him, 'Later, Harry. Do as you're told and sit.'

A hard-done-by look on his face, Harry sat next to Rosie on the black-and-white-tiled floor opposite the grand piano.

'There's aren't many Americans here, are there?' Alice, the other side of Rosie, craned her neck to see over the heads. 'Mrs Murray says they've been sent down—'

'Good,' Harry interrupted with a satisfied smirk. 'That'll mean more biscuits for us.'

Sir Henley appeared at the top of the staircase and Rosie, startled, had a stab of recollection when she saw the sheets of music in his hands. A vision materialised of her hands touching the keys on a piano. Excited, she turned to Alice to share her memory, then thought better of it. Whenever Rosie remembered anything from the past, it appeared to upset her friend. These days, Rosie was extra careful what she said because Alice was fretting about going to London and that made her touchy.

She watched as Sir Henley made his way towards the piano and, putting the sheets of music on the lid, he shook hands with the airmen, nodding and chatting all the while. Then he addressed the orphans.

'It's good to see you all and thank you for helping with tea which we'll enjoy later.' His eyes sweeping the room landed on Rosie; his head tilted back, he appeared to be looking down his nose at her and she would have cringed had it not been for his kindly eyes. 'We're here this afternoon to thank our American friends for the kindness they've shown to all of you over these past few months.' He turned towards the airmen. 'May God speed wherever you...' His voice faltering, he bowed his head.

Sir Henley looked how Rosie felt when she was struggling not to show how upset she was.

In the awkward silence, Miss Balfour, who by now was sitting on the tapestry couch, stood. 'How about we all show our appreciation to the airmen with a round of applause?'

They all started clapping and Sir Henley, after he heaved a big sigh, looked up and joined in. Then holding up his hand, instructing everyone to stop, he told them, 'I know you're all eager to get on with the singsong and most importantly tea afterwards – which I might add, the airmen assure me they have a treat in store, so without further ado we'll begin.'

As he walked over to the piano, some of the men dispersed and came to sit with the orphans on the floor. The laird sat on the piano stool and placed a sheet of music on the rest. One of the airmen came to stand at his side ready to turn pages.

At that moment, Mrs Stewart appeared through the open doorway carrying a fruit cake perched on a glass stand. Taking in the scene, she moved to the trestle table and put the cake on the table.

She turned. 'It's from the Yanks,' she declared, then hurried back the way she came.

The laird, with a nod, signalled to the airman that he was ready. His fingers poised above the piano keys, he turned and said, 'Everyone can sing along. And if you don't know the words just "la la la".' His fingers touching the keys, the sound of 'Run, Rabbit, Run!' filled the room.

Rosie with the rest began to sing; they all knew the words because Miss Balfour had taught the songs to the little ones. They sang shyly at first but when the men joined in, their deep voices booming out in tune with the music, the orphans became more confident and sang out. As the song was finishing, Rosie was surprised when words from the last line were changed to, 'Run, Adolf, run, Adolf, run, run, run.'

When the song ended, the atmosphere in the hall, with the airmen laughing and jeering and blowing piercing whistles, was on a joyful high. Sir Henley, delighted and smiling, bowed his head. Changing the music and giving the airman the old sheet, he focused on the pages in front of him. The room hushed as he started to play again and as the music filled the room, from the depths of Rosie's mind a memory stirred. The men began singing and as their melodious voices rang out, she recognised their words.

'You are my sunshine.'

As images crowded her mind, Rosie burst into tears.

# 32

Alice was taken aback when Rosie started crying. 'What's the matter, Rosie?'

A look of incredulity on her tear-stained face, Rosie came closer, raising her voice above the singing. 'I can remember who I am.'

Alice's body sagged in despair. Out of the corner of her eye, she saw Miss Balfour making a beeline to where they sat. Helping Rosie up, the mistress threaded her way through the children to the doorway and out of the Great Hall. Curious to know what was happening, the other orphans watched on. Alice, unable to stop herself, stood up from the floor and followed the pair all the way to the dining hall.

'Now then, what's all this about?' Miss Balfour asked once they were settled either side of one of the trestle tables.

Alice blurted, 'She said she could remember who she was, miss.'

A look of surprise crossed Miss Balfour's face. 'Is this true?'

Her tear-stained face picturing wonderment, Rosie

nodded. 'Yes, miss. I started to remember when I heard the song. Then it just came to me who I was.'

'You know your name?'

'Yes. Polly Pearson.'

Alice slapped her hand over her mouth. Her fear was coming true.

'But this is wonderful, Rosie,' Miss Balfour exclaimed, 'and nothing to cry about.'

'Miss, it's like you said. My memory came when I least expected. Honest, I'm not sad, I'm happy.'

'What about where you live?' The mistress looked intently at Rosie.

Screwing up her face, Rosie thought for a moment. Wide eyed, she stared at Miss Balfour, with a look as though she'd been given a bar of chocolate. 'I've been told if I get lost, I was to find a policeman and tell him I live at forty-six Whale Street.'

'Good girl.' The mistress beamed. 'And who told you?'

Rosie put her head in her hands as she tried to think. Looking up, she released a drawn-out sigh. 'I don't know, miss.'

'Don't worry, it'll come.' Miss Balfour gave a reassuring smile. 'It's remarkable you've remembered so much.'

Rosie's face positively glowed with happiness and Alice had never felt so betrayed. Thoughts whirled through her mind; disturbing thoughts that made her have a jittery feeling in her belly. Rosie's family would come and take her away, probably to a lovely home with her own bedroom. She would soon forget all about the orphanage and Alice would lose the only friend she'd ever known.

'I should think that's enough excitement for now, Rosie. How about we join the others for tea. But first' – her hands came together in a pyramid – 'how about we thank the Lord for the gift of your memory coming back.'

Rosie nodded.

As their heads bowed in silent prayer, Alice's resentful mind railed at a God who never allowed happy things to happen to her. She wanted to know who *she* was and have a family and a home too.

Later, as they made their way back through the passageway, Alice trailing behind, she tensed as she heard planes approaching. Coming closer, the thunderous noise sounded as if the planes skimmed over the rooftops. Rosie, ahead, stood rooted to the spot, eyes closed, hands over her ears. As the aircraft made their descent towards the airfield Alice relaxed and hurried to catch up with the others.

'They're ours, Rosie.' Miss Balfour removed Rosie's hands from her ears. 'You're safe.'

Her face gone white, Rosie looked dazed. 'I was in the shelter.'

'What shelter?'

'When the raid was happening, miss. Other people were there, a girl. The planes were screaming overhead.' Her face scrunched up as though she could hear them now. 'Daddy was outside and I had to go to him.' Her face changed, became terror stricken. 'There was a blast and I saw a wall starting to collapse and that's all I can remember.' She looked at Miss Balfour and then to Alice. 'Daddy would have come to find me if he could, wouldn't he?'

Seeing how heartbroken Rosie looked, Alice felt both bad and guilty. She hated herself for secretly hoping something awful had happened to Rosie's parents. She'd so wanted the two of them to be like family and live together – but that was mean thinking. In future she would try to be as bighearted as Rosie and be a true friend.

---

When all the children were in bed, Miriam entered the upstairs flat. At the sight of Mitch at the gathering that afternoon, a weight had lifted from her chest. It had been such a relief and she thanked God that both he and the crew were safely back at the airbase.

While everyone helped themselves to sandwiches, he'd sauntered over to where she stood alone. 'See you tonight, honey.' As his hand caressed her forearm, an electric jolt had hit the spot. 'I'll be in the flat ready and waiting after all the kids are in bed.'

It was rare these days for Mitch to have a night free and now as, wearily, she climbed the stairs to the flat, the thought of him waiting caused a rush of energising adrenalin to flow through her.

She entered her flat, where a fire blazed, a demure light shone from the standard lamp and the wireless played music softly in the background, and seeing Mitch's sinewy body dwarfing the couch, Miriam smiled joyfully at him.

His uniform jacket removed, tie undone, he sat forward, his features contorted in concern.

'You look tired, honey. I worry about you. You know what they say, "all work and no play makes Jack a dull boy."' He gave her a silly grin. 'Not that that applies to you but never taking time off will tell on you eventually. Promise you'll take care of yourself.'

Miriam gasped in delight. Never once could she remember anyone caring about her wellbeing and it was good to feel protected.

'Honey, how's young Rosie doing?' Mitch knew Rosie's story, as he knew most of the orphans' backgrounds. 'She looked kinda shaken.'

'She was.'

He patted the seat beside him. 'Come sit by me. It's time I had you all to myself.'

Moving to the couch, she sank into its cushions. Leaning in, Mitch tilted his head and gave her a lingering kiss.

Moaning as he pulled away, he drew his hand down his drawn face. 'Jesus, it's been an age.'

Miriam, heart pounding, looked deep into his eyes and, seeing the desire in them, the wary, insecure side of her couldn't give in. It was torture meeting like this, knowing they were worlds apart and this affair was going nowhere because when the war finished and life got back to normal, they would go their separate ways.

She sat up and smoothed down her frock. She couldn't look at him, see his reaction, but carried on the previous conversation instead, telling him about Rosie and the events of the afternoon.

'Wow! What a blow for the kid. You realise her parents could have died in the raid.'

'That's what she thinks, hence her shocked state.'

'Poor kid. What can be done?'

'Sir Henley's involved. He saw Rosie was distressed and when everyone was gorging on the cake you men kindly brought, he took me aside and wanted to know what was disturbing her.'

'The guy's heart is in the right place, even if he is a sir.' Yawning, Mitch covered his mouth with a hand.

Miriam knew it wasn't out of disinterest – Mitch's concern for the children was one of the finer points about him. It was the ceaseless hours he and the crew put in that had ground him down. He couldn't talk about it, she knew, but his strained face and the fact she hadn't seen him in a while spoke volumes.

She told him, 'Sir Henley insisted he took matters in his own hands and make enquiries.'

'Yep, there's nothing like money and contacts to set the ball rolling.' Hands behind his head, Mitch sank back against the couch's cushions, stretching out his legs.

Watching the mesmeric little flames as they leapt up the chimney, Miriam said, 'It helps she's remembered the address.'

'I bet it does. Let's hope it all ends happily.' His face perplexed, he blew out his cheeks.

They sat in contemplative silence for a while and then he looked at her, his lengthy gaze having a suggestive quality. Despite her misgivings, a long forgotten sensuous ache below took Miriam's breath away and a small gasp escaped her. Gazing at his broad chest, she found herself imagining slipping her hand beneath his uniform and touching his skin, running her fingers through thick hair. The thought shocked her but didn't discount the shiver of delight that swamped her. But again, the niggling doubts that brought the wall of reserve that never allowed her to go further than a kiss came to the fore.

Taking his hands from behind his head, an arm circling her shoulder, he rested her head on his chest. 'Miriam, we can't go on like this.' His husky voice held a plea.

Was he trying to scare her? Was there someone else? The traitorous thoughts upset her. Mitch was a flirt but she believed he was honest and would never two-time her. But the voice of uncertainty persisted. *That's what I believed about Terry Rawling, that he was earnest and sincere, and look where that got me.*

The internal fight too much, Miriam disentangled herself, stood and moved over to the wireless, where she turned up the volume and Bing Crosby's warm baritone voice singing 'You Made Me Love You (I Didn't Want to Do It)' resounded in the room. She looked over to Mitch, whose look had changed to pensive, and she wondered if the song's words were affecting him too. Paradoxically, the need to reassure him washed over her.

The song finished, Miriam no longer wanted to fight the desire she felt. This was now, she thought; the future could take care of itself – if there was a future for them. Moving towards the couch she sank down beside Mitch, and as he surrounded her with strong arms, she was restored to having faith in him. She had to be extremely unlucky if both men in her life turned out to be cads.

'You do know,' he said as he stroked her hair, his chin over her head, 'I'll be posted down south anytime.'

A chill of fear surged through her. 'I've tried not to think about it.'

'When the time comes, I mightn't be able to get word to you.'

She pushed away from him, sat up and analysed his face but his handsome features were inscrutable. The qualms were back. Twice bitten and all that. Miriam wanted clarification, honesty. 'Do you have feelings for me, Mitch? Or am I just another flame?'

He sat up and pushed her away from him. His expression contorted into one of hurt. 'Honey, is that what you think?'

Miriam's newfound confidence came to the fore, told her this was not the time to be meek. She had to know. 'I'm scared I'm just another conquest, Mitch.' Her heart pounded and she felt sure he'd notice.

He stared momentarily, then amusement flickered in those mesmeric green eyes. 'Yep, I sure did like a flirtation in the past... but it was harmless, the ladies in question weren't looking for anything lasting. And I've explained about Veronica.' His gaze turned serious. 'Being with you is different. I don't have to be lover boy or the life and soul of the party. I can just be plain ol' me. You don't know what that means to me.' He touched her face, his fingertips trailing gently down her cheek. 'I knew when I told you what it was like back home – as believe me that's something I've never told anyone before, excepting Joe – that you're the girl for me.'

Her head against his chest, she heard the thump of his heartbeat. Sometimes in life you had to trust your gut feelings, and hers knew this wasn't an act.

'D'you say that to all the girls?' she asked playfully.

He cocked an eyebrow. 'Only the ones I've fallen in love with.'

The joking atmosphere vanished and they stared at each other. *Fallen in love.* He'd said the words. A satisfying warmth flushed Miriam's chest. Cocooned in a world of newfound trust she put all her misgiving aside and relaxed. He must have sensed the change in her, because taking her in his arms, Miriam allowed herself to be pulled close. His lips when they touched hers were light, as if testing her reaction. The closed door within her unlocking, Miriam's body craved more. Pushing her lips against his, the kiss deepened and she felt the gentle touch of his tongue against hers. He tasted of fruit cake.

She pulled away and opening the buttons of his uniform she slid her fingers beneath and, feeling the firmness of his skin and thick tantalising hairs, she moaned.

'Honey' – his voice was husky – 'don't do this, you're killing me.'

Lifting her cheek with a finger as he looked at her, Miriam saw a need deep in his eyes. A terrifying thought struck her: what if this was the last chance they had? Hearing his strong heartbeat, the thought that one of these days it could stop made a physical ache of sorrow she couldn't bear stab within her.

*I don't want to live a life of regret.*

Taking his hand, she stood. Mitch cocked his head as he looked quizzically at her. In answer she led him to the bedroom door where a flash of enlightenment crossed his face.

'Honey, are you su—'

She put a forefinger on his lips, breathed, 'I love you too.'

# 33

## MAY 1944

As she stood before Miss Balfour's desk in the office, Rosie quaked. The mistress had sent for Rosie after breakfast, and the only reason the mistress could possibly want to see her was because she had news about Daddy. As she stood facing the mistress, suddenly scared it was something she didn't want to hear, the impulse to flee from the room overcame Rosie.

'Sit down, dear.'

Miss Balfour was being extra nice and that worried Rosie, too. Her legs weak, she sank into the chair.

'It's good news, Rosie.' Miss Balfour beamed.

Rosie let out the biggest breath she didn't even know she was holding.

'The police were in touch with Sir Henley earlier this morning to say they've found your father.'

'They've found Daddy,' she repeated, making sure she'd heard right.

Miss Balfour nodded vigorously. 'Yes.'

The full impact of what the mistress was saying

resonating with Rosie, images began emerging in her mind – Daddy tall and hunched, walking with a crutch. Just thinking about him brought a warm, safe feeling within her.

'There's no word about your mother,' Miss Balfour said, looking unsure.

Then all at once the memory of Daddy's stern face that night appeared in Rosie's mind. *Mam died*, his voice said. It was as if someone had punched her in the stomach. Rosie felt as though she was experiencing the loss of Mam all over again. Tears spilled from her eyes.

'Rosie, dear.' Miss Balfour stood and hurried around the desk to comfort her. 'It's a lot for you to take in for now but—'

'It isn't Daddy, miss.' Rosie hiccupped a sob. 'It's Mam. I can remember Daddy telling me now, she died at work in a raid.' She dissolved into sobs and cried and cried, her tummy hurting; she thought she would never stop.

Eventually, when there were no more tears left, Miss Balfour brought out a handkerchief from a pocket in her frock, a clean one that Rosie felt bad about using. Despite being sad, Rosie was glad she remembered Mam and somehow, she felt lighter now that she'd cried like a baby.

'I'm so sorry, Rosie.' The mistress squeezed her shoulder then returned to her seat where she gave Rosie that prolonged look grownups give kids when they aren't sure what else to say.

Rosie did what she normally did and, sniffing, tried to make things better for Miss Balfour. 'I'm very sad but I'm happier now I can remember what happened.' Despite saying this, Rosie struggled not to cry again because in her mind's eye, she kept seeing Mam and could feel a horrible ache of longing that wouldn't go away.

'That's the spirit, Rosie dear. At least you know now why

there's been no mention of your mother, but remember your father's been found,' she added quickly.

'We live in a flat, miss. Was Daddy there?'

'No, Rosie. The neighbours said he'd moved away. On further investigation the police asked at the post office who said they'd been informed to deliver your father's post to a different address.'

'Daddy moved?'

'Yes, to...' Miss Balfour peered at a piece of paper on her desk. 'Stanhope Road. Apparently, he runs a cobbler's shop and lives in a flat above.'

*Daddy mends people's shoes, I remember.*

'He knows about you, Rosie, and I've been told he's coming to see you as soon as possible.'

It felt unreal, too good to be true.

Then her newly found elation faltered. 'But he didn't try and find me.'

'Rosie, we don't know that.' The mistress shrugged. 'Those are all the details I've been given. Sir Henley spoke to the police on the telephone and related what was said to me.'

Rosie didn't know what to think. The daddy she knew would never stop searching for her. What if they'd got it wrong and it wasn't him after all?

---

Miriam, watching Rosie closely, knew by the way the girl's face blanched that the good news about her father came as a shock and it would take time for the reality to sink in. The poor child had been heartbroken at the memory of what happened to her mother and who could blame her. Her young life, like so many others, had been blighted by this war.

Speaking in a slow, deliberate manner, she told Rosie,

'Run along to the kitchen to see Mrs Stewart. She'll give you a cup of hot milk and if you're lucky a ginger biscuit. I'll tell Mrs Murray what's happened and when you're ready, you can join the others for the rest of morning class.' The idea was to keep Rosie's life during this trying period as normal as possible.

'Yes, miss.' As suspected, Rosie looked on the verge of tears again.

Miriam had warned Mrs Stewart about the situation with Rosie earlier and that she would be sending her to the kitchen, the only place Miriam could think of where the child would have space to recover, without the others pestering her with questions. She also knew that, although Cook was prone to have a good moan, she was an astute woman and would have the good sense to say and do the right thing.

'Don't worry, Rosie. As soon as Sir Henley hears anything more, I'll let you know.'

Rosie, ashen-faced and dazed, nodded. Making for the door, she stopped and turned. 'When d'you think Daddy will come to see me?'

'I don't know, Rosie, but as soon as I hear, I'll let you know.' Miriam stood. 'Would you like me to accompany you to the kitchen?'

'No thank you.'

Miriam's heart squeezed as she watched the child take a gulping breath before leaving. She sat for a while mulling things over in her mind. How come the father survived the raid and didn't come forward to claim his daughter? She let out a frustrated groan, too many questions without answers. The thing was, Rosie was young and had the resilience to overcome life's trials and for that at least, the Lord be praised.

But what about Alice? The two girls were best friends

and, indeed, as Rita once pointed out, Alice had changed for the better recently and the transformation gladdened Miriam's heart. She worried about the effect Rosie's good fortune would have on Alice. Especially now when Rosie would probably be leaving. Miriam rubbed the back of her neck. One day the orphanage would be returning to South Shields, and without Alice, and though she would be provided for in service, she wouldn't have the familiarity of someone who loved and cared for her – namely the mother she didn't know. Neither would she have a friend, and Miriam worried her daughter would go back to her rebellious ways and land herself in trouble.

Rotating her head to reduce the sharp pain that had now moved from her stiff shoulders into her neck, Miriam let out a disconsolate sigh. If only she could find a way for Alice to move to South Shields.

Her eyes strayed to the daily newspaper that lay on the top of the cluttered desk. Renewed anguish came to taunt her, making her stomach clench. These days, she devoured every item of war news from both the wireless and national newspaper because she knew whatever was happening down south would affect Mitch. A week ago, when she last saw him, although on the surface he had appeared natural, there had been an underlying edginess to him and the dark pupils of his eyes signalled a message of foreboding. Something was afoot, something he wasn't telling and she knew his days here in the north were numbered. They lay snuggled together in the middle hollow of the bed, Miriam's head on his bare chest listening to the thump of his heartbeat.

'When I go,' Mitch had told her, 'I'll get word to you somehow.'

There it was: the admission that he knew he would be going sometime soon. She'd known not to ask questions, but there were so many other things she wanted to say even though they were either too sentimental, or her fears talking.

In the end she said, 'Stay safe, Mitch. And come back to me.'

He inched away from her. 'Don't worry, honey. I don't intend on going anywhere.' It was said jokily but his sombre eyes told a different story. 'Always remember, you're the gal for me.'

It was a few days later, when Miriam riffled through the morning post, that she saw an envelope that had her heart skipping a beat when she recognised Mitch's handwriting on the front. Slitting the envelope open with a sword-shaped letter opener, she took out a sheet of paper.

*Honey,*

*We've just been told all furlough has been postponed till further notice, so I guess we know what that means.*

*Love you, take care of yourself.*

*Mitch xx*

Miriam re-read 'love you', then held the letter against her heart. Sighing, she indulged in a smile of happiness. But she was letting sentiment get the better of her. Mitch's crew, no doubt, were to be posted down south in readiness for the second front.

The smile was wiped from her face.

———

'What's up?' Alice asked Rosie. The two of them were in the sun after dinner on one of the grassy terraces in front of the big house. 'Why did Miss Balfour send for you? When you came into class you looked as though you'd had a fright.'

Rosie gave a wan smile. 'I did sort of.' She took a deep breath. 'Miss Balfour says the police went to the address I gave her but Daddy wasn't there. But guess what?'

Fearing what was coming next, Alice tensed.

'The police have found out from the post office that Daddy had moved.'

'And have they found him?' Alice's mouth dry, she swallowed hard.

'Yes. I can't believe it! He lives above a shop. He's a cobbler.'

'Cobbler?'

'Yes. He mends shoes.' Rosie's face clouded. 'Alice, what if it's a mistake and it isn't him? I mean, why didn't he come and find me?'

Staring up at the blue sky, Alice didn't answer because she felt mean that she hoped it really was a mistake. Watching as white clouds scudded past as if in a hurry to be somewhere else, she hated herself for not being happy for Rosie's sake. If the situation was reversed Rosie would never think of herself but be thrilled for Alice. She was reminded how Rosie said that she pretended to be an actress playing a part because people believed what they saw. Taking a deep breath, Alice decided to try it out.

A smile pasted on her face, she assured Rosie, 'Course it'll be your dad. The police don't get it wrong.' She saw hope shine in Rosie's eyes. 'This is what you've been dreaming of.'

. . .

As Alice undressed for bed that night beneath a tent-like nightdress so her nakedness couldn't be seen, she heard the dormitory door squeak open. Peering out, she saw Miss Balfour enter accompanied by a shaft of late golden evening sunlight. The mistress, smiling at orphans as she passed, made her way between the row of slim beds to where Rosie was undressing. Sitting on Rosie's bed, Miss Balfour patted the space beside her. Heads bent together, the mistress began to speak. As Rosie listened, she put her hand over her mouth and as the mistress put an arm around her shoulders, a stab of jealousy knifed Alice. In all the years she'd know Miss Balfour, she'd never shown an outward display of affection for her.

Remembering her resolution to put on a brave face, Alice steeled herself for whatever it was Rosie would tell her, drowning out the little voice in her mind that goaded, *Go on, you're really hoping it isn't Rosie's dad.*

Miss Balfour stood and, giving Rosie a broad smile, she retraced her steps up the dormitory, chatting to orphans as she passed and checking on the little ones who, oblivious to the goings on, were sound asleep. Making her way to the doorway, the mistress only smiled at Alice. Sorely disappointed, Alice sank down on the bed.

After a while, Rosie appeared alongside the bed, declaring with a hurt expression, 'Don't you want to know what Miss Balfour said?'

Alice didn't because she suspected it was something she didn't want to hear.

'Course I do,' she said, hoping her voice didn't betray how she felt.

'Daddy's telephoned Sir Henley. He's travelling up by train tomorrow. Miss Balfour says he can't wait to see me.'

'Blimey! I'm excited for you, Rosie.'

# 34

Rosie didn't sleep a wink that night and the next morning in class, she couldn't take in a word of what Mrs Murray said during the English lesson. She hardly ate any dinner and was told by the mistress afterwards that she was excused going to school because Daddy was expected anytime during the afternoon. Loathing the thought of spending time on her own, she joined Hazel and the little ones for an afternoon walk in the woods.

When she returned, Miss Balfour was waiting for in the office doorway.

'Come inside,' she told Rosie.

Following the mistress into the office she felt dizzy and weak.

'Your father's arrived,' the mistress told her in a bubbly voice. 'Sir Henley says you're to meet in his study where the two of you won't be disturbed.' Then her expression changed and her brow crinkled in concern. 'Rosie, I hope you don't mind but I've explained that you've remembered your mother died in a previous raid.' She gave a sad little smile. 'I thought it best that you both didn't have to broach the matter. That doesn't mean you can't talk about your mother, if you want,' she hurriedly put in.

Rosie nodded; she couldn't face having to talk about Mam. 'I'm glad you did, miss.'

That morning, she had dressed with care, making sure her boots were polished and tying the green ribbon Alice had given her that she'd never worn into a perfect bow in her hair. But feeling jittery, nothing seemed right – how she wished the white blouse she wore didn't look washed out, or her kilt hadn't lost its pleats and was so short she had to keep wrenching it down.

As she stood outside the study door, Miss Balfour at her side, Rosie felt sick with nerves. What if it wasn't Daddy, after all?

Miss Balfour rapped on the door and when it opened, the laird ushered them into the room.

Then, there he was. Daddy.

He was taller than she remembered and his brown hair had streaks of silver running through the sides and his grey eyes grew scarily wide when he saw her.

'Polly.' Using a stick, he walked over to her, and enveloped her with an arm. 'It really is you.'

As she stood stiffly in his embrace, all she could think of was Daddy didn't use a crutch anymore. Neither did he smell like she recalled, but a bit sweaty. As he held her tight, she disentangled herself because somehow, it didn't feel right. Feeling awkward and shy, she looked around the room but Miss Balfour and Sir Henley had disappeared. She was alone with him.

He stood back and stared at her, the white of his wide eyes appearing to bulge. 'I thought I'd lost you, Polly. Thank

God you were spared.' His voice wasn't the same as she remembered but faint and husky.

This wasn't anything like she imagined. She didn't know what to say or how to act. Maybe it was because she'd lost her memory.

She hadn't spoken, she realised, and said the first thing that came to mind. 'I couldn't remember you.' Then the question that burnt within her since she'd learnt they'd found Daddy surfaced. 'Why didn't you come and find me?'

His shoulder drooped. 'I didn't try, Polly, because I thought you'd died.'

So he hadn't searched for her. But why did he think she'd died? All he had to do was ask at the shelter and they would have told him a girl had been taken to hospital. Her tummy sank like it did when she slipped on one of the grassy terraces in icy weather. She didn't understand why Daddy was making things up. She remembered how different he was after Mam died. Maybe, he was better off without her.

'I'm Rosie not Polly!' she cried.

As he gaped open-mouthed at her, the walls in the room seemed to close in. Rosie needed to be away from him. She made for the door and, wrenching it open, she ran pell-mell along the passageway.

'Polly, come back.' His shaky voice echoed along the passage.

Making for the kitchen, she opened the door and found Mrs Stewart standing at the sink. Turning, Cook gave Rosie a look of surprise.

'Whatever's the matter with you, lassie?' she asked. 'You're as white as the pinny I'm wearing.'

As tears spilled from Rosie's eyes, Cook came and put her fleshy arms around her.

---

After meeting with his daughter, George Pearson sought Miriam in her office. Though thin, there was a solidness about the man and an air of sincerity about him.

Sitting opposite her, face strained, he told her, 'It feels unreal.' He sighed, his hands trailing down his face. 'You see, I thought she'd died in the shelter and there wasn't a day went by when I didn't think about her.' He appeared to struggle with his emotions. 'When I saw her, that she was actually here, I didn't know how to...' Overcome, he couldn't go on.

'The news must have come as a great shock,' Miriam helped.

'It did.' He stared into space as if reliving the moment, then his eyes connected with hers as he said, 'But a wonderful one. When the local bobby came knocking at the door, I couldn't take the news in at first and kept asking if he was sure of his facts. Afterwards, all I could think of was to head up here and see for myself.'

'To make sure it was your daughter.'

'Yes. It seemed too good to be true.' The man looked as though he was still in shock.

'It's perfectly natural you felt that way.'

'Can I be frank with you, Miss Balfour?'

Miriam smiled, encouragingly. 'Of course.'

'The thing is, I didn't handle the meeting well. I didn't allow for Polly's feelings. I just thought we'd pick up where we left off. But it was as if...' Swallowing hard, she watched his Adam's apple go up and down. 'As if we were strangers. She wouldn't let me explain why I didn't come looking for her. Why I thought she was dead.' His blue eyes looked haunted. 'She just ran off.'

Miriam felt for this man who couldn't hide his raw emotions. 'It's a lot for Rosie – *Polly* – to take in too, Mr Pearson.'

He looked at her levelly. 'I'm at a loss what to do. If only her mother was—'

'Mr Pearson, you love your daughter, and she loves you. Believe me, that's enough for now. She just needs time.'

Too choked to speak, he gave a grateful smile. After a while, his composure restored, he went on. 'When I saw her, realised that indeed she was my Polly, I wanted to take her in my arms and never let go.' His sad expression was heartbreaking. 'The intention was to take her home as soon as I possibly could. But that can't happen now, I realise.'

Miriam asked, bemused, 'Why? We'll miss Polly, of course, but she's rightfully yours and it's something she has no doubt desired, as all orphans do, to be part of a family.'

The idea of Alice longing for that very same thing made Miriam's heart squeeze. How she wished Alice could have this chance Rosie had been given – to be secure in the knowledge she was loved and valued. If only she could tell her she was. The sad thing being, the only person Alice had allowed to crack the shell of wariness she'd worn since a child, had trusted enough to call a friend, was now to be taken from her.

Mr Pearson was saying, 'Polly's attitude has changed towards me. I don't want to rush her into something when she isn't ready.' A beseeching look came into his eyes. 'I've lost my wife; I don't intend to lose my daughter too.'

'Mr Pearson, like you, Polly needs time to assimilate what's happened. You'll see, she'll come round to be the daughter you obviously adore.'

Shaking his head as if to clear it, he grimaced and sat forward in the chair. 'With all that's happened recently I can't think straight.'

'I'm not surprised. These past months have been difficult for both you and Polly. I would imagine you've both changed.'

'I've not been the same since Jane, my wife, died and I've reflected on how difficult that must have been for Polly when there was just the two of us.'

Miriam admired his forthrightness. 'Can I ask, Mr Pearson, what your plans are for you and Polly?'

He looked dumbfounded. 'I don't have any. I thought it was just a matter of taking her home and continuing as we were before. I realise now it isn't that simple.' He rubbed his eyes then looked up with a perplexed expression. 'I want to do what's right for Polly. D'you have any suggestions, Miss Balfour?'

This was his daughter, Miriam considered, but he was willing to swallow his pride and ask for advice. She liked this man.

She pondered for a while and finally said, 'Like you, because of all that's happened she's confused and it'll take time for Ro— *Polly* to adjust. How about you leave her here for the time being while you start spending time together? I've no doubt you'll know when she's ready to leave and return home.'

A look of hope crossed his face. 'By Jiminy you've cracked it. I could find digs and visit.' He gave a wistful shake of the head. 'Home wasn't the same anymore. I couldn't bear the memories in the old place and so I moved. It'll all be new to Polly and so all the more reason to wait until she's ready. She's had enough heartache. I don't want to cause her any more.'

Miriam couldn't help but ask, 'What about your business? Can you leave so suddenly?'

He stood, his tall lean frame overshadowing her. 'It's a

case of having to. I have some savings put by that'll see me through.'

Again, Miriam was taken aback by his frankness to share his affairs. This was a man of integrity, who didn't worry what others thought.

'I've taken up enough of your time, Miss Balfour. I'll bid you good day.'

There were all kinds of questions buzzing like inquisitive bees in Miriam's mind, especially about the aftermath of the raid and why he thought his daughter had died but these thoughts would keep for another day. It was important to see that for the time being things ran smoothly for Polly – she must call her that now as that was the way forward – and her father.

'About accommodation—'

Mr Pearson held up his hand to silence her. 'There's no need for you to be concerned. There's bound to be a room in the village where I can board. But thank you, anyway.'

His speech was formal but nicely so and his manners impeccable; Miriam liked George Pearson and was glad for Ros— Polly's sake that she had such a decent and loving father.

'When d'you think would be the best time for me to visit with Polly?'

Miriam, head to one side, thought. 'How about you meet after school in the afternoon. With the evenings being light for so long I've allowed the children an extra hour at bedtime.'

'That would suit me fine and I hope Polly too. I don't want to rush things. I'll return home tonight to put a notice on the shop door and to collect some things. But I hope to make it back in time for tomorrow's visit.' He moved towards the door. Then, turning, his affable smile a delight to see, he said, 'Thank you, Miss Balfour, you've been a great help and I appreciate it.'

Then he was gone, his amiable presence lingering in the room.

---

Alice found Rosie in the woods, on the other side of the fence that surrounded the big house. It was late afternoon and the Lumberjills' voices and the sound of sawing could be heard deep within the trees. Making her way along the earthen path and through the creaky gate, Alice headed for where Rosie sat beneath a sturdy sycamore tree. Her back resting against the tree trunk, when she saw Alice approach, Rosie sat up. Her eyes red and puffy, she looked as though she'd been crying but Alice didn't comment because, personally, she would die of embarrassment if anyone found her in such a state.

Deflecting her gaze, she said, 'I couldn't find you after class and I was worried.' When Rosie didn't answer she continued, 'I knew you'd be here because this is your favourite thinking place away from everybody.' Still no answer. 'Are you coming in for supper?'

Rosie dropped her chin on her chest and replied in a muffled voice, 'I'm not hungry.'

'I asked Miss Balfour about you. She said not to worry, you just needed time to yourself as you didn't feel too good.'

'I don't.' Rosie picked at the sleeve of the worn-looking cardigan she wore.

Initially, Alice had been dreading seeing Rosie after she met with her dad because in her imagination, Rosie would be excited and full of chatter about how wonderful he was and how great life was going to be and Alice was afraid she couldn't handle the situation but she never expected this reaction. She knew she should leave Rosie alone but, desperate to know what happened, she ignored the little voice inside that told her to be reasonable.

She blurted, 'How did it go with your dad?'

Rosie turned up her head and her tear-stained face held a dejected expression. 'Oh, Alice, it was awful.' Her pink eyes swam with tears. 'The worst part was he told me he didn't bother looking for me.'

'Why?' Alice was genuinely puzzled. The loving way Rosie had talked about her dad before had made Alice envious.

Rosie shrugged. 'He said he thought I was dead.'

'Why did he think such a thing?'

In a rare moment of obstinacy Rosie pressed her lips together before speaking. 'I never asked cos I ran away.'

Moving towards Rosie, Alice hunkered down beside her. She couldn't bear to see Rosie so troubled. Despite herself, she wanted Rosie to be happy. Rosie had taught her that: to think of others.

'Why did you run away? You were looking forward to seeing him.'

Rosie hung her head down and mumbled, 'He wasn't how I remembered.'

'Why? What did he do?'

Rosie looked up, her eyes round and anguished. 'He just seemed changed and nothing like how I remembered him. He smelt different and even his voice wasn't the same.' She shook her head as if blotting out the scene. 'It didn't feel right when he called me Polly.'

'But that's your name,' Alice said, bemused.

'Don't you see, that was before. I feel like Rosie now.'

Alice didn't see at all. 'But he's your dad. Did he say he wanted to take you back home?'

Rosie gave Alice a sidelong glance. 'When I was with him, I remembered what it was really like at home, how I felt hemmed in.' She screwed up her face as if perplexed. 'It's hard to explain. I loved Mam and Daddy and didn't want to disappoint them.'

Alice, even more baffled, asked, 'Why would they be?'

Rosie shook her head. 'It was just how they were. I've been thinking about it. Mam said second best wasn't good enough in our family. So, I tried to be the best at everything at school, playing the piano, tap dance competitions. The worst was when Mam volunteered me to do a singing act at church concerts, she told everyone I had the sweetest voice.' She clapped her hands on her cheeks to show how embarrassing that was.

'Why didn't you just say no?'

Her face earnest, Rosie thought for a moment as though trying to find the right words. 'I dunno. Somehow it seemed their happiness depended on me. But I never felt I made them proud and now Mam's gone...' Her chin trembling, she couldn't continue.

It was too complicated for Alice, who couldn't have cared less what effect she'd had on others – that is, until Rosie came into her life.

She linked arms with her friend. 'I'm so sorry.' And Alice was.

They sat for a while hearing the rustling of wind through the trees, birds tweeting and far-off sounds of the Lumberjills working.

'What are you going to do?' Alice finally asked.

'I don't know. It's like I'm frozen inside. I like being here where I'm Rosie and don't have to please anyone.' Her face became sad. 'I know deep down I love Daddy but everything's changed. He's never been the same since Mam died.'

Alice realised Rosie was scared and couldn't make up her mind. It came to her suddenly that her hopes for the future, that the pair of them could one day live together, could never come true. She had to grow up, accept the fact that after her birthday their paths would never cross again. Rosie had a chance that she could only dream about and she wanted to help because that's what Rosie would do for her, of that Alice had no doubt.

'Remember when you'd lost your memory. This is all you dreamt about, Polly. To find your family.'

Polly – as that's what Alice decided to call her from now on – gave her a peeved look. 'Don't call me that.'

'Polly's your real name and you don't know how lucky you are. I wish I had a dad who came looking for me.'

'I don't feel lucky, I don't feel anything. I want to stay here with you where I can just be me.'

Polly was mixed up and Alice knew what she must do.

Steeling herself, she retorted, 'It's my birthday soon and I'll be moving away. So, we won't be able to see each other anymore.'

'But you said you'd find a job and somewhere for us to live together.'

'You don't really believe that could come true, do you?' Hearing the scorn in her voice, she almost cracked and apologised.

As tears glistened in Polly's eyes, Alice hardened her heart. From now on this was how the future must be.

# 35

George Pearson descended the steep steps using a walking stick and, approaching the door, put the key that Miss Balfour, a charming lady, had given him, in the lock. He was tired after a tedious train journey; the train teemed with passengers and there were no vacant seats, so he'd stood in the corridor some of the way to the border country, until a soldier, noticing George's walking stick, offered him a seat. He'd returned to Teviot Hall, weary and hungry, in the early evening, so too late for his visit with Polly.

Miss Balfour greeted him and duly informed him that the gentleman (a sir, no less) who owned this grand place had asked how the meeting had gone between Polly and him.

'I told him you intended to find a place to stay so you could familiarise yourself with Polly again.' She held up a large door key and grinned. 'When he heard, Sir Henley insisted you stay in one of the bedrooms in the old servants' quarters.'

So it was that George had the good fortune to find

himself here in a room of his own. Dumping his suitcase on the squeaking bed, he surveyed the diminutive space. With crisp white sheets and a plumped pillow, the slim bed looked as though it had been freshly made. A chest of drawers and bedside locker, with a candle in a saucer, was the only furniture and with washing facilities down the narrow passageway, George decided this would do him grand until Polly came to terms with all that had happened and was ready to return home. He mused about what Miss Balfour had told him: that he could eat his meals in the kitchen of the big house. His appetite diminished these past months, it would be a treat to have food put before him that he hadn't cooked for himself.

A sense of longing for Jane returned – George corrected himself, the Jane she was before. He missed the companionship of having his own special person. What he didn't miss was her fastidious ways when everything had to be prefect. Nothing was ever good enough, not only was their flat too small and dingy, but it was also in the wrong area of town, and as for him – apparently, he hadn't outgrown his impoverished beginnings and had no ambition. Though he loathed to admit it, Jane pushed Polly to live out *her* dreams – namely to be noticed, to be a somebody. God help him, he didn't interfere mainly because he loved Jane and understood why she was the way she was. She'd had an invalid mother, and a dictatorial father who commanded that Jane forget her ambition to go to secretarial college and work her way up in an office. She was made to stay at home to look after her mother and so, he believed, it was this that led Jane to live out her aspirations through Polly.

Guilt stabbed him and George, sighing, massaged the area above his nose with his fingertips. He was at fault too;

he'd allowed Jane to get her way. He suspected it was laziness on his part; he took the easy way out and did nothing, convincing himself they were a normal couple with the ups and downs of family life but they loved each other and things would work out in the end. And if Hitler and his bloody war hadn't killed innocent folk like Jane, then he would never... A warning bell in his head told him to go no further and, slamming shut that particular door in his mind, George, defeated, sank onto the sagging mattress. As he sat there in the silence, and thought of the reason why he was there, his spirit lifted. He found himself thanking his maker every day that Polly, who he'd mourned over the past months, had been saved. Life was worth living again.

Opening the catches on the attaché suitcase, he took out the smart white shirt and pullover Jane had knitted for him, that he would wear tomorrow when he saw Polly. His intention was to build the relationship back to the loving father and daughter experience they'd shared before the raid.

A rap at the door broke into his thoughts. Wondering who the dickens it could be, on opening it he found a smiling Miss Balfour standing there.

'I just wanted to check you'd settled in and to tell you that Polly knows you're here,' she told him, her eyes taking in his attire. 'She's agreed to meet with you tomorrow after dinner before she goes back to school. It's forecast to be sunny and so she'll see you by the lake in front of the big house.' She hesitated. 'Apologies if I'm being presumptuous but I thought a short visit might be wise to begin with.'

'No need for an apology, I agree.' And George did. He couldn't bear the anticipation of waiting until school finished before he saw his daughter. 'Thank you, I'll be there promptly after dinner.' There was an awkward pause that he felt it only right he should fill. 'You've been most kind, Miss Balfour. I'd invite you in but it would seem servants of old mustn't have had visitors as there's nowhere for them to sit.'

She grinned at his attempt at light-hearted conversation. 'Poor souls were probably worked to death and would have hated the thought of anyone disrupting their sleep time.'

They both laughed.

'I must be off.' She made to move then hesitated. 'I do hope all goes well tomorrow, Mr Pearson.'

After she left, thoughts of Miss Balfour lingered in George's mind. She probably came from a well-to-do family with parents who adored her and were proud of all she'd achieved. There was no sign of a wedding ring, he considered, as he got back to unpacking his belongings, but that wasn't unusual because teaching was considered a vocation and teachers in general were married to their job.

Considering the events of the past few days, he gave a shake of the head. What with meeting a sir no less and now hobnobbing with a headmistress, he would have to watch his Ps and Qs. There again, in George's book no man was better than the other, and he didn't agree with all this cap tipping to supposed betters. He was a simple man from a working-class background, and as far as he was concerned, home was where his hat was. A job at the shipyard, marriage and a family had been enough to keep him content. As if he received a kick in the gut, George, hand paused mid-air with a pair of rolled up socks in it, remembered that then came the bloody war, his injuries, Jane having to get a job and the result— He sank on the bed as he recalled the moment of truth when his life changed forever.

. . .

As George sat on a grassy mound at the side of the lake beneath the shade of tall swaying birch trees, he saw Polly coming. She appeared on the top terrace in front of the big house and didn't appear to be in a hurry to meet him. His stomach now an anxious knot of anticipation, he wondered what he could do to make things right between the two of them. Polly's reaction when they first met had floored him. In his naivety, he had anticipated that there'd be a joyful and undoubtedly tearful reunion.

As a soft breeze swept her long blonde hair over her face, Polly brushed it back with a hand to reveal an angelic elfin face and George's heart melted. The reality sank in that, by God, against all the odds she was here and nothing else mattered. He loved her, and as Miss Balfour said, that was enough for now. Time didn't matter – George could wait as long as it took, his mission in life would be to provide for and protect her.

She was walking along the path towards the lakeside now and, spotting him, she paused, unsure. Using the walking stick, he heaved himself up and gave her a welcome little wave.

'I wish now I hadn't been so greedy and left the crusts from my sarnies and we could have fed the ducks,' he said in greeting. 'Then again I did them a favour, they'd probably sink if they ate a morsel of that national loaf.'

She didn't smile but hovered a few yards away. Biting her thumbnail, she turned and watched the ducks as they glided over the still water, leaving a trail in their wake.

He tried a different tack. 'Did you know that bakers can't sell a national loaf until it's a day old?'

She turned towards him, a flicker of interest in her ponderous blue eyes. 'Why?' She edged closer.

*That's my girl*, he thought, *smart and inquisitive.*

'Because stale bread cuts with no wastage, unlike fresh bread.'

She pondered then nodded as she stored the information.

He told himself to tread carefully and not say anything personal that would unnerve her, though questions teemed in his mind. Most importantly, did Polly still have nightmares concerning Jane's death? George cursed himself that he hadn't told her more sensitively at the time but for the life of him, he hadn't known how he could. He was reeling with shock himself and so mad he didn't recover for a long while. George was a straight-talking man but he would never tell her the facts of her mother's death.

'How are things at school? Are you doing well?' He knew immediately by her stiffening posture that he'd blundered misguidedly on a raw nerve.

She shrugged, noncommittally. 'Fine.' Then added, 'I don't play the piano or go to dance lessons no more.' A pause. 'Even if I could, I wouldn't want to.'

Was that a note of rebellion in her tone? What had happened to his little girl? he wondered. Polly was growing up but that wasn't all, he realised; she had changed and with all that had happened, who could blame her. Big events in your life do change you, George knew as once again he was transported back to Burma, and the godawful trek as his battalion carried a fighting retreat through the country. The scenes of that time, playing in his mind's eye, made him shudder.

'Dad, are you all right?'

Her voice brought him back from the torment and seeing her baby-blue eyes fill with concern, George relaxed. For there she was, his sensitive little girl, and instantly he knew his job was to be understanding, patient and honest. But the word 'Dad' disappointed because she'd always called him Daddy before.

'I'm fine, but how about you? You've been through a lot since the night of the bombing.'

He saw her flinch. Awkwardly, lowering himself to his knees, George manoeuvred his backside onto the mound of grass, patting the space beside him. To his delight, she came to sit next to him. How he wanted to wrap his arms around her, give her the biggest cuddle. Eyes averted, he watched the ducks as one of them, wings flapping wildly and skidding on the water, chased another to the other side of the lake.

'They say you were injured and had to go to hospital and that you lost your memory.' His gaze never left the ducks as they sailed hastily away in single file from the aggressor. 'Did it return all at once?'

For a long while she didn't answer and, chancing a glance, he saw she too watched the birds.

'My ribs don't hurt anymore now.' A pause. 'The first time I started to remember properly was at a teatime get-together with the Americans when Sir Henley played "You Are My Sunshine".'

George, overcome, because it was that particular song that she'd played for his birthday the last day he'd seen her, forgot himself and made to give her a hug. Polly, as only an agile child could, shot up to her feet and, like a nervous deer, she made to move off.

'Please don't go.' At a loss, he pleaded, 'Why are you behaving like this?'

She didn't move but stood with her head hanging down as though interested in her feet.

'Whatever it is, Polly, I promise I'll understand.'

She lifted her head and stared at him with uncertain eyes, as if deciding whether she should confide in him. 'I don't want to leave here where I don't have to be best all the time or be on show.' Her voice quivered. 'Mam died and I'm sad because I don't think I made her proud. You never talked about her and you seemed mad all the time and I thought I was the reason.' Pausing for breath, she looked stunned as if she hadn't meant to blurt all those things.

A blaze of outrage overcame George. This was his fault. Insecure in his marriage, he'd concentrated on keeping his wife happy and allowed their precious daughter to suffer. The worst was he had noticed, but had chosen to live in a make-believe world of happy families when life was anything but. What kind of father was he when his daughter would prefer to live in an orphanage than live with him?

'I don't feel like I did before. I miss Mam but I can't...' He saw her chin trembling.

'Oh, Polly.' He struggled to stand up, his intention to give her a hug, but then thought better of it. So much had happened to his little girl she was confused and didn't know what she wanted anymore. He realised that not even her home would be the same and she couldn't deal with the thought of another change. Polly was frightened and here, albeit an orphanage, was where she felt safe.

'How about you come home for a visit?' he suggested. 'See your friend, what's her name... Marjorie Binks, that's it, she'll be so happy to see you. Lots of people will.'

Polly's anguished eyes met his. 'I don't want any more friends; I have one here called Alice Blakely and I don't want to leave her.'

And with that she hurried off.

---

Picking up the newspaper from the doormat next morning, Miriam felt her heart rate quicken as she read the headlines. *Allied Planes Pound Europe.* The idea Mitch could be in *Alabama Beauty* in one of those raids made her sick to the stomach with fear. Along with the post, there had been a letter from Mitch saying he was now down south. Moving into the office and taking the letter from the top drawer of her desk, she re-read it, imagining his voice as her gaze scanned the words.

> *Sweetheart* (Sweetheart! Elation soared within her like a kite taking flight.)
>
> *Here we are in a place called* (the next bit censored was unreadable)... *somewhere down south. God almighty, the convoy we were in took forever with all the traffic driving south. Can't say much more but you can guess what's going on.*
>
> *I'm fine and dandy but wish I was with you and can't wait till this war is over when we can hitch up. Don't worry about me as only the good die young and I guess that counts me out.*
>
> *Love, Mitch*

Hitch up? As in get married? Miriam reeled.

That moment, the door burst open and Rita barged in. Startled, Miriam made to return the letter to the drawer but not before Rita's sharp eyes saw.

'I've left Hazel in charge of the class.' Her eyes never left the letter. 'Is that from your American chap?'

Miriam felt the heat in her cheeks. Of course Rita knew; she missed nothing. Neither did Walter, but the thing was, did they know the extent of the affair? Father would class her as a woman of sin (loose living it was called in these days of war) but Miriam didn't feel as though she'd done anything wrong but give herself to the man she loved. If that was sinful then she was guilty as charged, but in these uncertain times when the future for airmen especially was grim, you had to grab your chance of happiness while you could. If anything happened to him, Miriam would have suffered a lifetime of regret for holding back.

'Yes,' she told Rita. 'Mitch has been posted down south.'

'Oh, my Lord, you must be worried stiff with all the activity down there. I'll say a prayer he'll be safe and sound and back with you soon.'

Miriam could have kissed the woman for the concern she displayed both in her voice and expression. Rita, she knew, was principled and yet, here she was condoning Miriam's actions. But that was war for you – when people's behaviour was unfathomable.

'Rumours in the village are increasing about the second front,' Rita was saying, 'with most folk saying it could happen at any time now.'

Miriam didn't want to discuss the invasion as it would undoubtedly mean that Mitch would be involved, a thought that made her stomach plunge as though she were falling from a clifftop.

Obliged to change the subject, she asked, 'Have you taken an inventory from the store cupboard for what's needed for next week's meals?'

Rita, not usually one for subtlety, took the hint. 'I didn't but Mrs Stewart did.' She tore a page out of the jotter she carried and handed it to Miriam.

'Excellent, thanks. I'll get on with—' She paused as something caught her eye out of the office window. Recognising the slumped figure of George Pearson, head down deep in thought passing the window, she made for the front door. She told Rita as she passed, 'I'll get this off to Mrs Craddock. But first I'd like a word with Mr Pearson. He doesn't look very happy.'

'Nor was his wee lassie yesterday when I saw her.' Rita gave sympathetic sigh. 'Such a to do for them both to go through.'

# 36

'Mr Pearson, wait.'

As he made his way out of the courtyard, the voice from behind made George start. As he turned, Miss Balfour hurried to catch him up.

'I'm sorry, I didn't mean to startle you,' she said.

'I'm just having a stretch of the legs after breakfast in the fresh air.'

'I'll join you for a little way, if I may.'

He could tell by her business-like manner that she wanted a word with him. They strolled out of the gate to the path that led to Teviot Hall, him leaning on his stick, his lower spine troubling him after all the travelling.

'I just wondered how you got on yesterday,' she said.

He stopped. 'Not as good as I hoped.' Distractedly, he ran his fingertips through his hair. 'In fact, it didn't go well at all.'

She nodded as though she understood and he wondered if word had spread that Polly was upset when she left him. 'I don't mean to pry but if I can help in any way—'

'The thing is, you were right. Polly needs time to adjust. Losing her memory, this whole business, has upset her more than I realised. My little girl has changed and I don't know how to talk to her anymore.' He struggled with the emotions that welled inside. The last thing he wanted was to break down in front of this strong-willed woman.

'The main thing is you must stay a constant, Mr Pearson. Polly needs stability.'

'I agree but...' Feeling comfortable enough to share his fears, he explained, 'I don't know what to do. Polly doesn't want to come home; she wants to stay here where she feels safe.'

'Perhaps that's because here is familiar since she's regained her memory. Home isn't home anymore. She's had enough change and—'

'Doesn't know how to deal with it,' he finished for her.

Her face contorted with sympathy. 'Believe me, she was enthusiastic when she heard you'd been found.'

A glimmer of hope rose in George, then was dashed as he remembered her words, *I don't have to be best all the time or be on show*. He'd never dreamt that was the way she felt, but he'd known Polly was the same as him, liking her privacy, never pushing to be noticed, content to be behind-the-scenes. George had failed his daughter, preferring for peace's sake to keep his wife happy by telling himself Jane knew what was best.

'It would seem meeting me brought up uncomfortable memories of the past for Polly.'

'In what way?' Miss Balfour's expression was one of empathy.

In an unguarded moment, George felt the need to unburden his doubts. 'In those days I buried my head in the sand to a lot of what was going on. Jane, you see, came from a family of five children.' He winced as a pain shot into his hip and down his leg.

'Let's find somewhere to sit.' She led the way to a bench placed at the top of the sweep of steps on the first grassy terrace.

George, limping by now, followed, easing himself onto the wooden seat.

Squinting in the sunlight, Miss Balfour shaded her eyes with a hand and told him, 'You were saying your wife was one of five children.'

Though a sense of betrayal overcame George that he was discussing Jane in such a way, it was quickly replaced by the knowledge he needed help to restore the close father-and-daughter relationship he and Polly once shared. This intelligent and considerate woman was that very person, he felt sure.

'Jane was the eldest and her dad, a tyrant by all accounts, expected her to take care of the house, her siblings and an invalid mam, which meant she didn't have a life of her own. It was after her mam died that we met. Her dad remarried and his wife took to Jane's younger siblings but not her and it was plain she wanted her out of the house.'

It sounded as though Jane had used him to make her escape, he thought, but nothing was further from the truth. They were smitten from the start when they found themselves sitting next to one another at the cinema watching a Clark Gable film.

'After we had Polly,' he went on, 'Jane didn't want any more children. She'd had enough, you see, after virtually bringing up her siblings. Besides, she didn't want our daughter to have to share. Only the best was good enough and education was paramount.'

'That's not a bad thing,' Miriam commented.

George gave a despairing shake of the head. 'The thing was, not only was Polly expected to succeed at everything, she had to be the best.'

'Oh dear, that must have been hard for her.'

'That's her bone of contention now.' Rubbing his temples with his fingertips, he admitted to himself that if he found the situation difficult, how could he expect Miss Balfour to understand?

'Sometimes we are in the wrong but we do these things with the best intentions.' She surprised him by saying this, and looked as though she herself had personal knowledge of such limitations, which George found difficult to believe.

He felt it necessary to say, 'Jane couldn't help herself being the way she was but above everything, she was a good mother and only wanted Polly to have all the things she'd never had. I guess we're all products of our childhood and Jane was no exception.'

Miriam sighed heavily as though she agreed. They sat in reflective silence in the sunshine, staring down the terraces to the trees and the lake beyond, where water rippled in the breeze.

Miriam broke the silence first. 'Once Polly's back in a home environment and adapts to living with you again, things will change.' Her brow furrowed in concentration. 'How about you remind her of the good times, her friends and—'

'She mentioned a friend here, Alice Blakely?'

'Yes, the two of them of them are inseparable, but unfortunately Alice will be moving on soon. Sir Henley has found her a position as maid in a house in London.'

His brow creased questioningly. 'So far away and in a big city.'

Curiously, Miss Balfour blanched. 'Mr Pearson, these

children are not worldly wise as they've always lived in the confines of an orphanage. The main thing is, Alice will have a roof over her head and live in a decent residence where she'll be safe out of harm's way.'

*She sounds defensive but give the woman credit,* George thought, *she really cares about her charges.*

'I've never thought about what happens to orphans when they leave an orphanage. Doesn't this Alice have any relatives?'

Miss Belfour hesitated. 'She was found on the orphanage doorstep as a baby and no one's claimed her.'

Outraged, George exploded, 'My God, what mother would do such a thing?'

'A desperate one, I would think.'

'But still, never to be in touch, never to check how the child is doing is unbelievable.'

Crossing her arms over her chest, the mistress rubbed each arm up and down as though she were cold.

'The wind's chilly, Miss Balfour, I've kept you long enough.'

'Yes, I've things to attend to.' She made to move, then paused. Her head tilted, she said, 'I hope you don't mind me asking and please don't answer if it's too personal...'

'If it is, I can assure you I won't.' If nothing else, George prided himself that he was a plain-speaking man.

'Why did you think Polly had died?'

Like a wound being opened, the memory of that terrible time came to him like a sharp pain. 'Because a stretcher bearer told me she had.'

'Was this after the raid?'

'Yes.' At her baffled expression, he explained, 'Polly and I were returning home from the cinema when the first wave of raiders went over. A warden was passing and I sent her ahead with him to the shelter, an action I'll forever regret.'

'You did it for her safety, Mr Pearson.'

He gave a non-committal shake of the head. 'I followed, hurrying as fast as I could, but not quickly enough to avoid the second wave of planes. Amidst the whistling bombs and explosions, people started to panic and as they ran past me someone must have knocked me over. Either that or I was hit by debris because the next thing I knew a bloke wearing overalls was bending over me. He helped to get me on my feet and I remember him telling me that I was one of the lucky ones.'

'Were you injured?' Miss Balfour wanted to know.

George remembered the devastation: houses demolished, roads torn up, blazing buildings.

'It was as the man said, I was lucky with only a painful head wound. I felt groggy but hearing the continuous note of the all-clear sounding brought me to my senses and my first thought was to find Polly and so I moved on. The firefighters were at work and folk milled around looking as dazed as I felt. It was when I saw the shelter the real shock took hold.' George relived the slither of horror that had crept through his body.

'It had taken a direct hit. An ambulance and rescue squad were there and the entrance to the shelter was cordoned off by a barrier and had a copper standing on guard.' He shrugged. 'I don't know how long I stood there – minutes, hours. I watched as they brought out the few survivors, caked in powdery dust; the dead were lying on the ground. What I didn't know at the time was the first passageway had got off lightly and those that had survived had been taken earlier to the hospital.'

Miss Balfour's compassionate eyes looked as though she

understood that this was the first time he'd spoken of his experience from that harrowing time.

'There was a long wait as they moved rubble and shored up parts of the inner passageways.' He drew the deepest breath before going on. 'The stretcher bearers went down and when they reappeared, they were ferrying a body – a body covered by a blanket. The warden asked if there was any sign of life and one of the men shook his head.'

George hesitated before relating the next bit. 'The stretcher bearers were taking the body over to where the dead lay on the ground. It was the blonde hair flowing from beneath the blanket I saw first, then part of a multi-coloured scarf. The colours convinced me. No two scarves could have those particular colours. It had to be the one Jane had knitted for our daughter.'

His legs had buckled, he remembered, and if it hadn't been for his crutches supporting him, George would have sunk to the ground.

'If I did have any doubts, it was the sorry sight of Polly's music case that one of the men brought out that made me certain.'

'Oh, how terrible for you,' Miss Balfour cried. 'You didn't think to identify her?'

'I did try. I told them it was my daughter and made to pull back the blanket but one of the men warned me to stop, told me it was best to leave it for now.' His voice was gentle, George recalled and that's what made him hesitate. 'After they'd laid the stretcher on the ground, the man took me aside and told me heavy masonry had fallen on her and that she was gone and there was nothing I could do for her. His parting words were that it was best I remember my little girl as she was.'

The horror of that moment had stayed with George ever since. *And it is time to let go*, an inner voice told him.

'Later, at the funeral parlour, the stretcher bearer's words came back to me and I still couldn't do it, look at her crushed body, and so I left.'

They lapsed into a meditative silence for a while, when the sound of the clip-clop of horses could be heard.

'The Lumberjills taking the Clydesdales to work,' Miss Balfour told him, then looked at George questioningly. 'I wonder who the child was.'

George groaned. 'That's what will haunt me for the rest of my days. Because of me, whoever they were will never be known.'

'You can't blame yourself. You didn't drop the bomb that killed an innocent child. Besides, if no one came forward to claim her, you've saved them from being buried in a mass grave.'

George knew this to be true but the fact remained that a child lay beneath the ground with no loved one to mourn her. Come what may, George decided, he would continue to leave flowers on the grave for as long as he was able.

Mrs Balfour stood up and looked him squarely in the eye. 'The facts are, Polly survived, Mr Pearson, and you have a daughter to love and cherish.'

By Jiminy, she was right. The gods had been kind, given George something worth living for.

# 37

## JUNE 1944

Miriam felt sorry for the child walking beside her. Polly had been through a lot and Miriam didn't want to add to her anguish, but it was time for a heart-to-heart. Her father seemed a decent sort and Miriam understood his need to make peace with his only child. God willing, the same should happen between her and Alice one day. The reason for the two of them to take a walk in the woods after school was because Miriam wanted to broach the subject of Polly going home with her father but the child's closed expression was making things difficult.

Following the path into the woods, where Scots pine trees rose up to the heavens, Miriam came to a clearing and called out, 'Just look at that view.'

As Polly came alongside and looked out at the distant vista – the vibrant green fields and the copse of maple trees on the hillside, whose tops seemingly touched puffy white clouds that sailed in a powder blue sky – she let out a gasp of wonder. Standing in the tranquil silence, a soft breeze brushing their skin, a sense of peace descended upon them.

Seizing the moment, Miriam told Polly as she continued to gaze at the panoramic view, 'It was like your father told you, he thought you had died. A child was brought out of the shelter, covered with a blanket. Your father saw the blonde hair, the scarf the child was wearing and recognised it as the one your mother made and what clinched it was seeing your music case. He loved you so much, Polly, that he couldn't bear to identify you. So, all of this time he thought you had died.'

The air between them charged. Turning to observe Polly, Miriam saw by her look of comprehension that what she'd told her had registered.

'She was called Jenny.' Polly let out a sob. 'She sat beside me in the shelter. She had a cold and I loaned her a scarf. I remember now, her mam was called Sadie, she said I was...' A stricken expression crossed her face. 'Did she die as well?'

Miriam thought nothing but the brutal truth would do. 'If they were together, I would think so, yes. Otherwise, why didn't she search for Jenny?'

'I ran off to look for Daddy and the mam was worried and shouted after me.' Polly's voice was squeaky. 'I don't want them to be dead. I don't want any of them—' Her breath caught and, shuddering, she dissolved into tears.

Instinctively, knowing this was all the pent-up emotions from the past few months, Miriam took the child in her arms and held her tight. Polly didn't resist but clung on as though Miriam was a lifebuoy.

Her shoulders heaving, she sobbed, 'It's not fair. I should have—'

Miriam, disentangling herself from Polly's grasp, took her by the shoulders. 'Listen to me, Polly. You did nothing wrong, in fact if you hadn't escaped you would be buried under the rubble too.'

As the truth of the matter sank in, Polly's face contorted in dismay.

'And your daddy's heartbreak would be never ending. He's been so upset and sad over the months thinking that he'd lost you. He moved because he couldn't tolerate living at home without you—'

'And Mam.' Polly wiped her tear-stained face with a sleeve.

Miriam nodded. 'He came as soon he heard you'd been found. He loves you and he would never have stopped searching for you if he had known you were alive.'

Polly stared out to the faraway hills, her expression unreadable. Miriam wondered how she was taking the news – and, indeed, if it was her place to reveal all this? But she couldn't stand by and let the two of them suffer any more heartache than need be.

'I thought I wanted to go back.' Polly's voice was barely audible. 'Then I saw the pullover he was wearing that Mam knitted for him and I got scared that nothing had changed and it seemed better to stay here where nobody cares if I'm not top at everything.' Her chin wobbled and big fat tears leaked from her eyes. 'But I do miss Daddy and Alice will be leaving soon, so I've decided I want to go back and live with him.'

Teatime over, Miriam sat at her desk supposedly doing the accounts but staring out of the window where the sun shone brightly from a cloudless sky, ruminating that if the rumours were true, the second front could happen soon.

The end of the war. Could it really be? What would the end bring? The country was on its knees with houses destroyed and food in short supply and— A figure passing the window caught her eye. Rita. Hunched over, head in her hands, she looked in a bad way. Please God, no. Not one of Rita's sons. Miriam dashed from the room and out into the courtyard.

'Rita, what's wrong?'

Rita turned, the whites of her eyes pink, her face blotchy. She shook her head. 'It's our nephew, Roy. He's Walter's brother's lad. We've just heard the bomber he was in crash-landed in a field in Yorkshire. All the crew killed.' Tears streamed down her face. 'Roy was such a fine laddie. What Bob and Sarah must be going through doesn't bear thinking about...'

Miriam rushed over and put an arm around the older woman's shoulder. 'I'm so sorry, Rita. How's Walter?' *Such a silly thing to ask at a time like this.*

'It's hit him hard, I can tell, but he's from the ilk that believes men shouldn't show their emotions, silly sod. White as a sheet he is and just sits there.' Miriam felt the woman tense. 'Och! This bloody senseless war taking young lives in their prime and...' She turned towards Miriam with a tortured expression. 'God help me, all I could think is I'm thankful it's not one of my lads. To go through the war and hear the news at this late stage when I'm wanting them home is more than I could endure.' Her face crumpled.

Miriam gave her shoulder a squeeze. 'Rita, don't feel bad. You're only human and bound to have those thoughts. Is there anything I can do? How about taking some time off?'

Rita disentangled herself. 'Thank you, hen, but no. I'm wanting to go on as normal and look after me old man. Silly blighter. I didn't want him to see me upset and I just needed time to meself to absorb the news. It's Bob and Sarah we should be thinking of now.' She turned to go then added,

'Mebbes I might take a wee time off to see if there's any way I can help.'

Miriam nodded. 'Take as long as you like.'

She watched Rita walk away, mopping her face with a handkerchief. The thought of accounts now the furthest thing from her mind, Miriam made her way out of the courtyard, round to the front of the big house where she settled on a wooden bench that overlooked the trees and lake below. Closing her eyes, the sun's warm rays on her face, a blackbird's rich, mellow song trilling in the distance, Rita's words came to mind. *To go through the war and hear the news at this late stage.* Wondering at a world where happiness could change to tragedy in a heartbeat, she prayed for Mitch and the rest of the *Alabama Beauty*'s crew to make it to the war's end and come home safely.

A high-pitched child's voice alternating with a deep manly one brought Miriam back to reality. Seeing Mr Pearson and Polly walking up the steps of the top terrace, it struck her how much the man's appearance had changed. Gone was his gaunt, wasted look to be replaced by a more relaxed demeanour and with beaming smile and shining eyes, he looked years younger. The pair were making to where Miriam was sitting and she gave a heartfelt sigh of happiness. They were father and daughter again.

Her face animated, Polly said, 'I've told Daddy you've explained about the raid when he thought I'd died. He's promised I can be myself and to not worry about pleasing him or anyone else.'

Mr Pearson nodded. 'I've said nobody's perfect and I won't expect her to be and there'll be no more tap dance competitions or piano lessons unless it's something she wants to do.'

'It was then I told him I wanted to go back and live with him.'

They smiled at each other.

'And d'you know what?' Polly clapped her hand over her mouth. 'I can have a kitten.'

'A full-grown cat,' he told her.

'I could never have one before, because Mam was lergic to cats.' She looked down in the mouth at the mention of her mother.

'Allergic.' The two adults spoke at the same time.

'But I'm not leaving here till after Alice's birthday. It's not long now.'

The mood had changed and Miriam didn't want the child upset any more than necessary.

'Tomorrow's the last school day of the week.' Miriam checked her watch. 'And the extra hour's up. Off you go. Say goodnight to your father. You'll have plenty of time to visit with him at the weekend.'

'Goodnight, Polly.' Mr Pearson hung back, looking as though he wanted to hug his daughter but restrained himself. As they watched Polly walk away, he told Miriam, 'I really appreciate all you're doing. I don't know what you said to make her change her mind but when we met, she was transformed.'

'I just told her the truth of the matter as you explained it to me. I did worry it was not my place though.'

'Then don't. Truly, I can never thank you enough.' His expression became earnest. 'If there's ever anything I can do for you, Miss Balfour, you only have to ask.'

'That's very kind, Mr Pearson, but I assure you my reward is seeing Polly accepting of the situation and ready to return home.'

'Though,' he told her, 'it wasn't until I told her why I

hadn't moved to the countryside that she was completely won over.'

Miriam, puzzled, asked, 'You were planning to leave?'

'Originally yes. You see the night of the bombing, I told Polly we were evacuating to my sister's place in the country. I could tell she wasn't pleased, but it was for her safety we were going.' He wagged his head. 'If only I'd taken her sooner.'

'Life, Mr Pearson, is full of if onlys.' Didn't she know it, Miriam thought, raising her shoulders as she sighed. 'So why didn't you go to the countryside and live with your sister?'

'As I told Polly, I couldn't go because all the memories of her were where we lived, the park where she loved to feed the ducks in the lake, the swings at the playground, the beach where we built castles on the sand. So many places where I could visit that reminded me of her.'

Miss Balfour gave him an understanding nod, and they lapsed into silence as they watched Polly disappear from sight.

Then he turned towards her, his eyes glossy and bright with hope. 'I'll stay and spend time with Polly over the weekend and then return home for a few days as there are practical things I need to attend to. Organise a bed for a start. I got rid of her old one and most of her belongings. I couldn't...' He left the sentence open and Miriam understood.

'About the kitten?' Skilfully she changed the subject, raising a questioning eyebrow at him.

He grinned. 'I know, bribery and corruption, but it worked.'

His daughter wasn't the only one transformed, Miriam thought, smiling at him.

# 38

## JUNE 6TH 1944

Mrs Stewart burst into the dining hall wiping her hand on her pinafore. Her plump face was flushed pink and she looked excited. Prayers over, Alice, standing with the others, looked expectantly at her.

'It's begun,' Cook told Miss Balfour, who stood with a bible poised in her hand. 'The invasion, it's started.'

There was a communal shocked gasp from the orphans but all Alice felt was numb.

Miss Balfour, her free hand clapping onto her chest, appeared startled. 'How d'you know?'

'It's been on the news. That BBC announcer, Frank Phillips – I think that was him – reported the Germans were saying their naval forces were engaged with our landing craft. And Eisenhower has been speaking – they're talking to foreign occupied countries.' She folded her arms. 'That'll be our boys in the thick of the fighting and killin—'

'That'll be all, Mrs Stewart.' The mistress gave Cook a meaningful glare. 'Is the porridge ready?'

Cook bristled. 'I'd like to know when it wasn't ready in time.' Turning on her heel, she left.

After breakfast as they waited for class to start, the hall buzzed with speculation but all Alice could think of – and she felt really bad because as Mrs Stewart said our soldiers would be fighting this very minute – was her birthday in two days' time and life was about to change and though Alice was loath to admit it, the thought terrified her. The orphanage was the only home she'd ever known and Miss Balfour and Polly were the only people she'd trusted enough to touch her hardened heart. Would they miss her or would the mistress go on to make other orphans feel special? And Polly, once she'd settled into her new life – would Alice just be a passing thought once in a while?

A sense of despair overcoming her, Alice took a deep bracing breath. Tuning into the hubbub of conversations around her, she thought of the brave soldiers losing their lives. She wouldn't feel sorry for herself, she vowed, but make plans.

---

'Five elevens,' Miss Balfour called out. She was taking morning class as Mrs Murray was having time off.

'Fifty-five,' Polly chanted with the rest of the class. Her mind was far away, wondering about D-Day and a place she couldn't imagine called France where the fighting had started so that the war could end soon.

'That'll be all for timetables, class,' Miss Balfour told them. 'Your mind isn't on your work this morning.' She gave a rueful smile. 'Neither is mine, I'm afraid. How about we get the world map out and pin it on the wall and see where all the places involved in the invasion are.'

Everyone agreed and Polly sensed excitement rippling in the air.

'Please, miss.' Albert's hand shot up. 'If the war is over today, what'll happen to us?'

A cloud passed over the mistress's face. 'Albert, the war won't end today. The troops have only invaded. There's a long way to go yet.'

'When it does end, where will we go?'

There was a distinct change in the atmosphere and, looking around, Polly saw the orphans' happy faces change to ones of unease.

Agnes's hand went up. 'Miss, we can't go back to South Shields, Miss Black told us Blakely Hall's been bombed.'

'What if we can't stay here?' another voice piped up.

Voices rose as everyone started talking anxiously at once when, suddenly, the door burst open and Mrs Murray stood there and, clapping her hands together, she shrilled, 'Class, enough.'

Taking everyone by surprise, the children were silenced.

She turned to the mistress. 'I was only in the way. Bob and Sarah have got plenty of family around to see to their needs. Poor souls, it hasn't sunk in yet.'

Miss Balfour nodded as though she understood what Mrs Murray was talking about.

'Now what's this rumpus about?' Mrs Murray wanted to know.

'We were discussing the invasion and everyone started to think of the end of the war and what it would mean for the orphanage.'

'Och! That'll be some time away. Plenty of time for arrangements to be made. And, dearies' – she gave a reassuring nod as she looked around the apprehensive faces – 'I've no doubt Sir Henley won't let you go without a roof over your head.' Folding her arms, she turned to face Miss Balfour and said under her breath, which Polly could hear as she sat at the front of the class, 'My Walter reckons that evil man will have it in for us now and there'll be a price to—'

'I was just telling the class,' Miss Balfour interrupted in an overbright voice, 'that we'll pin flags on the map of the places where the invasion is taking place.'

Mrs Murray's face went a tomato-soup colour as if she was in disgrace. 'Good idea. I'll get the map out from the book cupboard.'

Polly was disappointed she wasn't chosen to make and colour in the Union Jack and American flag but when they got pinned on the beaches in France, like everyone else in the class, she let out a cheer.

Polly made sure she sat beside Alice at dinner time because it wasn't long before she was going away. Just thinking about her leaving made Polly wobbly inside. She couldn't imagine what Alice must be going through and mostly avoided talking about London because there was nothing Polly could say to make things better.

Though the cloud of dread at Alice going away hung over her, Polly couldn't help but feel a tingling of anticipation for what lay ahead. She could barely remember what peacetime was like. The idea of going into a shop with plenty of food and sweety jars on the shelves, and you could buy as much as you wanted, was unimaginable. Normally, she would talk things over with Alice and they'd get excited but she couldn't now because she would feel guilty. While Polly would be at home with Daddy, Alice would be working for a mistress and there would be rules and her life would be the same with nothing to look forward to.

Polly reflected on how Daddy seemed more like his old self before Mam died. Talking to him was easier as he really listened and she felt what she said counted. Though she would always miss Mam and pine for her in bed at night, Polly was looking forward to going home.

The clatter of cutlery dragged Polly out of her thoughts. Everyone had finished their corn beef hash and the dinner monitors were busy collecting plates.

While she ate her dish of semolina pudding, Polly's thoughts turned to the birthday card she'd made for Alice. Mrs Murray had allowed her to stay behind in class and use the yellow and green crayons to colour in the daffodils she'd drawn on the front page. She didn't have a present as Polly didn't own anything worth giving but when she'd been out on the terraces, an idea had struck and she decided it was better than nothing.

'Everyone, listen.' Mrs Murray's raised voice cut into Polly's thoughts. 'Seeing how this long-awaited day has arrived and is special, you're all allowed to listen to the one o'clock news on the wireless.'

There was a buzz of excited chatter. Usually, it was only the older boys who were allowed to listen to dinnertime news and no one thought it unfair because Miss Balfour explained that keeping up with affairs helped prepare them for the outside world. Not only did they have to find employment but also somewhere to live, whereas girls would work in a household as live-in housemaids.

Polly turned to Alice. 'Eee! We'll be able to hear what's happening in France.'

In answer, Alice pulled an uncaring face and shrugged. Feeling a little hurt, Polly thought about how this was the way Alice had acted when she had first arrived at the orphanage. She decided to ignore Alice's behaviour because she was probably nervous as the day of her leaving was getting closer and Polly knew that if it was her, she would be petrified too.

Dinner over, the tables cleared by food monitors, Mrs Murray moved over to where the mahogany wireless stood, opened its doors and twiddled with the knobs to tune in.

'D-Day, *the* day,' a man's voice said coming through the material grille. He went on to say in a posh voice, like Sir Henley's, that troops, ships and lots of equipment had been gathering along the south coast in readiness for the landings. Then he confused Polly by saying that ships, aeroplanes and tanks had been left in non-strategic places.

'Well, I never.' The news over, Mrs Murray clapped her hands on her cheeks. 'Aren't we the clever ones.' She turned the knob, switching off the wireless.

'Miss, what does non-strategic mean?' Polly asked.

'Basically,' Miss Balfour put in, 'the allies left those inflatable tanks and dummy landing craft in Pas-de-Calais—'

'Aye,' Mrs Murray laughed, 'only to flummox the enemy into thinking that's where our troops would land.'

'Miss, can we listen to the news tonight as well?' Agnes wanted to know.

Miss Balfour thought for a moment and, smiling, answered, 'You can all listen to the Forces Programme and we'll see what they have to say.'

---

After dinner, as Alice sat on the side of the lake in the shade of the trees, she heard a rustling behind her. Turning, she saw Polly emerge from behind a tree.

'I've been looking everywhere for you.' Polly hung back looking unsure.

Alice inwardly groaned – she wanted to be alone. She

was in a strange mood and the events of the day, the troops landing on the beaches, had only made her more confused. She knew in her heart today was extra special by helping the war come to an end but she couldn't get excited.

'I thought you might want company.' Polly edged closer, her voice holding that appeasing note she used when she was trying to please people which irritated Alice.

She was in a contrary mood that she couldn't do anything about and that was why she'd escaped and sought solitude here by the lake. She knew she should bite her tongue but she couldn't help saying, 'I came here to escape from everyone going on about the landings.'

Polly gave a little gasp of astonishment. 'It's super news and they're all excited – aren't you?'

Alice, watching the quacking ducks following their leader in single file across the lake, grunted in reply. She was, in fact, envious of the others and wished she too could feel elated instead of the dread lodged in her chest weighing her down.

Polly shook her head in disbelief. 'I can't wait to hear the Forces Programme and find out what's happened.'

The need to be contrary persisted. 'Huh! It won't be exciting for the troops doing the fighting. Or their families worrying if their loved ones are in the thick of it and getting killed.'

She heard Polly's sharp intake of breath. 'I never thought. I only meant—'

'Then you should have thought.'

Originally, when Polly was upset and didn't want to return home, Alice had put on an act of being scornful to make things easier for her friend. But she wasn't pretending now, she really did feel irritated – no, cross – with Polly. She could feel jealousy fizzing inside, waiting to explode.

She stood. 'I have to go. I've things to sort out.'

'I can help.' Polly made to move.

'I can manage.' Alice turned to go.

'You're not leaving till the day after tomorrow. Stay for a while and then we'll walk to school together like we usually do.' There was a plea in Polly's voice.

Alice made to move. 'I've nothing to say.'

'If you don't want to be friends anymore, just say so.' Rosie's voice was firm, startling Alice.

'What's the point of being friends when I'm leaving and we won't see each other again?'

Polly pointed an accusing finger at her. 'You've broke your promise, Alice. You said we'd always be like sisters.'

'How can we be when we live hundreds of miles from each other?'

'We can write. When the war's over I could try to come and see you.'

'Huh! All the way to London. I don't think your *daddy* will allow it.' She was being horrid, Alice knew, but the devilment inside spurred her on.

'Why are you being so mean?'

Alice ignored the hurt look on Polly's face. 'After the war's finished I don't know where I'll be. I've got plans and I could be anywhere.'

'Plans. What kind of plans?'

Alice wished she'd kept quiet about her hopes for the future but the words had come tumbling out as, childishly, she wanted to prove she didn't need Polly or anyone for that matter. But now if she didn't reveal her plans, she would lose face.

She blurted, 'When I'm used to living in London, I'll find a job and somewhere to rent then leave the house where I'm employed as a housemaid. There's lots of shops in London, fancy shops where the rich people go – Mrs Stewart told us, remember?' The memory of those days when Polly and she were pretend sisters and shared all their secrets made Alice falter. Then the thought of Polly going to her new home returned and so did the mean streak. 'By then, you'll have forgotten all about me cos you'll be living with your *daddy* and won't have time to think of me.'

Gawping at her, Polly looked close to tears. 'I won't ever forget you. I promised we'd always be friends.'

A twinge of guilt stabbed Alice but she took no heed. 'I'll have new friends and cats.' Why did she say that? she wondered. *To make Polly jealous*, a little voice in her head said. She was competing with Polly because her dad was allowing her to have a kitten. 'Lots of stray cats that have no home of their own.'

'Miss Balfour said people struggle to feed cats.'

Alice tutted and rolled her eyes. 'Dimwit,' she sniped. 'The war will be over by then. But what do you know?' she huffed. 'You're only a kid.'

Polly's eyes darkened and she stuck out her chin. 'Alice, I don't want to be friends with you anymore.' Turning, she ran off and was swallowed up by the trees.

What had got into her? As she trekked up the grassy terraces, Alice cupped a hand over her mouth. Polly's troubled face loomed large in her mind and, playing back the scene in her head, she was swamped by self-loathing.

*But what about Polly?* An incriminating voice spoke in her head. *She's guilty too, going around with a self-satisfied smiley face, not caring how I feel. She never talks about me going to London.* Feeling justified, Alice stomped up the terrace steps.

---

Miriam opened the gate at the side of the house and walked along the path that led into the woods. Finished her rounds in the dormitories and duly turning a blind eye to the excited and chattering orphans – for who could expect them to sleep on such a historical day – Miriam craved the solitude of somewhere she couldn't be disturbed. The Lumberjills finished their working day, the woods were silent and the heavens above, laden with angry clouds, threatened rain. Fastening her mackintosh, Miriam tried to no avail to banish worrying thoughts from barging, like a raging bull, into her mind. As rain began to patter on the leaves, she agonised at what was happening on those far-off beaches but more importantly to her, in the skies above.

*Don't worry about me as only the good die young and I guess that counts me out.*

She closed her eyes and as his handsome face with that lazy smile swam behind pink lids, a cry escaped her lips. Arms crossed and hugging her body, she rocked back and forth and made a vow. *Please God let him survive this day and the rest of the war and I promise I'll light a candle in church every Sunday.*

# 39

## EARLIER ON JUNE 6TH

*Alabama Beauty* made its juddering way along the runway and, taking off, soared into a canvas of blackness. Mitch, resting on his knees and sitting on a bicycle-type seat in the gun turret, had a moment of déjà-vu. Never a religious man, as he believed you made your own luck, he had to admit to a sneaking envy for the men who took holy communion given by the chaplain in the canteen earlier that night. He found himself wondering about the lucky sods who held the belief that some divine being watched over them, while he only had his dice. Aware he might jinx his lucky dice, Mitch acknowledged they'd seen him through to this day. D-Day!

General Eisenhower's words on the noticeboard in the canteen flashed in his mind. *The tide has turned! The free men of the world are marching together to victory.* Ike's speech had made *Alabama Beauty*'s crew jittery, as superstitions ran high before a raid and never a word was spoken about an operation's prospects in case the gods of misfortune were listening in.

The weather that night wasn't ideal with low clouds

prevailing but, as the plane flew towards the heavens, Mitch glimpsed a misty moon in the sky. As he flashed the Aldis lamp, used for take-off until assembly in the air was completed – as in darkness and inclement weather such as this it enabled planes to be seen from both in front and behind – Mitch wondered if Mildred watched from the parallel runaway as she promised she would.

Mildred, a dame renowned to be a flirt, worked in the canteen and, singling him out, it was as though instinctively she knew his weakness. Tonight, as she handed him a coffee from the urn, her enticing emerald eyes met his. Tongue provocatively wetting her lips, she wished him God speed. The canteen bustling, he told himself, where was the harm to thank her with a kiss. But a prolonged kiss on the lips? his conscience asked. In his defence, Mitch considered that he'd been carried away in the spirit of the occasion. He wasn't alone, the crew was the same; nerves jangling, they were all on a high degree of tension.

Low weather made assembling formations in the air difficult but worse was joining with the long column of bombers over England making for the south which entailed confusion and navigational errors. Finally, as *Alabama Beauty* followed the lead aircraft as it headed south, Captain Alexander's voice came over the interphone. 'Okay, boys, we're on our way.'

Hearing the gravity in the captain's tone, the hairs on Mitch's neck stood at attention. His mind focusing on his duty, he looked out of the cupola's central window and swore in frustration. How could he watch for enemy aircraft or protect the plane's rear end with nil visibility? Hedging his bets, he prayed to a God he didn't believe in for the heavy clouds to disperse, so that the groups of the Eighth Air Force could carry out the mission safely and effectively.

But if there was a God, he wasn't listening because low cloud persisted.

He strained to listen to the voices over the interphone but gave up as the noise from the engine made normal conversation impossible. The rest of the crew were close enough to be able to talk to each other and at times such as this, Mitch felt alone and left out.

As the flight followed the leader in formation, Mitch's mind, as he peered out to a sea of dense cloud, shifted to Miriam. He did love her – there was never a doubt about that – but a life of commitment scared him. His thoughts strayed back to kissing Mildred and as much as he denied it didn't mean anything, a warning bell of unease rang in his brain.

The doubts had started after Frank, the top turret gunner, received a Dear John letter from his wife stating she wanted a divorce.

'No explanation, nothing.' The letter still in his hand, Frank's shocked, bewildered face said it all. 'I never thought... she gave no sign.' Frank's features hardened. 'There's got to be someone else.'

Frank, solid as a rock, who Mitch would have wanted above all men at his back if there was trouble. But since then, the crew became wary of Frank, for he became a changed man, full of anger and vexation. The incident had dredged up all kinds of scenarios in Mitch's head. The main one being that it could be him in years to come. He trusted Miriam, but Frank had believed in his wife and gave the impression they were a devoted couple – and look where that had got him.

Mitch considered, was it not best to keep his independence than go through the agony of Miriam getting fed up with him? Jeez, even his own mother couldn't love him enough to stay and watch her son grow.

What with lack of sleep and the daunting effect D-Day

had on him, Mitch's insecurities fought for supremacy. His troubled mind thought of how devoted Miriam was to the orphans and jealousy flared within him. He didn't want to share her, not with anyone, and a lifetime of resentful paranoia was not something he could endure.

He understood the kiss now and it was no coincidence it took place in the busy mess. He felt nothing for Mildred but he'd wanted to be seen, shown to be the jerk he was. His underlying belief would come true: he wasn't worthy of anyone's love. Hell, the bottom line was, it wasn't Miriam he didn't trust; she was his one and only and deserved better than—

'We're getting close to enemy territory, boys.' Captain's steady voice came over the interphone.

Mitch's mind, switching off, became alert.

Captain went on. 'Time to focus on the job. Keep the communication free. Concentrate on the job in hand. Keep your eyes peeled for fighters.' A pause then, 'With luck this is it, boys, the beginning of the end then we can all get back to our loved ones.'

Spurred on by Captain's heartening words, Mitch concentrated. Daybreak now and as *Alabama Beauty*, still in tight formation, crossed the English Channel, he looked down through a momentary clearing in the clouds below and saw, from his advantage point at the tail, an armada of ships and landing craft waiting offshore in a grey, choppy sea. Along with the rest of the gunners, he couldn't help whooping.

'Be on guard for fighter planes.' Captain's tone held an admonishing ring.

Mitch's eyes scoured the skies. Nothing. *Christ!* he thought. *The surprise operation has worked, not a single sighting of enemy aircraft. The sky is ours.*

'Four minutes twenty seconds from bombing.' Captain's voice. 'I'm tuning to autopilot. Bombardier, you're flying the plane to target.'

As the bomber came closer to target, not only was the aircraft in danger from enemy fire from anti-aircraft guns and gun emplacements, but also as thick cloud cover returned, they were now at risk from friendly fire from the ground. Mitch said a prayer that the invasion stripes – black and white stripes painted on the wings and fuselage for easy recognition – would be seen in this foul weather and keep them safe. The order had been simple: *If it ain't got stripes shoot it down.*

'Bombardier, how's the target looking?' Captain Alexander's voice, as ever, was calm and detached.

'I can't see a thing,' came Wally Dickson's clipped reply. Wally was nicknamed Brains because of his remarkable memory and knowledge of countless – and sometimes useless – facts.

'We've only got one chance. Remember, no second runs.'

The warning at the briefing had been stark. Evade releasing the bombs prematurely to avoid hitting landing crafts offshore.

Holy cow! Mitch thought. That bombardiers had the unenvying task of worrying they might be hitting landing craft carrying GIs making for the beaches was enough to make any man hesitate.

'Bombardier, how's that target looking now?'

'Still no visual. Target totally obscured. Wait. I see smoke flares from the pathfinder aircraft.'

As clouds thinned, visibility improved, and seconds passed when puffs of flak exploded all around the bombers, unnerving Mitch as the jagged metal fragments they sent out could tear through an aircraft.

*Hell, Wally, come on. The specified seconds to release the bomb after the sighting of the target must be up.*

A further lifetime of seconds passed.

'Bombardier, what is the—'

'That's it,' Wally's grave voice interrupted. 'Bombs away.'

Mitch let out a long heartfelt sigh of relief. Physically and mentally exhausted, he craved being back at the base and a warm bed. Screwing up his eyes, he looked at the scene below and what he saw made him curse. The bomb had missed and dropped inland of the beaches. He reported to Captain Alexander and a telling silence followed. Looking below Mitch saw the first landing barges grounded.

'Okay, boys, that's it. We're heading home.' Captain's flat voice told of the devastation he felt.

As the aircraft flew further inland, puffs of black flak exploded around the plane, jolting the aircraft alarmingly. The blast when it came shocked Mitch and he registered instantaneously that *Alabama Beauty* had been hit. The thud in his chest knocked him backwards and, realising his flak vest had been pierced, Mitch panicked. Voices yelled over the interphone. Someone screamed. As red-hot pokers seared his chest, Mitch realised that someone was him. Touching his torso, sticky blood seeped through his flight suit but seeing the flames was when the real terror took hold.

Closing his eyes, his terrified mind sought refuge and thought of Miriam. As she smiled serenely at him behind his closed eyelids, she was the last thing Mitch saw before he sank into oblivion.

# 40

## JUNE 7TH 1944

'Miss, are those ships in the picture the ones that took the troops to France yesterday?' Tommy asked.

Curling up her nose in disgust, Polly watched as he made to wipe the snot away on his sleeve. Seeing Miss Balfour's look of disapproval, he gave a huge sniff and the green snot hanging from his nostrils disappeared up his nose. Polly's tummy turned over.

'Yes, Tommy, they are.' Taking a clean rag from her pocket and with a cross look, the mistress handed it to him.

Which wasn't like Miss Balfour because usually she was as 'as patient as a saint', according to Mrs Murray.

Mrs Murray gave the mistress a peculiar look as though she too wondered what was up with her. 'See, Tommy. The ships are approaching the French coast to take part in the landings.'

Breakfast over and prayers said for the deliverance of the forces fighting in France, Miss Balfour had joined the class and stood with Mrs Murray beside the blackboard where the day's newspaper was pinned with the headline: *Allied invasion troops several miles into France.*

Beneath the heading, which read: *Invasion of Europe: First pictures,* were black-and-white grainy photos showing lines of ships heading towards what looked like rows of tall trees. Squinting at the scene Polly couldn't make out which was land or sea.

'How many ships, miss?' Alan wanted to know.

Mrs Murray peered at the small print below the photograph. 'It says *an armada of ships making for the French coast.* There you go' – she pointed further down – '*four thousand ships with three thousand smaller vessels.* And before anyone asks, the picture was taken from an allied aeroplane yesterday morning and I don't know what kind of plane it was,' she quickly put in.

'I bet it was a bomber.' Alan again. 'There were bombers, miss, wasn't there?'

Polly noticed Miss Balfour's neck go blotchy pink.

Mrs Murray's eyes swept the page. 'It says that night bombers opened the assault and attacked in great strength and—'

'The paper also reports,' the mistress cut in, rubbing the back of her neck as if it ached, 'the first landings were successful and that Mr Churchill says the operation is proceeding in a thoroughly satisfactory manner.' She smiled overbrightly at the class. 'And who is Mr Churchill?'

'Our Prime Minister,' the class chanted.

'Enough of the war for today, let's get on with our work.'

Even Mrs Murray looked disappointed, as if she couldn't get enough of what was going on in France. She opened her mouth to speak but the mistress's shake of the head stopped her. Miss Balfour normally gave an account of what was going on in the war as she thought it important. Taking down the newspaper, folding it and putting it under an arm, the mistress left the room.

'Class, it's time to practise arithmetic,' Mrs Murray told them. 'Milk monitors are excused while they collect the crates.'

The small bottle of milk each day drunk through a straw was the highlight of Polly's day – except in summer when the milk curdled. She inwardly groaned. Wednesday mornings were spent doing sums, her least favourite lesson. She had hoped today, because of all the excitement of the invasion, lessons would be cancelled but as Mrs Stewart was likely to say, 'Well, you hoped wrong.'

As desk lids lifted, she looked around the glum faces of her classmates and realised they felt the same as her. The little ones were given slate boards and chalk but once Polly had learnt to do joined-up writing, she was allowed to use a pen with a wooden handle and metal nib which she dipped into the inkwell on her desk.

Polly's eyes scanned the class and met with Alice's. She felt peculiar and didn't know what to do, smile or look away – but that felt rude. Since their falling out, they hadn't spoken to each other and Alice ignored her. As Polly agonised, Alice gave her a deliberately long blink and, sticking out her chin, she turned away.

A flush of anger pulsed through Polly, and she could have cried. Not because she felt upset but she was hurt that Alice would be so mean to do such a thing. From now on she would do as Daddy said and not try to please anymore – even if Alice begged her to be friends again.

But the niggle in her mind, reminding her that it was Alice's birthday tomorrow, persisted.

---

Miriam's first thought when her eyes blinked open next morning was that it was Alice's fourteenth birthday. Where had all those years gone? As she lay beneath the floral bedspread that she'd found in the second-hand shop to make her bedroom cosy for when Mitch was there, her mind relived the fatal day she'd left her precious bundle on the Blakely orphanage doorstep, and the pain of loss, as fresh as ever, knifed her heart.

With effort she forced herself to think about today's plan to make Alice's birthday special – possibly the last one Miriam would get to spend with her daughter. The thought of Alice living so far away hit her like a hammer blow in the stomach. How could she live life without seeing Alice every day? Miriam missed her already.

Flinging back the bedspread and sitting on the edge of the bed, she slipped her feet into fur-lined slippers. Today, she told herself, was not for morbidity but a celebration and whatever the cost, she would put a smile on her face and do all she could to make her daughter's day a happy one. To combat any misgivings that she may have that all orphans should be treated the same, she would explain the surprise for Alice at dinner time was going to be a regular occurrence for all the orphans from now on.

Dressing in a navy summer frock with a white collar, belted waist and boxy sleeves, she decided to wear black brogue shoes as the weather outside looked uncertain and the puddles were still to be seen from overnight rain. Making her way down the stairs and over to the Little Theatre, picking up the pile of post and newspaper from behind the front door, Miriam walked to the office. She had plenty of time to deal with the letters and perhaps catch up with the news. Placing the post on the desk, she skimmed the newspaper's headlines: *Bayeux Is Captured – Official.* Further down the page an article caught her eye: *Shot RAF Men: Report.* Miriam tensed, painfully so in her shoulders which seemed to be on a level with her earlobes. She'd been like this since D-Day and, hearing about fatalities, sick with worry over Mitch, she didn't want to read, think, or speak about the invasion and neither did she want to be alone. So later, she decided, when she joined the class, she would veer the conversation away from any mention of the topic and make it plain she expected a normal school day. Ignoring the news and gossip was the only way she could avoid the what ifs plaguing her.

Alice's birthday helped to divert her troubled mind but that had repercussions too. She agonised whether or not to tell Alice about the history of her birth. What difference would it make now, when Miriam was losing her anyway? A picture presented itself in her mind – a picture she couldn't bear – of the revulsion on Alice's face when she discovered Miriam was the despised mother who'd left her on the orphanage doorstep. It was best, she decided, her daughter was left with the memory of her being the kind mistress who'd been her ally over the years.

Placing the newspaper on the desk, she noticed the envelope on top of the pile, the neat handwriting she didn't recognise. Intrigued, she picked up the envelope and, slitting it open with a letter opener, read the slip of lined jotter paper.

*Dear Miss Balfour,*

*This is to inform you that I've accomplished everything I intended to do in South Shields and I'll be returning to*

*Teviot Hall on Friday 9th of June mid-afternoon and will explain the outcome of my visit then.*

*I've a proposal to make concerning the future but it would be untimely for me to broach the matter here.*

*Once again, I'd like to thank you for your part in helping me regain my relationship with my daughter.*

*Yours sincerely,*

*George Pearson*

Her curiosity getting the better of her, Miriam tried to think what this proposal could possibly be. After many scenarios flitted through her brain, including Mr Pearson wanting to up sticks and move here as he'd confessed Polly was thriving living in the countryside and as a cobbler he could work anywhere, Miriam decided she really didn't have an inkling what it might be.

As she placed the letter in the envelope, she noticed movement in her peripheral vision. Looking out of the window she saw Polly and, looking closer, she realised the girl was clutching a bunch of daises to her chest. Seeing the cheerful little flowers, their central yellow discs surrounded by white petals, made Miriam smile. A thought prodded her into action. She must tell Polly about her father returning tomorrow.

As she made to place the letter back on the pile, seeing the handwriting on the envelope on the top, an adrenalin rush pulsed through. Mitch's handwriting. Her sigh of relief was heartfelt. She tore open the envelope and read the first line. The smile wiping from her face, she had to hold on to the desk for support.

*Honey,*

*If you're reading this, then I guess I didn't make it.*

Shocked, she slumped into the chair, staring at the words, praying their meaning would change. But as tears spilled over her lids, the blurry letters spelt out the same message.

Crumpling, Miriam's world as she knew it fell apart.

# 41

'What's up with your dinner?' Harry gazed longingly at the corn beef hash left on Alice's plate.

'Nothing.'

'Then why you not eatin' it?'

'I'm not hungry.' Alice gave him a *Don't bother me* glare. Nowadays the orphans could sit anywhere they liked at mealtimes and she'd had the misfortune of Harry coming to sit next to her but her dinner partner could be worse, she thought, glancing at Polly across the table.

Harry goggled at her in disbelief. 'Are you poorly or summick?'

'Here.' Picking up her plate, she exchanged it with his, which looked as though it had been licked clean. 'And don't ask any more questions. In fact, don't say anything to me. You hear?'

He looked deflated. 'I won't. I promise.' The youngster picked up his fork and, surrounding his plate with an arm, ate greedily.

A tinge of regret speared Alice at being mean to Harry.

After all, it wasn't his fault she was in a bad mood. Normally, Alice would wolf down her food as rationing meant food was precious and nothing went to waste and you'd starve if you were fussy. Mrs Stewart, with a stern look that would curdle milk, would quote from the wall poster to anyone who left a crumb on their plate, 'Fight food waste in the home.'

Polly was staring critically at her from the other side of the table and Alice realised that she'd probably heard her exchange with Harry. Alice blanked her and turned away. But the little voice of reason that balked at such behaviour persisted to make her feel guilty. What was wrong with her? She had reverted to the old Alice.

There was no escaping the real reason for horrible behaviour – Polly wasn't the problem, it was herself. Soon she would be travelling to London to be a skivvy for one of Sir Henley's rich friends. She wouldn't know anyone and from what little she knew of the capital, apart from it being forever away, she'd heard it was a busy city with huge amounts of people and though she was loath to admit it, Alice was scared.

Watching on as food monitors collected plates, clattering them in a pile on the trolley, she shook her head as Harry shovelled the last of the hash into his gob and, eyes bulging, swallowed it down in one effortful gulp. The others, pinning their eyes on the doorway, waited for pudding to arrive, hoping it wouldn't be tapioca – known as eyeball pudding – but invariably after corn beef hash, it always was.

'Ta-da.' Mrs Stewart appeared in the doorway carrying a large cake on a glass stand topped with a halo of brightly burning candles.

There was a collective intake of breath as she entered the room and set the cake in front of Alice. Mary, sitting the other side of her, clapped her hands in delight.

Alice blurted, 'For me?' No one ever got a cake on their birthday when Miss Black was in charge.

'I don't know anyone else whose birthday it is today.' Cook folded her arms, a smile splitting her face. 'You can thank Miss Balfour for her egg ration and with what I had stashed in the pantry, there was enough to ensure I didn't have to use that powdered stuff.' She nodded at Mistress, who stared from a white face into space as though her mind was miles away. 'And them candles are made from gas tapers, with the end sharpened to make a wick. But again, don't thank me.' Cook again nodded at Miss Balfour before she made for the kitchen doorway and stood like a sentry staring at the mistress with a look that suggested she should say something.

They all waited.

Becoming aware of Cook's gaze, her brow furrowing as though she was trying to work out where she was, the mistress noticed the cake with its burning candles. 'Alice, you'd better...' Her voice came out croaky. Clearing her throat, she continued, 'Happy birthday, Alice. Blow out the candles before they burn away.'

Alice sensed her classmates relax. Mary started to fidget, looking as though she might need the lav.

'Go on, Alice, blow them out, so we can have a piece.'

Alice stood, feeling self-conscious with all their eyes upon her. Bending down, her cheeks inflating like balloons, she blew. The last two candles stayed alight and Mary, who couldn't contain herself, bent forward and blew them out.

Realising what she'd done, Mary's cheeks reddened. 'Eee, I didn't mean to, honest.'

Everyone laughed and, head down touching her chest, Mary didn't recover until Mrs Stewart started cutting the cake. Alice got her piece first, then Mary, and when everyone had been given a portion, Cook disappeared with the remains into the kitchen.

Alice, halving her cake into two, put one piece on Harry's plate. 'I'm not that hungry.'

His mouth, already full of cake, dropped open, but it was his surprised eyes, that he couldn't believe such generosity, that made Alice catch her breath.

'Ooh ta, Alice.'

'Don't talk with your mouth full,' she told him huskily.

When everyone had demolished their cake Miss Balfour stood and, surveying them all, her gaze landed on Alice. 'Today's special because not only is it Alice's birthday but she'll be leaving us soon. Alice, we wish you well in your new employment.' For a moment it was as though she was about to say more but, swallowing hard, she gave Alice a little smile and sat down.

A painful lump came into Alice's throat and tears stung behind her eyes. She didn't want to leave all this behind. Little Mary and Charlie, all the others, even annoying Harry – they were all, she realised, her family. She was going not only to the big outside world, but to an unknown future where no one cared about her. Polly looked at her from across the table and the lump in Alice's throat grew bigger and tears clouded her vision. She didn't want to leave Polly like this; she'd grown fond of her and the thought of being separated hurt inside. But old habits die hard and instinct made it difficult for Alice to approach Polly and say how she felt.

'You're too headstrong for your own good,' Miss Balfour had once rebuked her. 'Don't let your stubbornness spoil your future.'

Alice had thrown off Miss Balfour's remarks as teachers' baloney, but now she wondered. As everyone climbed from the benches and made their way outside, Alice hurried after Polly and was surprised to find her waiting outside the door.

'Alice, I've got something for—'

'Polly, I want us to—'

They'd both spoken at once, then stood looking at one another.

Polly's expression was unsure. 'You go first.'

'Not here,' Alice said, aware of her classmates gawping as they teemed out of the doorway.

Alice led the way to the pathway leading to the woods behind the big house. Voices of the Lumberjills echoed in the distance. The pair of them faced one another. Polly's face was stony, as if preparing herself for what was about to come.

Alice took a deep breath. 'Polly, I don't want to leave with bad feeling between us. Let's be friends again.'

'You were mean to me.' Her lips bunched.

'I was a horrible cow and I'm sorry.'

Polly looked startled. Then her face curved into a smile. 'You've never said you were wrong before.'

'That's because I've never been wrong before.' Alice grinned cheekily.

Polly chewed the inside of her cheek and Alice worried that again she'd said the wrong thing.

'I was only trying to be—' Alice started.

'It's not that. Alice, it's not all your fault. I can't help being happy because Daddy's taking me home. I know I'd be jealous as well if it was the other way around.'

Alice's hackles rose and, about to vehemently protest, she swallowed the words. It was true, she was jealous. Polly had someone more important in her life than her and she had a future to look forward to. But the thing that stung most was that she couldn't wait for it to begin. But because of her jealousy, Alice realised, she had nearly lost the only friend she'd ever known.

'No, you wouldn't,' Alice replied. 'You're a softie and you'd be pleased for me.' Embarrassed at talking about feelings, she changed the subject. 'Anyway, what were you going to say?'

Polly reached into her skirt's pocket. 'I made this for your birthday.' She held out a daisy chain. 'It's not much, I know, but I wanted to give you something and it's the only thing I could think of.'

Overcome, Alice didn't know what to say. Not only was it the nicest of presents but – apart from the bible Miss Balfour had once given her – the only gift she'd ever received on her birthday. Taking the daisy chain, she put it over her head.

'It won't last long,' Polly apologised.

Alice found her voice. 'I'm gonna press the flowers in my bible so they'll keep forever.'

The two of them, silent, began to walk towards the house. The whinnying of a horse could be heard in the woods. Just as they were about to turn towards the courtyard and join the line that would be forming to head for the village school, Alice stopped.

'Are you still my make-believe sister?' she asked.

Polly nodded. 'Yes, even if you are a cow sometimes.'

It was Alice's turn to be startled by the use of the word by prim Polly. But then Alice grinned. 'Moo.'

It wasn't really that funny but catching Polly's eyes, seeing the merriment twinkling in them, Alice started to laugh. Polly, joining in, held her stomach as though it hurt and it felt good to be friends again.

Laughter over and cheeks aching, Alice said, 'We'll write

to each other. And one day when I'm working in a posh London shop, I'll save up for a train fare and come visit you.'

Instead of looking pleased, Polly's face clouded with uncertainty. 'Alice, I'm going to miss you and the others when I go home. I don't want to go back to being the only one.' Her eyes widening, she drew in her breath as though in wonderment. 'Alice, I've just thought of something. What if I ask Daddy if you can come and live with us?'

# 42

The next day, while the older children were at school and the little ones out for a walk with Hazel, Miriam sat in the solitude of her office in a haze of numb disbelief. She couldn't take it in that Mitch was no longer part of this world. It couldn't be true. He would appear like he always did with his broad lazy smile, telling her it was a mistake, his buddies posted the wrong letter.

Feeling a sudden limpness in her body, she opened the top desk drawer and pulled out the letter and re-read the ending.

*I left the letter in my locker so that when the crew empties it – that's what happens when there's a fatality and letters and belongings that are found are sent off to relatives – I'm confident this letter will be sent off to you and you'll know first-hand. The sad thing is there's no one else to tell, but sadder still is we can't be a couple. More than anything, I want you to get on with your life. Us, was never meant to be. My everlasting wish is for you to have a long and fulfilled life. Remember that always.*

*Love you,*

*Your Mitch xx*

Miriam looked into the bleak and empty future. How could she get on with her life knowing Mitch wouldn't be part of it? As a yearning dragged through her body, she rubbed the palm of her hand over her aching heart. Why hadn't she cried even a single tear? All she felt was angry and she wanted to scream at the fates who had denied her and Mitch a lifetime together.

Miriam's attention was caught by a noise outside, then a rap came at the office door.

A voice called, 'Miss Balfour, are you here?'

Mr Pearson's voice. The last thing she wanted was to engage in a conversation but common decency wouldn't allow her to ignore him.

Sitting upright, she called, 'Come in, Mr Pearson.'

The door opened and, his eyes sparkling, face flushed with enthusiasm, he appeared as though years had been stripped from him. Smiling, stick in hand, he limped into the room.

'The place is so quiet, I thought no one was...' As he came to stand in front of the desk, he looked closely at her. 'Miss Balfour, have I come at an inconvenient time?'

She opened her mouth to reassure him but seeing his expression of concern, ridiculously she choked up and didn't trust herself to speak.

'Something's wrong. Can I do anything? Or would you rather I left you alone?'

His solicitousness made matters worse. Her throat tightened and she feared she was going to wail and tell him everything. She fanned her face with a hand. Gasping, she collected herself. 'You've caught me at a bad moment.' Her voice was an embarrassing high-pitched squeak. 'I've had a letter,' she heard herself babble. 'Mitch, my... he's an airman. I've found out he...' She couldn't say the word died; it was too final. 'He didn't make it.' All too much, she slumped and couldn't go on.

As they sat in the dining hall facing each other sipping tea, made in the kitchen by Mr Pearson, Miriam squirmed at how close she'd been to bawling and didn't trust that it wouldn't happen again. Nodding to the cup in her hand, she hoped the smile she'd pasted on her face would reassure him the dramatics were over.

'Strange, Mr Pearson, how we think a cup of tea cures all.'

'George, please, otherwise it sounds as though you're speaking to my father.' His concern for her evident, he tried to lighten the moment with an attempt at a joke.

'Miriam,' she replied, feeling guilty. As if being so personal infringed some rule.

His gaze solicitous, he told her, 'Losing someone is difficult to cope with. It's only when you've experienced it yourself you know the true nature of the beast.'

Of course, poor man, he had recently lost his wife in tragic circumstance. Miriam's compassionate self came to the fore. 'Forgive me, you've got your own sorrows to contend without having me to...'

'Miriam, stop.' His eyes engaged with hers. 'You don't have to put on a brave face. I know what you're going through and, believe me, struggling with a bear would be easier.' He looked at her and, grinning, he shrugged. 'Where did that come from?'

The mood lightened and Miriam gave him a weak smile.

'It feels so unreal, doesn't it?' George sighed and shook his head.

'I know he's gone but I still keep expecting him to come walking through the door.'

'The reality does click but it takes a while and when it does it hurts like blazes.'

'The thing is' – she looked into George's candid eyes, feeling at ease to confess her troubled thoughts – 'I don't see the point of going on.'

His jaw dropped open. 'Don't ever think or say that.'

'Oh, I don't mean end it all. I just can't help thinking, what's the point of doing anything without Mitch? The future was looking...' Miriam realised she was revealing too much private information. 'There'll be no enjoyment without him.' The thought of Mitch – who had been so full of life – missing out on a future caused a sadness as deep as any ocean to overwhelm her. Despite her inhibitions, the tears came then unbidden, a tidal wave that brimmed over Miriam's lids.

He eased from the chair and came to stand by her side. Even in her misery she recognised his discomfort as he wondered what would be appropriate to say. His hand squeezing her shoulder was the physical contact she needed and, letting out a howl of wretchedness that seemingly came from her toes, Miriam cried and cried – not only for Mitch, but also for all the others who lost their young lives because of this senseless war.

When, finally, she dried her eyes on the handkerchief he offered, Miriam cringed, wondering what the man must think of her, baring her soul in front of him like that. Her a headmistress, who should have the good sense to do her weeping and wailing in private. But handing him back the handkerchief, she saw only empathy in his eyes.

'I'm sorry, I—'

'Don't apologise.' His lips turned upwards into a smile. 'I'm only pleased I was here and flattered that you felt comfortable enough with me to let go and cry.'

She thought about his predicament. 'I hope you had someone to be with you. You must have had a terrible time losing your soulmate and having Polly to consider. Poor thing, she was grieving too.'

There was a pause when George appeared to find it difficult to speak. A vein in his temple pulsed and she could see raw pain in his eyes.

Miriam hoped she hadn't overstepped the mark. 'I'm sorry if I—'

'It's nothing you've said.' His jaw tensed and, moving back to his seat, he faced her. 'My marriage was not what it seems. I've never told anyone this before...' His mouth twisted in a wry smile. 'Not that there's anyone to tell.' He looked unsure whether to go on, then rubbing his temples with his fingertips he took a deep breath and continued, 'Jane worked in a clothing factory at night. I felt bad as it was up to me to be the breadwinner but I consoled myself that working got her out of the house and the bonus was I got to put Polly to bed.'

Miriam nodded, wondering where this was going.

He drew himself up as though bracing himself. 'The night of the bombing, as soon as the all-clear sounded I left Polly with a neighbour and went to seek Jane. When I saw the factory was intact, I can't tell you how relieved I was. The staff had all been in the shelter but there was no sign of Jane and I thought our paths must have crossed and she'd returned home.' His eyes unfocused momentarily as though reliving the scene. 'Marge, a woman Jane had befriended, was still there and I could see she was uncomfortable when I asked her about my wife.' His jaw clenched and his hands balled into fists.

'She told me to check an address of a terraced house down by the docks.' He slowly shook his head. 'When I arrived, the street had taken a direct hit with some of the houses wrecked.'

An icy shiver went down Miriam's spine. 'And your wife?'

George nodded. 'I identified her body at the hospital morgue. I was told the man she was with didn't make it either.'

'She was with a man,' Miriam repeated stupidly.

'That's why she wanted to work evenings.' He looked up. 'I pressed Marge later and she confided Jane was having an affair and apparently only worked half the time I thought.'

Miriam couldn't help but wonder why a woman who seemingly had everything, a home, family, loving husband, would be crazy enough to have an affair and jeopardise it all. As the thought *You should never speak ill of the dead* went through her mind, Miriam decided it was wrong of her to judge.

'And you never suspected?'

'Not once. I was so angry I couldn't bear to speak her name. Polly had lost her mother and needed me but I let her down. We never spoke about Jane as I couldn't see past the anger and it coloured my judgement.'

'And now?' Miriam couldn't help but ask because it was an appalling situation for both Polly and George.

'I'm still furious with Jane but there must have been something amiss in our marriage for her to do what she did.'

'Don't ever think it was your fault.' Miriam was incensed the poor man should contemplate such a thing. 'We all have a path that could lead us astray but it's up to each of us whether or not we give in to temptation and take that first step.' Hark at her, Miriam chided her self-righteous self, with a shady past such as hers.

'The thing is.' He shook his head in despair. 'It hasn't changed how I feel about her. When you love someone, it isn't like a tap that you can simply switch off.'

His words caused a tightness in Miriam's chest. And she knew that the painful longing for Mitch that she was experiencing was everlasting.

# 43

George rubbed the middle of his brow with his fingertips. 'The thing is, how do I tell Polly?'

'Tell Polly?' Miriam's face crinkled in confusion.

'About Jane.'

Miriam reeled. 'You mean you'll tell her the circumstances of your wife's death?'

'How can I not? She has a right to know. Besides, the truth always comes out, usually when you least expect it. I couldn't bear it if she wasn't prepared.' He sighed. 'I'll wait until she's older, of course. Soften the blow by explaining I was overseas for years and Jane was alone not knowing whether I was dead or alive. Which, in retrospect, is probably the truth of the matter.' He nodded as if in affirmation of this thought. 'Jane was a devoted mother and Polly was her world. These things happen in wartime... and it had nothing to do with Polly and I want her to understand that.'

Miriam was flabbergasted. She didn't know if the man was admirable or plain foolish but whatever else, he was sincere and advocated honesty. They fell into a contemplative silence, his words hanging in the air.

*How can I not tell her?* his voice said in her mind. *She has a right to know.*

Was Miriam selfish by denying her daughter the truth? She professed she only wanted the best for Alice while allowing her to endure the agony of never knowing the realities of her birth. But could she suffer the revulsion she would see on Alice's face? A pain in the region of her heart made her gasp.

'Miriam? Whatever's the matter?'

George's face, a mask of concern, gave her the courage to blurt out, 'I've got a secret too. And I don't know what to do.'

There was a pause as if he considered what to say. 'Perhaps if you shared whatever it is, it might help you to resolve the problem.' He shook his head. 'By that I don't necessarily mean me. Maybe you'd be more comfortable telling your lady friend Mrs Murray, or perhaps the vicar as I know you're—'

'Oh, I couldn't possibly.' Miriam shrank at the thought. Her view of vicars was modelled on Father.

But the secret she bore burnt in her brain and she was in agony to know what to do. In the short time she'd known him, Miriam perceived George Pearson as one of the most trustworthy people she'd met. She valued his opinion, even though she knew what he would advise. His previous words, 'My God, what mother would do such a thing?', displayed his thoughts on the matter, therefore, he was the best person to test the waters on. Besides, she thought rationally, when he and Polly left for their home, likely she'd never set eyes on him again.

'It's your opinion I'd like.' And before he could reply or she lost her nerve, stomach plummeting, she dived in with the bare fact. 'Alice Blakely is my daughter. I was an unmarried mother and it was me who left her on the orphanage doorstep.'

She steeled herself. But the look of horrified disgust, abhorrence even, she expected didn't happen.

His expression became bewildered and he simply shook his head in disbelief. 'Miriam, I never—'

'Furthermore,' she interrupted, wanting him to know the full extent of her selfishness, 'I didn't tell Alice for her sake but mine. I believed the relationship I had with her was better than none at all. I realise now because of my neglect she suffered the most.'

There, it was done, out in the open, and Miriam felt a sense of relief regardless of the outcome.

'Neglect, Miriam, I don't think so.' His eyes glistened with compassion. 'You are a typical caring mother putting your child first. Making sure she's well cared for. You had no alternative, a woman alone with no means. Shunned by society.' As if a thought just struck, he raised his shoulders and opened his hands, palms up. 'Not only did you leave her somewhere safe but you gave up your life to be with her throughout the years. I think that's commendable.' He smiled.

Overcome by his reaction, she confessed, 'But what if I do tell her and she hates me?'

'I'll keep your secret, Miriam,' he told her, ever the plain-speaking man. 'I can't tell you what to do but you know my opinion on such matters. If you do decide to tell Alice, then her reaction is a risk you'll have to take.'

Miriam shrugged. 'The thing is, if I do say anything, there's no way we could be together. I have no means apart from this job. What would I have to offer when the scandal was known? I'd be sacked and have no chance of work.'

Bringing her hands together she entwined her fingers and rested her chin on them.

They sat awhile in silence as Miriam, concentrating on her recent disclosure, found herself exploring all kinds of disturbing scenarios.

In an effort to distract herself, she blurted, touching her cup, 'Gracious, the tea's stone cold. I'll make us a fresh pot.' She started to move, then a niggling thought made her remark, 'George, didn't you say in your letter you had a proposal to make?'

He thought for a moment, looking decidedly uncomfortable. 'I had decided to leave this subject for the time being but it has to be said and so why not now?'

He gave a reassuring smile, causing the laughter lines around his eyes to crease. 'You remember I asked what would happen to Polly's friend... Alice.'

Puzzled, Miriam nodded.

'I was appalled she was to be sent so far away when she had no knowledge of London and didn't know a soul. Then the conversation with Polly came to mind when she was adamant that she didn't want it to be just her again and I promised her a kitten in compensation.' As if to lighten the mood, he gave a mischievous grimace.

Miriam, wary, knew instinctively whatever he was going to say would be momentous.

'I decided to offer Alice a home.' His expression was uncertain. 'Think about it. Polly would have her best friend as a companion and Alice could find work that suited her in a familiar town. What d'you think?' He waited expectantly.

Shocked at the revelation, Miriam's thoughts whirled. Alice wouldn't be so far away and she would be able to see her; check that everything was all right. It would only be occasionally but it was better than the alternative. She would be there to witness Alice's future.

Suddenly, the full implications hit her like a runaway steam engine. Gone now was the dream that one day Alice could live with her and Mitch. Alice would become part of a family, and Miriam would be an outsider, of no consequence at all.

Then logic took over and her mind argued, *What's best for Alice? That's the priority.* With a sinking heart, Miriam knew the answer: a home with a family and a settled future.

In that instant, she made up her mind. She stood. 'George, I've decided that before Alice leaves, I'm going to tell her the truth.' She clasped her hands together. 'And suffer the consequence if that's the case.'

'That's the ticket.' George beamed. 'It'll be a lot for her to take in but I'll do everything I can to help.' He paused, his brow wrinkling in concentration. 'I wonder… d'you think it's best if you told her about coming to live with Polly and me? Imparting the good and bad news together as it were.'

Hope sprang in Miriam's chest. Hearing she was going to share a home with Polly might soften the blow.

*D'you really think so?* the voice of adversity whispered in her head.

Early afternoon, they sat on the bench that overlooked the lake on the topmost terrace in front of the house. The office for such news was too formal, Miriam decided.

'Honestly, miss, is it true?' Alice's eyes were wide in amazement and shone with delight. 'I don't have to go to London? Mr Pearson really wants me to live with him and Polly?'

'I promise it's true.' Her daughter looked so young, so incredibly happy, it gladdened Miriam's heart.

'I never dreamt such a thing could happen. I'll find work in South Shields and have a proper home to come to. I can't wait to tell Polly. She'll be as excited as me.' Not able to contain herself, she made to move.

Her stomach clenching at what must follow, Miriam put a hand on Alice's arm. 'Wait, there's something else.'

Alice's face clouded with suspicion. 'I knew it. There's a catch isn't there, miss?'

'No, Alice, nothing like that. There's something personal I want to tell you.'

Alice stared at her with trusting eyes.

God, how to go on. How much should Miriam divulge? *Everything*, her mind told her. 'Alice, you know how you were left at Blakely orphanage.'

'On the doorstep,' Alice corrected.

'Yes.'

'What has this got to do with anything, miss?' It was obvious Alice was impatient to be away.

'I left you there.'

Confusion crossed her face. 'You, miss? I was told it was me mam.'

Her heart thumping in her chest, Miriam was amazed it wasn't audible. 'There's no other way to tell you this... so I'll just come right out and say it. Alice, I'm your mam.'

Her mouth slack, Alice goggled in disbelief. 'You what?'

'I know it's the biggest shock but—'

'That isn't funny, miss.' Her eyes were uncertain.

'It isn't intended to be.'

'It can't be true. You're Miss Balfour. All these years you've been her.'

The silly logic could have tickled Miriam, had not the situation been so dire.

Feeling out of her depth, she reiterated it for the fact to sink in. 'I am your mother. I was young you see and—'

Alice jumped from the bench and, putting her hands over her ears, she shrilled, 'I don't want to hear.' Her face ashen, she glared at Miriam. 'Liar. All these years... How could you? I'm glad I'm going away, from this place, from you.' She stared in horror at Miriam, then sobbing, she ran off into the distance.

Shaken, Miriam stared up at the heavens. Dark clouds were blotting out the blue sky, fitting her desolate mood.

'I never once told a lie,' she whispered to the universe, 'I only omitted telling the truth.'

*The shock was too much*, a voice of reason said in her head. *She'll come round in time.* Miriam, envisaging those accusing eyes, the repugnance in them, knew she only kidded herself. The outcome, she acknowledged, was nobody's fault but her own.

Two days later, Miriam watched on from the Little Theatre doorway as George shepherded the two girls towards the truck that stood in the courtyard.

Before she climbed in the back, Polly turned, her eyes shining with excitement, and called to Miriam, 'Thank you, Miss Balfour, for everything. I'll never forget you.'

Alice's turn next, stiff backed, head down and carrying her pitiful few belongings in a battered suitcase, she avoided Miriam's gaze. George, hauling himself into the truck's cabin, sat in the passenger seat. Before he closed the door, he gave Miriam a warm smile, accompanied by an understanding nod.

Fran Patterson closed the tailgate, climbed into the driver's seat and, giving Miriam a little wave, she started the engine. The vehicle, transporting Alice to her new life, trundled out of the courtyard, vrooming its way along the path.

What was the point of her existence now? Miriam wondered. Staring into the black abyss of heartache and loneliness, she shuddered. She had nothing to get up in the morning for.

As she leant against the door jamb, the voices of the children, enjoying their after-dinner break, filled the air. With an air of conviction, Miriam pulled herself up to her full height. She had the orphans.

# 44

## SOUTH SHIELDS, OCTOBER 1957

As she closed the front door behind her, Miriam leant back against it. Thank God, she thought, no permanent damage was done.

Still in a state of shock, her body fit for nothing except to snuggle on the couch with a cup of tea, she told herself to buck up, he was in hospital – the best place for him. His injuries would heal. She toyed with telling the family; they would want to visit. Best to leave it till later when she was rested and more composed.

Making her way along the dim passageway to the living room at the back of the house and shrugging out of her coat, she looked out of the sash window to the back yard. Taking in the dismal scene – the cracked concrete, red-brick walls that could do with pointing, a coalhouse door that needed replacing – she concluded their home was too big for them now and needed love and attention. But with his ailing health, much to his frustration tackling manual tasks around the house had become beyond him. They needed something smaller, a downstairs flat or a bungalow perhaps where he had no stairs to climb— Stairs. Miriam shuddered.

Replenishing the dwindling fire with coals, she made for the kitchen, her critical eye noting the green distempered walls that were long overdue a coat of paint. She made a brew of tea then retraced her steps to the living room where she sat thankfully down on the saggy cushioned couch. In the eerie silence, she looked around the room and, a wave of sentimentality enveloping her, Miriam asked herself: could she really do it, move, leave their home behind?

Then a sickening image of him falling down the stairs and lying like a broken doll at the bottom came back to mind. The paralysing realisation that he could have broken his neck struck her. Resolve returning, she told herself it was time to let someone else love their home.

Yawning wide enough to give herself lockjaw, Miriam placed the empty cup on the floor, then settling back, she huddled beneath the patchwork blanket. The morning's events had taken their toll and she fought to keep her heavy eyelids open. Something at the back of her mind niggled. Something she needed to remember...

She woke with a start, disorientated, unable to fathom where the banging in her head came from. Looking around she noted the coals in the grate were burnt to cinders. Miriam wondered how long she'd slept.

The hammering started up again and it took her a minute to realise someone was banging the front door knocker. Struggling from the couch, she tried to recall what day it was and why she felt so anxious. As she padded to the passageway, clarity struck and she remembered his fall down the stairs, the ambulance taking them to hospital. With a sigh of relief, she recalled how she'd left him sleeping peacefully on the ward.

Fully awake now, it registered that today was Wednesday, of course, the day the American was due to call.

'All right, all right,' she called out as the knocking continued. 'I'm coming.' Smoothing her hair, her pleated skirt, Miriam opened the front door. She gasped when she saw him, an older man with grey streaks running though his hair.

'Miriam,' Joe Marino drawled, looking unsure, 'it sure is good to see you after all this time.'

The years fell away and memories, long forgotten and painful, buried deep within Miriam's mind, surfaced.

# 45

'When are you going to tell Alice?' Polly wanted to know.

Mary screwed up her nose. 'You know what she's like, she can't help blabbing.' Looking around, she scrutinised the tables to see if there was anyone she knew.

They were sitting opposite each other in Binns' upstairs restaurant in King Street. Waitresses, dressed in black frocks covered with white frilly-edged aprons and starched white caps perched on their heads, bustled between tables. It was Thursday afternoon and Mary's half day off from Woolworths store where she worked as a shop assistant. They'd ordered a pot of tea while they waited for Alice to arrive.

'Look who's talking,' Polly teased, as she withdrew her gaze from the waitress passing them with a silver-plated tray.

Mary, an affronted expression on her face, reminded Polly of Alice in those far off days when they all lived in the orphanage. Ever since the day Alice had come home with her and Dad, she'd become a different person. Gone was the unruly, self-destructive behaviour to be replaced surprisingly by a caring, considerate side. The more she became secure in her new surroundings, the more Alice became content with life, going to college to do shorthand and typing, finding work in a solicitor's office, meeting and marrying Teddy, having a family. A grin spread across Polly's face, but acquiescent Alice certainly was not. When roused, especially at any injustice, the old Alice emerged with all guns blazing.

But there was one problem that no one dared approach Alice about – she didn't get on with Miriam. Dad didn't approve of keeping secrets and so Polly and Mary were told early on that Miriam – Miss Balfour as she was known then – was Alice's mam. The how and why was never mentioned and discussion on the subject was taboo as far as Alice was concerned. She acted like she held a grudge against Miriam. In the beginning Miss Balfour visited as often as her duties at the orphanage would allow. After the war her visits became more frequent. She had an easy-going relationship with Polly and Mary but with Alice it was different. Miriam tried too hard to please and Alice met this with disdain but she hid her resentment when Dad was around – and this was the way of things over the years.

On the other hand, contrary Mary (the name Alice and Polly privately called her), who was once a timid little thing when she came to live with them, had grown in confidence over the years and she became more self-assured. She had the knack of twisting everyone, especially Dad, around her little finger.

After the war, with the fear the orphanage was going to close, Dad was convinced to give little Mary Millard a home. With her parents dead and no relatives to call her own, he took little convincing. Polly never regretted sharing Dad with the other two, especially as it meant he didn't have only her to concentrate on. And so, the two orphans and Polly became family and lived happily together – that is, for most of the time.

It was when Polly left school and was living in at nurse training school that Dad unexpectedly told her one day, 'Your mother would be so proud of you.' He had picked his moment to tell her, because it was one of those rare moments when she visited and they were alone together at home. Polly was rendered teary because it was special that he'd mentioned Mam. He went on to tell her about the events surrounding Mam's death, blaming the fortunes that he was away for years during the war, returning home a hopeless invalid who felt sorry for himself.

He finished by saying, 'The thing is, Polly. Your mam loved you; she thought the world of you and she'd never leave you.'

She was glad Dad had told her because it showed people were fallible and parents were no exception. All she knew was she loved and missed Mam, and she would make her proud by becoming the best nurse.

'What d'you mean? I never ever tell,' Mary was saying, dragging Polly out of her thoughts.

She gave Mary a meaningful *I know you so well* look.

Mary quickly went on, 'Besides, I've told Bobby I've changed my mind.' Bobby was Mary's fiancé and worked down the local mine. 'I told him there's no way I'm moving all the way to Australia.'

No one else knew about Mary's plan to emigrate except Polly and she dreaded the impact it would have when Mary told the family. The Assisted Passage Migration Scheme promised to ship migrants over to Australia where accommodation was offered, better job prospects, sun, sea. What was there not to like, Polly thought, as she looked out of the window at grey skies and the pelting rain. Most of the couples she knew had talked about the scheme but for most, like her and Bill, that's all it was, talk.

'Have you seen how far away Australia is? I looked it up on the world map at home.' Mary's eyes widened in disbelief. 'It's halfway round the world. And it takes weeks to get there by ship.'

'Seriously, you were thinking of going when you didn't have a clue where Australia was?'

Mary put on a huffy look. 'Geography bored me stiff at school. All those red bits on the map showing the British Empire.' She rolled her eyes.

Polly's eyes looked heavenward in mock despair. 'What about Bobby? He loathes working down the pit and was looking forward to an open-air job.'

'He says if I'm happy, he's happy. Besides' – there was always a besides with Mary – 'I've told him there's a job going at the hospital as a porter. He'll be good at that. He's always helping his old nana.' She gazed into space in a dreamy trance, no doubt thinking of the long-suffering Bobby Teasdale.

Polly brought her back to earth by winding her up. 'Did you think going to Australia was like going on a day trip to Blackpool?'

'Don't be silly, of course I didn't.'

The couple were getting married in the spring and then the intention had been to emigrate. Polly had a little snigger at the idea of Mary on the ship thinking she was only going a distance similar to crossing the English Channel.

Thinking about the wedding, Polly felt the need to get serious. 'So, you're still getting married as planned?' She knew Dad, particularly, was looking forward to the wedding when once again he would proudly walk one of his girls down the aisle. They were a close-knit family and he would be heartbroken, as would they all, if Mary went ahead and moved to the end of the world – because that's what it would feel like. Polly breathed a sigh of relief as this particular worry was nipped in the bud.

'Of course. Everything's planned. Maggie from work says her mam, who's a seamstress, says she'll do a fitting on Sunday at our house. Is that all right with you or are you working?'

Polly was a staff nurse at the local Edgemoor hospital and did shift work. She was married to Bill, who had been a year above her at high school. They'd met up again at the Majestic Ballroom when she was eighteen and they'd been sweethearts ever since. Her life was complete apart from not conceiving yet. As Bill said, there was no rush and it meant they could save for a deposit to buy their own home which would make their dreams come true as the tiny downstairs flat with an outside lav they rented was no place to start a family.

She told Mary, 'It's fine. As luck would have it, I'm on a late on Sunday. Though, don't make it too early as I'd like a lie in.'

'Is Alice still harping on about being matron of honour?' Mary pulled a despairing face. 'I thought she'd be thrilled when I asked. It's unthinkable getting married without the two of you at my side.'

A lump lodging in Polly's throat at this unexpected display of sisterly love – because being sisters was how they all felt about each other – she attempted to smooth troubled waters. 'I think she feels uncomfortable about her being married with three kiddies in tow and remember, she still has her baby fat. Crikey, the bairn is barely a fortnight old.'

In fact, Polly knew Alice's main objection was wearing a pink, Little-Bo-Peep frock at her stage in life.

'The wedding's not till spring. Plenty of time to get her figure back.'

'She's worried about Teddy looking after their kiddies when the baby will be so young.' This was in fact true.

'Surely Carol can help. She adores her little sister.'

'Carol's only seven, far too young to be taking on the responsibility of a baby.'

'I was only little when I was sent to the orphanage when Miss Black was in charge.' Mary pulled a disgusted face at mentioning the former mistress's name. 'And Agnes was assigned to be my mother when she was no more than a child herself. Of course, I'm not saying that it was right.'

A look of empathy passed between them, which happened occasionally when they remembered how it was. Then Mary's lips curled into a contented smile and Polly knew, like her, she was thinking how lucky she was with a home and family to call her own. There was Alice, who took her role as big sister seriously; Polly in the middle, the heart of the family; and Mary their lovable but annoying little sister.

Tuning into the hubbub all around, Polly, busy pouring hot water into her tea from the little pot, looked up and noted Mary's subdued face. 'What's wrong?'

Placing her cup in the saucer, Mary's eyebrows pinched together. 'I was excited at first at the thought of going to Australia but when I found out migrants have to stay for two years and if you didn't you have to pay your own fare back – money Bobby and me could never afford – I realised how daft I was being.' She looked discomfited, as if what she was about to say wasn't easy. 'I know I'm lucky, you know, to have...' She swallowed. 'What was I thinking of, I could never leave you lot behind.'

Sentimentality still difficult for the three of them, Polly decided this rare moment was to be savoured.

'What's all this about leaving?'

At the intervention of the familiar voice, the pair of them looked up.

'It's nothing,' Polly told a harassed-looking Alice as she hurried towards them. 'Where's the baby?'

'Teddy's mam agreed to have her but only if she was fed and asleep. She thought a little time off would do me good. I was nervous at first to leave her but the thought of a couple of hours of blissful peace convinced me. Plus, the fact Teddy's ma has had four of her own. But the little blighter took ages to settle and I couldn't bring her. Can you imagine the uproar if the minx woke up here and started hollering?'

'Crikey, I'd never dare show my face again.' Mary pulled a horrified face.

Alice gave an amused grin. 'Wait till you've got kiddies of your own, it's amazing how thick skinned you get.'

The three of them tried to meet up every first Thursday of the month for afternoon tea – Polly made it whenever her shifts allowed. She was glad Alice could make it that day as, pale and heavy-eyed, she looked as though she needed some time off from being a mam.

'What about a name?' she asked Alice as she took off her coat and sat down. 'Have you decided yet?'

'Me and Teddy can't agree. He wants to call her Wendy but the name reminds me of Wendy down the street who's a spoilt brat.'

'What's your choice?' Mary asked. 'If I remember correctly, Teddy chose names for the other two. It's your turn now.'

'That's the thing. I can't decide between Anne or Sally.'

'Ooh, I like Sally the best.'

'Anne for me,' Polly told them.

Alice groaned. 'You two are no help.' She eyed them both. 'So, who's leaving?'

'We were discussing someone who was thinking of being a ten-pound pom,' said Polly using the term Australians dubbed British migrants.

'And I was saying,' Mary cut in, 'there's no way I could leave you lot.'

Alice raised her eyebrows. 'Seems to me you couldn't get rid of us quick enough when we left home.'

'That was only so I could have the big bedroom all to myself,' Mary replied.

A waitress came over and took their order and when she was gone, Alice turned to Mary. 'How's George? Now I'm baby free for a bit, I'm thinking of calling in at home before picking the kids up from school.'

'He was still in bed when I left for work this morning but he seemed his chirpy self last night.'

Polly's dad suffered from stenosis of the spine and what with his war wounds and unsteady on his legs, he wasn't able to walk any distance.

'It's time they moved,' Alice told them. 'The house is too big for them now.'

The three-bedroomed terraced house in John Clay Street boasted a bath beneath the units in the kitchen and stairs which were fine when the family were growing up but not now for a disabled man.

Mary piped up, 'After the wedding I've decided to move into Bobby's parents' home but only until we can find a place of our own. What would be best was if they had a downstairs flat or bungalow.'

'I agree,' said Polly. 'Let's all go home and tell them what we think.'

'Here comes our order.' Mary eyed the waitress who was making for their table carrying a three-tier glass cake stand filled with mouth-watering cakes, rum babas – her favourite – vanilla slice, chocolate orange baskets and coconut haystacks.

The three of them alighted from the trolley bus platform, crossed the busy road and walked down John Clay Street. Polly stopped to stare at the ground floor converted flat Dad rented and where he ran his business. Strange, the shutters were down, obscuring the plate-glass window, and the shop door had a closed sign on it.

'Look. That man's coming out of our house!' Mary exclaimed.

Polly followed Mary's gaze down the terraced street. 'He is, and Miriam seems to know him well.'

The older man with swathes of greying hair down the sides was talking to Miriam at the door, then shook hands with her and made off down the street.

Alice gasped. 'I know who he is. It's one of the American airmen who adopted me during the war.'

# 46

## EARLIER THAT AFTERNOON

Collecting herself, Miriam told Joe Marino, who stood at the front door, 'It's good to see you too. Come on in.'

Looking uncertain, Joe stepped into the lobby and followed Miriam along the dim passage.

It had been a fortnight since she saw the private advertisement in the gazette with the heading: *US airman is seeking to identify orphans 'adopted' by US airmen in World War Two.* The advertisement went on:

> *Blakely Orphanage was evacuated to Dunglen, Scotland but returned to South Shields after the war. If you have any knowledge of the orphans' whereabouts, please reply to the box number below.*

Miriam had replied with her name and address and later received a letter. It came as a surprise to learn the sender was Joe.

> *Hi, ma'am,*

*We've been travelling in the south of your country but are now in the area and I've only just opened the box number. Thank you for the reply – the only one I got! I hope I'm not taking liberties, ma'am, as I sure would like to hear about those orphan kids, so the plan is to call on you on the afternoon of Thursday October tenth.*

*Joe Marino*

As she led Joe to the living room at the back of the house, she acknowledged how he had changed. Gone was the boyish, vulnerable look from those war years, to be replaced by this sturdy figure of a man who appeared both confident and mature. But his reserved manner bothered her; it didn't feel as if she'd reunited with the amiable Joe she once knew, but a stranger.

Looking around the living room, he took in the chairs in front of the tiled fireplace.

'Take a seat,' she told him. 'Can I get you anything?'

He smiled politely. 'No thanks, ma'am, if you're offering tea. I never did get used to it. It's always iced tea back home.'

'It's Miriam,' she told him. 'There's no need to stand on ceremony now, I'm not the mistress anymore.' She knew she sounded rather prim, but she couldn't help it as his stiff demeanour put her on edge.

He sat on one of the fireside chairs and Miriam, picking up her cup from the floor and placing it on the table, sat opposite him.

'It's been a long time,' she said to break the ice. 'What brought you back to England? Is your wife here with you?'

'Yes, *ma'am*...' His stress on the word was deliberate and seemed to say his intention was to keep this meeting on a business level only.

What had happened to change him? And why, when she considered that Joe was once a caring and thoughtful soul, did he act the way he did all those years ago when Mitch died? She had considered him a friend but after Mitch's death, she was not only confused but hurt when Joe didn't send his condolences or even try to contact her.

She tuned into what Joe was saying.

'... and over the years I'd often wondered what happened to the orphan kids after the war. When the folks passed away, we sold the farm—'

'You sold the farm?'

'My Katherine never took to farm life. So, when her pa offered me a job in the automobile business, I thought why not. I figured before I got started it was a once in a lifetime chance to travel and so we left the kids with Katherine's folks and travelled to Europe. I always wanted to return and see those beaches and Katherine had her heart set on visiting London.'

An awkward silence followed and it felt as though the subject was closed. As they both gazed at the yellow flames licking up the chimney, Miriam puzzled how to get the conversation back to the matter in hand.

She asked, 'How did you know to look for the orphans here?' To her knowledge back then, the Americans had no way of knowing the orphanage originally came from South Shields.

'Years ago, I wrote to Teviot Hall but got a short reply. It was a secretary and all the letter said was the orphans had returned to South Shields. No address. No nothing.' His disgruntled expression showed what he thought of that. 'When we came over here, it was Katherine who suggested I contact the local paper in South Shields and ask them to help. Which I did and one of the reporters suggested the advert.'

'You do realise the orphans could be anywhere by now and those that did see the advertisement mightn't want the exposure after all this time? But I can fill you in with what happened to them.'

'So, what happened, ma'am? How did the orphanage end up here?'

'It didn't.' Miriam drew in a sustaining breath. 'Shortly after the war Sir Henley had a heart attack and died.' Remembering the shock wave that consumed everyone at the time, Miriam paused. For her part, she was convinced that the laird never really got over the loss of his son.

'I'm sorry to hear that, he was a great guy.' Joe's eyes gleamed with compassion, and Miriam glimpsed her friend from the past. 'So, who inherited Teviot Hall?'

'A sister who wasn't interested in leaving the city life she led and her son, Sir Henley's nephew, got that debatable honour.' She blew out her cheeks. 'Teviot Hall, you see, had been badly neglected over the war years.'

Joe nodded. 'There certainly wasn't the staff to run such a big place.'

'It was a difficult time,' Miriam conceded. 'My hope was that we could stay at Teviot Hall but that proved to be impossible. Neither could we return to the original orphanage here because the buildings had been bombed during the war. I'd heard a rumour that because of all the bombing throughout the land many children were orphaned and crammed orphanages had to resort to getting the children adopted and it was a case of if you want them, take them.'

'Holy moly, poor kids. What about relatives?'

'In some cases, yes. That's what I had to resign myself to

doing. Luckily all the families I contacted were keen to take in their kinsfolk.'

'What about those who didn't have any next of kin?' Joe's eyes glistened. 'Little Charlie, for instance. He often pops into my mind, the thought of him at the Christmas party we held.'

'Charlie did fine. Rita and her husband took him in. You remember Mrs Murray?'

A smile spread across Joe's face. 'I do. I'm glad. She'll have made him a terrific mom. And the others?'

'Mrs Stewart—'

'The cook,' Joe interrupted.

'Yes, she and her husband took in Tommy and Alan.'

Joe laughed. 'That surprises me.'

'Believe me, beneath Cook's forbidding manner beats a heart of gold.'

His face serious again, Joe asked, 'And the others?'

'Little Mary found a good home.' Miriam didn't elaborate as she didn't feel comfortable enough with Joe to divulge such private matters. 'My biggest fear for the few that remained was that they would be sent to the workhouse. I was determined not to let that happen. So, Rita and I took it upon ourselves to get in touch with one of the Catholic churches in the South Shields area.'

'And?' Joe leant forward again.

'The nuns took in me and the remaining orphans. With the town having a bigger population to draw from, I managed to find good homes for all of them.'

'That's so good to hear. The lumberjacks, what happened to them?'

'Lumberjills,' Miriam corrected. 'They were disbanded in nineteen forty-six and though each member of the Women's Timber Corps was awarded a personal letter signed by the Queen, shamefully, no other recognition has been given to them.' She warned, 'Don't get me started.'

'Miriam.' Joe's look of admiration startled her as much as him using her name. 'Going back to your earlier admission, I wouldn't say it was good fortune but a great deal of persistence on your part in ensuring the orphans all have a decent home.' His smile was warm.

In the silence that ensued, Miriam knew by the guarded look back in his eyes, there was something Joe needed to get off his chest. As he opened his mouth to speak, she braced herself.

'I always thought you and Mitch were a sure thing. That you'd get hitched.'

Surprised, as this was something she didn't expect, she replied, 'Me too.'

*Please stop*, her mind pleaded. She didn't want to travel that particular route; she'd laid it to rest years ago.

His expression hardened. 'I never did understand you breaking up with him. Especially with his injuries. It was the worst time.'

Nonplussed, Miriam's mind reeled. Was she hearing right?

'Excuse me, I don't know what you're getting at but I think it's best you should go.'

'He never recovered.' Joe stood. 'I'm sorry, ma'am, if I upset you but Mitch was my best friend and I felt the need to set the record straight. But I do wish you well.' He made towards the door.

Miriam replayed the strange conversation in her head. She stood. 'What injuries?'

He turned. 'His wounds and burns after the plane was hit.'

'He died.' The words came from a place she didn't want to revisit. 'The letter he wrote told me so.'

They looked at one another in confusion, the reality beginning to dawn on them both that something was amiss.

'What letter?' Joe's voice mirrored the bewilderment he obviously felt.

'I received a letter from Mitch and in it he explained that in the event of his death, the letter would be sent to me. It was in his locker for the crew to find when they cleared it out.' Seeing the look of incredulity in Joe's eyes, she added so there would be no doubts, 'I've kept it to this day.'

Joe sank onto the seat he'd just vacated. 'Miriam, Mitch is dead but only recently.'

As a bolt of shock fired through Miriam, her knees giving way, she collapsed on her seat. A memory from the past sprang into her mind. *Joe was to write and say he'd been in a fire and burnt his hands. The letter ended saying recuperation would take a long time and he thought too much of her to ask her to wait. And that Mitch wished her to get on with her life.*

The words tore out of her. 'How could you, Mitch?'

She was aware of Joe kneeling beside her, taking her shaking hands into his. 'Miriam, this is the pits even for Mitch.' She looked into his devastated eyes. 'But if it helps, I think he spent the rest of his days regretting it.'

She straightened and, disentangling her hands, she pulled herself up to her full height. 'It doesn't. But I wish to know everything. I'm owed that.'

They sat opposite each other, a tumbler with a shot of whisky in his hand, a glass of sherry in hers.

Joe's eyes glazed as he remembered. 'It was on D-Day when

*Alabama Beauty* was hit by flak, disabling number three engine. The flight deck was trying to feather the engine and meanwhile we fell behind the formation.' His eyes landed on Miriam. 'Mitch was seriously wounded. It was a hell of a ride... sorry, ma'am, back. Being fired on by friendly ships in the Channel didn't help none.' He stroked his neck as though trying to calm the emotion that stirred within him from that day. 'Mitch was sent home in a bad way and after the war when I finally caught up with him...' He shrugged. 'He wasn't the Mitch I knew.'

'In what way?'

Joe puffed out his cheeks. 'The heart had gone out of the man is all I know. He withdrew, started drinking.'

'Drinking!'

'Yep, unbelievable I know. He started fooling around with the wrong type of women. *Love them and leave them* was what he said when I asked what was going on.' Shaking his head, he let out a sigh. 'Shucks, Miriam, the times I saw him I tried to help but it was useless, he didn't want any. I asked about you, thinking if I could get him back on track—'

'What did he say?' Miriam held her breath.

'That it was over between you but there would never be anyone else.'

Miriam groaned, remembering his letter.

> *More than anything, I want you to get on with your life. Us, was never meant to be. My everlasting wish is for you to have a long and fulfilled life. Remember that always.*

She'd believed he loved her and that was him saying goodbye. It was then Miriam understood. Mitch had known what he was doing. He hadn't wanted commitment and took no responsibility for his actions, whatever damage they caused. He had allowed his demons to rule his life. A well of sadness filled within her for him. Her first real love.

'He couldn't let go of the past,' she told Joe. 'Believe in a future where all things were possible.' And she should know. Her moist eyes met Joe's. 'How did he die?'

'I figured his wounds healed but not his heart. And, Miriam, I blamed you.' His tormented eyes sought hers. 'For being so callous as to finish it with him when he needed you most.' He rubbed his brow. 'He was stone drunk in his truck and skidded off the road into a tree.'

Ice flowed through Miriam's veins.

'They say it was quick.' Joe's expression showed the anguish he was feeling. 'I loved that man like a brother but I can never condone what he did to you.'

Understanding now Joe's treatment of her all those years ago and why he hadn't contacted her since, the hurt draining from her, Miriam allowed the sadness to flow through her – she had grieved for Mitch once but never again. That time of her life was well and truly over.

They sat in a contemplative silence, watching the dying embers in the grate. Then, as this morning's events returned, George falling down the stairs and taking him to hospital, and now this, she felt as though she'd been wrung through a mangle. But life today was what mattered, not the past. She looked at Joe – he had moved on in his life too and it was time for him to go.

'Friends?' she said, holding out a hand.

'Always.' His features softened as he smiled. Then, looking down at her hand, he exclaimed, 'You married.'

'I did. Very happily.'

Joe gave a sigh of satisfaction. 'I'm glad, Miriam.'

. . .

'We'll keep in touch,' Joe told her, following her along the passageway.

'Yes,' Miriam said, aware they both knew they wouldn't. They would go back to their busy lives, their paths never crossing, and time would pass and their friendship would become a fond memory. She opened the front door and standing back she allowed him to pass.

Stepping out onto the pavement, Joe said, 'Goodbye, Miriam.' He held out his hand and she shook it.

She watched him walk down the street, then turning to go inside, something caught her eye. Their three girls were walking down the street towards her.

# 47

Passing Sister's office, Miriam opened a side ward door and it did her heart good to see George propped up in bed with his eyes closed. As quietly as she could, she sat in the chair next to the bed and, placing her carrier bag containing his slippers, clean underwear and all the necessities for an overnight stay on the locker top, she gazed at his dear face.

He must have sensed her there as his eyes blinked open and, focusing on her, a slow smile of pleasure spread on his face. But it was those eyes, sparkling with love at the sight of her, that made her heart sing.

'How are you, love?'

'All the better for seeing you.' He laughed. 'Crikey, that sounds like the wolf talking.'

That was George, trying to make light of the situation because he couldn't bear to see her upset. But this was no time for light-heartedness, Miriam thought, noticing that though his colour had returned to normal, he still had a strained look; no doubt he was still suffering from shock.

'The girls called in after afternoon tea,' she told him.

'Blimey, has a month passed already? How's Mary? Did she mention the wedding and how the arrangements are coming along?'

'They're to have a dress fitting at our house on Sunday.'

'Will Polly be able to make it?'

'Yes. She's on a late.'

'And Alice?'

Miriam knew where this was going.

'Yes, she'll be there.'

'With the baby?'

The answer to that was most likely Teddy's mam would be asked to look after the bairn. But no way would Miriam voice her thinking as she knew George's opinion on the matter: that Alice should have more respect and shouldn't treat her mother as second best, only calling on Miriam when Teddy's mam wasn't available. It was the only time she and George fell out.

The truth was Miriam felt as though she walked on eggshells where Alice was concerned. But the reason she put up with her daughter's uncivil behaviour – and this she would never admit to George, as in his eyes Miriam could do no wrong – was because Alice was justified. And Miriam prayed each night that one day her daughter would find it in her heart to forgive her transgression.

'Who knows,' she told George now, then quickly changed the subject. 'The other news is Rita sent an acceptance card to say Walter and her and the two boys and their wives are all coming.'

'That is good news, we haven't seen them in a long while.'

Miriam couldn't wait any longer. 'The girls were shocked when I told them you'd fallen down the stairs and were in hospital. And they made it plain they agree with me.'

'About what?' said George. A knowing look glinted in his eyes.

She took a deep breath. 'George, I've made up my mind. It's time we moved to somewhere on the flat.'

George found walking difficult and negotiating the steep stairs proved to be downright dangerous. Stubborn man, he was prepared to put up with all the pain and discomfort if it meant staying in the home he loved, where they had such happy memories of their family.

'I agree,' he told her with a solemn face. 'You've been right all along.'

Miriam raised her eyebrows. 'I have?'

George winced as he struggled to sit up. 'I didn't want to lose what we had. But lying here thinking, I realised our girls are all grown up and while we'll always be there for them, it's our time now and we could find a home for us to live that suits the two of us.'

Miriam cast her mind back to those dark days when she thought Mitch had died and the worry of finding a home for the orphans. It was her faith and George that got her through. He was her rock and never failed her. They had exchanged letters and his supportive voice rang through each word on the page. When she moved back to South Shields to live with the nuns, it was George who took it upon himself to help her find each orphan a home. It was during this time their friendship blossomed into love. A different kind of love than she'd experienced with Mitch. A satisfying, contented love without the highs and lows of which Mitch was prone. George loved her for who she was and, for the first time in her life, Miriam could be herself and not try to meet what she thought were other people's expectations. And George, steadfast with his unique outlook of the world and heart of gold, provided a home for Alice and Mary and treated them as his own.

'Wherever we end up' – George's voice broke into her thoughts – 'I'm sure to find premises I could rent for the business.'

Over the years, George's cobbling business grew and expanded into handmade leather items, purses, wallets and belts, which all helped to maintain a decent living for the Pearsons. Miriam did the bookkeeping and had a busy but pleasurable life being a homemaker and helping out with the family where needed. Sadly, she didn't have the mother and daughter relationship with Alice that she craved and had to make do with the occasional request for babysitting when there was no one else. If Miriam offered to help in any way – ironing, collecting the kiddies from school – Alice treated Miriam in that aloof manner by thanking her kindly but she could manage. What was going to happen when Alice returned to work for two evenings a week at the old people's home when Teddy worked shifts at the pit, Miriam had no idea. Alice working disgruntled George, who reckoned a woman's job was running the home. Though he did have the good sense to keep his old-fashioned opinions to himself as he realised times were changing and he confessed to Miriam, 'I suppose, as long as she's happy, that's what counts.'

She eyed him now, wanting to make sure there was no mistake. 'That's agreed then. There's to be no arguments, we're moving.'

'I promise, sweetheart. But on one condition. As long as we have room to have family get together like we've always done at our house.'

'Agreed.'

George smiled contently. They chatted about this and that but the conversation seemed stilted somehow, as if they were both just filling in gaps and, knowing George, he sensed there was something Miriam wasn't telling. They lapsed into silence for a while.

Then George startled her by saying, 'Come on, sweetheart, out with it. No secrets, remember.'

'It's late, George, and you need your rest.' She'd avoided telling him about this afternoon's visitor because she wanted to spare him emotional upset – he'd had enough for one day. Of course, he knew about Joe coming but with his accident he must have forgotten. 'It'll keep for another day.' Miriam knew as soon as the words were out, she shouldn't have said them.

'Miriam, don't keep me in suspense. Whatever's bothering you I need to know. Or else I won't sleep tonight.'

With nothing for it, she began, 'Today was the day Joe Marino was coming.' She went on to relate a potted version of Joe's visit ending with his revelation about Mitch.

As he listened George's face, especially when she got to the part of Mitch being alive all those years, grew incredulous.

'That man wrote you a letter telling you he'd died when all the time he...' He shook his head.

'George, let's leave it. I don't want you getting upset.'

'Miriam, it's better we talk about it now, rather than having me lie here stewing for the rest of the night. It beggars belief what that man did to you.'

'You didn't know Mitch like I did. He was hurt when he was young and he couldn't leave his past behi—'

'You're making excuses for him like I did with Jane. We all have our crosses to bear but there comes a time when you have to take responsibility for yourself, for your actions.' He squeezed her hand. 'I saw what that man put you through and God help him, it was unforgivable.'

Miriam didn't argue. She knew how George felt about Mitch and the reason she knew was because she experienced the same anger about Jane over how the woman had betrayed his trust and hurt him badly. She'd wanted to protect George from the pain and this was what George was doing for her now. That's what you did for someone you loved.

'George, I'll admit I was shocked but my life has moved on. Mitch was part of my past and he's become a distant memory and that's where he'll stay.' And it was true that any feelings she had for Mitch had long ago been overcome by the perfect life she was living now.

George's smile was one of those smiles that made everything right with the world. 'That's the end of the matter, then. All I can say is the man did me a favour because his loss was my gain.'

Miriam inwardly smiled. Mitch would forever be 'that man' in George's mind.

'Did the girls see Joe?' George settled back against the pillow.

'Yes. Alice recognised him. I told her he was visiting England and he called in to say hello.'

After a reflective silence George's gaze strayed to Miriam. 'There's still something you haven't addressed. I think, sweetheart, it's time you did.' His voice was gentle but firm.

Miriam knew what he was speaking about as they'd had this conversation many times before. That she should tell Alice the full extent of her story – about Terry, Father and why she'd left her at the orphanage.

'Sweetheart, I don't want Alice harbouring bitterness against a mother she thought callously abandoned her,' George said.

He looked weary and she knew that this wasn't the time to argue.

'She's stubborn like you and never once has she asked about your life or who her father is. While you worry that by telling her the facts, she might think you're seeking sympathy to condone what you did.' He sank back against the pillow. 'Tell her the truth and let her make of it as she will.'

As his eyes pleaded with her, Miriam's thoughts returned to Mitch. His mother's actions had coloured his outlook of the world. He believed he wasn't loveable – and he could never be truly happy as a result. What if Alice entertained the same fears?

It was then Miriam made another important decision and she was prepared to take the consequence. 'George, you're right as usual. I'm going to be honest with her.'

The moment felt surreal but George's look of pride was real enough.

# EPILOGUE

'If Alice doesn't hurry up, she'll miss the dress fitting.' Mary, sitting on the couch filing her nails, pouted.

'She'll be seeing to the bairn before she leaves,' Polly told her. 'Then again, maybe she's bringing her here.'

'That's all we need.' Mary huffed.

The two of them were in their parents' living room with Maggie and her mam – Ma Turner as she was known – who was currently pinning up the hem on Polly's bridesmaid dress. Standing on the table, Polly gave a sigh of satisfaction. The room with the fire burning brightly had that secure, cosy Sunday at home feel.

Taking the pin from between her lips, Ma Turner shot Polly a harassed look. 'As long as I'm home by half two. The meat will be done by then and it's only a case of putting the veg on the gas and the Yorkshire puds in the oven.' She made a knowing face at Polly. 'The pub shuts at three, so me old man will be home at half past on the dot.'

Maggie, sitting next to Mary, looked over an old copy of the *Woman's Life* magazine she was reading. 'For goodness' sake, Ma, dinner can be late for once. You spoil Da rotten, you do. Puts me off getting married the way you run after him.' She shook her head in disgust.

Indignation flashed across the older woman's face. 'I'll have you know, our Maggie, your da works hard at the pit all week when never a drop of booze passes his lips. Weekends are his time to relax. And by God, he needs it working in the bowels of the earth to earn a livin'.'

Polly was thankful they were saved further argument when someone banged on the front door knocker.

'That'll be Alice now.'

Mary shot up and moments later Polly heard voices in the passageway.

'I had to bring the pram in.' Alice's voice. 'It's pelting down with rain out there.'

'Why didn't you leave the bairn with Teddy? The fitting shouldn't take long,' Mary said.

'He's taking the other two to a posh birthday party at the Thompsons' place. I'm lucky he's taking the kids at all. Can you imagine the scene if the baby starts yelling? Or God forbid, she needs a nappy change.'

The voices came nearer.

'Why not his mam?'

There was a drawn-out pause. 'I didn't want to bother her.'

Alice emerged from the living room doorway followed by Mary. Wearing a black plastic mac with a hood, Alice's sodden fringe was pasted to her forehead.

'Oooh, what's Teddy's mam done?' Mary plonked back down on the settee and snuggled beneath a patchwork blanket. 'Is she out of favour?'

Shrugging out of the dripping mac, Alice raised her eyes heavenward. 'Mind your own business, nosey.'

Polly hoped Mary didn't bite as she could tell Alice was in a delicate mood.

'I was only asking,' Mary retorted, burying her head in the magazine.

Oblivious to the tension in the room, Maggie asked no one in particular, 'Where's Miriam?'

The Pearson girls' – as they were known – background was no secret, nor that they were brought up by the former mistress of an orphanage. But it had been difficult at first to know what to call Miss Balfour when she and George became involved with each other. After the couple married, it was decided by vote, as most things were in those days, the girls would call her Miriam.

'She's at the cemetery,' Polly answered. 'I usually put flowers on Mam's grave but given I was tied up this afternoon, Miriam volunteered before she visits Dad.'

Ma Turner's face cracked into a toothy grin. 'That Miriam's a good un to you lassies and no mistake. A proper Christian. Not a hint of jealousy that you still want to upkeep your ma's grave and keep her memory intact.'

'Mam!' Maggie looked mortified.

Ma Turner gave her daughter a puzzled look. 'What have I done wrong now? I'm only speaking the truth as I see it.'

Maggie, about to retort, shrugged as though mentally giving in. The rest of the session followed without incident and once Maggie and her mam were away home, the three sisters sat comfortably in front of the fire. Polly, lounging in a wing-backed chair, knew she should make for home and spend time with Bill but, for the life of her, she couldn't find the energy to move.

'It's bliss having nothing to do.' Alice stretched luxuriously in an identical chair opposite Polly. 'With no "Mam can I have", and madam here now sound asleep in her pram.

I swear she's cranky because the other two keep her awake with all their shouts and squabbling. I must be mad having another one when I've got the other two at school.'

'I thought it came as a surprise.' Mary grinned.

Alice nodded. 'It was, a nice one. I wouldn't change things for the world.'

Polly eyed the swathes of brown under Alice's eyes. 'You look tired. Enjoy the peace while you can.'

'I intend to.' Alice gave another stretch with a yawn attached this time.

A contemplative silence between them reigned, while the clock ticked and a fire crackled and sputtered in the grate.

'It'll be strange,' Mary remarked.

Alice sat up in the chair, rubbing her eyes. 'I nearly dropped off then.'

'What'll be strange?' Polly wanted to know.

'If they sell the house. I mean' – Mary's voice broke – 'I didn't think about the reality. Not having this place to come home to. I'll miss it.'

'So will I,' Alice agreed. 'It's the only home I've known.' Her eyes glistened.

'Same,' said Mary. 'I can't hardly remember anything before the orphanage.'

They looked at one another. Their expressions said it all: how lucky they'd been.

'Can you remember when we first left and Dad took us to his flat.' Polly smiled at the memory. 'You couldn't believe it, Alice, when there was only us in the bedroom.'

Alice smiled and sighed. 'I'd never known such luxury. Though, I did find it strange at first not having all the others around me. The room felt a bit claustrophobic if I'm honest.'

'Everything felt peculiar at first,' Mary put in. 'Little

things like going into the kitchen and making a drink when you wanted. Having your own toys and books. The bliss of not having a schedule.'

'You were always a bookworm.' Alice smiled fondly at Mary. 'It's true though, we are the lucky ones.'

'Yes, I only hope the others did as well.' Mary gave a contented sigh. 'Things got even better when we moved into this house. It felt like we became a proper family. It didn't seem we were make-believe sisters but more like real ones with parents.'

Polly noted Alice stiffen. This was hard for her just now.

The previous night, Polly had heard a surprise knock at her front door and found Alice standing white faced and agitated.

'Are you in on your own?'

'No Bill's here, why?'

'I want to run something past you.' The words they often used over the years when something was bothering them.

'Come in, we're watching *Six-Five Special*.' The fourteen-inch black-and-white television with the grainy picture was the one luxury the couple had allowed themselves out of their savings.

'Are you sure I'm not interrupting?'

'No. Bill's glued to the television. He'll probably not notice you're here.' Polly led the way along the narrow passageway to the back bedroom. 'He even stares at the blank screen when broadcasting stops for the hour at six o' clock.' Her hand on the bedroom doorknob, she turned to Alice and raised her eyebrows. 'Every night's the same. Bill ranting that it's the parents' responsibility to get their kids to bed not the broadcasters'.' She grinned. 'All is well with the world in our house now the BBC saw common sense at last.'

She went inside, seeing the disarray in the minuscule bedroom. Items of underwear strewn over the unmade bed, Bill's work trousers, unwashed socks on the floor, makeup littering the chest of drawers. Mortified, Polly began gathering the clothes off the unmade bed and pulling over the covers.

'I was on an early, then I had to do grocery shopping and—'

'Polly, I came to see you for some advice, not to criticise your standard of housekeeping.'

Normally they would have looked at one another and laughed, but seeing Alice's strained and miserable face, Polly sobered. Dropping the clothes in a heap on the floor, she sank on the bed and patted the space beside her.

'What's wrong?' she asked.

Alice sat beside her. 'It's Miriam. She came to see me yesterday afternoon when the kids were at school.'

Fearful where this was leading, Polly asked, 'What did she want?'

Alice took a moment as though wondering where to start. 'She came to tell me her past.'

Polly, speechless, waited. Alice began to relate Miriam's life story, how her mam died when she young, her homelife with a strict father – a bible thumping vicar who abandoned her after she got pregnant and her baby was born. How she qualified as a teacher and worked in the orphanage where she'd left her baby.

'Polly, she kept calling the baby by the name she'd chosen,' Alice told her in monotone, her eyes blank of emotion. She was then silent for a while as though still digesting this piece of information.

'Then what?' Polly asked when she could stand the suspense no longer.

Alice's eyes widened as she was about to impart the biggest shock. 'You'll never guess. Miriam had an affair.'

'She never did. When? Who with?'

'During the war. With one of the Americans from Dunglen airbase. You remember them?' Before Polly could answer, she went on. 'They were in love and planned to marry. Supposedly, she planned for me to go and live with them.' Her voice held a cynical ring.

'What happened?' Polly asked, feeling uncomfortable because this was Miriam's private business and she wasn't sure if it was meant for her ears. Then she felt better when she realised Alice needed to share this with someone.

'She thought he'd died in the war.'

'Thought?'

Alice went on to tell her about Joe Marino's visit on Thursday and what Miriam had discovered.

'You know the rest,' she finished, 'she met your dad.' Alice flopped back on the bed. 'I'm confused,' she wailed. 'I don't know whether my mother is a wanton hussy, a deceitful bitch or—'

'A loving mam,' Polly finished for her and flipped back alongside Alice.

'I don't know how to react, Polly.' Her expression was anguished. 'I've built up this barrier of mistrust ever since she confessed to being my mother. I don't know how to think of her other than a devious liar.'

'She isn't though, is she?' She'd gone on to remind Alice of the sacrifices Miriam had made. How, as a qualified teacher she could have worked in a school for better pay and could have had a life instead of being subjected to the confines of living in an orphanage with a horror mistress ruling over her. The indignities to be near Alice, the heartache she must have gone through when Terry betrayed her, and then the American too.

Alice sat bolt upright and made for the door. Polly didn't try and stop her as she knew from old that if she said anything more, tried to make things better, Alice, in this state, would only explode.

*Fancy though*, Polly thought as the front door clashed. *Our Miss Balfour, all those loves in her life.* It only went to show you never really knew anyone. She smiled, thinking, despite what she'd heard, she was glad Miriam had found true love at last with her dad.

Polly's last thought that night as she snuggled into Bill in bed was that Alice never said what Miriam called the baby.

It was the bairn whimpering now in her pram in the passageway that brought Polly out of her deliberations.

Alice stirred and looked at her watch. 'Goodness, is that the time? She's slept for an age and she'll be starved, poor lamb.'

A familiar voice could be heard coming from the passageway. Mary cocked her head, listening. 'It's Miriam, she's back. I hope it's good news about George coming home.'

'Not a chance,' Polly said. 'There's no doctors' rounds on a Sunday.'

Miriam appeared in the doorway with the baby in her arms. 'I picked her up before she got upset in the dark. Is that all right?' Her tone held that defensive note she always used when addressing Alice about anything to do with the children.

As she saw Alice tense, Polly inwardly groaned. *Here we go.*

There followed a pause when Alice seemed flummoxed. Then a pink flush crept up her neck. 'Of course it is. She likes cuddles off Grandma.'

The look of amazement on Miriam's face was a picture to behold. Even Mary gasped.

'If you're not too busy tomorrow afternoon' – Alice spoke to Miriam – 'could you pick the other two up from school?'

'W-what about Teddy's mam? Is she busy?' Miriam looked tentative, as though she couldn't believe what she was hearing was true.

'I don't know, I never asked her.' Alice moved forward and took the bairn from Miriam. 'I'd best get home and feed her.' She made for the door, then turned. 'Oh, by the way, Mam, we've decided on a name. From now on she's called Gabrielle.'

Miriam visibly faltered. As it registered what Alice had called her, tears brimmed in her eyes and a smile of pure joy radiated her face.

Meeting Polly's gaze, Alice nodded her gratitude and grinned.

# A LETTER FROM SHIRLEY

Dear Reader,

First of all, I'd like to say a big thank you for choosing to purchase *The Orphan With No Name* and for your continued support. Writers depend on readers and there would be no book six without you lovely readers supporting me and reading my books. I'm truly grateful to all of you.

If you enjoyed *The Orphan With No Name* and would like to keep up with all my releases, just sign up at the following link. Your email address will never be shared and you can unsubscribe at any time.

*www.bookouture.com/shirley-dickson*

As is usual, the novel starts in the seaside town of South Shields, where I was born. While most of the locations are real, I did take liberties, inventing street names, towns (Dunglen) and bombings which didn't take place but were necessary for the sake of the story. Although there are many super stately homes in Scotland, unfortunately, Teviot Hall is not one of them. Though I have researched bombers and D-Day, if there are any errors they are mine alone.

If you enjoyed *The Orphan With No Name* and have the time to leave a review, I would be most grateful. It makes such a difference to an author and I do love to hear what readers think. Thank you to those who mention my name to family and friends as it helps readers find me for the first time.

Also, I would love to hear from you on social media.

Take care, and happy reading.

Shirley

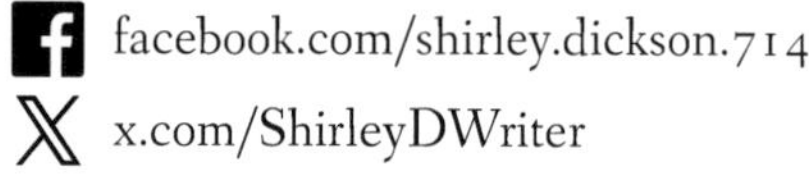

# ACKNOWLEDGEMENTS

As ever, thank you to my Wal for his love, support and encouragement. He never allowed me to give up on my dream of getting published. Love you, miss you more as each day passes – you were my solid ground.

Thanks to every one of the wonderful and dedicated Bookouture and PR team who have played a huge part in getting *The Orphan With No Name* ready for publication. Also my thanks for the kindness, patience and support shown over the past couple of years – you really are the best!

Heartfelt thanks to fabulous editor, Lauren Finger (who I probably gave a headache!) – the book is immensely improved by her input. Huge thanks to brilliant copyeditor, Natasha Hodgson, who did an excellent job that made the book so much better. Many thanks to proofreader, Becca Allen, whose keen eye for detail greatly improved the book. Special heartfelt thanks to fantastic Natasha Harding for taking me on and smoothing the waters. Indeed, her understanding, kind-heartedness and enthusiasm encouraged me to get the book finished, as there was a time when I doubted.

My lovely family – three daughters, their husbands, four gorgeous grandchildren, my granddaughter's husband, three delightful great grandchildren, (the newest addition, cutey, Maddison Grace) – I've said it before but I'll say it again, you all give meaning to my life and make it worthwhile.

Huge heartfelt thanks to all the reviewers and bloggers – I'm so grateful to you for taking the time.

Lastly, to my lovely readers, thank you for your support. I couldn't do any of this without you.

Shirley xx

# PUBLISHING TEAM

**Turning a manuscript into a book requires the efforts of many people. The publishing team at Bookouture would like to acknowledge everyone who contributed to this publication.**

**Audio**

Alba Proko
Melissa Tran
Sinead O'Connor

**Commercial**

Lauren Morrissette
Hannah Richmond
Imogen Allport

**Cover design**

Debbie Clement

**Data and analysis**

Mark Alder
Mohamed Bussuri

**Editorial**

Natasha Harding
Lauren Finger
Lizzie Brien

**Copyeditor**
Natasha Hodgson

**Proofreader**
Becca Allen

**Marketing**
Alex Crow
Melanie Price
Occy Carr
Cíara Rosney
Martyna Młynarska

**Operations and distribution**
Marina Valles
Stephanie Straub

**Production**
Hannah Snetsinger
Mandy Kullar
Jen Shannon
Ria Clare

**Publicity**
Kim Nash
Noelle Holten
Jess Readett
Sarah Hardy

**Rights and contracts**

Peta Nightingale

Richard King

Saidah Graham

Printed in Great Britain
by Amazon

53354594R00231